BREAKING THE MASK

Book I of The Fortunes, Fables, & Failures of Henry Game

ANTHONY JOHNSON

First published in 2020 by Komodo Books

Copyright © 2020 Anthony Johnson

Cover design by Myzizi Graphic Design

This book has been deposited with the National Library of Australia and is available from the NLA Catalogue record.

This book has been deposited with the British Library and is available from the CIP Catalogue record.

Paperback ISBN 978-0-6488475-2-6
E-Book ISBN 978-0-6488475-1-9

2nd Edition, June 2020

To my beautiful wife, Melissa, this is forever.

"What is history but a fable agreed upon?"

—NAPOLEON BONAPARTE

New York City, Present Day.

I t was a time of strange happenings and lost reasons; a time when things would never be as they were before.

Frank stuck to what he knew, and as a general rule of thumb tried his best not to do new things, or if he could help it, things for the first time. Repetition was the secret. It was the only way for him to fit in, unnoticed.

He maintained that the enemy of routine was change, yet, despite this fact, change would happen as often as the wind breathes and the sky cast its emotions, and it was something that he just had to deal with, as infuriating as it may be.

Sometimes it felt like existing in the world and its mercurial equilibrium was a battle he wouldn't ever win. Change harbours uncertainty and with it, darkness. With such fluctuations he could not foresee or predict the kaleidoscopic outcomes of random encounter. Yet, deep within the dark was a light, and that light was hope. While most events remained hostage to the law of perpetual variation, a few sacred practices defied this ruling and were a hundred percent, completely, unshakeably, change-proof. Frank was proud to have figured most of these out, and he employed them methodically. Small victories were enough to keep him from drowning in the white waters of fluid, city living.

The Way of Anonymity – the mantra of his entire life to this point – was one of the infallible systems he applied, guaranteeing the path of least resistance in almost every situation. The steps were simple: head down; keep his own opinions; don't engage others more than necessary; resist social trends; always take to empty sections, and fundamentally: keep out of people's business. The idea was to be truly unremarkable, to the *n*th degree. However, not standing out can only be fully realised when worked in cooperation with strict apathy. It completes the mantra. And over the years, he'd forged his discipline for lack of interest to the level of dispassionate perfection.

Care not, look not, pry not: the secret to an easy and predictable existence. Routine brings order to the world in its malicious uncertainty.

As you can imagine, Frank didn't get close to people; he didn't have friends and no real family. But recently, since he'd been upended and relocated to the far reaches of the city, his mobile phone hadn't buzzed and bleeped quite so often. An objective observer might say that he was popular, a man in-demand, except for the fact that almost every missed call was from Uncle Oddy.

Oddy, as Frank had always called him, wasn't a real uncle. His adopted parents had insisted on the familial title. But to a boy with no genuine family, an honorary uncle meant very little. And since the event, 'Uncle Oddy' had refused to leave him to wallow in the despair that had since become his life. The despair he believed he was entitled to.

Not quite human, was how Frank described himself in the sanctum of his own thoughts, but beneath the apathy and meekness, isolation was as much cautionary as any demonstration of reclusiveness. The truth was Frank trusted himself less than he trusted anyone else.

Routine was the only thing he could truly rely on, and the long and seedy route back from the new gym had very quickly replaced the old routine. He was at a new boxing club, in a different part of the city, staying in unfamiliar lodgings. A few weeks had passed already, but the sequences in life just have a way of clicking into place, if you work on them and remember to stay vigilant.

In the gym he liked to hit the heavy bag. Didn't need gloves. Not until one of the bags tore, leaving an unmistakable fist shaped hole in it. The damage was beyond repair. And also, it wasn't the first bag he'd destroyed.

Gym management suggested he should be wearing the appropriate bag-gloves from then on, if he wanted to continue using the facilities. Everyone should, they said. New gym policy. The first bag was ready to burst, and the replacement bag must have been faulty. The very next day, laminated sheets of A4 paper were placed around to remind everyone to wear the correct gear for the appropriate exercise and equipment.

No argument from Frank. Argument invites attention. Attention usually leads to conflict, then crisis, then change. And you know how he feels about change.

The gym was a little busier than usual, and as he moved on to the only heavy bag left hanging, one of the fight-team coaches shouted over, asking him into the ring as a stand-in sparring partner to "Slick-Rick-Hitter": an upcoming super-middleweight fighter, whose record stood at six and zero.

Frank continued to jab at the bag as the gym floor drew silent and the coach repeated his offer. People were looking at him and that was when he realised the coach was talking directly to him.

After an awkward silence, and a lot of attention from everyone on the floor, he declined with a shake of the head and retreated to the changing rooms, not meeting a single eye on the way. It was getting late, he reasoned. The gym was too busy tonight anyway, and winter drew nearer with every sunset. He figured he'd be wise to beat the frost underfoot.

In the changing room and Frank felt the stench from his clothes hit the back of his throat. It seemed that all of his clothes still choked-up thick with the linger of burn and disquiet. Twice he'd run them through the laundry at the hotel.

And even so, the smell remained unreasonably strong, and with it, every time he dressed, he would imagine being trapped inside his old bedroom to suffocate besides her.

Remorse isn't the right word for how he felt. Regret, perhaps, would be closer. It was never love for him, more like he felt responsible for not being there to help keep her around and breathing and useful to him and his routines. Maybe she loved him, but Frank didn't really think along those lines. Either way, her death was distressing and inconvenient, and as the nights came and went, the real and growing issue only matured into something more concerning.

When questioned he had told the authorities that he'd been working an extra shift at the hospital, cleaning the insides of operating theatres – a job he'd held down for going on two years – but the brutal truth was that he'd gone back to the Troll Thump Cages, beneath the George Washington Bridge, to fight, again.

Troll Thump hosted half a dozen fights every two or three weeks. The fight rosters were systematically posted on social media sites through bogus accounts. It was unlicensed and populated with angry folk that didn't say much about anything. Ideal for Frank: now a seasoned regular over the last eighteen months. And while he'd pulverised the latest faceless, almost toothless, opponent, the fire in his first-floor apartment had raged on. And Bethany had died from smoke inhalation.

Fourteen without defeat, so far, in the cages. But the last victory pricked at his conscience. He struggled with the feelings of victory in the face of what happened elsewhere that night.

Numbers and records are esteemed colleagues of routine, and at the Troll Thump, keeping the win count unspoiled by loss only increases the odds. Greater odds augment the monetary reward of the victor. Suffice to say that making a bloody mess certainly paid better than cleaning them up. And it even helped him deal with certain things – delicate issues of a mindful nature – but at the end of the day, his reasons for doing what he does, isn't, and never will be, anyone else's business.

Following the devastation of the fire, a benevolent building and contents insurance company provided him with immediate, temporary accommodation. They wasted no time at all in sourcing local building contractors and had quickly engaged them to get going with the repair works in his scorched apartment. A few weeks had passed already in a whirlwind of events. Frank being little more than an errand piece of debris sucked along for the ride.

It seemed as though the insurance company had sent him about as far away from the Troll Thump Cages as physically possible. His new lodging as far out to the city limits as he had ever been. And of course, Frank didn't drive. He just didn't have the composure for it. He barely kept it together when walking down a busy street, or when there were too many people at the gym.

Frank figured he was being punished by fate for not being there when it all burned to shit. The fire was a big surprise. Discovering that he had insurance, even more so. But regardless of the distance, the thought of going back down to the Troll Thump to fight on, only threw up a noose of guilt he felt he justly deserved to hang by. Not returning would have to be the new routine, he had already decided.

But it didn't stop him thinking about it all the time. In the cages he had taken the name "Kid-Reaper". Despite the fact he had told the organiser his name was "Reaper", when they announced him for his debut bout, the word "Kid" had been tacked on too.

Tonight, in the darkened despondency of New York City kerbside bin-lids held the glittering promise of a clear night sky. Leaving the gym early was probably a good move. Frank decided a nice jog would make up for lost gym time until he came across a parked car, only a couple of hundred yards down the backstreet.

The pearly silver colour coded bumper poking out from a narrow alley besides an old fenced-off power generator building. Frank slowed to a walk as he drew nearer, the engine was still running and the interior of the glass fogged up. As he drew level with the vehicle, he noticed the foil ducting that was stretched from the exhaust pipe, pulled tight over the hatchback, and trapped into the car through a narrow slit in the sunroof. Through the swirling fog of engine fumes within, he spotted two child car-seats housing the quiet tops of two small heads. He shook his hands to dispel the coldness in his veins, and despite his trepidation he had a closer look through the glass.

The driver was young and unconscious. Her face clawed by black streaks that faded down toward her jawline. The scene within the car was away from the world and life was leaking away with the vespers of exhaust fume that brimmed out of the narrow gap in the sunroof.

He tried the doors, he thumped his fists on the glass and shouted, but still stirred no response. Without much further thought, he punched through the rear passenger window, reached in and unlocked the door, brushing across the flakes of shattered glass, seatbelts tearing with little resistance as he pulled both of the car-seats free from the fumes.

They were twins by the looks of them, girls, and both still strapped in tightly, neither showing signs of waking up. They couldn't have been any older than two, he thought. The freeze that was crawling through each vessel in his hands caused him to fumble the clips and straps until he finally got the girls free, laying them both flat on their backs and in the middle of the frosty backstreet.

Looking up to the driver, still behind the wheel, engine still running, fumes wastefully washing away through the open car door, he rose from the frosted tarmac, reached through from the open back seat and opened the driver-side door. Then, reaching down into the footwell, he straightened the woman's limp leg out fully and wedged it down against the accelerator pedal. Grey fumes plumed in more densely than before through the sunroof and Frank firmly closed both doors again then returned his attention to the frosty tarmac and the silence of the two girls wrapped up tight in a damp gym towel from his rucksack.

They both had ice-blonde pigtails, and they could've been sleeping, but also, they could've been dead. He gently placed them up against the metal fence of the old generator house, figuring they would be safe from other cars at least, before calling the emergency services, anonymously requesting an ambulance for the girls.

Finally making it back to the hotel he slipped in through the foyer and immediately noticed the bubble-gum chewing girl behind the reception watching him from over the rim of her smart phone. Hawk-eyes tracked him from the moment of entry right up to the lift doors, and still as he waited for it to descend and rescue him from her judgement. Panic ensued. He wasn't getting enough oxygen.

Silently, while his heart thundered behind his eyes, he battled the rising terror threatening to spill over into something else entirely when the lift door mercifully opened, and he fell in, gulping the oxygen down like it was going out of fashion.

Through the mirrored panels on the interior of the lift, he noticed that his gym bag on his back was wide open, and with it, his dirty underwear hanging out, all twisted and sweat-soaked. Underpants dangling on the cusp, barely clinging from a plucked thread of elastic in the waistline caught on the zipper. Maybe that was what she was so interested in him, but the uncertainty of it all only increased the latest waves of anxiety that rammed against his defences.

As the lift climbed, so too did his paranoia. When at last he couldn't take anymore the doors opened and he escaped from the box of mirrors, scrambling to the solitary door of his top floor hotel room, fumbling keys in his iced hands and slamming the door behind him and locking it, sucking in as much air as possible in an attempt to regain composure again, if ever he had any to begin with.

The evening had been a touch out of the ordinary, and perhaps allowed a reasonable explanation for the case of mounting angst he was experiencing – but this was an all too common occurrence nowadays – especially since his world burned upside down.

His ticker box called to him from the bedside cabinet. In truth it had called to him since he decided to cut his workout time short, since before he went to the gym even. All day it had been drawing him along and into its blissful promise. Nothing else mattered tonight or wouldn't soon enough. Suffering, as they say nowadays, is a choice.

He picked up the old *Lord of The Rings* lunchbox and felt his muscles start to de-tension in the pre-pleasure promise of ignorant euphoria. The container was a seasoned and sun-bleached Eye of Sauron, scarcely winking back at him. The smell of smoke, fresher than memory stung as the lid cracked open. He assessed the remaining contents and tried not to worry that his stash waned, almost depleted. The fire took more than familiarity. There were two, maybe three hits left. Ten grams would see him through to the morning at least, he hoped. A gram for every hour was the general rule of thumb.

It wasn't that he was addicted to the drug 'per se', it was more that he was addicted to the idea of not having to suffer through the night, the day, week. It really depends on how much you take: the more powder you sniff, the longer your memory withholds from you, ergo the more time passes, and you leave the suffering behind, in theory.

Ticker was the drug that stole time. Yet time was said to heal all things. And to a man that sleeps maybe twenty hours a week, maximum, the opportunity to torture oneself had always been in abundance. Sleeping pills had never worked, weed, booze, sex, exercise, fighting, nothing had helped him sleep to a more frequent and 'normal' pattern or cycle. Not at least before ticker came along.

The hope was that by not having to lie awake and be tormented by demons, thanks to the miracle of the purple powder, the more time would pass and perhaps one day he could be whole, safe, and stable again – not that he could ever remember feeling that way – but now he was low on the substance and the only person who he knew could get their hands on it was also the same person lying in his bed when his apartment burned down.

The drug tin had been hers, Bethany's. She had started out as his supplier and then became his occasional lover, but it was more out of awkwardness than anything. He had never been attracted to her, or anyone else for that matter, not in a sexual manner at least. If anything, he had only felt embarrassed for her clear attraction to him. But she was tremendously useful. And of the people he had held any semblance of a relationship with, she was one of the few he could tolerate.

It was a shame she was gone, and not just because of her usefulness to him. Their relationship had been as such that sometimes he paid for the product, other times he didn't. She was also a cleaner at the hospital and that was where he had met her. She cleaned the floors and door handles. Things like that. Never entered the theatres. She wasn't meticulous, or serious enough, but that made up most of her charm and Frank would miss that.

He didn't get to see her corpse, in the end, but he did see the blackened messed-up bed sheets. The slight depression where she had lay…

He was doing it again: tormenting himself; suffering was a choice and he was making the decision to pass.

Rolling a dollar bill, he skipped the night his terrors had prepared with a single, long, sniff. And just like that he lay back, shooting each of his depressive thoughts dead while falling backward into the bliss of nothing and forgetfulness.

* * *

Frank wakened with the morning splashing through the thinning curtains. He assumed he'd slept, but of course could never really know what he'd done while under the influence of ticker, and that, of course, had always served as a part of the appeal.

The hotel wasn't up to much. Not when you looked closely at the finishes in the rooms, and common areas. However, the benevolent insurance company had gracefully taken care of pretty much everything, irrespective of Frank's concerns surrounding fraud or at the very least, an expensive case of mistaken identity, and therefore he had no room to complain. And the truth is that he had kept his mouth shut tight for fear of being sussed-out surrounding his non-existent policy, which he was almost certain he didn't have.

His claim handler was a very bossy lady called Selene, whom had an accent that he couldn't quite place. She seemed to start every sentence with "What will be happening next, is…" Truth is that she intimidated him a little, not that he would ever admit it. But something about her made him feel relaxed. In fact, he probably liked her for her blatant disregard for niceties and false sympathies. In a way she was just like him, although they had never actually met.

She had informed Frank by telephone, in the early hours following the fire, that he would only be allowed to go back to his apartment for one hour, and only after they had removed the corpse first.

When he arrived, he was surprised to see that the place was extensively damaged. But it appeared that most of the destruction to the walls, floors, and ceilings, had been caused by the firefighters in their attempts to snuff out the blaze. Everywhere holes were smashed through the plasterboard, spilling melted insulation and cables like guts. The extent of smoke damage was most surprising, even right out and into the back bedroom where the fire did not touch, it had started to turn the walls and skirting boards yellow.

During his one hour supervised visit, he was able to retrieve a few belongings, some clothes, toiletries, the old and dented *LOTR* lunchbox. His gym stuff was still in his bag as he'd had that with him at Troll Thump. And when I say gym stuff, I mean fighting gear, of course. Fist wraps and mitts and a chewed out gumshield to "protect his pretty little mouth", had said the guy who refereed all the fights, the very first time Frank had been down there to register. He didn't say anything else to Frank after that first fight.

His fighting gear was sparse and worn thin, and not enough to keep him warm throughout winter, especially not when the rest of his belongings were carted away by the restoration company. Selene explained that this was to clean the smell and smoke damage away.

Frank had one hour exactly to get what he needed, and he was surprised that they waited while he picked through the ruins. The men in white hygiene suits, all standing a little too closely to him, he thought. Their bright uniforms a contrast when everything else was tainted and devastated.

Hauling whatever he could manage to carry, he rammed his belongings into a couple of dusty rucksacks and left his beloved apartment behind to move to his new lodgings, the delightfully named Hotel Indigo, room thirty-three.

Again, to say hotel is a bit of a stretch. It ranked somewhere between a hostel, an Airbnb, and a half-way house, except it had a designated – albeit barely part time – reception desk and supposed concierge service. But only upon request and for prior bookings, apparently. Also, down in the main lobby was a sticky-floored, tropical themed liquor bar that boasted a proud and unplugged jukebox, featuring pop-icons from the early nineties. And if you looked closely, you could just about make out Peter Andre and his infamous six-pack.

Frank's first thoughts of the cold morning were for the two girls abandoned to the crispy night, wrapped in his damp gym towel. But his real concern was down to whether or not the police could somehow track him down through forensic investigation. Maybe his DNA would be in the sweat, he worried.

Ticker seemed like a good idea, even at this hour, but he only had one hit left. And distraction always came easier during the daylight hours. Routine would be enough to carry him through. However, the thought of having to endure the entire day was almost enough to bring on another panic attack.

Taking deep breaths, he watched the bustle of city life from out of his tall window. The night had been a cold one; ice had melted into a slush pile along the bottom of the windowpane and dripped out over the rotting timber ledge to the awning below. Winter had still not yet fully settled in, but the tail end of autumn often ushered in the cold snap. A grown man with a fur-coat might even catch their death out there all night. Especially if that fur coat was actually a damp towel and he couldn't move an inch because he was basically a baby, and unconscious.

Routine. Time to get dressed, grab his coffee from the truck on the corner, and his banana bread from the café opposite the hotel, then head back to his room to read the morning paper. Such was the new routine. He had been living in room thirty-three for almost a month now. Routines are inevitable; distraction is critical. And, of course, the best way to forget. Well, second best way, after ticker.

As always, the coffee would be average, banana bread soggy and sticky, but as he stood in the queue with his regular tabloid, he zeroed on a headline atop one of the local papers and suddenly the minimart became a confined space, filled with hostility and accusation. With the walls closing in, he stepped out of the line and swapped the tabloids and rolled it up in a way that you couldn't read the front page. His paranoia had him convinced that everyone in the place were staring at him, whispering, conspiring.

Taking deeper breaths than publicly acceptable, ignoring the ugliest part of himself, or trying to, he mutely purchased the newspaper, and avoided further eye-contact before clearing out of there, leaving over ten dollars in change.

Back in the safety of isolation, he popped the lid from the polystyrene coffee cup, tore the clear banana bread packet and unrolled the newspaper on the bed. The main headline, printed in bold letters:

"TODDLER TWINS RESCUED FROM A WIDOWED-MOTHER SUICIDE. POLICE ASKING WITNESSES TO COME FORWARD."

Beneath was a photo of the car tucked down the alleyway, broken glass from the rear passenger window glittering the tarmac all around it. No sign of the girls, or his towel, and no photo of the mother either.

It seemed the girls had survived after all. Frank wanted to feel good about that, but his anxiety had other ideas. He couldn't help but worry that the police were tracking him down, even as he read the paper-

A vibration from the kitchenette bench-top drew his attention. It was his mobile phone. The incoming number was withheld, he didn't answer no-numbers and before the phone stopped buzzing there was a heavy and ominous knock on his door.

This was it. The authorities had found him. The panic stopped trickling and instead just straight up flash-flooded and Frank couldn't swim. In blind panic he acted on instinct, not feeling his legs or even his feet moving, he hid the drug tin in a kitchen drawer, covering it with a tea towel-

Another knock on the door, this time much louder and less patient. Despite his survival instincts, Frank rushed over and yanked it open on to a squat delivery lady in a light grey uniform. She was trying to get a good grip on the brown boxed package she carried. The package looked old and the courier short of height and patience.

'Smith, Francis, that you?' she squinted through her fringe and blustered face, still clearly struggling with the package that was about a third of her overall size.

'Yeah. What's that?'

The courier didn't answer but instead bundled the parcel over to Frank then presented a tablet suspended on a lanyard tethered around her non-existent neck.

'Sign here,' she ordered.

With his free hand, Frank scored across the screen. Without another word the courier was stomping down toward the lift. Frank took the package inside and placed it on the coffee table that landmarked the lounge, albeit barely distinguishable from the bedroom and kitchenette. The address label on the top was handwritten in a cursive style. There appeared no return address, and nor was there an indication of where it came from. Naturally, he assumed that it was sent to him by the insurance company.

He grabbed his coffee and sat down to assess. The hospital he worked at had given him compassionate leave after the fire. After Bethany had died. Everyone at the hospital assumed they were romantically together… Frank didn't argue. In any event, intrigue almost always overwrites the self-loathing area of his thoughts, and already this parcel was the diversion his anxiety needed.

Inside were two items: the first being a large leather-bound book with golden tabs framing the outer edges of the thickened jacket. It had runes branded down the spine. He thought that perhaps it was Nordic in origin, but most obvious was that it was old, very old. The second item was a set of bound papers, tied together by paper string, and written in the same cursive English as the address stamp. It held a top sheet of paper with the words *"The Fortunes, Fables, & Failures of Henry Game"*. The paper looked old and thick, and it was smudged with black finger marks and smears of ink.

He lifted the bundle out by the string and placed it on the coffee table. The whole document was made up of varying shades of white and yellow parchment. Looking down the shabby outer edges of the bundle, bound by the wrapping and clipped through one edge to create a makeshift ring binding, it looked like it had been around the block a few times, and perhaps even via the sewerage system at some point. Frank placed it beside the ancient, and superiorly published book for a moment, returning to the empty packaging which had been lined with a red-purple velvet cloth material.

It looked too fine to throw away and a most bizarre box lining material. He wondered why someone would go to the trouble-

His mobile phone vibrated at a seemingly more intense frequency than ever before and caused him to jump from his skin. 'Oddy' displayed across the screen. He decided that he had avoided his uncle long enough.

'Hello.'

'Finally, Francis!' the speaker crackled on the handset from the roaring volume.

'Where have you sodding been for the past three weeks?' Oddy sounded a little stressed.

'At the hotel.'

'Hotel?'

'Yeah. The insurance company arranged it.'

There was silence on the other end.

'Look, I'm sorry. I've missed a few of your calls. I just needed some space to find my new routines.'

'Never mind that stupid bullshit,' snapped Oddy. 'Where is this hotel, tell me now what it is called?'

Frank had never known his uncle to be rude, and maybe only once or twice had he heard him swear. He'd never shown anything but confidence and awareness.

'Stupid bullshit?' Frank retorted but could sense Oddy's patience wearing thin through the tensioning static on the other end of the handset.

Silence is often a persuasive argument.

'I'm at Hotel Indigo. Down past the market end of the Takeaway Mile.'

'You're still in New York!' Oddy was laughing, and it clearly wasn't a question.

'Where else would I be?'

Oddy stopped laughing. 'Precisely, boy. Where else indeed?

Look, stay exactly where you are. I'll come and get you. I'm leaving Denver now-'

'Come and get me?' The words came out aggressive. But that was how Frank felt. 'I'm not fucking twelve anymore, *Uncle*. I need space. I'll call you when I am ready to see you, and not before.'

'And when your filthy drug stash runs out, what will you do then?'

Frank was dumbfounded. He looked to kitchen drawer where he had hidden it only a moment ago, thinking, or rather panicking about his secret so easily exposed.

'You know about that,' said Frank, but it wasn't a question either.

A drawn-out silence on the other end. Frank overheard a loudspeaker announcing the arrival of a flight to somewhere lost in the echoes.

'I won't be too long. Stay where you are. I'm coming for you.' He hung up.

Suspicious thoughts mashed with anxious chemicals as Frank tried to absorb some of the information he just received, and although it was a surprise, the truth is he was a little relieved that his uncle knew about the ticker situation. He reasoned that if Oddy knew about the drug in the first place, he most likely knew where to pick fresh quantities up. His uncle was undoubtedly a well-connected guy, everyone knew that. And by this train of logic, the threat of future suffering and worry was dialling down from ten to maybe a nine, or nine and a half.

The two books lay before him. Both of them equally intriguing and unexpected. Shutting his phone off, he unbound the document titled *"The Fortunes, Fables, & Failures of Henry Game"*, turned over the cover page and read the addressing line:

To my son, my flesh and blood, Francis,

Frank blinked. His heart triple jumping then plunging into his stomach to dissolve in acid. This wasn't written by the hand of his passive adopted father. The thick parchments, the cursive penmanship – everything about the whole package – the grimoire with Nordic runes, the pale-tan leather that looked like flesh, human flesh. He re-read the addressing line,

To my son, my flesh and blood, Francis,

Had his biological father finally reached out to him? He was doing it again: overthinking, tormenting himself.

Taking a deep breath, he returned to the manuscript:

I decided to attach this letter as a companion to my chronicles past, present, and recollected. My life is far too complex and protracted to present in a linear narrative, especially given my current time precious situation, we would literally need a lifetime…

For me to start at the beginning and write through to the present day would perhaps take more from me than I can give you right now.

Therefore, I give this to you in a way that will help make sense of the disarrays I have made.

I divided this companion throughout the entries, placing it where I see best to help you understand and perhaps empathise with my journey throughout the many centuries gone.

My earlier years I have had to recall my story through memories alone. The last two hundred years, however, I was able to call upon my journals.

There was a period of time when I guess you could say I was 'not alive'. And it was in the wake of my alter-death

experience I began to collate my experiences as they happened, committing them onto paper for posterities sake, or perhaps, my own vanity.

The original intention was to keep an accurate recording, as I experienced them first-hand. They are often not the same version of events as you will find documented in your public libraries. But the reasons for mistruths, especially on a governmental level, are vast and varied and usually calculated.

But of course, my writings for my own benefits all began long, long before you were born. However, recent proceedings honed my intention into purpose and that purpose is to do what I can for you before I am forever and finally no-more.

You must forgive my lack of precision with dates, especially in my 'early' years, as one might call them, should you find error or discrepancy. The day a thing happens is not what matters, only that a thing did happen and in what order, regardless of whether it was a Tuesday or a Thursday, a June or a January.

By the time you receive this package, the most recent and final entries, including this companion, will be no more than a year past, maybe less. The important thing is that by the time it reaches you I will hopefully have done what needed doing, and in doing so I will be truly dead, and you will be closer to safety and anonymity for good. Come what may, I dare say that these words will be my legacy.

As I said, my original intention was to record history, yet it is whilst I write in the here and now that I see the real reason for my final act of penmanship is to give you these words as a personal apology, an explanation even, or perhaps just something for you to have in the gaping void that was my absence from your life.

By engaging with my histories, I hope to educate you and

hopefully prevent you from making similar mistakes. These journals are the grand sum of regret, because remorse is all I am left with.

After all the riches, all the adventures: what remains, here in this lonely chamber of mine, is everything I have come to wish could have been different. Everything I wish I could change or undo. The end approaches me like an old friend, and as I open my door for her, I fear what is to become of the things in my wake.

Here I scribble across the blank page suddenly plagued by questions that have never before haunted me, but now press down like an anvil dropped atop a house of cards.

It is ironic that whilst I outwardly question the things taken for granted, here and now, in the quiet before what is to come, I finally discover that the answers are within, and I fear they always were.

Maybe this is what happens when one lives too long. Perhaps I have become complacent in my longevity. But what is life without the promise of death?

If time is the most valuable currency, I spend what little I have left on you by committing word to page in an effort to finally, and fully, document my story as a collection for publication, and hopefully provide you with a blade sharp enough to cut the bowels of the suppressors and spill the secrets of the powerful.

Trust that if I ever did one thing right, it was to complete this historical recollection and ensure it was safely delivered to you, so that you will know the truth of events, and I can die knowing that I have done my part in setting the record straight. But, this letter and these pages of accounts serve more purpose than just a whistle-blower. The main reason for my redemption is accomplished by telling you the truth about who and what you are.

Hopefully by now you have been able to accept that you are different. Certainly isolated. However, I hold fast in my belief that this has moulded you into the man you are today and now implore you to embrace this difference. It is distance that preserves you when all else fails. When the walls crash down around you and the fire takes all in its relentless embrace, you, my son, will be the last one standing. It is preparation for what you may become. This is your gift.

I am telling you this because my truth is a part of your truth. And in the end, whether you are sound of mind or completely delusional, what we hold as truth is all there is to it.

Hear my words. Read this account as it has been written for you. Research my claims. Question everything. Judge nothing. Do not for one-second think that I am any kind of a hero. I hope my confessions will help you better understand the demons that most plague you.

Who am I?

Let me start by saying that my name has been redacted from most historical records. I am your biological father. And until present, anonymity has suited my lifestyle. But now not so much. Seems I traced a faint line. My trails cut like a scalpel through the flesh of civilisations. Look close enough and you will see the scars I left for those who seek the truth.

I do not fib, nor exaggerate. Myths were forged from the shadows of the truths I leave for you. Falsehoods through propagation are reserved for the faithless and self-consciously needy.

I have been told about your violent exploits. I know only too well that you will know the feeling of Chaos. Through no fault of your own you battle everyday against your aggression, only so that you can exist within a society that was never meant for you. For this unequivocal failing, and many more besides, I am deeply sorry.

Suddenly wishing I had more love and happiness to ease my passing, let me tell you, it seems that all I have for company is stiff guilt in a shallow and sandy grave, while a contemptuous wind never relents to unearth my sins. I will not pass with a smile on my lips. I've taken enough lives to know how to die, but now that it is here and the spotlight is on me, I am afraid. And I am not ashamed to admit my flaws.

I will try to make you see the way my cards were dealt. Maybe you will learn from my mistakes and find empathy for a savage cunt like me.

I wasn't born a monster. The fiend grew upon me like a cloak of fungus. The darker my deeds, the denser my jacket.

My story started long ago in a quiet and unassuming village in Yorkshire, England. It is difficult for me to pinpoint the exact year, but what I do know is a new king had been crowned, and his name was Henry, the eighth of his line. Yet the place where my path was altered, and presently bringing me back to you, was as recently as last summer, amongst the pomps and toffs of British aristocracy. I never did like those dinner parties.

Last Summer's (L. S.) Solstice.

To keep the plates spinning, the wheels in rotation, and whispers pregnant with threats; my life had become one of maintenance, management, and juggling. The days of fool-hearted adventure and bathing in the blood of my defeated enemies were behind me. The monumental collection of scars and dents, the missing bits, the clicking and popping joints, my face, were all that remained of the mysteries I had carved into the folklore and legends that shadowed my own histories. These days I was cruising through the decades at top speeds and all I needed to do was apply a little throttle to maintain high velocity.

Truth is, by this point, I thought I'd seen it all, and most recently it was thanks to the wondrous and all-seeing Internet. Furthermore, and largely due to my many long years wherefrom, I had witnessed the cyclical nature of human failures, and, perhaps, had even stretched so far as to believe I had seen all that there would be. Yet, as ever, my ignorance never fails to get the better of my convictions.

Last night, my impression of who I was and where I fitted into this world shattered around me when I discovered that I, eternal and damned to walk a lonely and destructive existence, have a biological brother. And not just a brother, a twin, whom was also 'found', as the legend goes, in the depths and darkness of the well at St Oswald's Abbey – metaphorical or otherwise – many, many years gone by.

The abbey was once the proud home of The Order of St Oswald's. But today it stands as little more than an isolated church, its walls sinking into the shadows of the mountains that loom over the village of Horton in Ribblesdale, its congregation following suit as the years continue to pass by.

For centuries The Order has been the official keeper of secrets for governments, feudalists, and conglomerates alike. Their vaults are said to secure historical records that stretch back as early as the 8th century, preserving secrets only rivalled by that of the Vatican.

Well or no well, wherever I came from, all I know is that I was taken in by The Order from being too young to remember anything else. By the time I figured out what any of that meant to me, or the significance of it all, my hands were decently red and thick with sin and The Order were all but diminished to titles and ceremony and scattered throughout the United States of America.

So, it was upon arriving at yet another highly privileged event that I happened to come face-to-face with the current head of The Order – a scrotum of a fellow – the Archbishop of Canterbury.

And whilst I do submit to the pomp and sanctimony of these ritual gatherings, if not purely for the gossip, I elect to keep to the darkest corners, from which I am able to monitor the affairs of men. Such things are expected from me. Wars being old hat these days; I mingle with the heads of various multi-national intelligence committees, keep my hand in and learn of potential threats or opportunities. But whilst these *spyders* are not the loosest of fellows, they sure can tell a good "knock, knock" joke, and they make the evening rather more palatable.

Things were moving along as predicted when I clocked the archbishop chomping away, a pig wrapped in blanket in one hand, and a spilling wine goblet in the other, making an industrious beeline straight for me. His bald and wrinkled head bobbing the reflection of the overhead fluorescents. The fact that he headed in my direction at all drew various glances.

Plus, given my history with the religious zealot establishments, it really wasn't the kind of attention I welcomed, nor he either, I would imagine, but come my way he did.

He stood before me and waited, staring at my scars like a child gawps at an invalid in a wheelchair at the supermarket. Meanwhile, chomping and swilling, he ended my conversation with the Germanic *spyder* prematurely and altogether quite rudely. And as my wurst-loving-collaborator bolted, I realised that left just the two of us: the archbishop and I, alone, with each other.

With the last piece of bacon-wrapped-sausage devoured, he offered his gloved hand out, very proud. 'Lord Game,' his liver spots glowing with the warm reflection of the ceiling.

I didn't reply, nor shake his hand, and instead continued to frown at him like I couldn't remember his name, then I settled for clenching my teeth and peeling my lips back.

He dropped his hand. 'May we find some privacy?' He was gesturing to one of the many side rooms down a long corridor away to our left.

I nodded and as the party watched on, we made our swift exit from the main function and selected a doorway that stood out in no way, shape, or form.

As the door shut behind us, we stood in total darkness, the soles of our polished shoes buried in plush carpet. Seconds stretched on until finally, I found the light switch.

'Your Eminence,' I said, my words dripping in sarcasm.

He waved a clicky wrist. 'Let us not get overly weighed down within the extravagancy of our titles, or we'll be bloody at it all night-hargh!' His chortling turned into a phlegm filled donut of bronchitis, stuck in his throat.

I didn't laugh, it wasn't even remotely funny.

'You must forgive me,' he recovered, holding a hand to his chest. 'I have heard many stories about the great Henry Game and how-' he touched a hand to his cheek, 'and how you came about your…'

If I disliked the guy before I had even met him, which was in fact true, then I was moving closer and closer to just straight up hating the little fat cunt with each second that passed.

'Scars.' I finished the sentence for him, my arms folded across my chest because I didn't trust my hands not to reach out and strangle him.

'Oh, but I don't mean to offend you.' His words slurring a little, 'I am honoured to finally hold an audience with the real Lord Game. I mean, you're a legend!'

He blinked hard and stumbled, a little unsure on his feet. 'I think I might be a little tipsy,' he moved to sit by a small reading table that backed up one of those floor-to-ceiling bookshelves: the type that comes with a ladder on a rail. Perching on the edge of the desk, hands folded atop his crotch he seemed at ease.

'But tonight, humbled, I come to you under the advisement of our brotherhood: The Order.' He stood again, maybe not so relaxed after all. 'And please, I urge you to hear me out before you react.'

He pulled at his collar as if to loosen it up. 'Brother to brother.'

I perked a little, stepping closer. Now he was just pleasantly irritating me. And I do love a good puzzle.

'Can't promise anything,' I said.

The archbishop looked far from satisfied, but he nodded anyway.

'The Vatican has cut the ribbon around Ian Mulliti,' he said, and then watched me with woozy caution. A few awkward seconds passed before he continued.

'Now, I know the two of you have nothing to do with one another, and never have, but just as a courtesy, I wanted to let you know, to deliver the news personally, even...' his words lost as he swayed from side to side, struggling to keep his eyes on me.

'The bounty calls for him dead or alive,' he continued, 'but I heard more if dead. Not unusual when dealing with your lot. One must take precautions-hargh!'

'Ian Mulliti.' I repeated the name, interrupting his solemn nodding and chest patting. 'Never heard of him. And I honestly couldn't care less what the Vatican does to the poor bugger. Now, you have a good night, and maybe save some of the wine for rest of the party?'

As I turned for the door the archbishop's sigh and subsequent peering from atop his wire-frame glasses held me in limbo.

'Never heard of him?' He folded his arms and drew his eyebrows tight, blinking long and drunkenly. 'Look, your brother has a bounty on his head, and I just wanted to pay you the courtesy of letting you know. I don't play games as you damnwell know, Henry. As the head of The Order of Saint bloody Osw-'

'Brother?' I cut across his tripe. 'Is this a wind up?' I looked around the room, a playful half smile. 'Do you have cameras in here or... Hang on, who put you up to this?'

He blinked and opened his mouth to say something before flapping it shut just as quickly. His face flushing of blood, suddenly blinking faster than usual.

For a few moments he did nothing except allow his beady eyes to reach beyond the room. Several seconds later he returned to the present and swallowed. He was drunk and he looked like he wished he wasn't.

'Brother?' I advanced and immediately he threw his hands up before him, stumbling backward and tipping the small reading desk over in the process, even dislocating the ladder from the rail with a crash. I heard the door struggling against the carpet to my rear when a sudden darkness fell in and I wasn't standing upright anymore.

Light returned in sharp blinks. The seldom trodden carpet was intimate with my face, and I was sprawled belly-down upon the burgundy plushness. Slowly sound returned with clarity and definition. I registered two sets of feet shuffling, tiptoeing around my head space. A piece of furniture being dragged across the room toward me.

'Mason, quick, stick him with the needle…' The archbishop's words slurred heavier than the weight of furniture being shifted around. 'The sodding sedative, man, quickly!'

'Argh!' complained another, deeper voice. Something dropped to the floor. 'These stupid fucking safety lids, they get me every time.' A statement that resonated with effort and little intelligence.

'Why do they make these stupid things so fucking hard to open?'

'I told you to get it ready before you came in here, you fucking idiot!'

More shuffling and dragging. 'Just give it to me, you bloody tool…' That was definitely the archbishop.

I was still getting my bearings, but I think I had the room and their positions mapped out in my mind.

'Safety caps are made to stop children, or in your case, absolute retards, from getting into the dangerous bottle. Here, now quick, stick him with this before he wakes-'

'Too late,' I whipped my arm out, punching the archbishop in the side of the knee from my prostrated position.

His bones knocked together with a crack and he folded like human origami and I leapt up and on top of his crumpled sack of religious bones. It had been too long since I had last had such fun. Before he had time to cry out my forearm was across his windpipe and my free hand on the back of his balding pate, exerting enough force to choke him, slowly, I didn't want to kill him, yet. But what I didn't foresee was that such an action would also make him dribble all over my new tuxedo.

The back of my head hurt and itched at the same time, but scratching it was out of the question. Somehow amongst the mania, I'd forgotten about the cunt that hit me with something heavy from behind. That was until he pricked me in the neck with an almighty war-cry. It was like something straight out of a Mel Gibson movie.

He pushed the plunger down as spittle arced through the air around me and my adrenaline kicked it up a gear. Before the plunger had depressed enough for it to matter, I had the needle out of my neck and in through the black of his eyeball. It was a big, big fucking needle mind you, I half expected it to shoot through the other side of his skull and pin him to the door. I waited to squeeze for a heartbeat or two, allowing his senses to catch up to reality. It was only fair. Didn't want him dead before I could enjoy his final realisation.

He screamed again but this time it was more befitting of a Wes Craven narrative. I administered the cloudy substance as forcefully as possible, before leaving the dopey fucker to slide down the door slab in the throes of death. He wore the clothes of a houseboy, but from the looks of his thrice-crooked nose, the droopy eye, and gap-toothed grimace: he looked more accustomed to cleaning up blood and teeth than he was cleaning houses.

'But. But…but,' he gawped, the essence of an idea scribbled over his unbeautiful mug, before abandoning him along with his consciousness and limited life force.

Meanwhile the old cunt behind me was hawking and spurting on his hands and knees. I finally turned around and advanced on him.

'No, Henry. Please don't!' he pleaded, wrinkly hands shaking in front of his face in some pathetic attempt at fending me off.

'Don't what, kill you?' I laughed as the wrinkled sack of piousness flinched behind his pink palms in a prayer of mercy. 'Certainly not yet.'

I perched on the edge of the desk, opening a little distance between us. 'And definitely not before you've answered my question.'

'I don't know anything!' He continued to curl into a ball of puss and cowardice.

I turned away and retrieved the bedded needle from Dickhead's oozing eyeball and smiled like it was my birthday, which it most probably wasn't, but certainly felt like it could've been.

'Okay, you were saying,' I held the needle up to the light and picked a little lump of red goo from the end. 'If I recall correctly that is' I continued, 'something about a brother of mine that I clearly know nothing about…' I held the syringe up and blood frothed from the pointy end as I pumped the plunger to the top.

'Brother! Yes, he's your brother, Henry.' The archbishop's eye wide and his cheeks pale. 'Ian Mulliti, your brother, very dangerous…'

'Oh, so you do remember!' I crouched down beside him.

He flinched, tightening back into a ball, like a hedgehog. I wielded the syringe no more than a few inches from his pocked face and made a suggestion.

'Now then, let's see if you can help me understand all this a little more clearly then, yeah?'

Good Friday. Horton in Ribblesdale, England. Early 1530s.

'Ow, enough Henry!' The look in Francis' eyes told me he was fed-up. 'You're too quick, and you keep hitting me in the same places.' Francis rubbed at the flushing patches on the tops of his bare arms.

We were out on the fields by the kitchen side of the abbey. The smell of broiling fish driving up a forgotten appetite in us both. The sun hanging low over the mountain that loomed, and the chill of night blowing its way toward us with the promise of a thunderstorm. Dark clouds gathered in the next valley with just the beginnings of rumble in its guts. I always knew when rain was coming. My tongue was sensitive to it, could taste the humidity brewing.

'You've got to be tougher, Franky,' I said, crouching down a little to bring myself to his level. 'Be willing to take a hit, or two if necessary. Sometimes it's the only chance you'll get to hit them back. And when you do,' I made my fist as tight as I could, my knuckles white and pitched, 'you hit them a lot harder than they hit you.'

'But it hurts!' he still rubbed at the red patches, the makings of a little bruise showing through; clearly not convinced that fighting was at all necessary.

I nodded and corrected his form again, un-tucking the thumbs from beneath his little fingers. 'You'll hurt yourself more if you punch like that. And yes, it does hurt. But it will hurt more if you do not fight back when they come for you. And they will come for you-'

'But what if I don't want to fight?' Francis looked up at me, serious frown dressing the question.

'As you grow up, you'll realise that standing up and fighting for the things you want is the only way you'll ever get it. Father says there are two types of people: the strong and the weak.'

Francis nodded and lifted his arms up again, ready for another round, his bony and pale fist bunched, thumbs on the outside.

'Remember, when you are up against an opponent who is equal to you, or maybe even a better fighter, you will have to-'

'Take a hit to hit back, harder.' Francis stepped toward me, determined in his position.

I threw a soft punch and he took it on his forearm, using the movement to manoeuvre himself closer to my body. I swung again, leaving my defence down on my left. Expecting him to block again, I was surprised as my fist bounced off his head with a crack of knuckles, and Francis moved closer still, throwing a right-straight of his own and striking me in the ear on my unguarded side.

It hurt more than I expected, and I let my legs go, dropping like a sack of grain on the grass. Francis grinned like a fox in a chicken pen, standing proudly over me.

'Good punch, Franky! Think you may have busted my eardrum.'

'Did you see it? I took your punch by head-butting it. That way it doesn't hurt as much, and I could hit you back where I knew you couldn't block!'

'Eh?' I wiggled a finger in my ear.

'I said that I took the hit on my head-'

'Sorry, I can't hear you! You must've broken my ear!'

A long rumble of thunder from above the valley rolled over us. Seemed the sun was of the same opinion as it too had decided to call it a day and disappeared, but not before the night could arrive.

'Okay, okay, help me up, punchy,' I teased, my hand out, still playing the wounded fighter. 'That storm sounds grumpier than old Brother Elliot during Lent.'

Francis laughed and we slowly made our way back to the abbey. I watched how he practised making fists with his thumb out. He was a good kid.

The purple twilight made everything look different. I had always imagined that it was the time of the day when the world cooled down and transformed into the night lands. Francis' hair looked blood red; the grass a brown blue.

Bells rang out, signalling the conclusion of Vespers, mingling into another yawning of thunder. The bells indicated that it was time to light the lanterns and prepare for the ceremonial meal of Christ's last supper.

* * *

The table was set traditionally except, of course, Brother Glen's fork was on the right, not the left.

After setting flame to the dinner-light I rang the bell. Back then I didn't have to wait long between hearty meals and the equally mouth-watering smells that prepared the way before them. Today it was the boil of fish-stew that washed over me, given that Fridays we always ate fish, but especially so on the holiest of Fridays.

A few moments later the door opened and in entered our resident cook: Brother Thomas, carrying the stew pan and carefully setting it on the centre tray.

The monks filed into the room until every chair of The Order was filled. The abbot: Father Game, sat at the head of the table, and I by his left with little Francis opposite my place on his right – Francis' toes still swinging above the stone floor. I was small for my age, or so the brothers told me, but I could at least sit in a chair like a man.

Before food was dished, we bowed our heads in prayer but a noise at the door disrupted our worship. Hard knocks echoed through the darkened hallways and a follow up rumble of thunder sent tremors through the floors of the abbey and into my feet. The storm was closing in.

Gossiping murmur circulated in the absence of routine prayer. I focused my concentration, drowning the brothers out, straining myself further still until it happened again: another hard and purposeful knock, only this time I knew a little more about our uninvited guests.

I could hear the sounds of rain pounding against the timber shutters; a muffled conversation between hoarse men; hoofs scratching at the cobbles; and then, loud and clear, the scrape of wet steel. The guests weren't welcome or looking to join our prayer.

Pulling at Father Game's sleeve, I struggled to get his attention through the cacophony of presumption filling the room.

'Soldiers" I shouted, 'at the door!' My words bringing a moment of silence.

'Nonsense!' Brother Elliot scoffed. 'It'll be one o' those townsfolk again. Hands out beggin' fo' grain, I'm tellin' thee,' his round eyes circling around the table, resting upon Francis' golden hair, betraying the conviction in his voice.

I heard our visitors again, and they didn't sound like townsfolk to me. I tugged at Father Game's sleeve, but he only looked out at the brothers, his cleanly shaved jaw and mouth forming a hard line.

'Or maybe Papa has finally come to claim wee Francis, now that he's a strong lad. An' if he has,' Brother Elliot pointed his well-fed finger at nobody in particular – his barrel chest swollen – 'I'm tellin' thee now, brothers, if he has: well, he'll be bloody handin' over fo' all the upkeep o' the boy, and that's for a starters.'

'Please!' Father Game stood, quietening the room with open palms. 'That is not the knock of a beggar. Listen!'

The Order stilled to a quick silence. All could hear the pounding storm beyond our fickle doors as the clouds rolled again and sent power through our feet and into our table.

Father Game looked around, nodding as though he was agreeing with a statement that no one had made. Or perhaps it was a statement that I didn't understand in my younger years.

'The moment the dissolution order passed we knew this day would come. Or did we not?'

I didn't understand the words but the reaction throughout The Order was clearly one of fear. I looked around, confused, as one or two of the brothers made holy crosses, whispering private words to God.

'They already pillaged St Andrew's,' Father Game's words waded through the rare silence. 'And Andrew's are independents, as are we. The gold, silver, and bronze we wear and decorate our halls with are why they come. No other reason. We must hide our treasures, or fear losing them.'

Father Game's warning rang hard and all were deep in their own fears, meanwhile I could still hear the visitors growing less patient as the wind and rain beat down on them with righteous violence, or so I imagined.

Brother Elliot flared up again. 'It's the land they're after, I'm tellin' thee now. Mark my words, all o' yee…' He leaned across to the pot and dipped a crust into the fish-stew. Straightening back up he blew on the steam, ate his food and sat back down, seemingly nothing more to add to his open-ended statement.

'Father,' I turned to him as the rest of the table continued anxiously predicting their futures or that of The Order and abbey. 'There's more than one of them out there. I hear hooves, and steel-'

The banging on the doors echoed out again, only this time louder and immediately followed by a wilder set of thuds much like boots pounding wood.

'Brother Thomas, take the food back and hold it a simmer, let us see if we cannot postpone this charade until a more reasonable hour. That being said, brothers Elliot, James, please see masters Henry and Francis to the upper section of the stables. They'll be safe there whilst we deal with whatever blasphemy dares intrude upon this holiest of occasions.

'The rest of you know what to do, leave just enough treasure around for these scavengers to steal. We wouldn't want them looking too hard, would we?'

Chairs scratched against the stone floor as The Order followed instructions without delay. I grabbed a roll of bread as I understood that we were to leave and hide.

I tried to get Father's attention again, but he was already heading toward the visitors at our doors. Without time to think we were swept away in the opposite direction and out of the back exit.

At the stables, Brother James stood as lookout by the doors whilst Brother Elliot rushed us up and onto the mezzanine level, way out at the back. An area usually "out-of-bounds" to children. Once up there, Brother Elliot ordered us to hide amongst the dusty saddles and broken tools, I noticed the rusty scythe with only half a handle.

'Right, listen up, Henry lad, you think yee can help us keep the little one quiet?' Brother Elliot looked a little more flustered than usual. He looked worried.

I nodded and put my arm around Francis.

'We'll be back fo' yee soon enough lads,' he said, and gave Francis a pat on the head before starting back down the ladder.

'What do the soldiers at the door want?' Coldness had started to work into my bones.

He frowned at me. 'It might not be soldiers-' he snatched his sentence and looked back toward the stable doors as suddenly as Brother James had an over-exaggerated coughing frenzy. 'Listen, the crown's just about lookin' fo' excuses to raid our wealth. Catholicism is not welcome in England anymore. If they could close us down fo' good, they will. Yee understands me?'

I tried to understand but didn't, nodding as solemnly as I could. Brother Elliot looked tired, and more worried than I had ever seen him.

'Havin' two unregistered young lads here,' he continued, 'that'll certainly be the end o' Saint Oswald's as an abbey. Yee understand that, surely?'

I didn't but continued nodding along anyway, sitting low amongst the dust and old leather, placing a hand on Francis' shoulder, pulling him lower behind the saddles with me.

A drip had started and was catching Brother Elliot on his arm where he held the rung. The sounds of wind and rain revved up as a boom of thunder rumbled out and vibrated through the timber framing. It sounded like the storm was directly above us now.

Brother Elliot gave a lasting nervous grin and descended the ladder. I watched him exit the barn, plunging us both into darkness as soon as Brother James pushed the barn door closed and left into the night and the storm and the fear of ignorance.

I tried my hardest to hear what might be going on in the main residence, to hear something about anything, but failed to penetrate the sounds of wind and rain lashing the derelict barn. After a while I grew tired from the effort of worry. Meanwhile Francis sniffled and fidgeted, curling tight-up against my back. I couldn't take my eyes from the barn door.

'They are not in trouble because of us, are they?' Francis's soft words had a way of disarming me.

I turned away from the doors. 'No, Franky, don't be silly. We're just…playing hide and seek. But shush now. They'll never find us here. You get some rest, okay?'

'But I'm hungry. We didn't eat. Can we go back? I don't want to play anymore…'

I grimaced. My own stomach clenching suddenly. I'd forgotten about the fish stew. Reaching into my overgarment I produced the bread roll I'd grabbed earlier and took a small bite, passing the lion's share to Francis who accepted it hungrily, wordlessly, like all five-year-olds do. It wasn't much, but Francis was satisfied enough not to complain or ask for more. Somehow, in the stormy darkness, we both managed to fall asleep, half-hidden beneath the dusty saddles and discarded tools of years spent.

Torchlight and heat woke me stone-cold and alert. I panicked as I registered the towering form of a royal guardsman above me, blood of the Tudor Rose across his dented breastplate, glinting in the firelight. A dagger longer than my spine loose at his hip.

He frowned down at us both but said nothing for a few moments. I was only grateful that Francis was still asleep when he reached down to grab him.

That was when I kicked out at the guardsman's legs with as much force as I could muster. To both of our surprise, my efforts managed to knock his footing straight from under him and he ended up crashing down on top of us both, which in turn caused the mezzanine floor to split and give way.

All three of us fell and I'll never forget the whelp that Francis made as we hit the earth, the guardsman atop of him, his belted dagger lodged firmly into child's flesh, fatally sticking Francis through to the mud.

The horses scrambled. Bolting only as far as the stables would allow them to scatter. I bounded to my feet unharmed, desperately trying to reach Francis as he continued to slurp in desperate gulps of clotted air. And in my haste of scaling across the wood and debris, one of the horses kicked me whilst my arm was lodged between two of the partially collapsed mezzanine floor joists.

I remember a flash of black, then a pop. Moments later I was lying next to Francis. He reached out toward me, dirty fingers brushing against my own numb hand. Once. Twice. I could not feel his touch, but I could feel his fear. I watched helpless as he could no longer find the strength to breathe in. I remember screaming when his body started convulsing before finally shuddering still.

In the silent moments that followed I realised that my arm had been entirely ripped from my shoulder, and it was that which lay beside Francis, his dead fingers maybe an inch away from my separated arm.

The guardsman started to rise, coughing, looking down at us both, but the blood that smeared across his pale forehead looked black, blacker than his eyes, and the splintered handle of the rusty scythe jutting awkwardly from out of his ribs, deep within the side of his chest plate. He coughed his own death, looking down at what had killed him then back at me, surprise, more than anything else on his face.

The barn dimmed. I blinked slowly.

The guardsman was gone.

I blinked again and tried a smile as I recognised the weathered face of Father, hovering above me. He looked worried.

I blinked a long and tired blackness.

Loose-Lips, Caviar, and Service Stations. (L. S.).

It was time to leave, and preferably before anyone noticed the archbishop was missing.

We took- I'm sorry, I'm making it sound as though we skipped away hand in hand. Let me rephrase, I dragged the weeping sack of shit out of the service entrance and stuffed him, and all of his flappy robes, into the backseat of my car. Then, with no raised alarms, I calmly exited the grounds, passing the gatehouse with a wave and a wink, and silently accelerated off into the heart of the English countryside.

Rain was in the air. I could smell it. Muffled sobs and sniffles from the back seat reminded me of that dirty old bastard slavering on my dinner jacket. Then I imagined him drooling all over the fabric interiors. I'd just picked up this cute little number: Tesla Model S, 100% electric, great for the environment, and supercharged to the nuts.

'Don't you fucking dare make a mess back there, or I'll make you lick it up.' I thought about the threat and decided that it was empty and that I wouldn't make him lick anything up, not from the car at least. That would probably just make more mess. No, most likely it would be a microfibre cloth and maybe a little soap and water, but I wasn't going to tell him that.

We merged on to a dual carriageway from out of the winding darkness, smoothly cutting across the deserted lanes at silent top speeds. We headed north-east, back toward the "Vault of Records", as the archbishop had put it when I demanded evidence of my sibling's existing.

He assured me there was such proof, but the truth is I already believed him. Evidence was merely academic at this stage. Only an absolute fool would make such a thing up, and despite the archbishop's allegiances to the Church of England, he was no fool. Pursuing it was the distraction I needed whilst I digested the fact that I was not alone in my extraordinary longevity, and never had been.

A services station approached and, annoyingly, I realised that I was in desperate need of sustenance, so I pulled in.

'If you try and escape, or make any sound at all whilst I'm gone…' I finished the sentence by slicing my forefinger across my throat, then emphatically stabbing it at him, to emphasise a purposefully over-emphasised point. I am nothing if not thorough.

The archbishop stopped his mumbling and nodded, wide-eyed.

I opened the door before cursing myself. 'Where are my manners?' I leaned back in, half-in: half-out, 'do you want a drink, something to eat, maybe a sandwich, coffee?'

He declined, and I slammed the door, carefully of course, and locked the cunt inside with my fob from several yards away. Fucking technology.

I rushed my food more than I would have liked, but I just didn't trust my hostage, and especially not in my new machine. I'll admit that I was proud of myself for buying an electric car. And of course, when I say "buying", that is stretching the truth a little. Let us say it was a gift made in earnest, under duress, and against the will of the previous owner, but a gift that broke no law of the land and now it legally belonged to me.

I'd enacted countless wrongs in my lifetime but driving an electric car is not one of them. If anything, I figured, just by driving a Tesla, I had already become a better person with zero emissions. I deserved a badge.

Rain had begun to fall as I climbed back into the driving seat and it didn't look like letting up anytime soon. Thankfully the archbishop had regained some semblance of self-respect, as the blubbering had dried up, and he'd even managed to sit upright and fasten his seatbelt.

This was a good development because whilst I ate, I had considered beating him unconscious, and stuffing him into the spacious boot. I reckoned it was better than listening to his pleading and crying and sniffling and drooling. I had my satellite navigation hooked up through the central digital screen, my music and hot air blowing through the futuristic vents, I really didn't need the old cunt in the back seat...

Fed and watered we set off again towards the Vault of Secrets which contained, according to the archbishop, irrefutable evidence that my *brother* had left with a troupe of missionaries to explore the recently discovered Americas, way back in the early 1500s.

I promised the archbishop I would let him live should I be satisfied with the information – assuming it provided a current address for brother dearest – but we had a countdown clock on this mission, owing to the Vatican's fatwa, obviously. Let's not forget that little detail.

Truth is that this was the most exciting thing to happen since the fiasco in the Gulf. It would surely be a shame if he was assassinated before I'd had the opportunity to meet the bastard. I wondered if he was anything like me: a monster in a world of well-dressed horrors.

The archbishop had said that my brother most commonly went by the name Ian Mulliti. Kind of average, I figured. I reckoned he kept himself to himself with a name like that.

'P,p, pull in on your left and take the fourth exit on the roundabout,' stuttered the archbishop through his flaking veneer of self-dignity. I could smell his sweat. I considered turning the heat up, but in an act of true altruism, decided against it.

We pulled onto the exit lane, double-checking my speed as we passed a sneaky unmarked police car in the lay-by. I'm not psychic but I would have bet my left nut that the bastard was going to flag me down and within ten seconds the wash of flashing blue made pursuit.

Weighing up my options, I decided that keeping the law off my trail would be the best route, given that we had a good few hours of driving ahead of us. I came to a silent stop directly beneath the exit sign for *Malmesbury*, *Cotswold Water Park*, and *Tetbury*. The deserted roundabout a hundred meters in front.

'Keep your mouth shut.' I warned without turning, 'make a fucking peep and you'll die first.'

The plain-clothed police officer exited his vehicle, looking on at my car from a short distance back. He wasn't wearing a raincoat, which was odd, and it looked like he was talking into a mobile phone. Flashing lights still going, loud with colour, especially given the time of night.

Something didn't feel right. Coldness was creeping into me. I unfastened my seatbelt, ready to open the door when suddenly two shots fired, shattering my rear window.

I could have cried right then and there if I wasn't so afraid that this *Terminator 2*-style-cop was in a mood to put more holes into my car. I smoked my tyres down to the metal fibres in a frantic bid to escape, and it wasn't for my benefit, but obviously this cop-cunt had the proclivity for shooting first, second, and if required, shooting some more until everyone was dead and no questions could ever be asked or answered.

Gunshots harrowed around us as we tore away to the roundabout, drifting the road around ninety degrees and taking exit four. I checked my rear view but couldn't make out much from the puncture wounds steadily spraying rainwater onto the ruined parcel shelf. Something else was wrong, but

I couldn't quite put my finger on it, but for the moment I had a duty to protect my vehicle. I figured the bastard would no doubt be after us by now. I needed to get off of the main road and disappear down an unremarkable street.

'How are we back there?' I asked over my shoulder, checking the side mirrors for signs of pursuit.

His response was delayed. The kind usually reserved for the dead. I glanced at him and really wished I hadn't. My car didn't deserve this at all. The front of the archbishop's head, his grey matter, bone and all, was splattered all over the back seats and the ceiling.

I wanted to scream. In fact, I think I did. I'd had this fucking car for a week. One week! In the swelling rage of injustice, and at the smell of blood, I started to think more clearly. Traffic police don't carry guns. Nor do they shoot at innocent, good for the environment electric cars. But if they did carry guns, and they were targeting me specifically, meaning they knew who I was, they would definitely not be shooting at me with mere pistols. That would just piss me off.

No, I was missing something obvious. I thought it over again: if they knew who I was, and they were shooting bullets at my car, the only two possible outcomes would be that they want to fuck my car up, or, they wanted to shoot me down and capture me. Or, the third possibility occurred to me as I waited at a red light, I wasn't the target.

'Holy fuck!' An involuntary outburst. And yes, of course he was a holy fuck, but also, I couldn't believe my own stupidity and cowardice.

I just took it for granted that whenever situations got a little stabby, or just outright murderous, I was the target. Obviously, not this time.

That got me to thinking further. It seemed that thinking would be featuring heavily on the agenda for the foreseeable future. And when thinking has traditionally been secondary to the action, it was time for a change in the paradigm.

My brain shifted into second, then third and as the red light switched to green, I didn't move from the mark. Clearly no one was following. And I had just driven away from the only tangible connection to whatever the fuck was going on.

Temper got the better of me and I let the steering wheel take the brunt of it. I'm ashamed to admit it but the car was already besmirched.

Pulling over to the side of the road, I clambered into the back with the dead man. No two-ways about it: this was an assassination for sure. Turning the dead cunt over, I peeled back his collar upon collar, turned out his pockets and flaps and robes. So many pieces of fabric. I had another moment of devastation as I looked around the back of my car. It was ruined; desecrated. The archbishop was turning up empty, and with no clues I was starting to think that all of this madness would be for nothing. Sometimes shit does just happen.

My temper got the better of me again and I pulled out *Abatu* and stabbed the fucker in his wrinkly face, a good dozen or so times, until his skin hissed and crackled like pig skin on a hot plate.

When he was sufficiently blistered and defaced, I put away the dagger and continued my search. The release in frustration gave a return of clarity, allowing me to think outside of the square. Out of places left to search, I pried open the heel of his church-issued loafer and found the motherfucker, finally.

It was a tracking chip or maybe a listening device, or both. It looked a little like one of them pill-batteries you get in watches, and it had words lasered onto the outer casing: 'ATLAS, NV, USA'. I figured they knew we were going to the Vault after all, and clearly didn't want to let that happen.

The riddle was maturing. I sensed the old ways flexing their muscles within me. Sure, I was pissed about my car; discovering that I had a brother was certainly interesting and infuriating at the same time. But what was done was done. This wax version of Henry Game would melt away as soon as the heat turned up.

I touched the sharp edge of *Abatu* across the seats and footwells before hopping out as fire engulfed the interior, the Archbishop of Canterbury's corpse along with it too. The Tesla was only a fucking machine after all.

I dropped the listening device down a storm water drain and picked up the pace as the sounds of sirens neared the scene and set off running into the night just as lightening flashed and thunder rolled distant and softly. All compasses pointed west. I was going to the States again.

* * *

I had an apartment not too far away, maybe a twenty-minute run. It was an upmarket little spot that I'd purchased some time ago for my rare getaways to the Cotswolds, which of course, never seemed to eventuate.

My plan was to stay at the apartment after the dinner party, maybe even spend a couple of days down there, for once, but things being what they were… I didn't have the time or the motivation to rest. I was way too excited, even stimulated, with America on the horizon and the lingering stink of burnt hair and shit stuck in my nose.

Dark memories from my time spent in the land of the free came sprinting back at me like a gold medallist Olympic champion, of the waking nightmare event category. And being the person of slow decay that I am, sleep does not come my way somewhat as often as it does the next man. Perhaps once a week is all I can manage. However, never do I sleep quite so easily as when danger and adventure is afoot, or, as happens more often than I care to admit, when I am perilously wounded.

I had a new quest on my hands and in memory of my beloved car's desolation, I couldn't help but retain a smile for my loss, like a teenager almost, because if I needed something to avenge, then of course it would be the Tesla, for the time being at least. I am nothing if not a habitual creature with the proclivity for righteous murdering sprees.

From the shower I could hear distant sirens and assumed that they must have reached the burning wreckage by now. The hot water nipped at my scalp and I noticed a faint red-blue trickle down my left arm, tracking it back up to my shoulder, then my neck and into my hair until I found the wound. The purple swirling about my feet and escaping into the shower drain was telling me that maybe I had been nicked by a stray bullet, or, perhaps it was from when I got thwacked by the moronic house-boy back at the dinner party. Either way, blood was in the water, and old habits led me to strategising a quick cover identity to take control of the crime scene from the local constabulary. Preferably before any evidence could be stored or sent away for testing.

I wondered how they would handle the news of a dead archbishop, killed by gunfire and burned along with the Tesla. But this time I was the victim: my car had been murdered and desecrated by the blood and guts of the Archbishop of Canterbury, and I had been attacked and wounded for no forth coming reason. Fucking let the police come, I would avenge the injustice done to me should anyone be stupid enough to try and compound my misery with insult, uniform or not. I had a score to settle.

I had scarcely dried myself and stepped into a new suit when I heard a faint creaking in the deliberately loosened floorboard just outside of my apartment door. I approached silently, listening and picking up nothing but calm breathing. I held my dagger in my left hand, the other rested on the handle.

'Game, less of the nonsense and just open up, eh?' urged the familiar voice from the other side. 'Before I huff, and I puff…' the voice trailed, and a moment of silence passed. I hesitated in my response as memories flooded. The person whom I feared to be standing on the other side of my apartment door had died years ago, or so I believed.

'Look, I don't have all night. Hurry up!'

Of course, I knew the voice but couldn't make sense of it. Any of it. I wondered if I was having a flashback, or finally some sort of mental breakdown. They said my sins would catch up with me one day. Perhaps that day was finally here-

'Open the sodding door!' The door and frame and wall shook from the force of the impact. I felt it in my hands and feet, even the paintings on the wall rattled way over on the opposite side of the living room.

'Grim?' I dared to whisper as the handle began to turn, even as I held on to it with both hands. It was opening whether I stood there or not. I let the door swing inward and stepped back as *he*, my formerly dead friend, Grim Catspaw, filled the doorway, entirely, and then some.

'Same holes; same clothes; maybe even the same pigeon bones…if you get hungry enough.' He grinned, all eye and big teeth, like this was a perfectly normal evening and he hadn't been dead for the last twenty years, or so.

'Is it still raining then?' I kept it casual, like I knew he had been there the whole time, 'Certainly alive, I see.'

The towering form of Grim Catspaw bowed beneath the header of the doorframe and stepped into the room, dripping all over my polished wooden parquetry.

'As always, my friend, you underestimate, well…' He kicked

the door shut with his booted heel and looked around the apartment before settling his bright eye on me again. 'Just about everyone, actually, but me, most of all.'

'Please,' I said, 'come in why don't you.'

'That face,' he shuddered, 'time hasn't softened those scars, eh?'

I eyed him. He knew too well what I'd been through.

'I paid the price for what I became. What you brought me into.' Watching him as he candidly picked up the ornaments dotted around the room's perimeter and flicked them back down, out of position.

'I did what I did because it was the right thing to do,' I reminded him, adding a steel into my tone that warned off the topic.

'Cut your nose off to spite your face, really?' He didn't look at me as he asked the question, and the amusement in his tone wasn't fooling either of us. I caught the flicker in his eye when he saw I held my dagger in a ready fist.

'Where have you been? I mourned for you.' Grim stopped at that and looked at me with a squint in his remaining eye, the other was covered by a black eyepatch with no visible strings or attachments. It was pretty cool and very villain esque.

'Didn't you know that it's rude to stare at a man with cyclopsosis,' he said and resumed his inspection of my 'off the grid' safe house.

I held back the smile. 'Fuck. You're looking a bit fat, old friend.' It wasn't a compliment, more of another running joke between us. Truth is I was glad to see the massive cunt, but also angry at the same time.

I slid *Abatu* away, holstered within a specially made pouch attached to the belt hole on the back of my trousers. Just holding a weapon like that, I found, dramatically increased one's chances for death and carnage and amputations, and this was not the time for anything like that.

He ran his fingers around the rim of his dripping fedora. 'I realise you will be pushing me for answers, but I have come to tell you that you must go to America, but not to find your brother.'

'Yeah?' I slipped my winklepickers back on, tucking the laces down the sides of my feet. 'Find my brother,' I repeated. 'The thought never occurred to me.'

'Ian Mulliti is no joke, Henry. Make that lapse in judgement at your own peril.'

'Tell me,' I rose to my feet, my blood beginning to rush, 'because, this is pissing me off a little: how long have you known that I have a fucking *brother*?'

Grim stopped his prying for a moment and smiled in the face of my annoyance. He shrugged. 'Tell me, what happened to the fearless Game? Time made you soft I see.'

'No bullshit,' I snatched my sunglasses case out of his hand and returned it to the sideboard with a slam, probably breaking them, by the sound of it, 'and just tell me what you know for once, one old friend to another.'

There was a long pause and plentiful serving of smug grin, and after a shrug, Grim continued skirting the edges of the room, all fingers, not looking at me as he spoke.

'Fine, let's start with tonight.' he moved on to the vinyl record collection, picking random spines out for a closer inspection, then dropping them back into it place.

'You attended one of those old-money swingers parties you're so fond of,' now showing interest in one of the candles. He picked it up and smelled it. 'Amazing, isn't it? I mean, how do they get the smell just right? Exactly like apple and cinnamon. Amazing.' He gave it one more sniff then moved over to the window and peered out.

'At which there was a situation with the archbishop. Then the situation evolved and ended in a sodding wild-western gun battle on the main road, over near the Priory Roundabout.' He returned to the candle and breathed in deep. 'Bet it doesn't taste as good though, eh?'

'First of all, I didn't shoot anyone, and secondly, you should try it.'

He sniffed deep again and put the candle down, out of its proper position. 'Then you came to this place, quite possibly the most well-known safe house of Henry Game, in the history of all safe houses, worldwide.

'Then I thought I'd better get off my arse and come and warn you that it's most probably a set-up. The whole thing, I mean. I reckon they killed the archbishop to stop him from telling you more than they wanted him too.'

'So how long have you known about my brother?' It was the third time I'd asked him now, and the starting of cold creeping into my bones.

Grim met my eye but said nothing.

'And why is the upcoming assassination of my supposed long-lost brother, an obvious set-up to get to me, tell me?'

'I only know what I know, Game, and it is obvious to me that someone told The Order, knowing that they would eventually tell you. But I think the whole thing is just a distraction.' He peered out of the window again. 'Because the real reason for our reunion tonight is more alarming, and most concerning.'

He stopped his casual act and looked at me honestly. 'Our friends from across the water have sent word that they think Francis is being targeted, maybe. But either way we shouldn't take the chance. He needs bringing in.' Grim crossed the lounge and checked the other window.

'You're still looking out for him?' I was touched, truly.

'Of course.' Grim looked at me for moment with a disappointed frown. 'But look, stay clear of your brother, seriously.

He just isn't the sort of person you get to have a nice family reunion with. By all accounts he's a nasty piece of work. I'd say he's a totally different breed altogether that one, but so were you.'

I ignored the last comment and focused on what was really important.

'Who's looking for him, The Order? The Tyrant? The Vatican? The Iron Mask?' I realised my length of suspected enemies were longer than any sane person would welcome. But with longevity, comes an even longer list of adversaries.

I didn't know whether to be glad or furious that my friend was alive and standing before me, messing up my ornaments and leaving pools of muddy water all over my floor, so I settled for dumbfounded. I had it on good authority he was dead. But of course, I've been dead before too…

'My people have reported that Francis is being groomed at an underground fight club. Several known affiliates of the Illuminati have been connected to it in the past. The two are unlikely to be coincidence, of course.'

My previous encounters with the Illuminati had been brief and bloody, and I heard it that they had fled Britain's shores like a wounded dog, back to the Americas.

'How would they know where he is if I don't even know?' I suspected everyone and everything as the only living person who I knew in possession of this information was directly before me, and of course, for the last twenty years or so I thought he was dead and buried.

I couldn't entertain the possibility that Grim would betray me. Especially not to then just come and warn me about it. My enemies must have got lucky, I figured. All good things must come to a murderous and gore-splattered end.

'We are not sure which entity is targeting him, but the obvious guess is the Illuminati. But whoever it is, if they know *who* Francis is, then all we have done for him was for nothing. The only option is to relocate him. Maybe even bring him to England, with you.'

I sat down, deflated as a sail without a gust. 'Easier said than done. You know that my problems with the Illuminati started and ended with The Iron Mask. I paid the price of removing it, everybody can see that.'

'Old wounds fester, and these New-World-Order sort hold on to grudges longer than anyone else. But look, a promise is a promise, Game, dead or not, and I've made good on my end. So…'

'How is it that you know about this brother of mine, Ian-fucking-Mulliti, and I'm only just finding out now?' I crossed my arms to keep them busy for fear they might try to attack my estranged companion.

Grim smiled and sat down. I couldn't decide if he looked older or not, but he certainly looked decently weathered. 'It is not the time for me to answer that question.'

I looked at my friend through the last strand of my patience and saw sadness through his smile. How could I feel relief, betrayal, anger, guilt, jealousy, and love, all at the same time? Grim had altered somehow, even though he looked exactly the same as always. Whatever deal he made he chose the wrong devil, and for that I hoped he suffered every day. We'd had our differences for sure, my face was evidence enough of this fact, but in the end, we'd always had each other's back.

'What exactly are you doing here then? You could have simply had one of the *spyders* tell me about my son's situation. Why come out now?' *Abatu* weighed heavy in its sheath and for a moment I considered using it on my so-called un-dead *best friend.*

Grim looked out the window again before taking a seat. 'Look, you need to protect him. I'm out of play. My promise was kept to you, but now I must disappear. It's time for you to take care of him now. And you should try to stay clear of any contact with Ian Mulliti. At least that would be my advice, for what it's worth. Despite what you think of me, I keep my promises, even if that means coming back from the dead.'

I was lost for words. Anger remained however, but I knew he was right and more importantly I respected him for that.

'But if I reach out to him directly, then surely that would be confirming his connection to me?' I searched Grim's bright eye for one last favour, but his response was little more helpful than a shrug.

Weariness sprinted at me and bowled me over. I felt exhausted and almost allowed myself to venture close to the realm of self-pity. Grim reached for the candle again and resumed his sniffing.

Not looking at me he started his instruction. 'So, here is how you will get onto US soil with your head still on your shoulders, and most importantly, unfollowed.

'Heathrow Airport. Your Uber arrives in three minutes; you'll be flying from terminal two, at 6.35am, boarding the A3380 flight to Dallas-'

'Dallas?'

'Let me finish...once you have made yourself comfortable, you'll need to get off again, before it takes off. The tricky part is that it will have to be after the doors have sealed shut. For all intents and purposes, you need to be on *that* flight, if you know what I mean?'

'But Dallas?' I couldn't help myself. All I could think of was cowboys and outlaws and moonshine-

'Look, just be on that plane, understand?' He handed me a printed eTicket for the 6.35 am flight to Dallas, eyebrows raised. I didn't understand, but kept my mouth shut and pocketed the ticket.

'Right, back in the terminal you'll need to find the Costa Coffee. It'll have a wet floor sign across the entrance. From there someone will deliver you your next set of instructions. Just follow the steps and take note of the address. It'll be a current address for Francis. You'll be given a new passport and the next available flight to America, just to get you out of the country. Really simple stuff.'

Grim checked out of the window again as sirens wailed past and off into the distance. 'Once you land in the States you'll be on your own. All I know is that your son is living in New York City with his girlfriend.' His smile didn't reach his eye as he offered out his huge paw of a hand.

I hesitated. 'Where will you go?'

He let his hand drop. 'Next time we meet, we'll both know the field, the players and the game we're playing, but for now just get to the States and take care of your business. You have two minutes before the Uber arrives,' and with a tip of his hat he gusted out of the door.

I wanted to reach out to stop him. Make him answer more of my questions, but fear of learning what he had become prevented me. Clinching my grab-bag and US passport I left the anonymity of my not-so-secret, safe house. My excitement had been replaced with anxiety and my vengeance replaced with a sense of overwhelming dread when I thought about the mountain that stood before me.

I really shouldn't have gone to that fucking dinner party.

Grim.

I must admit, I've never been blessed with an abundance of friends. And if the wealth of a man is measured by the number of friends he keeps, then I would be the beggar amongst paupers. The 'acquaintances' which I do keep are all out of selfish need or want. People in useful places are what make up my circle of associates, so to speak. And it is precisely this proclivity for people manipulation that enabled me to amass the type of wealth that guarantees obscurity from most circles.

I do not hide the truth, whereas liars live in fear. It is a quality that very few can stomach to witness as shame often enshrouds the guilty. No, I tell the truth, it's way more fun.

Over the many and long years, I have maintained one or two close alliances. I would even call them friends. And foremost of which is the infamous Grim Catspaw: a sledgehammer of a gentleman, and the only person I entrusted your safety and anonymity to.

I have since learned that he has in fact been active in your life and you know him as Woden, or, Uncle Oddy. And how I came to meet him is tale all unto itself, and decidedly worthy of sharing:

The year was 1913, and the world was charged with an over-ripe evil. It was, as the cultured would say, ready for the pallet. And for all I had done, I could've been crowned head chef at the devil's dinner party.

The Order of St Oswald's had packed up and shipped over to the United States of America. Perhaps in the wake of my actions, or perhaps they too had started to fear the monster

I had become. However, the bishop who was left behind to caretake – can't remember his name now – had it that The Order had dashed away to re-connect with its counterpart association. A group from the original Abbey of St Oswald's that shipped out as missionaries, way back when the land barrens were relocated to colonise the Americas, back before my memories began even.

Seemed, as I was once again out on my luck, and deserted by The Order, that I had time to kill, at least until they returned to answer my questions. The truth is that I was at a point in my life when I had no pressing vendettas to be exacting, nor any other insult to justify, other than my questions of origins, and with nothing left to hold me back, or want me, or need me, I put the halls that raised me at my back and crossed the Pennines into to the Red-Rose County of Lancashire. I felt liberated and I decided that once again it was time to re-invent myself, wherever my feet would take me.

At an aimless wander, I returned to a piss-soaked shithole of a town where I had once made a name for myself, for reasons not unbecoming of my old proclivities. And as is the way with long absences, I wondered if perhaps half-century away from the place had soured my memories, particularly regarding the weather habits. But no. Every day I ever spent in that place was fucking sodden and miserable. It rained from the crack of dawn to the bubble of dusk. Every. Single. Day.

With what little cash deposits I managed to retrieve along the way, I found cheap shelter in a disreputable drinking establishment, along the tumbled outskirts of the industrial town of Bolton. The tavern was called The King's Bastard, and it was a place which offered third rate whores, and any number of nefarious services to the bearer of the correct sum.

The place was shady even on the rarity of brighter days, and it had a reputation far and wide as the best place to hire the worst kind of Bastard.

A Bastard being the kind of fellow willing to perform particularly violent services for, and on behalf of, the punter with a few coins, and most often a heart wrenching story to accompany it.

And whilst I frequented said establishment, I was not a punter. My speciality was bounty hunting, or, for a few extra coins, making sure people were never found, ever again, including those under bounty. Easy business for a cunt like me, and it wasn't long until I earned the respect of the other Bastards.

Better paying punters often tried to sell me their sob stories and given my ruthlessly earned notoriety, I was able to pick and choose my jobs. In fact, I had even stopped paying for digs because the generous landlord threw in full board after I had threatened to start drinking in the competition's bar across town.

Truth is my name drew all manner of shady. All paying and often wealthy. And should I have decided to stay elsewhere, the wealthy shady punters would no-doubt follow, along with the rest of the Bastards for hire, I reckoned. They called me the Bastard of Bolton, and they weren't wrong.

One fine miserable evening, I was sitting by the edge of the bar, sticking to the hard stuff, when I heard a deep and rumbling question sneak up on me from behind.

'How many?' It cometh from the darkest corner of the room, and from a face completely shrouded in shadow, save for the occasional red flare of a puff pipe.

Despite the low-lighting, I could tell he was a big one, and he wore a round hat with a rim, even indoors.

People who wear hats indoors have always confused me.

'How many what?' I knew exactly what he meant, but the sudden question and spooky appearance had pricked my temper, slightly. I'm not fond of surprises.

'Amassed quite the reputation, and you're barely even a pup. How old are you?' Again, the bulb glowed.

I had to think. I mustn't have looked any older than my late twenties. What a bizarre question to ask a Bastard. Unless, of course, he knew precisely who I was, which disturbed me even further.

If I dislike surprises, then I despise uncertainty. So, naturally, I slammed my glass down on the bar top and approached the big man in the corner who, to give him credit, stayed exactly where he was, calmly puffing away.

'Are you going to answer any of my questions, Mister Game?' Now he leaned forwards, face still hidden beneath the rim of his hat, but clearly wearing one of those jewelled eye-patches that I'd seen some of the rich folks sporting recently.

'Not until you have answered all of mine first, cunt. And think carefully, as the answer to this next question could determine the rest of your life, or to be more precise, how much of your life you have left to live.'

His response was raucous laughter, which must have cleared the bats out of the loft. And, despite my anger, after a moment of two, in which his laughter only intensified, I found myself laughing along with him.

'I heard you were a sodding wild one, but shit boy! Go on then: ask away!' He clapped his big hand down on the table. I was impressed with the size of this man, but far from intimidated.

'How do you know who I am, and who said I was wild? Am wild'. I corrected myself.

'Now, now! That's two questions Mister Game,' he continued to chuckle. Something was obviously very funny about all this.

I forced myself to relax. The lack of concern from the big guy undermined my confidence, a little.

'Just fucking talk.' I sat down.

'Okay, punchy, okay. You ever heard of the Iron Mask?'

I hadn't, but I didn't want to admit to my ignorance, so I continued to stare at him.

'Course you have,' he knocked back a whiskey like it was honey-milk. 'Look, I have orders to bring you in for a proposal.' He put his hand up for another drink and the landlord snapped too. I'd never seen old Gerald do that before... not even for me.

'Orders from whom? And what makes you think I'd be interested in any kind of proposal that you might be offering?' I let the question hang and attempted to hold conviction on my brow – but the truth was I was desperate for something 'real' to do.

The big man narrowed his eye at me and leaned in even closer. Suddenly we were conspiringly close.

'Come now,' he glanced around the room, seemingly to appraise but coming up short of impressed. 'You could stay around here, keep earning a shilling or two for beating up bullies. Or, you could come with me to London at first light, listen to a real proposal. One only worthy of the legend that is Henry Game.'

I was sold. Truth is he had me at Iron Mask. I love nothing more than a mystery – except maybe killing people that deserve it.

'Okay,' I leant back and knocked the dribble of my own whiskey back. 'Okay, Mister One-Eye-Big-Hat,' I said, 'I'm in.'

'Grim.' He held out his huge hand, a gleam in his eye patch and a puffing pipe in his great bearded jaw.

* * *

The next morning, I arose and exited my lodgings fresher than the stink I left behind for good old Gerald. I reckoned he'd have to crack open a few windows.

Grim was already outside, hunkered in his soaked trench coat and dripping fedora. Looked like he'd been waiting for some time. But one never could tell in such a dank and despondent place. After two minutes, wet is wet.

'You better have a decent horse and carriage or we're not going anywhere-'

'I'm driving,' he interrupted, then walked away, and obviously I looked at him sceptically; cars were a rarity, but people willing to drive the kind of distance from Bolton to London, even more so.

I kept my mouth shut and waited by the curb. Not so much as a bag packed as my pockets filled, dawdling on the mudded verge out at the front of the King's Bastard – a place I had existed in for somewhere close to six weeks by that point.

Grim told it that the Iron Mask was most interested in my stubbornness to dying. "You seem to be most reluctant," were Grim's exact words, if I recall correctly.

Purring, a vehicle approached and came to an unusually smooth stop before me.

'Mister Game, if you please,' gestured Grim, from the cockpit.

I instantly fell in love. This was where my admiration for the automobile began, and I sure as shit recognised a Silver Ghost when I saw one.

It was marketed through tabloid and radio as the 'Pride of The North'. Regular people daydreamed about this exquisite machine while I daydreamed about overcast skies, and I was lucky enough to be sitting in one whilst the skies overhead drizzled and sulked despite my sudden euphoria. I climbed in alongside my chauffeur. Grim looked ridiculously big in such a regular sized cockpit. I wondered if one-eyed people were safe to drive.

'So, where exactly in London does Mister Iron Mask live?'

Grim forced the gear stick down. 'She's at the palace of course!'

'Pardon?' I was shocked. For a moment I feared the worst: royalty.

Grim just smiled and kept his singular vision on the cobbled road ahead.

* * *

It had been years since I last fought an opponent that didn't crumble and die within the first ten seconds.

As night drew close, we pulled in to rest at an old manner house called Wollaton Hall in Nottingham and welcomed by dozens of pale-faced minions. It appeared Grim was their superior, which wasn't strange in itself, but the ceremonial robes they all wore certainly were. It reminded me of my childhood back at the abbey: of the brothers, of Father. Except this place was not holy, at least not overtly so.

As the evening meal was being prepared, Grim loudly invited me down to the "Pit" for a challenge, if I wasn't too tired from all the site seeing.

With everyone watching, I accepted and followed the congregation down to a room with a padded floor and leather punching bags hanging from the floor bearers. As the doors were finally closed, Grim made a show of proclaiming my alleged fighting prowess, in somewhat a patronising and insulting manner.

Most, if not all, of the robed followers were gathered along the edges of the room, the challenge was described as unarmed, non-lethal, combat. The winner would be decided by submission or knockout. Grim seemed unreasonably confident. Truth is, his confidence undermined my own a little, but I have never been one to back down from a challenge.

I stepped into the circle to meet the huge fucker. The crowd drew silent around me and I could hear my own pulse in my temples.

'Let's have some fun, boy!' roared Grim, and he attacked with a leaping knee that struck me cold in the stomach. It even hurt a little.

The crowd gave a polite applause. Yet another strange occurrence. Grim capitalised on my hesitation and barrelled into me with a flurry of punches, much quicker than you would expect from a man of his size, and way more accurate than a one-eyed man should be capable of.

I ducked and rolled to come up quick behind him and punched hard to the base of his spine, which he managed to parry with a back-swing of his arm, setting me off balance, and, only to be on the receiving end of another sharp knee to the solar plexus. I imagined such an impact would typically incapacitate a man, but I am not typical. And instead of absorbing the force of the attack, I used it to propel me away and upward, simultaneously deploying my own knee to catch him under the chin in the process of my boosted arc.

Both of us stumbled backwards to regain our balance and once again locked horns. I tried to take him down by spearing across his knees, but before I could connect cleanly,

Grim's hands clamped on my shoulders, forcing me down to the mat.

I tried to resist but could not outmatch him for strength. This was certainly an unsettling development, and a first for me. Holding myself on my knees, trying to stop myself from being completely prostrated, I suddenly gave into the pressure and rolled with it to my side and away to a safe distance, sending Grim crashing to the mat and forcing another roaring laughter from him as he stumbled. Grim staggered to his knees again and smiled at me, and I back. He was correct: this was fun.

We'd been sparring a little over two minutes, and to give him his due, Grim could damn well hold his own. He swung a great hairy chunk of an arm toward my head in a feint, before quickly front kicking with all of his weight to catch me flat. But I had clocked his slights and tricks by now, and as his concrete slab of a foot blurred past me — the force of which would have probably felled a tree — I sidestepped; both avoiding his decoy punch and rendering his kick redundant, making him vulnerable in his overly-committed position.

I even had time to wink at him before my fist crashed down in to the recess between neck and shoulder, shattering his clavicle, followed by a thunderclap to the mastoids as I stepped around to his rear and watched him broil over like a de-finned shark being discarded back into the choppy blue.

Grim's shoulder slumped and his eyes bounced around before he folded onto his side. This is when I would end him, under normal circumstances, but seeing as though we were merely "having fun", a broken collarbone and concussion was sufficient.

The room drew silent as Grim crashed to the mat. No applause for me.

I stepped away from Grim and looked around the room

in a challenge of my own. Suddenly a strange, high-pitched moan caught my attention. It was coming from the balled-up form of Grim: he was laughing.

He rolled out onto his back and smiled through his pain. He held out his good arm and I pulled him back to his feet. I could see respect, and it was reciprocated. I don't know what he thought before, but if I'm being honest, I couldn't give a fuck what he thought of me, or what any of these other fuckers thought. I turned and headed for the doors; I was starving.

'Game…' he called at my back. 'Almost had you there!'

I stopped by the door to look at him. He had his arm folded across his chest.

'No, you didn't,' I informed him and left to find the cook, leaving Grim to dwell in his pain and the silent judgement of his apostles.

I wondered why they didn't clap for me.

The next morning, with Grim's arm being slung up, I had been promoted to driver. It was actually my first time, and I can't tell you how much I loved it and Grim hated it, but what I can tell you is I enjoyed every single minute, mile, and complaint from my new best friend.

* * *

We arrived in London, relatively safe and unharmed. I was fuelled and still coming down from my high when I belatedly recognised the interior of the palace. I had been here before, and had once again found myself before a throne, ushered in a flurry that trampled all over my euphoria.

It was the very same throne that fat Henry VIII resided upon, it seemed we had come to Hampton Court Palace, long since repurposed, and apparently now the headquarters for the Iron Mask.

Being ushered into the hall by metal-faced ninjas, I had to restrain myself from laughing, especially when Grim slid his ridiculous metallic mask on too, only one eye hole, the other side just plain as if it never existed.

The Lady of the Mask sat upon the aforementioned throne. A face of sorrow looking a long way down on me, expectantly. Grim had fallen in line with the other metal-heads. Each and every one a different expression. Grim's portrayed a winking defiance, but then again, I reckoned that was Grim to a tee, except for now of course, now he was clearly submissive.

The other faces lined the walls, shoulder to shoulder like barriers between towering marble pillars on each side of the throne. I didn't see any weapons, but I suspected that these Iron Maskers weren't bothered about getting a little bloodied. Maybe that was why they insisted on wearing robes.

I looked up at The Lady of the Mask, after assessing the surrounding threat levels, and to my surprise she was leaning forwards, perched on the edge of her sanctimonious seat. To be honest, it unsettled and aroused me in equal proportions.

'Well? Now you have me!' I announced, obviously.

'Now I have you,' she echoed. I flinched when I heard her voice. I did not expect her to sound so sweet. It was a little menacing, and alluring.

'Look, ah…' I ran out of words and resorted to a shrug.

She laughed. The rest of the room stayed silent, unnaturally silent. That was the moment I realised that I wouldn't be able to leave of my own free-will.

She had me. Check. And although my new acquaintance had loured me into this web of hers, I did not blame him or hold a grudge, which was also disturbingly uncharacteristic of me.

'Your adventures are quite the stuff of legend, Henry Game.' Her words reverberated off the hard walls. 'I believe

that you are even the primary subject of research for privately funded scientific communities.'

'I was told you have a proposal?'

The Lady stepped down from her throne and circled me, her hand trailing across my shoulders and chest.

'I do have a proposal,' she admitted, her voice trill and fleeting, like the song of a bluebird.

'The Iron Mask cordially invites you to join and help carve the future. We have a task specifically suited to one such as you, the Eternal Lord Protectorate. Despite what they say, I see your potential.

'The Bastard of Bolton is not worthy of your time. I see this as but the tip of the iceberg. Together, with our resources and your skills, we will shape the course of histories to come.' She sat back down, still perched, and leaning a little too far forwards for it to be comfortable, or even safe, for that matter.

'I'm not cheap,' I said, taking another look around at the row upon row of shining masks. 'I hope you realise that.'

The Lady laughed but did not move from her position, and of course, her mask remained cast in sadness. 'You will have every luxury afforded to you; every desire met. None will stand in our way with you beside us. None would dare!'

They say flattery will get you everything. Not true. For me it was only part of the deal, flattery with a heaping of wealth was the trick to securing my services, and this Lady was fluent in the arts of persuasion, and, truth be told, I suspected her to be a fox beneath the mask. I'm a sucker for a sexy voice.

Easter Monday, 1532. Morning Birdsong.

I coughed through the wafer crisp seal of dry blood and gulped in the cold air by the lungful.

I remember pain, a deep and soul scattering pain. I looked over to my left; my arm was back in position, attached to my shoulder and plastered with seeped bandages that stretched from my neck to my elbow.

I could see the twinkling of the sun through the thinning thatch in the roof above; it was early morning. Trying to swallow the fluids in my mouth I almost choked as congealed chunks of blood-vomit forced a way up and out of me. I ended up soiling the dressings further, only now with a brightness over the hardened black blood.

A sudden movement behind me made me jumpy and I flinched with a full-body jerk, and a tremendous agony spiked, surging to an unprecedented level. I saw rainbows before my eyes, and through the agony I realised I was in the stables and the movement was just a horse. For all I knew it could have been the same one that kicked me and landed me on this cot of infirm.

Distant sounds alerted me to people approaching the stables. Two sets of footsteps struggled through the mud before the stable's entrance, I knew who approached: one I recognised through his laboured breathing, and the other from a habitual irritating clicking noise he made with his jaw.

I tried my best to sit up but all I could manage was to roll my face toward them as they entered through the large and loose stable door. Brother Glen edged in first carrying a pail of water, and behind him, Brother Thomas carried anointing cloth, oils and candles.

Both of their faces whitened as they noticed my eyes open, watching them, awake, alive. I dared not speak for fear the pain would betray me and send them fleeing when I so needed them desperately.

Brother Thomas dropped the cloth, oil and candles, the latter rolling about the splinters of wood and hay, his eyes swimming as he headed toward me. 'Henry, my boy, you're alive! A true miracle. Bless the Lord, truly-'

Brother Glen put out an arm to stop Brother Thomas in his advance, the pail hefted in his white-knuckle grip.

'You, you died…you're supposed to be dead. Blue blood. Abomination!' Brother Glen's breathing labouring even further under the pressure of his accusation.

I couldn't say why but that look of fear on his face, the judgement, really cut through me. I surrendered to the pain as it erupted from my lungs and I roared with everything I am and was.

Pain laced with fury and washed through my veins, beneath my skin, through my bones, down my arms, my fingers. Behind closed eyes I saw Francis' death boring into me, his mouth askew in confusion as his life abandoned him. Anger took over and I locked tight, weeping as my suffering carried the strength of the injustice for both of us. My conviction enamelled and became latent purpose.

Brother Glen dropped the water and fled. Brother Thomas lingered a moment longer before following in tow, my screams chasing them out. Even the light of day abandoned me, and darkness swelled to fill the vacuum I had become. My throat cracked, and I drank my own blood.

Through the dark I heard Francis whelp; his ribs cracked under the sudden impact. I pried my eyes to resist the darkness and saw that blood dribbled from every orifice on his trusting, sweet face. He reached out to me. Reaching into me.

* * *

Muted and muffled chanting carried with it the smell of corned beef hash, lifting me from the veil of the un-possible and back into the tortuous peril of the present.

The glint of the falling day hung sentinel and framed low between the open doors of the stables. In that moment, the warming glow of the sun felt personal. Both my physical and emotional beings warmed and strengthened – tingling sensations coursed across my palms, not unlike that of stinging nettles. I winced and clenched my hand instinctively when I realised that I could once again, somehow, move my left hand and form a fist.

The chanting suddenly ceased. That was when I realised that The Order, clad in full ceremonial robe, surrounded me. Father Game stood by my head and smiled, tears of kindness spilling down his cheeks. He held a book. It looked ancient and I would not see it again for many centuries to come, a book that holds much importance and power, and turmoil.

'Brothers, Henry...' whispered Father Game, and the light seemed to fade faster and faster from the open room, frost catching on the edge of his breath.

'Pray ye', and stand witness to the Blood of Almighty, the Flesh of the Cursed, and Soul of the Free. We offer this as tribute to your greatness...'

'To your greatness,' the brothers echoed.

In the failing light I caught a glimmer from a dagger suspended above my chest. I panicked and tried to move but couldn't. That was when I realised that I had been tied down.

Father Game shushed as he put his open palm across my eyes, plunging me into darkness, forcing my head to be still.

He whispered, barely even loud enough for me to hear him, 'trust me my son, it will all be over soon.'

A burning screeched through my chest and escaped my lungs as I felt my heart open up, bared to the heavens above. Hot life leaked down my twig-thin ribs as the darkness once again washed me away upon the whitecaps of slumber.

* * *

The events of the ritualistic evening had abandoned me when I finally woke again, three days later.

My body appeared fully healed and bared only a thick pinkie-purple lashing of a scar around the circumference of my shoulder joint, and also a suspect looking thrice-pronged marking across my chest. Of course, I remembered the shoulder injury – remembered that little Francis didn't make it... They later told me that his body had been buried down by the rose bushes.

It would be many years until the importance of that night would return to me, but as it were, I awoke tentative and with pain induced amnesia, only to find Father Game by my bedside who kindly delivered a version of accounts that omitted the suspicious and sadistic ritual. And while I still bore the scars across my chest, I did not think anything of it. In fact, I thought myself the lucky one.

I dreamt dark and often. But mostly I was carried along the river of regret in a boat lashed from self-loathing. It was my fault Franky was dead. My actions had brought the guardsman down upon him. It had landed me in a new world of colder winds and the living promise that I would be punished at the end of it all and punished during it too.

If only I could return to that day on the fields – untucking Franky's thumbs, telling him that he needed to be tough. I would have grabbed two rolls of bread and made sure that he was hidden better, like Brother Elliot had asked me to.

Father Game explained that the king had passed a new law

that gave them the power to close down the monasteries. That was why the soldiers arrived and of course why Francis and I were sent into hiding.

He explained that if the guardsmen were to discover us both, unregistered, orphan boys within the abbey grounds, things would not have ended well for anyone. These things were often the cause for cruel conspiracy that left abbeys, brothers, and communities in ruin. He ordered us to hide for our own protection and for the good of the whole village.

Father tried to tell me that Franky's death was his fault, said he shouldn't have sent us up into the mezzanine: too dangerous. He looked older than ever right there in the fresh light of the morning, beneath the thinning hatched roof of my medical bay.

I knew that he was a good man and I believed every word he said, apart from the blame. I healed remarkably quick, and before the day's end I was hobbling around again and joining The Order for evening meal, although the only thing I could bring myself to eat was half of a hardened bread roll.

After morning prayers, I visited the rose bushes. The sun was wrapped in a thinning cloud, threatening to burst free. Standing over the freshly turned earth I felt breathless beneath the weight of what I had done.

The brothers had had been right about me: I was an abomination. A monster.

I remembered Father Game bringing me down to the rose bush one summer's day and explaining the lesson behind the rose, that God had sought to teach us that perfection was never part of his design, and the rose was just one of his many examples. The cruelty of the thorn, a sharp reminder, lurking beneath the magnificence of the rose petal.

Yet, as I stood there atop of Francis' grave, I couldn't help but disagree in my heart. Perfection did exist. Or it did once. Now it lay buried beneath my feet.

Francis was made from goodness. He knew no sin, nor cruelty, or thoughts of malice. Only love and wonder lived within his soul. But the fucking king had taken that away from me when he decided to send his soldiers.

Perhaps when that guardsman decided to climb the mezzanine, or maybe when he tried to snatch us, a small but very important piece of me was broken. Whatever innocence had been in my soul was fractured and had escaped upon the winds of shame. All that remained now was regret and anger.

But anger hurts less, and even at a young age the rage of injustice felt good and was strong enough to overpower the feelings of guilt. It was a straight-up swap, and fuck was it liberating. It was an alternative energy source, but more importantly, it would be the glue that would keep me together for many a century to come.

The sun had lost its battle and the sky had turned corpse grey. As the thin veil of rain began to fall, soaking the freshly turned mud beneath my feet, my tears became lost upon my cheeks. I left brother Francis alone, at rest, in peace, forevermore.

If any should deserve to sit by the side of the Almighty, it was he.

May 1534.

A couple of years had passed since Francis' death, and my wounds looked little more than silvery scars across my skin. I healed fast, unnaturally so. But for all my hyper-healing ability, the emotional lacerations festered and continually bled, never healing.

I reckoned that Francis was probably little more than cloth and bones in his casket six feet deep, but still I maintained the rose bush upon his burial mound, that had since become a garden, and the garden that had become my place of solace and reflection.

The abbey had spiralled into a state of poverty since the Vatican had cut all funding to England. Given that King Henry VIII cared only for his own church, the brothers had resorted to accepting handouts and charity donations from the villagers, or of what few remained of them.

Father explained that the downturn was a reflection of God's anger, anger that England's greedy king had turned away from Rome. He said that throughout the Craven Parish District, throughout the entire country and Europe even, a relationship not unlike a marriage was formed between the community and its church or abbey. The more involved the church in local commerce and government, the more prosperous the township. A cap-in-hand situation. Therefore, it came as no surprise to him that as the abbey fell into poverty, so too did the village of Horton in Ribblesdale. For richer or for poorer, he said.

I often saw contradictions in the teachings and scriptures. Father preached that God only gave us the burdens we had the strength to bear, and my very own burden was keeping the stables clear of the copious amounts of horse shit, but then I heard him tell the brothers that if the king did not repent and return to the old ways, we would not survive.

I reminded Father of his teachings and his response was a long stare and a tight line in his mouth that told me he was displeased. Since then I stayed out of their discussions and focused on clearing the stables and re-provisioning, as currently the horses were now in surplus, through an ill-thought up investment idea by brothers Glen and Thomas. I reckoned that it had landed the abbey in further dire straits, and that now we had more mouths to feed, and more shit to clean up. The months that led on were grey and bleak. Even the sun and spring couldn't coax the flowers to blossom and bloom.

It was mid-May and overcast the first time I saw a man murder another in hard determination.

I was mucking out when I noticed a silhouette in the barley field, cresting the horizon. I recognised Father Game as he hobbled on in his age, hands held up to greet someone at a distance and not in my line of sight.

After a few more minutes, with horse manure on shovel in mid-swing, I noticed the arriving glint of armour reflecting the coldness and despair of the day. It was a battle-ready guardsman advancing toward Father, and Father's hands were held up in a defensive gesture, not in greeting, and my stomach twisted as I noticed the soldier's sword already half-drawn.

And in that void – that negative second between heartbeats – I was paralysed. It was all I could do but watch as his sword was fully unsheathed. The blade high and striking true.

I dropped my shovel as death embedded in Father's chest and suddenly everything refocused around me and in me. Everything that I am became further magnified in the horror that was transforming into pure rage.

An intense charge grew inside, and for the first time I saw the world and life around me and judged how fickle it was. It was like I could see everything, everywhere, all at once. Yet all I wanted to see was the pig-fucking-guardsman die in extreme agony.

Father gasped as ribs cracked and flesh tore, the soldier pushing his blade in further and further to the hilt.

I broke through the paralysis with a scream as my young legs took flight toward Father, just as he toppled backward, the sword red and slipping out of him in murder. Anger overrode my pain as I zeroed in on the guardsman still standing over him, cleaning his weapon on Father's tattered robes, now scarcely visible through the crumpled barley.

He saw me coming and laughed as I advanced. I remember taking a small amount of satisfaction as his forehead creased, his throat clenching tight when he registered the immediate danger that I was.

I'd covered the distance between us in the space of a dozen heartbeats, faster than our quickest horse even, and he readied himself, retreating a step to square up his footing, roaring something at me, but I couldn't hear him for the wind rushing past my ears and the hot blood in my purpose.

Before he could swing his sword, my fist impacted just below his ear sending him slack jawed and wobbly and vaguely aware of reality. His tongue lolled with blood and in the microseconds before my other fist hit him, his eyes begged me for mercy. The next blow landed, concaving his nose into his face.

The guardsman staggered, his sword scattered amongst the crop, a thick red slug of goo dribbling from his gaping, blooded mouth. His gauntlet scratching at the crater where his nose once was. He fell to his knees and I pushed him onto his back with the flat of my bare foot, then mounted his chest plate.

Locking my fingers around his throat, I squeezed, the bones of my grip carving into the cartilage and bone that made for his neck. His flesh tore as my fingers and grip clamped down tighter and tighter. He squelched a little and even managed a nonsensical gargle before I forced the life to abandon him, my fingers squeezing little more than tendon and spinal cord, the rest of his neck turned to mulch in the gaps between my fingers and all over the backs of my hands.

The last legible words he ever said were lost in the wind. I laughed down on his corpse, spat, and then I cried. Now I was truly alone.

I couldn't stay at the abbey any longer. Doing so would only put the rest of the brothers in danger. I had killed one of the king's men and I knew that meant someone would pay, and probably more than one someone. More like a whole abbey of someones, and especially if they were Roman Catholic someones.

Anger imbued me and sent me on my way. I knew from experience that it was far better to focus on revenge than settle and wither with my loss. Mourning would have to wait, and the longer the better, I convinced myself.

I didn't have a plan, but I knew I was going to kill the King of England for sending his soldier to kill Father, and for that I would probably need a sword, so I took the cunt's whose throat I'd just squelched into slush, and whilst I was pillaging, I removed the large, square golden ring he wore on his sword hand that showed a depiction of two horse riders bearing shields, the red cross of Saint George between them in the righteousness. I vowed that the king could eat the fucking thing right after I'd made him lick the shit off my boots, which I was also lacking at that moment in time. Still, dead men don't need boots, and they fitted my feet well enough.

Rolling the guardsman over and on to his front sent a

jingling of coins, somewhere beneath his chest armour. I wasted no time in relieving him of his redundant protection until I found the purse, suspended from around his neck, and tipped its contents on to the folded crop of barley around us. I spent a few moments counting the coins, knelt between the guardsman and Father.

I had to recount them again as it was the most money I'd ever seen. At collection, especially on the most holiest of occasion, I had seen the odd tuppence thrown in to the bowl, sometimes even a goat, but I'd never seen a sixpence or an actual shilling, and this fucker had been carrying almost half a years' wages for the average hard-working man. I wondered how many people he'd cut down to gather this amount of money. I turned the shilling over in my red hands, reading the words stamped around the edge of the coin: "𝕳𝖊𝖓𝖗𝖞 𝖇𝖞 𝖙𝖍𝖊 𝕲𝖗𝖆𝖈𝖊 𝖔𝖋 𝕲𝖔𝖉 𝖆 𝖗𝖔𝖘𝖊 𝖜𝖎𝖙𝖍𝖔𝖚𝖙 𝖆 𝖙𝖍𝖔𝖗𝖓."

I thought of Francis, how his and my father's death were both sanctioned by the king. And now Francis slept beneath the roses whilst the king preaches of his perfection. A fucking rose without a thorn! I held that fire and swore that I would make the cunt swallow a mouthful of thorns before he died.

Gathering the coins, I slipped them back into the purse and hung it around my own neck. The weight felt comforting. I spared a moment for Father, his eyes scattered across the overcast skies, a painful surprise on his face.

I closed his eyelids and left streaks of blood down his cheeks from my fingers. The devil filled me, and in my anger, I felt safe, empowered, righteous. It felt good. And it was good. And I was bad, but for all the right reasons.

Francis,

Now, as you're reading this, I wouldn't blame you for not believing these accounts. Hell, if I were you maybe I wouldn't either. Except I know better and so do you.

I know you are faster, stronger, and intellectually superior to those around you. I know others envy you and as such you view your gifts as the curse that has driven a wedge between you and the rest of them. They are jealous, nothing more. Pity them for they are the scum of all humanity.

You see clearer, hear better; you even look better. You rarely become sick, and if you do the cause is always a medical mystery that heals in its own time. The fact is your ailments are purely metaphysical, and modern medicine is just not equipped to diagnose it, nor capable of treatment.

In the right light, one might say that your blood is almost purple, perhaps. You are overly sensitive to the sunlight and your skin burns, no matter how often you apply sun cream.

If you have ever felt like you don't belong, like you're a part of this race on the surface, but beneath you're a whole different species — something not quite human — keeping the world at arms distance because they don't think like you do or see things as you do, you are not alone, trust me on this.

I know this because it has also been the way for me. My biggest regret is not being present to help you understand this barrier, as you have doubtlessly grown to loathe, as I once did. Just know that as you age, I curse the reasons that continue to enforce my distance from you.

I had just killed my first, the guardsman, for what he did to Father, and this is when the boy Henry first started to mutate into the monster I became. This is where the trail of blood leads back to: upon those deep green fields on that overcast day.

Everything that happened from this moment forth was ignited by my need for vengeance. Every fibre of my desire was laced with the fury of my destiny.

Perhaps this was my activation. Or is it that maybe no matter what happened to me back then, my path would have been no different. Still, one cannot look back. Yet looking back is all one can do when that all that waits before you is oblivion.

Yet, whilst the flames burn up behind, forcing me closer to the cliff's edge, I look deep beyond the inferno and into my past in the hope that my way out is in there, through there.

Maybe this is the true reason for this grand and final recounting. Does my sub-conscious rebel against me? Am I writing to re-live in the hope of salvation through another, through you? Do I dwell upon these philosophies to achieve some semblance of a heightened stage of enlightenment, just before the final curtain closes?

It is now I admit that I am afraid to die. And it is in my fear that I take the greatest comfort for I know that I am part of something bigger than myself, a thing that lives on through you.

I ask these questions as an act of contrition. A flagellum device to keep wounds from healing. I maintain that it is all a bastard like me warrants.

I know that I deserve nothing from you for what I have done. But I believe that only you can be the one to give me the relief of forgiveness, should you deem my confession as worthy.

End of Spring, 1534.

All I can do is thank my lucky stars it wasn't the middle of winter when I set out to bring about the end of a monarchy. If it was, I would have surely frozen in the wilderness, alone but for my trophies and anger.

I set off in an easterly direction at a furious pace, crossing the treacherous terrain of the Yorkshire Moors, my fire soon burning out when I realised that I was completely and hopelessly lost.

The nights were cold; the wind unrelenting. I tried my best to stay on course by keeping the sunrise in front of me each morning. I was aiming for York City, but my inexperience left me stumbling, desperately, into the township of Harlowgate, beyond hungry and feeling more foolish and inexperienced than I undoubtedly looked.

Trotting through my ineptness of escaping the moorlands by design, things finally took a turn for the better when cresting the peak of Meugher, relief tingled through my water-logged toes, and hope was renewed as I looked down on the promise of warmth and food in the form of an actual civilised town.

Either side of Harlowgate's entrance road boasted iron plaques mounted on timber stumps, each a panel of three golden lions painted on a red background, signalling that the land thereof to be the property of the Duchy of Lancaster.

I took it for a victory, although I had been wandering hopelessly lost, I had made it this far, to the lands of the Duke of Lancaster. Although not quite Hampton Palace, it was still the king's territory and therefore I was one step closer to my revenge.

From my position, I could see that the roads looked well-kept, and several taller buildings clambered up from the evanescence of the freezing-fog to thaw in the yellow morning sunlight. I remember thinking that the town must have been a place of considerable wealth, as nothing spoke of affluence like the twinkle of glass in windows.

Although I still had quite the way to go to get back on the road to London, my baser desires decided that my quest for vengeance would have to play second fiddle to my appetite for food. Besides, I was clearly a fish out of water, ill-prepared and not at all likely to ever make it to the palace without a little direction and maybe a good travelling cloak.

The knock of the purse around my neck had weighed heavier and heavier since hunger had reached its bony hand up to tug at my focus. A meal and a warm sleep being as important as anything, including revenge.

I took the main road in, catching suspect glances from the watchers at the gate and awkward smiles from the women. I still carried the sword across my back and with my common woven clothing, and a washed-out look about me, I most definitely presented as low hanging fruit, albeit a prickly one that would need to be washed and cooked before consumed.

Thankfully the rain over the last couple of days had cleaned the blood from my hands, yet had left me taut with the chill, but the sun was on the rise and with it, the promise of warmer climes. Hope can be as effective as any fur coat, except for the times when you are cold and wet. Even a hopeful traveller with a belly full of optimism and no jacket will freeze to death or catch the sweats, and I didn't want that, not at least before the king had died by my hand.

Down the main causeway I spotted a tavern and headed over to it. No glass in those windows, however, just tattered rags coated and hardened by linseed oil. I immediately felt more comfortable amongst displays of lower class and entered through the splintered door.

My age had never been a subject broached in my days at the abbey, but I knew that I was at least twenty-five summers to the good, yet I barely looked old enough to enjoy a real ale, never mind carry a man's sword. Either way, the landlord kept his concerns to himself and allowed me to settle behind one of the tables near the blackened fire-pit.

Other than the landlord behind the bar, and two fellows sat before it, the place was empty, but then again it was a still a good few hours before midday. I untied my sword and lay it across my lap and closed my eyes for just a second. I was just about ready to sleep right where I sat.

'An' what can I get fo' a young buck like yerself then, a cup o' child's mash?'

I startled and grasped for my sword, which was still across my lap. The landlord was standing across from me, the table between us, drying his hands on a cloth, then hanging it over his broad shoulder. I reckoned that I must have fallen asleep. I blinked and looked around again, checking for threats.

'Intrestin' ring you've got there...' the landlord continued. 'Seen one o' those before on the hand o' one o' those special Roman Catholic guardsmen-'

'I'll have a proper pint,' I cut across him, my voice strong, tone serious, 'and a bowl of something hot and salty, and a decent bed for the night.' I dropped a sixpence on to the wooden top and sent it rolling toward him. The other two men glanced over at the teasing sound.

'I can do ye' the drink. But the scoff's still cookin'. Couple o' hours yet.' He picked up the coin and inspected it closely. 'Only room left is the duke's own suite. That'll cost ye' extra.'

I lifted the sword up and laid it on the table-top, my hand over the handle and the ring winking back the sun as it edged in on our affair. 'You better make it two beers then, and that sixpence is twice as much as your best room for the whole fucking week! Keep the drink coming and I'll think about letting you keep the change.'

The landlord grinned rotten gums and a stump or two. 'Alright bucky, alright then. You got a deal. But only 'coz I like you!' And with that he tapped the coin against the wood and returned to his place behind the bar.

I noticed the other two gentlemen had continued their interest in me.

'Hey!' I shouted to the landlord, 'and pour a round for those two fellows, whatever they want, yes?' I casually removed the sword from the table but rested it in its scabbard by my side, safely within arms-reach, then I hung the purse back around my neck and tucked it under my tunic.

The two men raised their glasses in my direction as their drinks arrived and I nodded, but neither of them uttered another word for the next couple of hours. Meanwhile I did my best to satiate my hunger with liquid.

* * *

The food came hot and sudden, and with it my table was more densely populated than I had previously calculated. Perhaps it was the beer, but I had thought the other two gentlemen were precisely that: just two, and also, I thought that they were supposedly sat way over at the other end of the bar. Now there were four of them, and all sat at my table, mumbling to each other, and looking down on me like a pack of hyenas over a stray baby wildebeest.

I recognised the two I had bought a drink for, lurking on the shoulder of a yeoman warder, and also the local sergeant at arms. The former clad in white and green, and both of the king's men wore hats, even indoors.

Fear jolted through me as they inspected the sword I had taken from the guardsman. It was now on the table between them and far out of my arms reach. I was awake, but for show I stirred and groaned, and they all turned their attention back to me.

I had heard stories of the yeomen warders, of course. Occasionally travellers would pass through the abbey and share far-fetched tales of the warders' close bonds to the royal families of Europe, and how they were each hand-picked for service by the king himself.

The warders were said to be berserkers, every man one of them. And I noticed that even the sergeant at arms deferred authority to the man in white and green with the single thistle and a shamrock stitched into each of his lapels, and between them, woven in crimson, sprouted the Tudor Rose of King Henry VIII of England.

I reached for the steaming bowl of stew set before me, all eyes still watching as I tucked in.

The landlord looked around the table, his hands ringing on the manky cloth now tucked into the top of his apron. 'Can, can I get anyone else a bowl?'

'Leave us.' The tone of the yeoman left little room for confusion or argument.

The landlord gave me a nervous look before backing away and disappearing into the back rooms. Meanwhile I continued to wolf down my first meal since the morning of my father's murder, my throat and chest burning as the lumps of duck fat and gristle slid down, slowly.

The two lawmen looked unimpressed by my ravenous appetite, but I cared not for their thoughts, my wooden spoon scraping the bottom of the bowl. I could smell bread, but there was none in sight.

The two men I had bought a drink for looked amused by

my lack of fear, or perhaps it was my ignorance to my current situation. I looked up at them, my hunger subsiding enough to allow my present condition the presence of thought. I don't know why, but I suspected these two had ratted me out, and I was of the mind to tell them what I thought of tattle-tales-

'Oh no, you carry on boy, don't mind us here…' smiled the yeoman, albeit straight-backed and eyes narrow.

I took the hint and abandoned the last remnants of stew, feeling better than I had in a long while. I must have slept for a few hours because I felt energised and ready to go again.

'I reckon you've some explainin' to do, boy,' said the sergeant as he tapped his grubby fingers against the scabbard of the guardsman's sword, way over on their side of the table.

I pulled my hands beneath the table in an attempt to hide the ring from them also. A fellow entered the tavern and stopped in his tracks as he witnessed our congregation. With only a slight hesitation he turned around and exited again. A decidedly smart fellow, and clearly not thirsty enough to drink with a yeoman and company.

'The sergeant here has received a reporting that a soldier and a monk were murdered over in Ribblesdale, not three days back. Reports say the guardsman was relieved of his sword, his ring, and his boots, and almost his head-'

'He killed Father Game!' I shot up to my feet as the blood rushed and realised my mistake as the two lawmen shared a look with one another.

'But his head was only hanging on by a thread…' the sergeant looked on at me, a heavy frown. 'You are little more than a boy, how could you possibly-'

'Are you admitting to murder, boy?' The yeoman started to rise to his feet. I looked around, assessing my options for the possibility of escape and came up flat.

'You'll hang on the gallows for that,' added the sergeant, his hand over the sword hilt now. 'Only way out of this is if you tell us who helped you kill him.'

'Helped me?' I remained standing.

'Was it one of the monks, then, more than one?' The sergeant persisted. 'He had just killed the father of the abbey, hadn't he? This, this Father Game, you say?'

The two rat-cunts that I had bought a round of ales for were smiling widely, three steps back and watching on in suspense, I wanted nothing more than to stuff their wooden tankards up their arses, lengthways. Fear was climbing up my back and making me feel small and weak. I was out of options, but I had killed a man and I would be the only one to take the blame for my crimes, righteous as they may be.

'It was just me.' I slumped back down upon my chair, I was addressing the yeoman, but it was the sergeant who spoke next.

'No matter boy, we'll haul the lot of you in for conspiracy to murder, murder, assistin' a murder. You'll all hang together, if you want to be a hero.'

Fear stepped aside, and my outrage burst forth and I flipped the table upward and sent it toppling on to all four of them in a shriek of rage. The yeoman skipped away but the sergeant and the two other fellows fell back to the ground as the table landed atop of them with a crash.

Ale and tankards scattered to the stone floor and the guardsman's sword clattered away to my left, equal distance between myself and the yeoman. He met my eye and I noticed his pupils dilate to the point of paranormal. He was smiling at me, making my blood rush cold. I saw him, and he I: suddenly opponents, the sticky tavern floor our battlefield.

With deathly intent he unsheathed his blade and stepped toward me, closing the distance by thirds with each stride. No time left for hesitation. I darted for the sword, but then the world flashed black and suddenly my face was wet with ale and hugging the floor. My limbs weighed me down and the last thing I remember seeing was the landlord's filthy dish cloth drop to the ground besides my face.

* * *

A strong smell of urine attacked my senses as I awoke to ice in my bones.

I was in a small room containing little more than four walls, a caged door, and a high ceiling baring floor joists and the underside of half-rotten, mouldy floorboards. My head prickled, touching the bulbous wound on my crown, I remembered that I had been squaring off against the yeoman warder and shivered.

Climbing to my feet I looked around. Along the floor by the back wall, the stone had been chiselled out to form a gulley-drain at one end, the shallow gutter spanning across to the other wall from which a fist sized hole in the cell's party wall drained in to. From the smell it gave off – and from the yellow-brown trickle of liquid that was creeping along the ditching – more like a puddle than a flow – it was clearly a place to relieve oneself. Only I didn't fancy that the hole in the centre of the gulley would be wide enough to allow an adult sized turd to pass through, at least not a healthy one.

In the distance I could hear the agonising cries of a man, chorused by the slow tensioning of rope. I refocused on my own situation and looked up as the ceiling creaked under the weight of two persons in motion. I centred myself again and tried to decipher the muffled words in a mumbled conversation from another distant set of voices.

A bang from the floor above, immediately followed by a

tirade of scummy grey water flooded through the gaps in the floorboards. I jumped across the room but could not escape the deluge. Moments later I flicked the rancid wet from my matted hair and face; the faintest smell of blood mixed with sand and lye.

I was clearly in a prison. That much was clear, only I didn't know which town, nor for how long I'd been resident, nor whether it was a debtor's prison or criminal. I had been relieved of my purse, boots, and the ring with the two horse-men. And it was the latter that disturbed me the most. The ring had become my totem of revenge, and also a reminder of what I had done; what I was becoming.

I approached the bars, my hands still wet and sticky, testing the metal, pulling with all my strength until surprisingly the iron flexed, but for the width of a spider's leg, and I hesitated: I knew I was strong, but I never imagined I could be strong enough to bend iron. Not until that point anyway. Buoyed by my minor victory, I adjusted my grip and set myself to prize open the bars wide enough to allow me to slip through when two sets of footsteps clocked down the narrow hallway beyond my door.

I stopped my attempt at escape and listened, holding my breath. The footsteps reached the end of my hallway and stopped. I hid from sight with my back against the wall to the side of the door.

After another murmuring only a single set of steps contin-ued onwards toward me. The iron bars rattled, and a key was inserted, creaking, and the door opened against rusted hinges.

My head still pricked from the bashing, and a cold washing of blood passed through my arms and down my spine as I looked up at the green and yellow tunic of the yeoman warder, the same one from the tavern.

The yeoman stepped into my small and hellish confinement

and looked at down his long and thin nose, clearly not comfortable in such surroundings. He held the same narrowed eyes and the same sword in his hand.

'No more tricks, not in here. This is the end of the road for you,' he said. 'If you talk, you'll get to die quickly, painless. Otherwise...' he trailed, and the distant cries of agony echoed, as if on cue.

'Where am I?' I had a hundred questions, but that one seemed most important.

'Not that it makes any difference, York, the castle prison.' He held a finger up as the screaming started up again on the echoes. 'But listen, that noise is coming out of one of the other treasonous scum we collected from your little abbey.' He attempted to spit on the floor but missed and completely got my feet.

'That one,' he put a finger to his ear. 'That one is on the rack, right now. A big-fat-juicy one, he is.' He nodded as if the screaming was making a good point. 'Everyone talks on the rack, though. Big, small, old, fat... everyone, and especially the younger ones.'

My heart burst in my chest as I listened, desperately putting a face to the howls. The yeoman was laughing as he stepped around to be square in front of me.

My apprehension was melting away. 'But I am the only one responsible for kill-'

He cut me off with a pinch of his fingers and another cry reverberated from wall to wall. More creaking overhead followed by a scrubbing sound. We both looked up to see bubbles lathered between the gaps in the floorboards.

'I killed the guardsman. Just me. Please, the brothers are innoce-'

'Not a single person alive is 'innocent'. The rack consistently proves that point. Never fails.'

The distant tensioning of rope followed by another cry set my fury to boiling point. The yeoman was but a man, and I was…well, I didn't quite know, but I was something more than ordinary. And although small in stature, I had the strength of a horse, and enough anger to bring a whole castle down.

Whatever fear I'd previously held for the yeoman had all but evaporated. The crying and torture only seemed to get louder and louder and I adjusted my position to set my foot against the wall. My back straight and tensioned to strike him down. I couldn't cope with the noise and the yeoman was lapping it up.

I was aware that another guard was positioned somewhere down the hallway, so I would have to be fast, ruthless even, and hopefully quick enough in my attack before the guard down the hallway entered the fracas.

'Anyway, I came to tell you that you're up next, considering you still want to play games. Now get up. Let's see how loose we can stretch that tongue of yours.'

I looked him in the eye, more serious than I'd ever been. 'I'll kill you if you-'

He smashed me in the mouth with the pommel of his sword and I had to spit out the rest of my threat with a gob-full of blood and the chunk of cheek-flesh I'd bitten off.

Enough was enough and my anger boiled over to save me from my hesitation. I'd taken enough hits and unless I fought back, I'd surely find myself on the rack as he'd promised. I held my hand up in submission and started to get to my feet, the yeoman's smile faltering – suspended somewhere between a grin and a snarl – when I pushed off from the wall and punched him harder than I had ever hit anything before, connecting clean under his jaw with a crack.

The yeoman whelped as his head arced backward and away from me, his entire body lifting from the floor until the back of his skull split against the ground like an ostrich egg, and his legs clattered, limp.

Without a moment's pause I jumped on top of his chest and was about to strike again when I realised that he definitely wasn't getting up again, at least not anytime soon. The yeoman's eyes rolled white and dark blood pulsed from his nose. His jaw jutted octagonal and his arms twitched unnaturally. I snatched the sword from his white-knuckle grip and turned to face the incoming castle guard.

Sprinting footfall chorused by shouts of "escape!" gave me the advantage of knowing he was merely seconds away from entering. But the guard's panic was starting to cause quite the stir amongst the other prisoners, and before the first echo blended into the next, the walls trembled with the howls and barks of the incarcerated rebellious. Every one of them lending me strength and courage.

The castle guard came into the cell swinging his short sword and struck the wall beside me as I sidestepped his attack and sent my own blade deep into his soft and exposed ribcage, all the way to the hilt, and in the blink of an eye, his moment to save the day was over.

I caught the guard and lowered him to the ground, leaving his head in the piss gutter. But still I lowered him, gently, and he struggled to gulp enough air to keep living.

'Tell me where they keep the prisoner's possessions, now, and I won't kill you-'

He coughed, blood pluming from his wound of a mouth, reaching my face.

I thought better about my promises. 'Tell me, and I won't cut your cock and balls off and stick them down your throat, then,' I corrected. That got his attention.

His eyes wide and grey, every breath a fight he was clearly losing. We didn't have long.

'My belongings: the purse, sword, boots, the ring. Where will I find them?'

The guard coughed again, and his eyes rolled for a moment before I grabbed a fist of his balls and twisted.

'N, n, no. No…' he had life enough to beg.

I let go but showed him the sharp end of the sword I had already killed him with. 'Fucking talk.'

'The Earl of…' he trailed, then coughing awake again as the point of the blade pressed against his groin. 'Earl of Huntingdon!' he fell into another bloody cough and the whites of his eyes clouded red.

'Where is he?'

"H, he, here…' and with that his breath left him, a heavier stream of piss passing around his head and soaking his hair from the hole in the cell wall. The piss gutter did work quite well after all.

The walls were still alive, and I realised that it was only a matter of time before the reinforcements would arrive to join me in this little cell of mine. Taking both swords available to me and jumping over the convulsing body of the yeoman warder, I escaped out and into the darkening hallway, choosing passageways that led toward silence and darkly away from the ruckus.

I had just killed my second and third victim. And one of them was a yeoman warder! I needed to gather my thoughts and figure out a way through the castle that did not end up with me back in the cell or worse, strapped to the rack.

Night was coming fast, and I would have to use it to my advantage. Distant sounds of alarm and armoured footfall told me that they knew I was out, and also that they were heading in the opposite direction I was.

I had no idea who this Earl of Huntingdon was, nor why he would have my belongings, but I sure as shit was going to find out.

* * *

The commotion was spreading faster than I could sneak through the dark and damp hallways of York Castle.

In avoiding the thundering searching of guards, I had worked my way closer to the inquisition wing. Here, the rope tensioning was as loud as the screams that almost always followed. It was when no cries could be heard, that I shuddered at the thought of what was being done in there, and to whom. My caution was failing me, and fast, as with every step I took I grew less concerned with my own situation, including the risk of recapture, and more frantic with rescuing the brothers.

I reached the torchlit hallway whence the torture certainly ensued and was most surprised to find that no guards were stationed in the passages leading up to the double doors. I imagined the opening needed to be extra wide to get the instruments of torment inside and assembled. Even this deep into the labyrinth of passageways the walls quaked with revolt. I could only see fury as I sprinted at the door, in the lull between screams, and burst through to the shock of all within the torture chamber.

Reactively I swung both swords at cross-paths to meet the neck of the first responder: a grubby looking shit who'd released the tension on the wheel to turn toward me; whilst simultaneously I kicked out with bare feet to meet the heavy gut of the second and more deliberate responder: a fat and sweaty fucker to my right.

It was a room of sick bastards. Six of the cunts, all watching on with erections as a naked man was stretched past the point of dislocation from each of his four major extremities. Except now they were all looking at me. And in the heartbeats between the first guard's head hitting the dirt, his neck blood shooting all over the walls, the fat fucker who'd attacked from my right stumbling backward and falling over, and the collective call to arms amongst the other four guards, I realised one very important detail in all of this: the man being stretched out was not a brother, nor had I ever seen the bastard before in my life. Odds were, I reckoned he was probably in there for good reason. Still...

Fat guts fell backward with flailing arms and bowled over two other guards in the process, conveniently leaving just the two others totally unencumbered and free to slice me up. Or die trying.

My blood was pumping, and a little smile crept on to my face as I watched their slow and obvious movements in a motion that I call 'half-time', when each second feels like two, and to put it simply: I can move quicker than most.

Blood still gushing from the standing headless dead-cunt-guard, I took him around the waist and proceeded to swing around in a full circle arc, spraying the whole room and everyone in it red and dripping.

All the tension from the wheels of torture were spinning backwards as I let the headless fucker fall and vaulted across the stretched-out criminal to land in the thick of the guards' indignation as their worst fucking nightmare: me, with two dripping blades and a new-found proclivity for decisive and deadly action.

With blood in their eyes and on their faces, they had less than no chance as I slew them both with a simultaneous, cross direction thrusts. The hilts of each sword buried deep through their rough tunics – memories suddenly flashing back to Father: his hemp robes stretching through his back and the tip of the sword poking through-

A loud roar from the fat one as he lurched over me and sliced down with all his might and menacing intention. I leaned away. But not far enough. Suddenly my left shoulder was on fire and missing a fist-sized chunk of meat.

I spared a moment to look at the damage and immediately wished I hadn't as the white of bone gawped back at me and one of my swords dropped to the dirt. Meanwhile, the two with holes in their hearts had slumped to their knees and keeled to opposite sides, a murder in perfect synchronicity.

Fat guard was carried off balance as his sword ricocheted from my shoulder and into the thigh of the stretchy prisoner – who then looked down at the sword, lodged not two inches from his nut-sack, like the day couldn't possibly get any worse, but then just had, and let out a panicked cry – which was then moments later backed up by a torrent of additional pain and anguish. The poor cunt.

I turned my body to lead with my right foot, my injured shoulder behind me. The three enduring gaolers looked on with blood-red faces, the whites of their eyes wide. They clearly didn't fancy their chances and I started to laugh at how things had changed in just a few days.

The fat one rushed at me slow and clumsy and tripped over the dead body of his fallen comrade only to land at my feet, face down in the mud. I looked at the remaining two as I stamped on the back of the fat one's neck with bare feet, and very audibly broke his spine. Barely even a gurgle as his blood-ied sword scattered in the dirt and his legs shook out in a similar way to how the yeoman convulsed.

I advanced on the two gaolers and they backed away in unison.

'Where are the brothers?' I asked, but I already knew the answer. They were back at the abbey, right where I left them.

The guards looked at each other then back at me but said not a word. Meanwhile, the cries from the poor bugger on the rack were failing as the torrent of blood squirting from his accidental wound lessened to a dribble. The wound was bright and not at all healthy looking.

'That fucking yeoman cunt!' He'd played me for the gullible boy I used to be, back when I was locked in that cell, maybe an hour ago.

The door was less than ten feet away from the guards, and I was fewer than six from them. Their chances of escape from me was non-existent.

'Only one of you will leave this room alive, and with me.' I looked at the swords they both carried and back into their eyes. 'Only one of you can help me and live to see the outside of this room.'

I jumped up to sit on the rack, my arse a few inches from the head of the delirious stretched prisoner who was blabbering now, his speech so slurred I couldn't understand a word. And if I'm honest, I just wanted him to hurry up and die already.

The two guards looked at each other and backed away half a step. Both raising their swords tentatively towards one another, flicking nervous glances my way.

'Fucking get on with it then, I don't have all night.'

* * *

The fight between the perverted guards was over as quickly as it began.

The first to strike was decisive and did not mince his intentions, especially not with his sword lodged firmly through his former friend's sternum. And that was exactly where it stayed.

We left the torture room and headed away to locate the Earl of Huntingdon, along with my lost possessions, but now at a more careful pace. I held the tip of my blade against the spine of the guard leading the way, as a reminder of the threat I made to him just before we left the torture chamber. We wandered for less than ten minutes when the stone floor we walked upon gradually became covered in animal fur, and paintings or various religious artefacts populated the walls. It was clear that we were approaching the nobility wing of the castle.

The noise of riot didn't reach this far, not even for my ears, and instead of guards we encountered servants with heads down and rushing, quietly, often with brimming silver wine-pitchers or buckets and lathered water; they took little notice of us in any event. One of them was in the process of carting away soiled bedsheets from a decadently furnished bed chamber, evidenced by the smell as we passed, and the grey look on the young girl's face doing the dirty work. Eventually we reached a large arched timber door, skilfully carved and emblazoned with a coat-of-arms of an upside-down scorpion's tale.

The guard turned to look at me. 'Shall I knock?'

I thought about it. 'But what if he's not in?' The sarcasm was heavy enough for him to realise my question required no answer and he immediately tried the handle and the door opened just like magic.

As we entered, the heat from the open fire was too much a contrast to the cold halls, and the sounds of sickly sex were enough to set my discomfort far beyond my young tolerance. I slammed the door as sharply as I could, causing an immediate cessation of sweat slaps, followed by a moan of outrage purely reserved for the entitled.

'What the bloody hell?' he snapped off his indignation as he rushed out from his curtained fourposter bed, his briefs still around his knees, and registered the current situation.

The guard was covered in congealed blood, and I smiled broadly with a sword and intent, and also with the death of eight armed men upon my ledger. I was ready to make it nine, maybe even eleven if things didn't go exactly as I hoped, and quickly.

Ruffles from the curtains on the other side of the bed chamber and a servant lady darted toward to door on the opposite end of the room.

'No, you don't…' I warned her, pointing toward a fur covered bench beside the fireplace. 'Not until I am ready to leave. Nobody is going anywhere until I get what is mine.'

I turned back to the pant-less, balding noble-cunt with scant ginger hair remaining to his head, and a laughable, pathetic attempt at a beard.

'Earl of Huntingdon, I presume?'

As if reminded of his position by my question, his posture strengthened, and he strode clearly from his bedrest, still no underwear to cover his manhood.

'That I am, and who may you be, and what business have you?'

'I just told you.' I said, advancing a step or two towards him in a rush, my left arm still trailing and starting to itch like crazy.

The earl nodded to himself, pulled his trousers up and slowly skirted laterally toward a silver wine goblet, pulling two tankards and pouring full servings.

'Yes, you are the one charged with the murder of the guardsman at Horton in Ribblesdale.' He offered out a tankard to me. 'Also, it appears, the very same person who escaped his cell and killed one of my guards and most likely killed the yeoman warder!' He smiled as he finished his sentence and I accepted the drink. I had an insane thirst on me for sure.

'So that was you.' He looked impressed, interested even, but not at all concerned.

I just wanted my stuff, and to be out of the castle and back on point.

'My things.' I demanded then finished the tankard and threw it back to the earl.

'Yes, yes of course, of course. I remember now, curious possessions for a young murderer. The yeoman had grave concerns about you, justifiable after all.'

He turned to the servant he had just been having sex with. 'Send for the young man's items, it would be that of a ring, a fine pair of boots, and a…well.' He looked back at me with a guilty smile. 'The purse will be surely emptied by now. Never mind that, I am sure I have enough around here to reimburse our young friend. That will be all, go, and say not a word of this situation to anyone!'

The servant left the room and I did nothing to stop her. But I was more than a little upset about my fortune having been pillaged, and suddenly unsure of the situation myself. The earl handed me another helping of wine and I accepted it and with that, I started to relax a little.

The evening had taken a turn for the bizarre indeed. I was convinced that I would be cutting my way through this earl to get my belongings. I even fantasised it as we traipsed the extravagant hallways and corridors. But now, it seemed, we shared a drink together and held polite conversation.

The earl had retrieved a small wooden box from atop a reading desk by the large stained-glass bay and was selecting a variety of coins and dropping them into a fine leather purse. I almost coughed up my drink when I saw an angel and a golden sovereign drop in, along with an ample dosage of goats and shillings.

'Pray ye tell me,' he said, his back to me as he continued to restock my lost fortune and then some, 'how is it you plan to escape the law once you leave my modest lodgings? Life on the lam is no life worth leading. Especially not for a young and passionate gentleman such as yourself.'

'I have no interest in running.'

'Oh, is that so?' The earl's eyes were round and full of delight.

'I'm taking my things and heading for London. The king will pay for my father's murder and my revenge will be exacted. After that, who knows what I will do. But that fat bastard will be dead, and it will be by my hand.'

The earl's face lit up like the sun. 'Well now, that is quite the vendetta.' He dropped another angel in and pulled the strings tight, tossing it to me as his servant quietly returned through the door with my boots and a ring in her fragile, trembling hands.

'The guardsman I killed was in retaliation for my father. The king must suffer for sending him, and anyone who gets in my way will fall too.'

The servant placed the items by the side of the earl who snatched them up and brought them over to me with sheer excitement dripping from his face.

'Get in your way you say? Hell, I'll send you with my finest horse and the harrowing tales of how you single-handedly annihilated my castle forces and held my throat beneath your blade before you spared my life, but only so I may pass on the promise of treason to the king directly!'

I took the boots and slipped the ring back on my finger. 'You will help me, why?'

The earl's face grew darker. 'That ego-driven shit of a king tore my family apart when he took my mother as a mistress and my father had to stand by and just accept it… Who do you think bore the brunt of that injustice?'

I bent to fasten my boots. 'We have a common enemy then. Only you pretend to be his loyal subject.'

'I play the part. But I am only one man, and as you can see, I am not built for lethal combat.'

I finished the second goblet without coming up for air and passed the silver back, then turned for the door.

'Wait, please, take an escort with you. Him!' The earl

pointed to the guard who looked back wide eyed and not at all keen on the idea.

I stopped and considered, walking over to the guard until I stood behind him, looking at the earl as I drew the sharp edge of the sword across the cunt's throat and he dropped into a slush of blood. The servant let out a sharp scream but shut her noise at a sharp look from the earl.

'This man liked to watch people get tortured. The castle will be better off without him. I'll go alone and make the king answer for what he's done, even if I have to burn the whole fucking country to the ground to do it.'

'Yes!' the earl's words and movements were filled with passion. 'Yes! They will fear your name. Tremble in the dark as you cut your way to the festering core!'

I headed back toward the door as the earl jumped up and down on the spot. I think he was unhinged.

'But what is your name, young lord?' he asked.

I turned, thinking for a moment, I hated my name because of who I shared it with. 'Henry.'

'Henry what?'

I didn't have a family name… 'Game, Henry Game.'

It was decided, that would be my name, and with that I left the castle, its prison, torture chambers, decadence and all, calmly through the front door towards the stables. The earl followed, hot on my tracks and drooling from the idea of his own revenge finally playing out.

As we approached the wooden outbuildings the earl shouted for the stable boy to bring his personal horse and a finest travel cloak, immediately and without delay.

I thought the two words were both one and the same, but I said nothing as we waited by the steps. Dozens of armed guards watched on with hands on hilts, all of them stopped in the midst of whatever they were previously doing before we trotted along, shouting commands and storming around all seriously.

I mounted my horse and set off without another word or a backward glance, but I could feel the earl's gaze follow me out and into the night.

Early Summer, 1534. Lost in the Woods.

I put it to you that one cannot spend a significant amount of time aback a steadfast horse, and not form a sincere bond with the animal between your legs.

In my ignorance I formed an opinion of the robust animals as being little more than a beast of burden. Employed to keep the grass short; or clacker the brothers down to the village and back. I'd spent most of my life surrounded by horses, of course, but I was mainly concerned with the mucking out and changing of the water troughs to think of them as animals with emotions or awareness, and far be it from the intelligent beings that I had since appreciated them to be.

I named the horse Constance, as she never gave up, or faltered to my demand. Except when she did, of course, which was probably around half the time. I started to think that she only ever did what she wanted in any event, and that I was little more than a companion to her. She was a beautiful dark brown hackney, with a band of grey, narrowly hooping her mid-section, and tipped white on each leg to the hoof.

Naturally, it served as no surprise that the Earl of Huntingdon would be in possession of such a fine specimen. I was only grateful that my journey south had led me into the deep appreciation that I now bore for Constance.

I trusted her too. More than once on my journey south had she steered me clear of ambush, or rather as often, barged straight through it without hesitation and regardless of danger to herself. It was endearing; she clearly cared for me. Whereas a dog loves their human unconditionally, Constance was more like a cat in her affection.

Along the mainly wet and long route down to my destiny, I took boarding for us both each night at the various taverns and guest houses along the king's road. The coin I carried was enough for me to simply hand the reins over to a stable boy and concentrate on hot meals, warm sheets, and strange folk, knowing that my horse was being looked after.

In the din of a drunken wet evening, I would often drink quietly in a corner and listen to the inflated stories of the one they called "Henry Game". And each night I would keep my silence, except for the evening when I heard it proclaimed to all within the tavern, that Henry Game was none other than the secret bastard son of the king. His mother being a witch-whore from up north. And, as the legend continued, Henry was returning to the palace to claim his birth right, deposing of the fat king and ruling the country alongside his witch mother!

The ejection of mead through one's nostrils was often a sure-fire way to get the attention of those around you. The clearest sign of disagreement.

The fellow sharing his 'secret and privileged information' was marginally wider than he was tall, and I wondered if he could see his own dick anymore. He scowled at me and called for silence, challenging me to enlighten them all with my own "Henry Game facts".

And after a moment or two in thought, whilst I cleared my nose of liquid, I spun them a story, but only as "I had heard it from the local bishop" who had said that the man known as Henry Game was in fact a prophet from God, sent to execute the king for his blasphemies toward the Roman Catholic Church.

When I had finished the whole bar was holding their breaths… It seemed that my version of the legend made sense, or at least more sense than of bastards and witchcraft. At least judging by the general head nodding and banging of tankards on tables.

The big guy pursed his lips and stared into the warren of his own concentration for a long moment. With a firm nod and a knock of his tankard on the bar top, he returned to the business of tall tales and frothing ales. As the quarrel was quickly forgotten, it wasn't long before more false accounts of the infamous and indestructible, Henry "God-Sent" Game" came back to the forefront of conversations. I kept my peace and hid my laughter at the absurdity of it all.

The next morning came with a birdsong and I was back on my way, passing just south of Grimsby and into the dense forestation of Lincolnshire Wolds. Two aimless and desperate nights later, I conceded to myself, and more specifically Constance, that we were thoroughly and utterly lost, again. Thankfully the weather had been fine. I dare say nice even. But, the feeling of actually being lost is not good for the mind or morale, and even the damned horse was going crazy.

Finally, we reached a point where Constance would not let me ride her in any direction at all. She simply would not move, yet only agreed to accompany me if I went on foot. So, robbed of choice, I jumped down and started walking in what I hoped was a southerly direction.

Since leaving York Castle, I had quite become used to the lavish lifestyle of the rich merchant traveller, so after wandering all night through the never-ending dense forestation; resting and shitting in nothing but prickly divots; worrying about the moans of the forest whilst Constance rested and I remained on high-alert; at the first sight of an actual cottage with a roof and walls and probably beds, understandably I ran toward it. Regardless of Constance's reluctance, we were going, even if I had to carry her on my own back.

The cottage was built from stone, with a foliage-littered thatch roof. It sat in the thickness of shade where the trees over-head had formed an almost impenetrable canopy. Ivy cladded the front wall, parting only for the half dozen twinkles of glass, here and there. The windows were of strange and fascinating shapes, and the entrance door was squared and bark brown, banded by a harsh iron boarder. I figured that the opening was probably wide enough to let two full grown horses pass, side by side, though not quite tall enough to enter without ducking. Pale grey smoke chugged from the small stack over the other side of the ridgeline and the sudden and overwhelming smell of freshly baked bread lured us closer still.

My stomach has often been known to override my brain, for if it hadn't, I think I may have found this whole situation remarkably odd. Glass was reserved for the rich and privileged, and being way out into the deep, deep woods, where the trees almost completely block out one's view of the sky entirely, it sure seemed a long way removed from civilised folk. Further compounded by the smell of fresh bread and possibly cakes, when again the nearest food markets must be days away at best; the lack of well-trodden tracks to and from the cottage; the lack of a horse and carriage even; the lack of a garden boundary wall or fence; and then, of course, the precipitous appearance of three, twig-thin, and wide eyed women in severely moth-eaten dresses, appearing as if from thin air, and following silently behind us as we moved closer to knock on the door... My powers of observation were far from optimum. Yet, one must not look a gift horse in the mouth.

'Look sisters, look,' said the one in the middle wearing a long, long mud-brown dress with frills about the collar and wrists, the trail of leaves and muck set into the fabric train behind her. 'A young man.'

'He must be lost. Is he, sisters?' asked the one on the left, wearing a dress similar in frilliness, except black and scandalously short on the leg. She turned to the other one on the far right who suddenly sucked one of her grubby fingers and held it up to the wind.

'When a horse is about to...' said the last sister, this one in a very dirty white dress of the same design but of middling skirt length.

All three of them nodded and smiled at me, in unison, grey stumps hatching through swollen banks of gums. She never did finish that sentence. I tried not to dwell on the strangeness of folk and instead turned Constance around to face them.

'Good afternoon...' I looked up to locate the sun. 'Or whatever time of day it may be, I wonder if you could provide me and my horse lodgings for the night, a warm meal, and set us off again in the morning, in the direction of London?'

The middle lady, the sister in brown, stepped forward and held out her left hand, palm up. I took it and after a moment of awkwardness, I bent over to bow.

'We have lots of food, yes, and a bed for you too.' She looked at Constance and frowned, who in turn snorted back. 'But not a bed big enough for your horse.'

'We have a trough and a storm shelter.' The lady on the left. I wondered if they always took it in turns to talk.

'That would be perfect,' I said, 'and thank you. I will of course reimburse you for your hospitality...' the sister in brown, closest to me, had started to dig deep into her ear canal. 'And your troubles, naturally,' I concluded.

The final lady, sister in white, stepped forwards now and batted her sister's hand down from scratching her ear. 'Now, now boy, we have plenty to go around. You are too thin. Follow me, you can settle her for the night. A storm is coming.' She set off at a cripple's pace and I wondered if all three of them were senile.

Besides, I am usually very astute at detecting changes in the weather, but I tasted none of it. With only the waft of a fresh bake to think about, I followed and within a few minutes was seated, boots and cloaked removed, stuffing my face with gingerbread before a warming stove.

The three sisters watched me intently, they looked hungry. I wondered why they watched me so appreciatively, when there was clearly way too much gingerbread for one man to handle.

* * *

The next morning came late and confusing and I struggled with the static white sheets, wrapped around me a little too tightly. I couldn't remember coming to bed, but my boots, cloak and sword lay neatly beside me. I had the feeling that I maybe had slept too long, although the trees were so thick outside there really would be little way of telling the time of day at any hour.

Smells of fresh bread hooked my appetite again, over-riding my desire to relieve my bladder in fact, and as soon as I was booted, I stumbled out of my room and along to the kitchen once more, my sheathed sword in-hand, and travel cloak draped over the crook of my elbow.

'Good morning, I, I think. Is it late? I must be…' I noticed another guest. She was a much younger and prettier lady, but bloated and rounder than Constance's hind even, just about swelling out of her comically undersized dress of frills and bows.

She was seated on one end of the table with the three hags watching her intently from the other, all the cakes and breads piled up before the fat girl. She looked up at me between mouthfuls. Her eyes wide and watery.

'Sit down, eat, you must eat,' said the sister in brown, offering an empty chair besides the fat girl.

The sister in black turned away from gawping to remove the freshly baked food from the oven. My mouth watered as

I watched her popping hot muffins and loafs of gingerbread onto a wooden platter.

I sat and nodded warily to the girl as she continued to engorge herself unashamedly. 'You have another sister then?' I asked, and the three crones turned to face me together, small eyes and seeping gums. I spared another look to the girl on my left, still wide-eyed and eating herself into a frenzy.

'Eat up, eat,' said the sister in black as she slid a platter before me.

'Gretel is a guest. Lost, like you.' The sister in white winked at Gretel and slowly scurried to stand behind her, resting a long and withered hand on Gretel's ripe shoulder.

'How very kind you all are,' I said. Resisting the delectable aroma from the scones and muffins and loafs stacked high on the table before me.

I leaned a little closer to Gretel. 'So, where were you traveling to? I was lost for two days before I found this little beauty.'

She said nothing with her words, however, her eyes screamed at me. Just not sure what she was trying to communicate. Still, the oddness of folk, and especially strange ones, will never be something to stand in the way of a man's breakfast.

Without further ado I tucked in to my first scone, tearing the little delight in two and spreading a heaping of strawberry jam and cream into the fold.

'Won't you stay with us another night, Henry?' The sister in brown looked tense through her hideous smile. She looked to be starving.

'Nonsense. I am afraid that I have a king to murd… I beg your pardon: pressing business in the capital city.'

The sisters slumped in unison, as if somebody had unplugged their drain and suddenly their humours were leaking away.

Sister in black was next to speak. 'You continue to eat, and I'll fetch a map and compass that you can take with you.'

'Thank you kindly.' I cut a slice into the gingerbread loaf and reached for the butter.

'Why did I not think of gathering a compass before I set off?' I laughed at my own stupidity and ignorance, shaking my head as the sister in black hobbled away, slightly more mobile than the sister in white.

'Perhaps you didn't intend to get lost.' The sister in white was gently squeezing Gretel's round shoulders now, digging her fingers into the fleshy mounds.

'Nobody ever does.' Gretel's first words, and I noticed that she had a decidedly Germanic accent.

I nodded. 'Quite right. Tell me, has my horse been kept as well as you have kept me?'

The sister in brown wrinkled her nose as she spoke, 'I'm afraid we don't have suitable food for horses-'

'Nonsense!' I showed her a fresh scone. 'Many a time I have fed a horse bread, even if a little sugar is present. Poor girl, Constance must be starving. I'll take her some bread now then, before we-'

'No!' interrupted the sister in brown, her voice rising to a trill. 'You just stay where you are, eat your food. I'll take it.'

The disgust across her face was bothering me somewhat unreasonably, but I handed her the scone and continued to eat as ordered.

As she left the room at a much slower pace, I looked back toward Gretel and the sister in white hovering over her. My stomach was getting full, and in all this time Gretel had not stopped loading cake after cake into her gob. I scooped the last of the jam into the open scone and reached for the cream again only to find it empty.

'May I have some more jam and cream?' Gretel asked the question slowly and almost breathlessly, her eyes never leaving mine. I was thinking the exact same thing.

'Yes, yes. More gingerbread in the oven too my sweet Gretel.' With agonising slowness, the sister in white scraped her feet away and into another room leaving just we two.

'Good these scones, hey?' I nodded to Gretel and shoved the last bit into my mouth with my thumb. It was time to be going, I decided, but just as soon as the sister in white had vanished from view, my hungry companion reached out and grabbed my hand.

'Please, Sir, you must take me with you!'

I shook her hand away and scraped back my chair to stand. 'I'll do no such thing-'

'But you must!' Tears started to flow now, and I wasn't surprised: I'd be weeping too if I'd eaten that much cake.

'My, my brother...' she said between sniffs. 'Hansel. We came together. He's gone, the witches, I think they, they-'

I'd heard enough now. 'Look, girl, I have my own problems to deal with and I suggest you stop eating all the sweets and start figuring out your own.' I couldn't believe the ungratefulness of this greedy, greedy girl. I stood and swept my cloak over my shoulders.

'You know what, a little appreciation for the sisters wouldn't do you any harm.' I stood behind my chair and brushed the breadcrumbs from my tunic. 'Well then, Farewell. If I see your brother, I'll tell him I saw you-'

'No.' She tried to stand up but failed and flopped back into her chair. 'You do not understand; they are not sis-' her words broke away like a dried-out twig from the branch of a rotten tree. The sister in black had re-entered the kitchen and she was carrying a small leather pouch with a rolled-up parchment.

She looked tired and, if it were possible, like she had aged another ten years since she had left the room.

'Leaving so soon?' She slowly handed over the compass and map.

'Thank you again, but, needs must,' and with that I left the kitchen and the house through the back door, but not after giving the greedy girl a look of contempt and a thoroughly judgemental shake of the head.

Outdoors the sister in brown was painfully making her way back inside and startled as she saw me, stopping in her tracks. I breathed in the fresh air and held it for a moment, tiredness shedding from me like silk sheets over marble.

'If you ride south, south east for a few miles, you will come by an old farmhouse, wedged between two hills.' She stood straight and looked visibly annoyed with something. 'From there you need to ride due west for one day and you will reach the town of Lincoln.' Without even a smile she started to hobble past me and back into the kitchen.

'Thank you again.' I reached out to stop her and snatched my hand away as quickly. Beneath her mud-brown sleeves, I saw that her arms were little more than leather wrapped bone. She turned and met my stare with a great sadness.

'Please, allow me to pay for my lodgings.' I pulled out my purse from around my neck. 'And the compass and map, I beg your pardon.'

'A storm is coming,' she said, again, although I sensed none of it. 'You best be on your way.' And with that she slammed the door, much more forcefully than any elderly woman of her build should be able to.

Constance was shaking. The long grass around her had not been touched. Not one blade. I put my hand on her nose and she tried to bite me. She was pulling on her stay so violently that I thought she might break it. My stomach was starting to hurt a little from all the cakes and it made climbing aback a horse harder than it should've been.

I opened the leather pouch and looked upon the fine silver compass, marked with foreign symbols in exquisite detail and finesse. That last slice of gingerbread repeated on me and I wondered if I had perhaps eaten too much, but then thought nothing more of it as we headed south, south east, in search of civilisation once more. After all, I had a king to kill. And it was high-time I got back to it.

Late Summer, 1534. Another Wet Evening.

My personal crusade against the English monarchy had to come to an end one day. I just never thought it would be whilst submissively kneeling at the feet of Henry VIII, surrounded by his armoured soft-tin polished yeoman warders.

Of course, the warders' reputation was enough to make any man hesitate, but reputation only gets you so far, especially on the battlefield, but in my case, my reputation had brought me here, and here I knelt, thwarted.

Inside their tall suits they stood brave, shiny, and rattling. I shot them filthy glances, expectorating as often as my dry mouth would permit whilst they aimed their crossbows and their polished wheellock hand-guns at me, all hands a shaking. I took about as much notice to the threat as bears do to bees when raiding for honey. Though I admit that if they managed to shoot me it would hurt, at least for a while, but I would turn them inside out for the inconvenience, and that would hurt them to death.

It appeared that the tall tales and bards' poems boasting of my invincibility had preceded me. *The York Castle Riot* had been my rise to fame, and since then the stories had grown darker and more far-fetched. I had become the myth; the monster in the night… Now only to be kneeling, subservient, before the glutinous king, because of course, some legends overshadowed even my own, and I knew that most of mine were invented.

'I dub thee, Lord Game, Eternal Protectorate of the Church of England. Rise, Lord Game!' declared the King of England with all the pomp and ceremony that such an occasion required.

Heat surged to my temples as I stood, and the king passed his needle sword to one of his nameless bearers. I could've squashed the fat farce of a king, if not for the unexpected presence of Dr Mirabilis, and I would have done, without hesitation.

"Doctor Marvellous", as they had recently taken to calling the ominous wizard, was inspecting my ring in the light that drained down from the glass dome overhead. His ancient eyeball practically kissing the metal, his other hand aloft and in a suitably mystical fashion. I was expecting forks of lightening to snap and pop from his claw-like-fingers.

I had come to squash the king along with anyone who was foolish enough to die for him. Excluding, of course, terribly famous and dangerous magicians.

The grin spread across the king's sticky face as I rose to my feet. He waved a hand to lower the rattling crossbows and polished gunpowder weapons, deflating the tension to a more acceptable murderous level.

'The guardsman,' I said through gritted teeth, 'an agent of the Vatican, you say?'

'I'm afraid so, young man.' The king nodded, emphatically. 'Solitary times lay ahead of us all now that the Roman Catholic Church has shunned our beloved, and most godly nation.'

He leaned forward, closer to me, more on a level, as if we were in this together. 'Rest assured that our forces hunt down these cowards of *Knights Templar*.' He held his hand out for the ring which I had pried from the dead Guardsman's hand.

Dr Mirabilis obliged, placing the ring down gently in the king's sweating palm, watching me with a blank expression. I could not guess his emotion and that unnerved me. I looked back at the crowned one.

Henry squeezed the ring tight in a fist, making a real show if it. 'And when my men find those foreign agents who dare to invade my lands,' he clapped his hands together, the crack reverberating around the halls. 'Together, young Henry, we will have squashed the threat, and saved countless more innocent lives. You have no enemies here, my boy. Justice for your father will be had. God demands it so, and so do I command his judgement on this land!'

He stood and limped down the steps until he stood beside me, enveloping me in a supportive embrace, whispering into my ear. 'For the scores of my men you have killed,' his embracing arm turned quickly into a throttling squeeze, 'I should chain you up. But Doctor Marvellous here, well, he convinced me otherwise.' He placed the ring in my hand and gave me a cruel grin, before hobbling back up to his worn-in throne.

'The lie of Catholicism is no longer welcome on these shores; I assure you of that.' He clicked his fingers and a fruit platter was presented. Without pause he shoved grapes into his mouth. 'The pious flee this country, even as we speak...' his mouth too full to say much else.

'The continent,' suggested Mirabilis at a whisper. His eyes never leaving me.

Henry nodded and chewed noisily, suddenly holding up a remembering finger. 'Ah! Yes, yes. Henry Game, your real enemy hides behind the incestuous walls of the Vatican. Only the pontiff himself can order the Knights Templar into service. Everyone knows that.'

'And the Vatican is in Rome, Italy?'

Dr Mirabilis bowed his head at my question and turned away. His metallic-purple robe glimmering as he trotted off. Within a few moments he had left through a small dark opening behind the throne wall. I wondered if the old man was senile and perhaps it was tall tales that followed him also...

'Rome.' The king answered after following my gaze to the wondering wizard. He dropped more plump red grapes into his mouth, frequently spitting out pips onto his tunic without shame.

'I will arrange passage for you on a trading vessel travelling to France. However, from there you must travel alone. England can have no 'overt' part in the assassination of the pope.'

'England has no fucking part at all in what I'm doing, whether I travel by your boat or not!' I turned on my heel and headed straight for the barricaded doors, the three yeoman warders scattering like gazelles before the lion.

'Yes, yes of course, of course,' he laughed and spat pips. 'Oh, and Lord Game?'

I shivered at the title. I was bored with him now. 'Yes?' I may have let my impatience leak a little.

Only reason I wasn't tap-dancing on his face was because if his crazy old wizard bodyguard. Dr Mirabilis was said to be over two hundred years old, many a passing traveller through the abbey would share tales of the one they say can control death, and even reverse it.

The king smiled again, showing his grey teeth. 'Tell him idleness is the chief mistress of vices all. Oh, and also that we know he's a nonce, and that—'

I turned and stormed out of the throne room, blood boiling behind my temples as the king's laughter morphed into a phlegm-filled coughing frenzy.

I really did not like the man. Still, I couldn't ignore the facts. All the king's guardsmen and all his servicemen bore the Tudor Rose proudly, mostly painted upon their breastplates or tunics, but the one who killed Father and subsequently mulched beneath my grip did not. Also, the ring he wore signified a secret ancient order known as The Knights Templar.

Henry told it, or Mirabilis told the king in loud and slow whisper, that the 'Knights' were once the foremost military arm of the Vatican, and now served in secret as the pope's protection detail. Mirabilis went so far as to fetch for a scrolled document to prove it, not that I could read the ancient and faded ink.

And how I had become a lord was equally as surprising to me as discovering about the secret sect that had been implicit in the murder of my father. But as for the reason behind my father's murder, I would need to ask the pontiff in person, they said.

The king celebrated me for "chasing out the covert catholic assassins" and thus named me the Eternal Lord Protectorate of the Church of England. It was a public relations exercise, as most things are, but it was also one with which the king could still save face.

I didn't give a shit about the king's reputation. All I needed was revenge, and I was one step closer to exacting it. It wasn't until after the blood had stopped boiling, and I was aback Constance, heading for the ports, that I realised how far I had come. To receive a direct audience with the king and his secret warlock had only confirmed that my legend had preceded me and stricken fear into the heart of the powers that be. Yet, to the appearance I looked little more than a child and already the myth had it that I was half-devil. The legends whispered into the ears of my enemies that no earthly weapon could kill me. Which was partly correct, but still they tried always their best, and I have the scars to prove it.

* * *

The wind and rain threw me a leaving party as I boarded that miserable bastard of a ship. It would be my first time at sea, and damn did that ship roll some.

I figured the higher powers had it in for me. Ill omens preceded my murderous mission in the form of vomit by way of severe sea storms, and all we crossed was the bloody English Channel!

If I wasn't hanging over the side heaving my back out, I squibbed, hopelessly, like my feet were covered in oil and my leg muscles like chicken fat. I was a landlubber removed from the mud and dirt and dust, and I hated the taste of salt on the wind.

The crew watched me and kept their distance. Never known a more superstitious bunch of pansies. Them being the king's men, my reputation had paved the way which didn't help matters on the social scale. I had the death of thirteen men under my belt, adding a few sailors wouldn't be too taxing, but I let them have their dark looks, for I hoped the journey would be short.

The sun invaded the afternoon, and I spent it unseen in my storeroom chamber. My purse had been made heavier yet with silver. I felt no value, only burden for the extra weight it promised me. Another goodwill gesture from the fat-bastard-king in his fat-bastard-palace, and, they said, I should have been grateful to have left with his blessing.

I studied the crumbling map parchments they provided. Most definitely out-dated, and I hadn't the foggiest what I was looking at. I took a bearing of east, south east and hoped for the best.

My vulnerable days in the Yorkshire Moors and Lincolnshire Wolds were behind me, but still, memories of being so hopelessly lost and desperate picked at the frayed stitching of my convictions. My compass and my will to kill would have to be enough to chase away my fears.

That night I lay awake. Closed eyes showed overcast skies only, and so instead I wandered, ghosting the decks whilst the anchor had been lowered. My stomach had settled and now all I had to contend with was a slippering sway and a cool breeze.

The cedar deck did not complain as I snatched between

the deep shadows, catching the scraps of conversations held between the crewmen.

Whispers in the dark about the half-baked fables of Henry Game and the fear they harboured for me actually set a smile to my lips. "Let the fucking French have him!" one of the deck hands boldly convicted. "I heard it, that they killed his whole family and made him watch whilst his mother and baby sister were tied down and..." words zipped off as I emerged from the darkness to be amongst them, enjoying the warmth of a small fire.

'No please, you were saying?' I waited, but they did not wish to continue.

I left them to their conspiracy. Let England and the greedy bastard king have them. My kill list was populated enough, gobshite sailors were the least of my concern. Besides, I reasoned, if I had killed them all, then I would surely be stranded at sea forever.

* * *

As the coast of France broke the horizon, I found that I yearned for it. I longed for the thing that kept me awake night after night; the itch that never ceased; the need for blood; the need for justice. Or to put it even simpler: old fashioned revenge. Nothing more, nothing less.

The skies darkened with the promise of blood as I realised that a welcome party awaited me on the northern border of France, a busy little spot called Calais. I began to entertain the idea that my legend had spread across the channel and felt my self-swelling even further.

The idea of my escapades spreading fear, even across waters, was a boost for my ego. A fool's boost to be sure, as even I started to believe I was invincible. I breathed in the salty promise of adventure and set my sights on the mission. The glint of my militarised host, ranked, waiting by the pier, armed to the teeth.

The twelve-man entourage sent to chaperone my passage through France was evidence enough of my reputation. In the very least it showed respect. And respect stemmed from fear and fear from the unknown, or, to be more precise, fear from the possibility that some of the legends were true. Either way, never has a man jumped over-board a moving ship quite so confidently as I did that day. You can never make too good of a first impression, even if wet socks are the price to pay.

I squelched up the sandy shore embankment, my hand resting on the pommel at my waist, and straight past the static holy guardsmen, my smile wider and easier than it had any right to be.

After a moment or two I heard them snap into shape and advance upon my rear, trailing my purposeful stride toward justifying my vengeance. I stopped walking and drew my blade, inspecting it in the sunlight. The squad came to a halt behind me, watching and waiting with bated breath.

I sheathed my sword and whistled on my jolly way. Rome bound, but damn my feet were cold. Wet feet, socks, and boots are definitely not the ideal way to start any long journey – but damn if I didn't look fucking spectacular, and like something ripped straight out of the *Iliad*.

Stateside Secrets (L. S.).

Word arrived just as my plane landed that the commercial flight to Dallas was presumed to have gone down somewhere over the Atlantic.

I wondered who was following my movements so closely as to believe that I was now destroyed with the plane and chum for the fish. The mystery and danger had me pitched, like a teenager, and I took my complimentary whiskey at the front of the plane on my connected flight to Grand Canyon West Airport, lay back and enjoyed myself in the recess of my own thinking.

I had an address in New York City, but of course, an entire country to travel to get there. I worried that the passport I used to board the Dallas flight would get flagged if I used it again to take a plane to New York, so I resigned to the idea of a good old road trip, and then pondered on my options of American muscle and the famous Route 66.

The last forty-eight hours had been like the good old days, back when Death and I were on first name terms. I was living again, and I had purpose, reason, and righteousness on my team.

I stepped out on to the dusty pavement of Peach Springs, Arizona and breathed the far-western wind into my lungs; I was enamelled, and this adventure was fresher than a newborn's fart, and trickier than a barrel full of oiled up horny monkeys on LSD. Getting to America would not be the end of my journey. Not by a long shot. However, as I marched purposefully along the pavement, I realised that I had absolutely no idea where to rent a car from. I had no smartphone on me and only the false passport, *Abatu*, and my money clip in my possession, along with my shabby looking winklepickers and my dishevelled suit, of course. I needed to regroup, and the first thing I saw was a big dirty burger sign, jutting from out above a shop front window.

"Wet Paint" signs littered the immediate area around the entrance and so I was careful not to get any on my clothing. My stomach had always been a harsh mistress. And currently she threatened to go all out cannibal if I didn't fill her with greasy shit to soak up the belly of malt whiskey I was running on.

As I entered, I noticed the two dozen rows of computer monitors, with mainly old folk driving them, varifocals on, heads tilted back, absorbed. Adopting my best manners, I asked the exceedingly happy lady behind the counter for their biggest, dirtiest burger, with two fried eggs on top, a heaping of crispy bacon, coffee and an available kiosk.

She looked me square in the eyes, all the while smiling like she meant it, called me sugar and handed over a card with a code printed in the middle, and told me my food will be right with me, honey.

I sat down in the corner booth. Strategically, it was the only place from which I could see both the monitor and the rest of the room. By the time I had figured out how to log-on properly and opened an internet search engine, the food arrived, and man was it filthy and hot and unhealthy. Exactly what I needed. My teeth sank into the grease and yolk, egg dripped down my shirt, but I really didn't care in that moment. I mean, I looked a little ruffled to say the least, and with a face like mine, people rarely paid attention to my clothes, regardless of my best efforts. After a good few bites, my ravenous appetite choked with a cholesterol bomb, I typed "Ian Mulliti" into the search bar and hit enter.

An umbrella appeared in the middle of the screen and after a minute it reloaded and was filled with a list of website links.

I scanned the information quickly but found nothing obvious or apparently relevant. My arms felt heavy of a sudden and my stomach glugged happily. The second half of the burger was drooling over my fingers. Rising to the challenge, vowing I would not be defeated, three large bites and the monster was gone. Devoured. I clicked onto page two of the "Ian Mulliti" search results.

A key word match for "Mulliti, I." stood bold in the middle of the list of irrelevant links. I double clicked the keyword match and waited again as the umbrella swirled round and round and round. My coffee was still hot, but the excessive salt had me gagging and I skulled it, again missing mouth and getting my shirt – I looked like a tramp, I decided, but still didn't care. I would buy a new suit once I had escaped the museum of dusty Peach Springs and returned to the real world of high streets, 5G and anime porn.

My screen flashed a dark and violent red. Slowly an image of yellow circles faded into full colour and became connected by straight lines of black and white. All the lines and circles faded in and filled the screen on the red background. The circle in dead-centre glowed and pulsed, inviting. Thirteen circles, I counted, and the lines that connected and inter-sected and divided, dissected, and added layer upon layer of complexity, drew me in. The longer I looked at the image the more I saw.

I clicked the glowing circle in the centre when the computer fans started to whir, loudly. The image on the screen froze, the circle no longer pulsing and the loud noise revving out of the back of my ancient computer was drawing looks from the old folk, most of them now scowling over their monitors.

I was pressing every damned button I could when finally, the whirring stopped. I relaxed a little and winked at the lady across the aisle from me when suddenly the screen began to bleed purple, then blue, then cracked as the monitor split down the edges of the monitor and gel dripped on to the keyboard and desk.

At this point I figured that I probably needed help. Looking up, I noticed a decidedly noticeable looking fellow enter the internet café, his serious eyes scanning the room with a decidedly serious purpose.

I reckoned that my computer was seriously fucked, with smoke escaping the huge black box that made up the cranium of the dinosaur. Without a doubt, I figured they were on to me. Mr Serious was here to make me pay, no doubt, so I lowered into my seat as much as my cubicle would allow, but, inevitably, he approached. My belly was so full. I really didn't want to have to beat anybody up.

Mr Serious wore a black suit with a metallic silver tie. His curly hair and long beard were also black, blacker than his suit even, and he straight up reminded me of a bad guy out of a Bond movie. Not a specific villain, but more of the generic type to fit the mould.

My screen had gone past sizzling and finally given up, still in the throes of fading out to black. Meanwhile, smoke continued to escape the vents in tendrils.

Without invitation Mr Serious sat beside me, his fingertips steepled in front of his nose and mouth, saying nothing, expectantly so, however. And so, the silence stretched on between us until around a minute later, after coming to the conclusion that he wasn't the internet café security guard, I pointed at the computer.

'Your handiwork?'

'Yes,' he replied, without moving his hands from in front of his mouth.

'Well I'm not fucking paying for it-'

'You try to find Ian Mulliti.' It wasn't a question. His dialect was thick and harsh. It sounded Arabic, but he looked Rus-sian-ish, if such a thing is possible.

'Ah, yeah,' I admitted, growing just a little tired of his lack of manners. 'Who are you, Mister Serious?'

'I am sent to take you to *Him*, Mister Game.' He rolled his Rs and almost spat his Hs.

'Sent,' I asked, 'by whom? And take your fucking hands away from your mouth when you talk to me.'

He sat back, straightened up and lowered his palms to his ninety-degree lap. The way the light caught his face made it look like he had a mouth full of peanuts. Then he smiled, fully, and I recoiled away from the dozens of pointy white teeth.

My first thought was of a fucking man-shark. But I'd read somewhere about these freaks who modify their anatomy, sharpen teeth and have fucking horns and other weird shit implanted. Stuff like that spooks me. Gives me the willies. My silence was probably a key indicator for my distaste, hopefully not my unease.

He placed his hands back in front of his face and this time I didn't say anything. He stood and gestured toward the door. It seemed we were leaving so I stood up and followed him out.

A long blacked out car was waiting a dozen inches from the cracked pavement. Mr Serious held the door for me.

'You have dinner reservation. Long drive. *He* cares not for tardiness, Mister Game.'

'Route sixty-six?' I hoped, but Mr Serious kept his mouth shut and looked at me with impatience and reserved aggression.

The Iron Mask.

'Seriously, you've more chance of them electing me to be the next pope than you do of convincing me to agree to wear one of them ridiculous iron masks!' I said, but the silver-faced drones delivered the bundle anyway on my bed, my 'assigned' robes and mask gleaming from atop of the pile. Purple fucking things, none the less. Worst colour there is.

'Look, just do as your surname suggests and play along.' Grim unfolded himself from the tiny chair nestled in the corner of my living quarters. I noticed he wasn't wearing his mask.

'Sorry,' I shook my head, 'but I'm just not doing it.' Holding the metal face up I spied at Grim through the eye slits. 'If they want me to wear it, they'll just have to make me. And I'd like to see them try as well-'

'No, you wouldn't...' Grim looked his namesake of a sudden. He reached out for the mask and studied its features. 'How would one describe it, then? Disdainful, untrusting. Quite out of character for you, wouldn't you agree?'

I snatched it back from him. 'More like sceptical or defiant, I'd say.'

'O' for the many faces of Henry Game!' he laughed, and with that his humongous frame made to leave my twenty cubic meters.

'And Game,' he said, turning in the doorway 'just wear the sodding mask, and don't make too much noise about it all.' He lowered his voice. 'Because if you don't follow the rules, I promise, you will regret it, no matter how tough you think you are.'

He leaned back again, checking the hallway either side of him, lowering his voice to barely even a whisper now. 'Ask around about the Blade of Northwood. That should be warning enough for you.'

'I am not wearing it.' I tossed the mask back into the corner of my prison cell. 'They'll just have to make me.'

Grim laughed and walked away, shaking his massive bearded head, and I laughed too, and much louder. I wasn't sure what he was laughing about but it felt like he was one-upping me. I'd like to say that I was laughing on the other side of my face. But…well, suffice to say that my face was no longer my property, I just didn't know it yet – and laughing on one side or the other wasn't a thing easily done when you no longer owned one. And a face is a thing we take for granted. It is also a thing to attach identities. When you lose one; when it is taken from you; when they force another upon you…

I have more regrets than you could shake a stick at, but, if I had just listened and submitted to wearing the damned mask, or even if I had taken Grim's advice and tried to find out about the Blade of Wherever, then perhaps I wouldn't have found myself in immeasurable pain. Still, there is knowledge in all things, especially in pain.

I learned that there is a kind of pain that reminds you that regular living is a delight that we all take for granted, only to be reminded of this knowledge after it is swapped out for agony. I took it for granted.

I deduced that these bastards knew they couldn't kill me, and it's also my guess that they knew I wouldn't wear it. Not by choice anyway. I thought it by design that they manipulated me into such a situation that I had no choice at all. And I had played straight into their hands.

So, when I publicly challenged The Lady of the Mask to make me wear the stupid thing, she cordially accepted, had me restrained in an instant, and then proceeded to have the fucking thing melted it onto my face. It was as if I watched from afar as my skin smoked and hissed as it was seared and replaced by the white-hot, inside coating of my new identity.

The feeling was truly unique and unforgettable. They kept me tied down for what must have been weeks. Dripping water and soup through the straight slit that protected my teeth from the iron. I couldn't even speak. To try and move my lips, before they became healed and fused to the mask, caused a feverish phenomenon that paralysed me from even thought.

Lying there, alone, I explored the recesses of reason. I allowed myself to turn inward and acquire the perspective of subjective objectivity. Whatever selfish desire I once allowed to ravage my purpose was dissolved and replaced with a mandate of directive.

For what felt like long enough to scrape the crusty edges of eternity, I was nothing. Less than equal; I was little more than the plants they watered and fed daily. My ability to free think suspended as they conversed about me. I smelled the scents and tasted the water but paid no opinions to the source or outcome.

We all break.

I'd wager that one cannot truly get to really understand one's own character until it is shattered, then reassembled. That was when he came in and showed me kindness. It started with him just talking to me, directly, as if I was a real person again. Telling me about the weather outdoors and then of events that were occurring around the globe. I latched on and took interest, hungrily. He wore the mask of wrath and he was known simply as Sin.

Months, or maybe even years, passed before they eventually released my restraints. The mask was one with my face; was at one with me; and I with it. I attended meetings, routinely, and was gradually given free roam of the palace.

From time to time I noticed them following me, but I no longer resented their mistrust. Instead I yearned to be of use to them, to be accepted as one of them. Whatever I was before had been completely replaced with this new veneer of subservience.

Stories of Grim Catspaw's expeditions in Europe echoed like gossip in the Halls of Obedience, the palace to which had become my new home. The name Henry Game had been burned away with my face. They referred to me as the Bastard of Bolton, or just "The Bastard". My trade name would be plied with purpose towards the greater good, they versed me, and I welcomed it.

My mask, looking at it in the mirror, bore the face of dedication. At the meetings I was given an honorary position, seated by the side of Sin, one down from The Lady of the Mask herself. After a time, Grim returned from Europe to sit opposite me, and decisively I was activated. My time had come.

It was the spring of 1914, and finally they released me to wreak havoc. My outlook on existence had changed, but of course there are some things that never change, and my proclivity for ending human life is one of them.

Germany was war mongering and spreading the disease of rumour. There was a potential for large-scale war, and we were sent to make sure it happened. Grim and I were partnered as the sword and the shield to enact the will of the Iron Mask. Money was to be made from war and empires needed money to rise up, especially clandestine empires.

Needless to say, it wasn't long before tales of 'The Bastard' began circulating; propagating and spreading fear into the hearts of those who braved to oppose the Iron Mask.

Our mandate was singular and clear: to administer our influence upon another secretive society of contemporaries, another continental collective aimed at political warfare. They were simply referred to as the "Black Hand", and after a couple of well-placed mutilations, we had them where we wanted them.

* * *

'For the last fucking time,' I was growing rather impatient, 'ich spreche kleine Deutsch!!' I think I pronounced the words correctly, but this fucker insisted on speaking to me in harsh German, that of course I did not understand a syllable of.

The man frustrating the hell out of me held the rank of Lord Hand, and he wore gloves, black ones, and an expensive smoking jacket. His people had patted me down for concealed weapons, twice, before admitting me entry to his personal library and war room, or at least that was what I thought the place was from the looks of the maps and plastic soldiers on the tables.

The overtly armed guards at the gate had the skull symbol of the Black Hand emblazoned on the backs of their soaked, knee length over-coats. The nuzzles of their automatic weapons peeping from beneath. Even the driver, who also didn't seem to understand that I did not speak German, wore plain black gloves.

I thought the Black Hand insinuated something more sinister, at least more than just leather gloves. I suppose it is not much different to my own twisted and nefariously clandestine organisation, whereas we literally wore iron masks. These simplistic names for societies of secrecy seemed ridiculous. At the time, however, it certainly wasn't, and still isn't.

'Ich weiß. Du bist eine unwissende fotze,' said Lord Hand, smiling at me.

I stood up to leave, sending a fine spray of rain from my anorak. 'Forget it. I'm done. It would be easier for me to talk to a-'

'Mister Game, please, sit,' he interrupted my dramatic exit.

'Seriously, after all this time, you speak English?'

He laughed and popped open a polished wooden cigar box on his desk. 'Come now, sit. Ve have much to discuss for ze future. Zigarre?'

I accepted and felt all the better for it too. Whilst I had been mentally planning a fight path exit, what with all the bullshit and games, to talk like gentlemen and enjoy the fineries of life was preferable when the business of world war was afoot.

He filled a crystal tumbler glass with a substance most like brandy and offered it to me first, then proceeded to fill another for himself. Again, I accepted his hospitality and relaxed even further whilst the fire roared in the background and the wind and rain howled against the stained-glass windows to the northern front.

'Bitte, let us take your coat.' He clapped, and a servant appeared as if from thin air.

'Lord Hand, vill zee guest be staying for dinner, heute abend?' The manservant spoke with his head high and proud.

I laughed and made myself comfy in my chair. I could absolutely get used to this. 'Of course,' I announced, holding the tumbler against the mouth slit of my mask with a clank. 'As long as you can make it fit through a straw!'

I thought my quip was funny but neither of the Germans laughed, and within seconds the manservant placed a straw in my drink. Without even a nod of appreciation I sunk back and drank deeply, well, as deeply as the straw would permit.

* * *

Perhaps I had sozzled one too many brandies, even though I was only halfway through my second, I suddenly couldn't find my straw or feel my tongue anymore. The brandy was pretty potent stuff, but I doubted the alcohol content was the cause of my sudden total body paralysis.

The Lord Hand had happily sat behind his desk, smiling at me as my eyes began to swim in panic, and my arms no longer moved under intention. I was rooted to the comfy chair and as the tumbler fell from my grip, the Lord Hand jumped to his feet, wasting no time at all before rolling up his sleeves and moving the heavy furniture around the room with a purpose that both intrigued and worried me equally.

The manservant reappeared and together they lifted the war map table and waddled from my view, muttering ugly and harsh words at each other all the while. Whilst my entire body was paralyzed, my eyes, unfortunately, weren't, and I could see that the pieces of furniture they moved around were all connecting together with clinks and clunks.

They collapsed two of the legs on the chair beside me and folded the back down and carried it away. From as far as I could tell, they were assembling a contraption, very much like a torture table.

I gurgled my displeasure at seeing such an archaic device, even if the engineering and genius design of it was impressive as hell. It looked like a relic from an era of darkness, albeit a well-used and regularly oiled version, that doubled up as regular furniture when disassembled. The German really were efficient in engineering.

The wrist restraints had large bolt heads with sharpened grub screws to pinch the flesh. They looked like they could be screwed in slowly; I reckoned it was for screwing into the bone without shattering it. I farted. It was totally involuntary, but I held their looks all the same as they stopped assembling for a moment, their faces somewhere between disgust and surprise.

I laughed, in my head anyway. In reality it was another gurgle. The fart was thick and rich and perfectly horrible and lingered closer to me than I'd hoped for. With little choice in the matter, I was resigned to torture. I would have felt better about the whole situation if they had captured me in battle, like real men.

I always thought it a coward's tool: poison. But I suppose karma catches up with us all in the end. Napoleon would certainly vouch for that if he could've seen me then. They say what goes around comes around and I continued in this line of thought as they flipped the war map table onto its end, the plastic soldiers sliding off, and began unstrapping the wrist and ankle clamps.

Suddenly the footsteps of a larger, if not heavier, beast entered the fray. I couldn't see whom this late comer was from where I was drooped, but I could see how far up the Lord Hand had to crane his neck to look him in the face.

A shadow dropped over me from behind, breathing heavy and close to me. I could sense the moisture from a wet coat, hear it dripping to the floor. A foot squelched and the timber moaned as he advanced further. Now just inches behind my chair.

The manservant's eyes went wide, and the Lord Hand nervously eyed the torturing table that was damn near ready *for me. Suddenly the sneaky servant darted from view, toward the fireplace when a loud bang rang in my ears, and a portion of the manservant's chest and guts exploded like a party popper into my line of sight and all over the torture device. Flames hissed and spat in the fireplace.*

'Game, you comfortable?' It was Grim. I whooped for joy, but again just a gurgle.

The Lord Hand backed towards a window. 'Please, vhen ve heard that Ze Bastard vas coming, ve, nyth just assumed he vas coming to kill uz!' He looked pathetic as he scrambled and fell over the upright torture table.

I hadn't thought of it that way.

Grim didn't speak immediately and after a moment or two he walked around into my field of vision. His overcoat was thick with blood and, what looked like, mud. He either winked at me or just blinked normally, it really is impossible to tell when they only have one eye.

Reaching over he kindly straightened my slumped position somewhat, allowing me a broader view of the room, and of the disgusting diplomacy which was about to unfold.

* * *

Eventually I regained the use of my faculties, by which time Grim and the Lord Hand had peacefully worked things out and come to an arrangement. To say I was disappointed that my previous situation had not rewarded the Lord Hand a delightfully creative death was an understatement.

My fury brewed and stirred like a proper cup of tea. To put it plainly, I sulked whilst I sat, still in the same chair, bottom lip out (metaphorically speaking) and huffed often and empathically. And if I had a dummy, I would have spat that out too.

Grim still held the shotgun diplomatically across his lap. He maintained a giant hand across it, the threat carrying the weight of promise as they came to a solution in ensuring that the Great War would happen, and more importantly, happen precisely as planned. They toasted to exciting times ahead.

The Black Hand's first mission was to assassinate an Austro-Hungarian fellow, whom I had not previously heard of, some aristocrat by the name Archduke Franz Ferdinand.

Precautions were taken in ensuring that the Black Hand had their end covered. Meanwhile, the Iron Mask would nudge the British government, when the time came, into declaring war against the Germanic evils, and thus a climate would be born that would help usher the way for the Iron Mask to seize control of policies and decision makers, but most importantly, to seize upon the financial gains of expensive war.

Looking back now, I regret not killing that bastard with his stupid fucking gloves on. At least the Iron Mask created anonymity and mystique.

* * *

As you will know through the histories available to you, the atrocities inflicted during the first half of the twentieth century proved to be a true reflection on mankind's de-evolution. Even I struggled to see past the displays of anti-humanisms all across the globe.

Humanity hated itself and countries turned on each other for little more than financial or political gain. Friends stabbed each other in the backs; brother turned against brother; fathers against sons. Looking back, I wonder if this is where my mask first began to slip free.

It wasn't too long after the great violence that another masterful deception was introduced. The Treaty of Versailles. It was as the Allied Powers made Germany sign the concocted document, especially Clause 231, that I really started to see what a machine of oppression I was helping steer. And such an efficient machine it was, more efficient than even the Germans... But something had flipped inside me and I knew the machine had to be broken. The parts scrapped and melted down or buried as far and wide as possible.

Regardless of my efforts to unearth the truth, the Second World War happened, sooner rather than I had thought possible. Grim argued that there was no stopping a thing once it is decided, and that we must let the nightmare play out to see the rise of a new day.

Grim had been responsible for the relapse in Russia, as was to be expected: as Grim is very effective. The idea was to prolong the fighting... The longer the war would continue, the more power would be secured.

My feelings had changed entirely. I worked as a double agent and reached out to The Order in the States, begging them to persuade the Americans to abandon their commerce and neutrality and join the war to help save what remained of the world.

The American government and economy were the true victors of the World Wars. The model had been set after the first for financial gain, but this time it was the USA that profited exponentially. Calling time on a winning streak was the key to capitalisation and Allied victory.

As my involvement with the Iron Mask came to light, I believed my bridges burnt with The Order. So long had passed since I had returned... The reconnection reminded me of something I had almost forgotten. I remembered what I was and when I returned to my chambers, I was *delighted to see the re-emergence of my book, the one passed down to me a long time ago. The Order knew I was being used and must have had agents of its own amongst the Iron Mask. I wondered whom but wasted no time in securing my freedom. I had a home, a history and was part of something much bigger.*

Wheels were turning and like just like clockwork my face rebelled against the separatist ideology I was a part of. Opening the book, feeling the lost language of the symbols on my tongue, I once more remembered who I was; remembered the overcast skies, my anger; the Iron Mask would remember soon enough too.

Good and strong relationships were broken and ripped apart. Such is the way with doctrines. I gave a thought to Grim, still deep in Europe as the last of the war's fighting died out. If I knew I would have to kill my way out of the Iron Mask, I felt immensely grateful that Grim would not be one of those standing against me.

It took me almost two full years to be completely rid of that bastard mask. I mean, of course I'll never be completely free, not now. The mirror reminds me every day. But eventually I did manage to peel off the last section beneath my left eye. It was a process accomplished piece by fucking piece, which each and every time demanded a pound of flesh with it.

Smashing the mask was bad enough, what with it still being attached to my face. But if nothing, through all the pain, I learned to bide my time. Relationships could mend, skin could regrow, especially with time on my side, for he who does not grow old is forever young, if not unreasonably impatient.

La France. Late Summer, 1534.

I had the twelve-strong, fully-armoured, welcoming party trailing about a day and a half behind me – not that I was moving quickly by any sense of the word – but of course they were mostly on foot and I had the good sense to purchase the first horse I laid eyes upon, from the very first farm encountered.

The mare was considerably older than Constance, and she cost me a full sovereign, because it was the only golden coin in my possession. Of course, I didn't speak French, and apparently, the dairy farmers didn't speak English either, but gold speaks the language that everyone understands and so the business was done and consummated with a frothy mug of warm milk, surrounded by tiny-toothed Frenchmen.

She was a chestnut brown Breton, I suspected bred with a gypsy's pony by the extreme shortness of her legs and the length of her mane; and for all the bloody money she cost, she didn't take kindly to the saddle. But after half a day struggling with her, she finally conceded and from then on, she went steady enough.

My French chaperones laughed at my struggles to mount her, but not so much when I finally set away at a canter. I called my new horse Mary, and each night as the sun would set, she made it clear that it was time to make camp, whether I liked it or not. My alternative was walking to Rome, which was about eight-thousand furlongs, give or take a few hundred.

We were a few days into the French countryside when we came across the pope's first and most righteous responders. I had made camp early for the day, taking shelter in a derelict farmer's outbuilding in the bowl of a depression at the foot of a saddle between two ridges. My compass directed the way, and the steep incline to make it through the pass would've been too much for Mary after particularly arduous going. She was no Constance, and I needed to take care of her if she was to carry me to my destination.

We had rested the last three nights out in the wet and open, so taking the opportunity to sleep beneath a partially collapsed roof was an opportunity not worth passing up on. Although the ground was drying out, the grass around the barn was still considerably boggy and riddled with broken ankles. It really was a stupid place to build an outbuilding, and I only hoped the rains held off for the evening as I imagined the depression to fill up like piss in a pot jar.

I decided to leave Mary on firmer ground, tethering her beneath the only tree close by, I didn't want her to get stuck in the bog, so it seemed like the best option. We were maybe a thousand furlongs into our long journey, and so far, the way had been danger free. I knew it was only a matter of time before my enemies caught up with me.

The outbuilding was crumbling away and back into the mud, storm after storm, stone by stone. The masonry was sticky with moss and the lime mortar had bled out and down to the stone slabbed floor. It was wet, but after pulling up a few sections of the thatch roof that had fallen in, I was able to make a semi-dry cot for myself. The day still had a couple of hours and the skies were open and blue and cloudless.

In the warmth of the late afternoon sun, I lay and closed my eyes to rest, realising that I hadn't slept since the evening before I stormed Hampton Court Palace and ended up kneeling before the king. I thought back to the long road to the capital, and how it had taken the lives of eight men to get me there; whilst the journey I was on now was easily five times as long. I hoped that I would not have to total the same ratio of dead men on my ledger. But if my first few days were anything to go by, I was starting to feel optimistic about the whole thing. Only the pope needed to pay for ordering the guardsman to kill Father, and I was the collector of that debt.

I fell into dreams of dampness and celebration and turmoil. Thunder shook the fabric of my imagination and anxiety pricked my conscious. I reached for my dream sword and bolted back to reality as the cacophony of drums and trumpets dispersed throughout the valley around me in a full-circle echo.

Mary whinnied, thrashing against her tether, and I bolted to the open doorway just as the bronze cross of Catholicism crested the saddle of the hill to cast the reflection of the falling sun back into my eyes. The pope's defenders had come to meet me head on, and with fanfare. And I would've been flattered, but I had literally just woken up and wondered if I was still dreaming or not.

The corporation of Catholics waited upon the hill, presenting into two units. I watched from the doorway as they funnelled down the draw and into the valley around my lowly position. A Bishop in red rode at the helm of the eastern flank, directly in my path. He bore the bronze cross abreast his ceremonial, and not at all practical, battle robes.

'We 'ave you surrounded!' The declaration echoed around the valley. It was the bishop-warrior, now front and centre of my latest obstacle. "Enry Game, errr, ze pope ordures your immediate surrenda!'

The sun was blinkering out behind the dip of the saddle pass, casting us all into a deeper shadow. One by one they set flint to stone, casting fire-lanterns before them like I might be some feral beast and they had come to cast out the evil.

'Hired men,' I tried to make my voice as deep as I could, but in my head, I still sounded like a child. 'Abandon your weapons now and you'll live to see another Sunday! Only the pope must die!'

Their response was a barrage of rock throwing. One came through the decaying thatch roof and landed a few feet away.

'Go home.' I pleaded with them. 'My fight is not with you men.' I gave them as much opportunity as I could. 'It is with your pious-'

'As you can see, err, monsieur Game, we 'ave you totally out numbered. Give-up! While you still can, ay?'

A kindly darkening hue cascaded across the skies like a short-tempered omen. It was almost time to act. In darkness I hold a damning advantage over my average enemy. My speed and enhanced senses would be more than a match for this rag-tag band of sell-swords and disreputable cunts. I'd had my fair share of scrapes and holes poked in me, and learned, painfully, that swords, arrows, and bullets could only wound me. As was sang by the bards of the time: "Henry Game is immortal and cannot be slain".

I wore very little armour and I was aware of how inconveniencing such injuries could be to a man travelling inter-continentally. I figured the best thing I could do was to keep trading insults with them until they eventually stormed the barn, where then I could pick them off a few at a time as they bottlenecked in my doorway.

'I was about to give you cunts the same deal.' Another rock crashed through the roof and struck the wall beside me. It seemed the men were making a sport of hitting the barn, hitting me.

'Zis is your last chance, get outs, or we come in!!' The bishop sounded very confident, behind all of his men.

I retreated back into the barn, priming myself for battle. The sun was almost a memory in the skies when I heard the sickening cry of Mary, quickly followed by the cheers of men.

I peered out of the door again and saw several arrows jutting from Mary's back and hind. I gritted my teeth and stepped back into the shadow of the derelict outbuilding.

I heard the march of men closing in. They sounded confident. I heard the final cry of Mary as she collapsed. Lit torches washed orange and yellow across the doorway, pooling the entrance in a hellish glow that matched my growing laughter. The cold pumped into my arms and my muscles trembled.

The first brave/stupid cunt entered, his pokey sword rattling in both hands with his arms fully outstretched and I unleashed upon him. Before the moon reached its zenith, each and every one of them were dead and in the beautiful process of decomposition, once again feeding the very earth that sustained them. I counted their corpses as twenty-six in total, some of them in several pieces, but only twenty-six heads.

I ended up with a few unwanted bumps and grazes and most annoying was the bullet to the calf, as I now faced several thousand furlongs on foot. I designed it that the last of them to die was the warrior-bishop André.

He died slowest out of them all and I made up a poem from the information he spilled as his faith and conviction drained away quicker than the piss in his bladder. I wrote it down:

> *Faithless André*
> *had lots to say*
> *about the pope*
> *not-so-secretly gay.*

> *And, so I hear,*
> *as the sun disappears,*
> *he would ring for vespers,*
> *albeit with queers.*

For within his tower
the pontiff has power.
And he shields this discretion
through daily confessions.

I remember humming that tune all the way to Rome, and the Holy City, with my calf strapped and my mind set, my will enamelled. In my mind the plan was all too clear. And for once, I would be counting on my childish good looks to win me access to Vatican City.

André disclosed that the pontiff was quite fond of the young and less-fortunate men in his service. He said that all I needed to do to gain access would be to present as a construction worker on the new site. From there I should ask any bishop to be pointed towards his tower, pardon the pun. And the rest, as they say, would be history.

The Devil You Thought You Knew (L. S.).

The pigeon bopped and pecked amongst the street-light-glittered pavement, visible to me through the floor-to-ceiling windows at the front of the restaurant. My eyes tracked the movements as the bird skittled, scratched, and pecked. Pigeons were remarkably predictable, I mused.

After three days' worth of surprises, back when I thought nothing could astonish me ever again, I now sat opposite the brother I didn't know I had, but, as it turned out, I had indeed met before. Only this time he went by the name Ian Mulliti, instead of the benevolent man that I knew as Father Saxon.

Since being 'accidentally' informed of my brother's existence at the old-money dinner party two evenings ago, I had kidnapped an archbishop, who was unfortunately assassinated along with my car, been on three aeroplanes but only two flights, broken a relic of a computer that was still running on Windows 95, back at an internet café that was also stuck back in the late 90s; I'd eaten a fully-fledged heart attack breakfast burger, and then been collected by the ominous Mr Serious, only then to be driven directly to the decidedly unremarkable town of Limon, Colorado, which is a fucking ten hour car ride I might add, in order for me to dine with my actual long-lost brother.

The waiter made eye contact as he approached our table. The pigeon wandered from the window view and I sat up to follow it, hungry as I had ever been. The not-so-famous "Route 160" had passed by the car's darkened windows in an airconditioned blur, thankfully. Mr Serious was a man of few words, and a very poor listener.

The waiter had "Freddy" on his nametag. 'Sirloin, rare, Sir.'

The plate was placed perfunctorily before me as the pigeon bobbed back into view. The waiter cleanly swivelled and presented my brother with a fillet of charcoal and a smattering of sautéed vegies.

'Something distracting you, brother?' asked Ian, following my interest, turning in his seat to look out of the window behind him. He turned back around, sipping at the head of his lager.

'You rather enjoyed whittling, right?' he grinned, transitioning from the Queen's English to redneck American in the same sentence, keeping it casual and easy. I just watched him as he tucked into his disastrously over-cooked tender.

'*You* can't shame me…coward,' I said, holding out my hand, 'so, if you would be so kind?' I nodded my head to the condiment by his elbow, 'be done with the sanctimony and pass the fucking salt.'

'You used to do it with the leg bones, right?' Ian continued as if I hadn't said anything at all, his eyes alive with memory.

'You scratched the thigh bones against the stone walls, sharpening them. I remember now. It was the femurs, right?' His fork scratched at the porcelain.

'I heard that the main section of the old abbey still stands today. Do you visit often?' The salt stayed by his elbow.

I clicked my fingers toward the condiment and ignored his words.

'I mean my god, man!' he carried on, heavy chewing and a large gulp of frothy lager between words. 'That face.' He spluttered out bits of his food as he talked. 'Oh no, yep that's it! Ha, yeah, that's it, I remember now. It was the Iron Mask!' His voice rose to a volume that had quietened the rest of the restaurant.

Ian imitated hitting himself in the face with what I could only imagine was a hammer. Cocky cunt. He sprinkled salt on his sautéed carrots then put it back down besides his plate, still out of my reach.

'Has anyone told you it looks like hardened custard skin? Your face, I mean. It looks like a pinched up, crinkled nut-sack!' He chortled away to himself, stuffing the meat in, laughing at his own jokes.

People were leaving, their dinners unfinished. I noticed the waiters return to the kitchen with plates of hot food still not served. I fixed my brother with my coldest stare, fantasising all the ways I could corrupt his perfect face forever.

'Relax, cranky pants.' He sipped at his lager, producing that easy, betraying grin once more. 'Eat, for Christ's sake. Fucking custard skin. Classic!' He smacked the empty pint glass down on the table then waved for another, tilting back on his seat, easy as you like.

If he knew how I fantasised about gutting him, his posture betrayed no hint or perceived threat. And that just irritated me more. I wanted to cut the smile from his pretty little mouth and make him eat his own flesh. But most of all, now that I knew who my treacherous 'brother' was, I suddenly, and unequivocally, wanted back what was rightfully mine, but accusing him without proof would be child's play, so I unleashed my hunger upon the bloodied fillet, impatiently.

'You know, Ian,' I said, my fork halfway to my mouth, 'it is Ian these days, right, not Bishop Saxon?' His eyes twinkled, and I knew I was playing straight into his hands, but I couldn't stop myself.

'It's a bloody good job you weren't around when we were being brought up in the abbey…' I trailed; my thoughts not as convicted as my words sounded. Came across more as a statement than the threat I intended it to be.

The silence that followed was filled with scratching forks and thoughts that scratched back.

'Daddy issues, Henry?' He lifted his thick and unscarred eyebrows with the question, whilst still working at his crispy steak, cutting in clean movements.

My gut told me to keep my mouth shut, stop playing into his hands, but my mouth ran away with my senses.

I decided to change the subject. 'Rumour has it that your organisation-'

'*My* organisation.' He held meat on his fork, now watching me.

I was confused by his interruptive confirmation. 'Yes, like I said, your organisation, are the ones behind all the wars and such things. There was a time when I was a puppet, just like you.'

He held a fork of dry steak suspended, watching me, his mouth ajar and squinting in exaggeration. I couldn't tell if he was amused or confused. The pigeon bopped over his shoulder again, my eye was drawn momentarily before I reigned it back in.

'You really are ignorant, brother.' He said before stuffing the steak in his gob and chewing. 'And jealous, and vengeful. Totally self-absorbed. You're an arrogant and honourless bastard,' he sipped at his beer, 'that cannot let bygones be bygones, can you? And here I was thinking you were coming to save me from the pope's hitmen!' He drank deep, half of the pint in one gulp.

'What is it they say? You can't pick your family, eh, *brother*?' He continued to cut into his steak, separating the meat from the fat in quick, precise cuts.

My turn to smile. 'Well clearly you have me at a disadvantage. You already know about the Vatican's death warrant.' Ian smiled as I continued talking. 'And until two days ago I didn't know I even had a brother! Then I see you and it's, well, it's fucking you!'

Ian continued to eat and smile like a proud peacock. In the absence of words, a coldness crept along and filled my heart. If any were brave enough to remain eating their dinners, they were either completely deaf or couldn't hear a fucking thing.

I leaned forward, fixing him with as much sincerity as I possibly could, civility be damned. 'You, Ian, are the twisted cunt, and I should cut your fucking head off and stick it up your-'

'Ahh, there he is!' fork abandoned across his plate with a clatter. Ian stood and gestured both hands toward me like he was seeing me for the first time.

'Here is the Game. The Eternal Lord Protectorate; The Bastard of Bolton; The Anarchist; The Monster – for how the list of accolades precede you: oooooh, for they say Henry Game cannot be slain by King or Country or God! And any man foolish enough to try, will end up cold and dead in the clod!' He sang the words from the bards of old in a thick northern accent and then sat down again, wiping his mouth with a serviette and dashed it on top of his plate.

The meal was over.

'Or do I dare rhyme off some of your more sinister titles and deeds?' He asked but for a beat then continued. 'At last, after all this time, brother, again we meet, officially this time and honestly, and damn if I'm not excited to get to finally know you.'

He pushed his plate to the table's edge and leaned forward, pointing his finger at me, wagging it: 'But you, you old snake you. Come now, don't toy with me, I know that you have your own angles in-play, surely you didn't come all the way over to the mighty US of A just to be my knight in shining armour? I never heard a bard sing that Henry Game saved the day. As easy as that rhymes, even. But tell me, what other business have you, brother? Tell me what you really want. I am here to help you. I mean, we are blood after all, right?'

'What I really want?' I shook my head. I had only come to

the states for two reasons: one to find my cunt of a brother, and two: make sure my son was out of danger, again. The former mission was complete and now more of an irritation and distraction to the latter. But I couldn't let the bastard slip away from me without taking back what I believed he had stolen from me, what was rightfully mine.

Plus, I didn't like the way he was looking at me; I worried that perhaps he knew about everything. I suspected that he was manipulating me, and the only way to really protect myself would be to play along, play the subordinate.

Ian continued to smile like a weatherman on a fine day.

'What I want is simple, Ian-fuck-face-Mulliti,' I made sure I held both of his eyes as I said my next words. 'Now that I know who you are, you thieving twat...' I shook my head to scatter the regret that had once lingered over me after this cunt's tragic death. I looked him square in the eye. 'I want my fucking book back, thank you very much, and I'll take it tonight. Then I don't want to see you ever again.'

For the first time since we sat down, I saw him dumbfounded.

'Your book,' he repeated the words slowly, thinking deep and frowning hard. Then he frowned some more for another minute or two before suddenly gulping down the remainder of his lager, flashing me a smile and tilting his chair back on to two legs again.

'Your book.' He said, clearly on the same page as I was, but still I didn't like his smile any more than I like a sharp stick up my arse.

When in Rome, Autumn 1534.

Even in those days seven was a revered number. Held in the highest esteem by the pious for its heavenly importance. So, I suppose it goes without saying that they thought Pope Clement VII was going to be something very special indeed and maybe even succeed in bringing humanity closer to God. How quickly he fell out of favour in times of continental unrest and upheaval and of course, the Reformation.

Gaining access to the Holy City proved to be less of a challenge than I first feared. I was young enough to still have my boyish features yet weathered enough not to be questioned when I simply gestured that I was working on the rebuilding of St. Peter's Basilica. And it's true that assuming a cover identity to gain access wasn't part of my original plan, but as I arrived at the gate to St. Peter's Square and was almost flattened by a cargo wagon carrying dozens of lengths of cut timber, it was abundantly clear that getting in would not be quite as simple as it was to get into Hampton Court, or any other place I had ever visited. The faithless bishop had tried to warn me after all when he suggested I get in as a construction worker.

The crazy Swiss Eidgenossen that guarded the Vatican were known throughout England and Britain as "oath brothers". And if the yeoman warders were a bunch of lunatic berserkers on the battlefield, well, then the oath brothers were straight up demons of war that had been dragged out of Hell to massacre everyone and everything.

Despite my confidence in combat, I had just walked the best part of three thousand furlongs over the past couple of months – the rest aback a horse or two, thankfully – but my feet were fucked, my bones rattled, and I didn't have the energy or will for a fight at the gate. The fight I had actually come for would have to come later and against a maggot of a man, preferably after I'd found a tavern to replenish myself in.

I tried to slip through unnoticed, as many a traveller and workmen were having documents assessed by the dozens of soldiers on the gates around me, and of course, I had no such thing, but my slippery footwork was not good enough and moments later I was penned in by three towering Swiss Eidgenossen; all clad in shiny breastplates and frilly trousers of red, orange and blue; all of them holding halberds of intimidating proportions.

The guards questioned me in a language that I did not speak. The easiest answer to their aggressive questioning was pointing and gesticulation, a skill that I discovered on my travels through foreign lands, I was most proficient at.

The guards looked annoyed, and after a few moments and a lot of heavy sighing and gobbledygook, they waved me past without so much as a second glance and just like that, I was in, and my revenge at hand.

The sun had not yet reached the zenith, so I had at least half of the day left before I would scale the pope's tower and exact my revenge. I was in the beating heart of all Catholicism with time on my hands and a will to explore; to wander through the buzzing swarms that flocked throughout the Sistine Chapel; and to ponder within the rooms of the Stanze di Raffaello.

Already the day was hot, much hotter than I was used to, and still laden with a wealth of silver, I thirstily sought-out a tavern. After wandering the dusty avenues between close cropped ancient walls, I finally spotted a table and bench with a plethora of empty wine goblets sitting on top, shining the rays of the day into my eyes, green-bottle flies coming to feast on the rims. I wasn't sure if the place was a tavern as I drew closer, noticing that the timber bench was top splashed with various shades of paint and smudged with what looked like clumps of dried clay.

Nobody was sat outside, however, but the open doorway looked cool, dark, and inviting. I reckoned it must be a tavern of sorts as there was a bar inside, and of course all the empty wine goblets outside.

I walked in, noticing there was only one other patron inside. He was a scrawny and haggard fellow with a half-eaten apple on a plate before him. The exposed apple flesh was brown and festering and long forgotten, as clearly the gentleman had his thoughts deep into his sketchbook.

I sat by the bar, knocking twice on the stone countertop, pulling my purse from around my neck and waiting, impatiently. Minutes went by and still nobody arrived to serve me, so I knocked again, but this time louder and continuously.

'Aiuta te stesso, amico mio.' It came from the guy still scratching away in his papers.

'I don't understand you. Where is the barkeeper? It's hot and I need a drink. Ale, mead, wine, anything, for crying out loud!'

He stopped his scribbling and put his papers and chalk down on the table. 'Parla Inglese?'

I glimpsed the scene he drew on his pad, recognising the Garden of Eden and Eve being tempted with an outstretched apple by a succubus with a lizard-like tail, the length of it wrapping the Tree of Knowledge, tightly.

I mulled the two words over in my head for a moment. 'Yes, Inglese, English. You speak English?'

'A little,' he pinched his forefinger and thumb together. 'Bevi vino?'

I shrugged, clueless again. Since I'd left England, I'd had nothing but people trying to speak to me in languages that I did not understand, and it was starting to get old.

The man grabbed a hold of an empty goblet on his table before him and pretended to drink. 'Vino?' he gestured.

'Wine? Yes. Wine. I want wine. Please, give me wine. I can pay, look, purse, money.'

He pointed to the racks of wine jugs behind the counter, frowning. 'Solo aiutare te stesso allora.'

I felt like banging my head against the bar. Well, actually, I felt like banging his head against the bar or against that weird picture he was sketching out. I turned away from the idiot and knocked on the counter several times in harsh, quick raps.

The sounds of papers being dropped again, followed by the scrape of chair meant that my new best friend was joining me. I reckoned it was probably time to leave and find a new tavern. I pushed my stool back to leave-

'Amico mio, nessun servizio.' The man looked more dishevelled than I had initially judged him. He looked like he was literally starving to death, and probably just a little on the unhinged side of the door frame.

He shook his head at my blank expression, frowning heavily then walking around to the other side of the bar. I sat back down again. The stick-thin artist stood before me with two jugs in his hands.

'Rosso o bianco?' he gestured to each jug as he spoke the words that meant nothing to me.

I was fed-up with people not believing that I didn't understand them. I snatched one of the jugs off him and saw that it was filled with white wine.

I pointed to the other jug. 'Is that red?'

The man looked more annoyed than he had any right to be. 'Sì, vino rosso,' he let out a big sigh. 'Ne vuoi qualcuno o no?'

I frowned at him and gestured for a drink by sipping at an imaginary cup.

The man wasted no time in slamming a wooden tankard

before me and filling it right to the very top. 'Grazie al signore. Il mio ritorno alla mia arte ora?'

He was asking me something again. I accepted the drink with a nod, then taking a groat from my purse, as it was the smallest denomination I had, I slid it onto the counter, begrudgingly.

Suddenly the man's expression changed. He picked it up, inspecting the king's head then the portcullis on the reverse. Then, without providing me with change or even another word, he wandered off, totally absorbed with his new coin, back to his papers and empty goblets.

I resisted the urge to further converse with him and instead focussed my mind on what I had come here to do. The pope's tower was barely a minute's walk from the tavern. And in my mind, I had already mapped my route out to scale the outer edges of the wall and up to the chamber window.

In the dark it would be easy: my clothes were dark and my hair blacker still. I still wore the ring on my thumb, but I had hidden my sword outside the city walls. This murder would have to be done with my bare hands.

The wine was strong, and in the hot afternoon I reminisced about how far I had travelled since seeing my father slaughtered just a month or two previously; I had transformed entirely. I wondered that if he was still with us, he wouldn't even recognise me anymore.

* * *

As the sun set, I left the tortured artist to continue wasting away in his scribbles of lizard women and forbidden fruits. I never did see a barman, nor anyone else enter the tavern, which led me to consider the possibility that it was not a tavern at all.

With the darkening sky creeping over the day like a superior invading army, I knew I had work to do and so set about it without hesitation but with a tingle in my tummy much like butterflies. I had always enjoyed climbing. Something about the fear of falling thrilled me in a way that I could never explain.

It is fascinating how often a child follows the same road as their fathers before them, only to suffer the same misfortunes, time and time again. Experience the same injuries, the same assassinations. It is almost as if they ignore the warnings history projects for them. And as I climbed through the pope's open window and perched patiently upon the edge of his grand bed, he entered the room and didn't look at all surprised or alarmed by my presence.

I, meanwhile, held my breath a moment or two as I saw the spears and halberds of the oath brothers positioned directly outside of the bedroom door, but still the pontiff saw me and closed his door softly, relaxed, smiling down at me with large eyes, locking it.

Maybe he expected I was his next 'special communion', especially considering the way he was undressing me with those scaly eyes of his. The master teaching the pastor: a story old as sin. He got what was coming to him. Sometimes history isn't obvious enough for some.

I knew it, and maybe he didn't, but time was over for unlucky number seven the moment I slipped in through the window of his tower, and he locked the door, naively, perversely, not raising the alarm.

I crossed the space between us, the pontiff misreading the signs as he met me halfway, breathing quick and shallow, the blacks of his eyes spilling out like dark oil. I acted decisively and ruthlessly. Before he managed to out a single syllable, I had the point of my outstretched fingers stabbing into his throat, and my travel hardened foot bursting his perverted bollocks with a kick.

Hopelessness fleeted his eyes and I nurtured my paranoia to explore the darkest nooks of my psyche as he keeled over, mutely nursing his injuries. I slammed him to the ground with his head, the walls shaking with the impact, and for the next couple of moments the pope's eyes swam like fish in a bowl. I waited until finally they rested on me again, I wanted him to be lucid when I killed him.

It seemed that the pope had finally realised what was happening to him as he started to thrash and struggle against me, his eyes desperately searching over my shoulder for something that was never going to help him.

From then on silent tears were all that passed between us. I mounted his chest and squeezed his stubbly throat for the insurmountable weight of injustice that had been served upon me and my family by his corrupted orders.

God's man, apparently. If this was the best God could do, then hope was definitely...hopeless. If this was God's man, then I vowed to kill that cunt too, and I paused my choking for a moment to allow me to remove the ring from my thumb: the guardsman's ring. I had carried it with me for a reason.

The pope's eyes were bloodshot, and drool splodged out from every orifice. I took the ring and rammed it into his mouth, smashing it through his front teeth in the process and lodging the ring as deep into his throat as my fingers would reach. Then I returned to the throttle and squeezed as hard as my fury would let me. It wasn't until his lips turned blue that the murder gave way and I finally allowed myself to unclench.

As I removed my hands, I realised two things: one, I had forgotten to deliver the king's message. And two, I had left sickeningly deep impressions in the late pope's neck, that of course could never be mistaken for anything other than handprints, and by extension: murder. After I had finished, there could be no denying that the pope was assassinated. Like father like son, as they say.

I climbed up off him and thought about what to do next. The whole thing was a decidedly anticlimactic moment. I felt numb. I still hurt for the loss of Father. I still hated the dead cunt at my feet, his neck shaped like the letter "S" and long like a giraffe.

Something caught my attention as I turned away from the justice I had wrought, it was an energy that called to me in a way that nothing had before. I felt the frequencies within me both repel and attract at the same time. It was a mixture of dread and delight, of liberation and alarm.

I turned, remembering the pope had been looking over in this direction just before his accident. The irresistible vibrations reaching into me again as I walked over to the other side of the room. I wondered why I had only just noticed it. I couldn't help myself as I reached out to the solitary wooden box upon the mantle to uncover the source of my newfound infatuation.

My fingers reached out and brushed the box, perched above the extinguished fireplace. I felt sparks at the touch and snatched my hand away for a brief moment, then reached in again, entranced, but aware of a danger somehow. My heart rushed as I released the golden latch. The box barely even opened a finger's width, it just loosened somewhat, and allowed a red velvet cloth to spill from the seams. I held my breath as the lid creaked back and my eyes were drawn in.

Lay within was an object that was as infinitely ordinary as it was not. It was a dagger with carvings around the handle, written in a language of scores and symbols.

I reached in and stupidly picked it up by the blade when an

intense hiss and searing pain gripped me tight. It took me a moment to realise that my own skin was crackling and popping like chicken flesh where flesh touched metal.

I released it and it fumbled awkwardly from my burning hand as it fell, tearing clumps of tissue from my palm and burning through it like wildfire as it descended to the wooden floor and bounced, twice, before rolling to a stop. After a pregnant pause the polished floorboard began smouldering, churning up a thick smoke in a furious fashion. Within moments the smoke was thick and choking the room. I could hardly see anything around me.

Banging and shouting from beyond the door set my nerves like maggots to dead flesh. I scurried to the box and retrieved the red velvet cloth. It seemed it was the only thing that the dagger didn't burn.

Blue-white flames had erupted from around the metal of the knife where it met the timber floorboards, and the door rattled in its frame to the sound of armoured panic. My left hand was pouring with blood and slick with agony. Fumes distorted my perception of distance as I reached forwards with the cloth in my good hand and scrabbled through fire and smoke to retrieve the mysterious and beautiful weapon.

With an almighty crash the door swung inward. I didn't have the time or the inclination to hang around any longer as my fingers found purchase and I fled, through the flames and out of the window, followed by white smoke.

I had travelled over eight thousand furlongs, slaughtered thirty-five men in total just to get to this point. And now I didn't feel anything at all except a great sadness and loss and nothing and shame. And in this void, I embraced the hollowness that nestled within the centre of my extinguished need for vengeance and purpose. Anger fled and all that remained now was grief and vulnerability.

Disappointment wasted no time before morphing into a confused cocktail of righteousness, delusion and total desolation. Maybe, if the overcooked impressions of grandeur had never manifested within me, maybe I would have allowed myself to just feel and mourn my father as a wounded young man should.

The fear of accepting loneliness, I have come to believe, was too strong to allow the great Henry Game to succumb to such wallowing and self-pity, no matter how much I needed it.

I fled that tower bearing a weapon of tremendous potential, and if I had slipped or miss-placed one step, or failed to find purchase on loose footings, maybe I would have fallen upon the blade and ended it all. Maybe I would have saved the world from what I was about to do.

If the blade was a weapon of tremendous potential, then I can only be described as a weapon of terrible consequence.

But weapons are passive at the end of the day... They do not choose to be bad or cause harm. Some weapons are tools as well. And some tools are used as weapons. People are like this, never completely one thing or anything else. It really depends on one's own proclivities for such things, when all said and done.

Estranged Sibling Rivalry (L. S.).

'Do you even know what it is, *exactly*, that you ask for?' Ian's head cocked like an intrigued dog.

'Just don't,' I warned, 'I know you have it.' I searched his face as I said the words but gleaned nothing. Ian was at least as good as I was. Maybe even better.

'I heard you're writing a book of your own, a collection of memories and old tales. Too far-fetched for my liking.' He picked up his fork, removed the napkin and resumed fussing at his dinner, the glee over his face even clearer than his smarmy tone.

I had no idea how he knew about my journals, but I wasn't going to let him have the satisfaction of seeing my surprise, and anyway, he was avoiding the question.

'The. Fucking. Book. Cunt.' I didn't think I could be any less ambiguous.

After a shrug and another swig from his pint he put his fork down again. Arrogance and manipulate in equal measures; he opened his mouth to speak, but then didn't, and instead picked up his fork again.

'I know you took it from me, back in the seventies.' I persisted, teeth gritted, 'you even took a piss on me in the process, if memory serves…' that got a bit of a raised eyebrow from him as he continued to push his carrots over to the far side of his plate.

I was losing what little patience I ever possessed. 'It's mine and I'm taking it back from you!'

He quietly placed down his cutlery and chewed thoroughly, then had another large mouthful of lager, still managing a half-smirk all the while.

'Say I know what you're talking about. Say I know *exactly* what you're talking about. The fact of the matter is that you, dearest brother, clearly do not.' He was laughing when he spoke but there was nothing funny about any of this and we both knew it.

The pigeon bopped along the curb outside again until a stuttering toddler stomped along, trying to catch it. The approach was just wrong. Amateur. One does not simply charge at a pigeon to catch-

'However, and with that being said, my most ignorant, isolated brother, I know that you know it has *potential*. So, I won't bother wasting my breath trying to deceive you on that score. And if truth be told, I actually stopped you from making the biggest mistake of your life. And I just don't think I have it in me to do it again.'

He swigged from his dripping pint glass before continuing. 'Religion is already losing potency. We are considering other avenues now. But this!' He gestured vaguely toward me with scorn and judgement and a whole manner of things sanctimonious. 'I mean, consider the damage something like this would do to our reality. Never mind the likes of us, but to the order of the entire world-'

'Look,' I cut across his tripe with a raised hand. 'Just stop with the bullshit. Are you going to hand it over, or am I going to have to make you?' I spat on the carpeted floor by his feet and pushed my plate to the side without finesse. I'd more than had my fill already, and I'd barely even touched my meal.

Talking with snakes makes my bones vibrate. Coming to see my beloved brother was always going to be a risk, that was why my insurance policy was securely strapped to my back, slightly above the waistline for optimum comfort and ease of access, especially when one is wearing a rather expensive dinner suit. I pretended to adjust my jacket, un-tucking my shirt from the back, just in case.

Ian shook his head then rolled his eyes, stuffing another fork full into his smooth face, quite the appetite, clearly. He held up a condescending finger. 'You know not what you ask for, *brother*. Didn't they teach you in that abbey of yours, not to bite off more than you can chew?' He chomped and waited for an answer to his question, I think, but I really wasn't sure where he was going with any of it and he was really pushing my buttons.

'Over two-thousand years ago now, time was reset. That is how diabolically bad it all got the last time the scriptures were used by ignoramus fools, like you, no offence...'

I said nothing and maintained strong eye contact. He looked a little warm under the collar of a sudden. Now it was my turn to cock my head at his lip service. I smiled at him and he smiled back: mask back in place.

'Actually, Henry, I've got to say that I'm a little disappointed...' he waved his fork around aimlessly, 'with you,' he clarified, now patting the napkin at his mouth. 'I really thought you had more gumption than the rest. But of course, you come here and judge me with conspiracy and holier-than-thou remarks. But *them,*' he pointed out of the window, late night shoppers rushing past, oblivious. 'Those farm animals out there, well, I expect it from them and their small minds. Hell, we often profit from it, but not you, one of the blood.'

'Not me...' I let my words drag, retrieving the weapon from behind my back. I watched him blink between sucked breaths and chewing.

That was when I seized my moment. No going back until it was bloodied.

Maybe I should have waited a little, been more patient with him, tried to find amicable routes to get what I wanted, but the truth is I'm not well known for my diplomacy, patience, empathy, sympathy, or anything other than exacting vengeance, and with as much blood and violence as possible, or convenient.

I unsheathed *Abatu* with my left, pulling swiftly yet unavoidably blistering my back in the process, reaching across the table, pulling Ian toward me and across his half-eaten dinner with my right, I hammered the exo-metal deep into his suited forearm with a smoky squeal of glee. With him pinned to the table-top like a dying moth, I sat back, relaxed, and enjoyed the sweet music of his shock and agony. I looked back to my barely touched tender, my appetite perking a little all of a sudden. Happiness brings hungry bellies.

Ian screamed like any regular person might do in such circumstances, but it was a bit of a let-down. A victory, nonetheless. Bitter-sweet. I couldn't help but show my enjoyment and disappointment and as Ian roiled and swore and smashed everything from the table, including my untouched meal, I sighed.

'You know, I expected more,' I said, and kicked the legs out of Ian's seat beneath the table.

He roared as his body weight pulled on his forearm. The table was smoking intensely now, and I imagined that his arm was cooking nicely, like pork. Ian continued to flop and scrabble and scream and lash around at everything he could reach. I wondered why he didn't reach up and pull the damned thing out when something ate into me like lava through green grass.

My eyes whirled as fire took a hold of my leg and burned. He'd got me from under the table and I tried to pull my leg away from the heat but found I couldn't. It seemed that my unsuspecting dinner guest was not as unsuspecting as I suspected.

I had felt pain like it only twice before and I knew that only one kind of reactive metal could inflict such destruction and pain: it was the same kind of dagger that had almost burnt through the table-top, but still lodged through Ian's arm. However, this motherfucker's exo-blade was firmly imbedded through my shin, muscle and bone, by the feel of it. I was just waiting for my trousers to set alight, then it really would be a party.

Ian had himself an exo-blade too… That was a surprise, I had only ever come across the one, and that came from the pervert in the tall tower. I believed it was the only one on the planet. Except here I was, painfully, horribly, wrong.

Regardless, there we were: one howling over the table and one snarling beneath. Proper brothers. Like two babies locked in merciless combat: one biting the foot of his enemy while the other one pulls hair in fury, neither one giving in.

Suddenly I noticed a shadow of order closing in around me, surrounding our little pathetic charade. I realised it was the suits. The same suits I had seen lurking on the peripherals since Mr Serious had delivered me to the aging restaurant. I knew they wouldn't be far away from Mr Mulliti. This was his territory after all.

As the shadows closed in around me and the pain rose in intensity I lay back and tried my best not to show my discomfort.

'Truce!' I just about managed to gasp as I leant across and pulled *Abatu* out of my dinner guest's forearm.

Ian growled as the blade left his body and he thumped down on the table with his good arm, splintering the charred and smoking top, embers of wood burning new holes into the faded carpet.

Conveniently, the other blade was still in my shin, my skin hissing and spitting as my trousers finally flickered into a blue fire. I pulled it free and as I did the shadows closed in completely and my arms and legs were stretched out to their full capacity. I was spread eagled on the restaurant floor.

'That!' hissed Ian, wrapping a napkin around his arm, 'was very impolite – ah, ah!' he winced as he bent over to retrieve his own bone-handled dagger and slid it into the inside of his dinner jacket. Then, he relieved my other hand and took *Abatu* from me. He clearly knew what it was and didn't seem at all impressed by it.

The men holding on to my shoulders and neck, my arms and back, were just about beginning to annoy me. 'Get these fucking maggots off me now-'

Ian's shiny loafer to my temple finished the sentence for me and the night went away in a blink.

Late Autumn, 1534. A Chilled and Dewy Morning.

A peace settled over me as I idled my way north through the continent and back to *Mother* England.

The ponderous pace allowed me time to consider my actions and my potential to wreak death and destruction, all seemingly without consequence.

The last few months having undergone the metamorphosis from an innocent boy into...well, into whatever I had become, had given me a dark and realistic perspective of the world and I was at least grateful for that. Even though the last few months had been the cruellest, they were undoubtedly the most educational and enlightening moments of my early and sheltered years.

My unique outlook on the world around me was clearer than ever before, but also much darker and brimming with jealousy and spite, and insecurity. I saw it exactly the way it was.

My vengeance satisfied, thoughts of loss and mourning started to settle within. Anger abandoned me deciduously, and now I was left with the bare branches of a mundane existence, not sure at all how I felt about my new reality.

The road north had brought with it the harsher conditions, which I absolutely preferred to the fiery southern reaches of the continent. Heat and humidity only brought thirst and flies and shit. Never had I seen as many starving beggars, more poverty and desperation, as I did upon the doorsteps of the Holy City.

My singular experience of that place had left me wondering if we had not got it all wrong, and that perhaps the Vatican was in fact Hell, and the pope the devil. Otherwise, why would God allow so much suffering in his holy capital?

Give me a naked tree and the crisp crunch of frozen grass any day over a warm and putrid goblet of wine with the heaping of flies and disease that come with it.

As I travelled through the remnants of the Roman Empire, through the straggling of Imperial Free Cities, I was surprised by the lack of scandal or outrage at the assassination of the pontiff. Through the various taverns I stayed in, never once did I hear of any suspicion of murder. Not that I often understood a word any of the bastards said, but body language alone, it suggested that the people seemed pleased to be rid of the perverted cunt.

I kept myself to myself, and often I wondered if God truly approved of my actions in my quest to deliver justice for Father Game.

Given the lack of hostility or suspicion from those I passed on the road, I believed myself to be clear of danger, but I was little more than a child at the time and still so ignorant to the desires of life and energy, and the malignant attachment of consciousness to flesh and need.

I wandered through the eye of a hell-storm in the green and peaceful lands of Germania. Ice-cold nipped at the nape of my neck followed by a sudden outpour of sweat from my arms, shins, chest and face.

I now know that this was a reaction, a very specific and unique symptom that occurs when one happens across spectres: a pride of nasty and malicious inter-dimensional entities that have a wholly different agenda to the rest of us. My quests for revenge pales in comparison to those nasty cunts, let me tell you.

Often, they group together and linger as a pool of poisonous energy in a specific area. Most people can recognise the dark energy and tend to steer clear, naturally. And sometimes spectres are small enough to go by unnoticed in fact, but this specific group of seriously nasty bastards that I wandered into, had accumulated together as an ocean of malintent, and they set upon me in my ignorance and vulnerable state of reflection.

Most individuals, most of the time, have nothing to fear from such energised evils. However, those who are susceptible to spirited effect can be drove to great immoralities whilst 'under the influence'. Tales of husbands suddenly murdering their families while they sleep are often heard of, and always to the befuddlement of those who know them and their families.

But like I said, most folks are perfectly safe from these malevolent entities, most of the time. Unfortunately for the town of Hamelin, I am not most people.

Truth is, I had absolutely no idea what was happening to me when they latched on. It felt like my insides were being liquefied and my skin friction-burned from my muscles. I tried to resist but didn't know what was happening and the curtains of consciousness closed in around me.

Next thing I knew, I was dancing through a sleeping town, my new-found dagger wrapped in the resistant red cloth tucked into the front of my trousers, and a fucking ivory and silver flute at my lips, playing a tune to die for.

My thoughts caught in my mind suspended, my conscious locked away as I played, dancing straight into a waking street, the instrument caressing the moisture of the morning fog as tune and intention weaved a magic most unholy and unjust and brought people from their homes and toward their ends.

I played a melody so entrancing, so inspiring, that what little hope of control I still held over my body was carried away also to follow the piper, just another amongst the townsfolk. Off and away we floated into the dark, dark forest; it was a cold and hard morning.

* * *

I awoke to the stillness of death. Not even the forest dared breathe. No bird flew over-head and no flower braved to blossom.

I felt…dejected, abandoned. The last several hours had forsaken me. I sat up, my hair pulling from the soft grass with sickly separation. From head to toe, I was saturated in blood, surrounded by the corpses of dead-eyed strangers: women, men, and children, all corpus-indiscriminate.

I wondered if I had truly woken in Hell. Perhaps I was being punished after all by God for murdering his most trusted servant on Earth.

An amalgamation of body parts settled as spread and scattered. Like something had torn them all to pieces and thrown them away again in boredom. Some upper bodies had attempted to climb the silver birches to the west of the clearing. I imagined it was an attempt to escape the horrors foregone.

The sun was setting over the upper most reaches of the clawing branches. Whatever had brought me to this place had unceremoniously dumped me and left. In my haziness I searched for the flute that I now only vaguely remembered.

I forced myself to shut out the nightmare that decorated the forest around me. Distraction is the only painkiller for such situations; my moral compass still pointed west, north west. Blood soaked or not I had to get back home. I needed to get back home. There were questions to be unearthed and answers to be forged. I wondered if the brothers were still alive and continuing to struggle, especially so after Father had passed, and I had abandoned them. I wondered if they would they help me after what I had become.

I thought back to that overcast day, the image of Father,

slain, for nothing more than believing in a higher power and trusting that Catholicism was the purest way to worship a God that doesn't care a damn.

I clambered out of the tree line and on toward the French boarders. I scratched at the nape of my neck; still confused by the fact it had been my hands that held the responsibility for the nightmares hiding in my ever-growing shadow.

Smoke rose from a nearby village and I paused for a split-second. I didn't even want to know the source of all that smoke. For the first time in my life I was afraid of myself. Regardless of my actions, however, I forced myself to believe that what lay in the smoking village beyond the thicket of trees was nothing more sinister than that of a smithy's forge, staunching his furnace at the end of a long day. Or perhaps even the local baker, hard at work preparing for the morning bread; or maybe it was a village in ruins, dead and charcoaled skeletons in the wake of my hands and the evils they are capable of committing. Whatever the case, however, I decided I would be better off not knowing, and also, safest bet was not going anywhere near them.

The sun was setting in my path and I used its light to chase away my worst fears as I trudged on, feeling dirty on the inside and ashamed of myself for being weak.

Dungeons and Dickheads (L. S.).

In the void of conscious I lay suspended, peaceful almost, before the tide of present situation cascaded over me in the form of a tuneless whistling.

Echoes brought me back into the present and the all too familiar jangling of chain-link, iron scraping stone, imprisonment accompanying my waking movements.

I was in a very dark and damp place. Possibly underground. I maintain an uncanny ability to determine my altitude from sea level, and wherever I was, I was deep into the earth. My eyes had just started to adjust to the absence of light when no sooner had I sat up and my head stopped swimming, my cell door opened and in stepped my finely suited dinner guest, his sickly smile wide and genuine.

Ian had changed his attire and looked as though he had not been stabbed through the arm just recently. Meanwhile, I imagined that I resembled something that had been thrown into the gutter, washed down a storm drain, been contaminated by human waste and then fished out again and left in the darkest and dampest place imaginable to fester.

I looked for subtleties in his movements as he stepped over the threshold, from thick carpet to damp stone. If his arm still wounded him, he didn't show, but my leg sure did.

Ian's teeth were perfect. 'Well, are you going to stay in here all day or what?'

I was about to demonstrate the inconvenience of my chains, by giving them a good old rattling, when I realised there were none. Or, at least none on me. I swung my legs off the stone table and eased down, casual. My jaw a little stiff, the intense throbbing in my leg causing my concentration to wobble somewhat, but I made no complaint as I hobbled out of the room, doing my best to give no indication of injury, but failing, terribly.

I heard the chinking of chains again and I turned by the door to peer back into the darkness where I saw a great mound swelling ever so slightly as it breathed, backed into the furthest and clammiest corner. Five chains trailed from it, each one anchored against a loop bolted into the stone floor in the middle of the cell, an arm's reach from the cot I had been laid upon. It watched me with a glint that sent shivers through me. Without acknowledging it, I exited the cell and shut the door.

Ian was clearly trying to fuck with me, and I would not give him the satisfaction of showing him anything like a reaction.

I stepped out into a decadent hallway that housed another dozen or so cell-doors matching the one I had just slept in. The ceiling was arched, and every surface apart from the cold cell doors were covered in a thick, slate-grey carpet. A light shone from one end of the hallway, showing a spiralling staircase that led up and away. The other side of the corridor led into blind mystery only.

Ian led on toward the staircase, his footfall as silent as I have ever known, whilst my wounded leg dragged along with my tattered trousers. I spared a look to the other cells and noticed one or two desperate hands hanging, hopelessly, each of them filthy and damned, contained through the tiny barred windows at the top of iron cell-doors.

I asked no questions and said nothing as we reached the end of the softened hallway, and started up the metal spiral-staircase, which seemed to climb for much longer than reasonable.

After a painful five-hundred steps, we eventually reached a chequered tile landing before two lift doors. A large and ornate mirror hung between the smooth metal doors and gave me a glimpse of my current appearance. I turned away from the reflection and noticed the umbrella stand with both a long and short umbrella hanging, and two chairs between a chequered tile table, along with an old and silent rotary telephone on top.

Ian pulled a chair out for me and smiled, grinning like a cunt. I reckoned he'd had dental; his teeth were too perfect. There were two buttons inset into the plaster wall: up and down. Pushing the chair back in after I had ignored him, Ian pressed the down button and gave me a cocky little wink then turned to face the doors.

I started laughing. 'You have a lift, and you just made us climb that bastard of a staircase. Fuck me...'

Ian smiled. 'Oh Henry, why would I do that?' And in he stepped as the door opened with a soft beep, a glass floor suspended over a void of steel wiring and counter lever weights. He held his hand across the threshold and gestured for me to enter.

'Back to the dungeons then, dickhead?' I paused at the entrance, shin still burning. I didn't think I could do those stairs again.

Ian laughed. 'Oh no. No no no, no; this time we go deeper, much, much deeper. Now come on, quickly. Much to see, just you wait.'

His face told me he was positively delighted by my total obliviousness to the situation.

I had to give it to him, my brother was way better than I was at the game of fuckwittery.

Summer, Mid 1550s. A Dark and Terrible Storm Raged On.

I t was around 1535 when I finally arrived back at Horton in Ribblesdale, and the sky was perhaps no-less miserable and filled with turmoil than when I left.

I had limped home, ashamed and hollowed out, at the conclusion of the long and questioning journey that had taken me across the width of a continent, and then some. Naturally, I sought shelter within the abbey, from where so many of my earliest and most pleasant memories were made.

Where Father was buried, or what eventually became of his body, I'll never know. The abbey was deserted, a fragmented husk, some of its pieces missing. I assumed that the brothers had dispersed amongst the new Church of England as mushrooms will always find the darkest places to grow.

I didn't blame them. In most instances surrender is absolute when the alternative is execution, especially so for the soft ones and those without backbones. I pictured brothers Glen and Elliot drawing swords to save the dignity of the Abbey of St Oswald's. The image alone was almost enough to bring a smile back to my day, but not quite.

The exaction of revenge had all but taken the wind from my sails. I had no will or energy left to investigate the fate of the brothers any further than the thought I had already spared them. I needed to rest and recuperate. My days of righting wrongs were over. The business of revenge is as relentless as weeds, and I reckoned I deserved some time off, at least for a while.

What had once served as the main hall still remained intact

and relatively whole. It was as stumped with age as it ever had been, but under the spring-grey skies that ushered in my homecoming, I looked around and decided that it was not the same hall I remembered. Perhaps eighteen months had passed since I left, and it was as if I was in an entirely different era of time. In a shadow reality. In a shadow abbey.

The once thriving community of trade and produce, the pride of the Three Peaks District of Yorkshire, was now little more than an overly large farm and a scattering of elderly folk too fragile to move on to pastures new.

Spring had traditionally meant an influx of commerce for the harvest of root and leaf vegetables, garlics and cabbages. Now all I could see was an abundance of abandoned houses. I thought of them as scarecrows to those Ribbelsdalers still I enough to believe in free will.

Two of the abbey's outer buildings and the stables were gone. It amazed me how that in such a short time they had been greedily recaptured by nature. Only the charred stumps of the stable doors stood tall enough to be seen as a reminder of the burning that befell this once great place that I used to call home. And alas I had returned: the banshee haunting the tumulus into the decay of time and the afterlife of the good days gone by.

An oily priest from the exotic Kingdom of Portugal whom went by the name "Juan" was the new head priest at the abbey when I arrived back, but of course, he was the only priest in the entire Craven Parish still brave or stupid enough to worship despite the Reformation.

Stretched thin, he said that he serviced all of the surviving six Catholic churches. One for almost each day of the week. So, when he opened the abbey up on that first wet Sunday morning to find me hunkered amongst the box pews, it was as if he were expecting me, or so he made it seem.

I had been back in town only for a couple of days, and I

latched on to Juan's kindness like an alcoholic stranded in the desert would suck the piss out of a camel's dick to quench his thirst.

It felt good to be home and back amongst real people with simple lives. Within mere moments I had started to feel normal again, and thankfully I didn't have to suck or drink anything that I didn't want to.

During first Mass I realised how much I had missed the old ways and customs of the village. The place had drastically changed, but some of the faces remained the same, mostly elderly folk, but any friendly face is welcome in the heart of a runaway.

In the few dark days before the arrival of Juan, I searched for forgiveness in the Holy Book. Combing the scripture for deeper meaning. Searching to find an example of righteous justice that resembled my own actions. I wanted to find a god that could accept my sins and allow me to find forgiveness. I wanted a god to clean away the dirt within my soul, the residue of evil that had been left within me after Germania. I read and I prayed, and I tried my damned hardest to convince myself that I truly believed in The Word and to thank Christ for his sacrifice. But it was a lie; an act. It lasted no more than a couple of delusional and conflicted days. My new-found Christianity ended when Juan entered my life.

I was proud that the priest knew of my legend. He seemed very welcoming and humbled before me like a hyena demeans before the lion. I wondered if he knew that my hands had killed his beloved pope, and if so, did he care at all.

He preached that I had been weak; that my sins allowed the devil a foothold in my heart. I doubted I had a heart at all, and he said that only God Almighty could cleanse away my filth. Said I was too corrupted for any earthly man to save, and that following scripture was not for the likes of me. Said I was a

Heaven-sent instrument and that my actions were not for men to judge, not even holy men similar to him.

Almost immediately I liked the new priest. He was kind and relaxed and accepting of my self-loathing, but he was certainly not like any priest I had encountered before.

During Mass he would often talk of his friend, another European fellow by the name Paracelsus, and how his good friend had a magical sword that commanded the hordes of Hell for the good of all mankind. Juan said he had been shown a great number of miracles on the continent and that he had been hand-selected by the new pontiff to save Britain from the wicked greed of Reformation. He really had the villagers hooked with his evangelisms and quickly the congregations grew into a full house.

After maybe a week or so he showed me another path to righteousness that came as a milk that was able to numb the pain of my previous actions and my present chastising, but mostly it was able to numb my mind to guilt and regret and thought.

Juan called it "Poppy Tears", and it swiftly became my new source of worship and dedication, and in this respect, Juan was pontiff to me.

I eventually figured out that The Order had moved on and was not coming back for me, and also that Juan wasn't anything more than a drug dealer, and he clearly had no authority at the Church of St Oswald's. I, however, had unwittingly become his protection and bodyguard while he had wormed his oily way into the pockets of the wealthy families of the parish. So, when he raised the prices for his poppy tears, none dared to cross him for fear of me, and so paid up, hand over fist.

I was kept topped up with the milky-sedate for my troubles, and of course, completely oblivious to how dire the situation was getting. It wasn't until I overhead a conversation one evening at the local tavern that I finally came to my senses and kicked Juan out and into the gutter. I relieved him off his poppy-tears and shut the great arched doors of St Oswald's once more to him, and to the villagers.

The poppy tears only lasted so long, and when stocks started to dwindle, anger and resentment began to fill the void of anguish left by the devastation of my life. I found that the drive of rage sustained me more effectively and vividly than any drug ever hoped to, and I believe that my fury burned through the sickness that took me to see me alive and bright-eyed and hungry again.

Anger was the key to kicking the habit. I just needed to find enough reasons to stay angry, and so, I reopened the doors to the church and let the world roll-over me once again.

* * *

Eighteen years since I returned home to attempt a normal life, the English monarchy reeled me back into their webs of egomania and duplicity.

The summons arrived at the door by way of six decoratively armed yeoman warders under order of Her Royal Highness, Queen Mary of England and Ireland.

Apparently, the fat bastard King Henry VIII had died a death of putridity and ulcers, and I was mortified that I wasn't present at his funeral to shit in the casket before they tucked him in forever with a dirt blanket.

As the decades started to roll by, the legend of my adventures had taken on more of a mythical context. Even in the local tavern, as from time to time a conspiring traveller would pass through, the boasted tales of how the legendary Henry Game had single-handedly defeated the Neo-Viking uprising in the far northern reaches; or how Henry Game had been sent into heart of the Ottoman Empire to choke Suleiman the Magnificent into submission and force him to surrender the Spear of Destiny and deliver it back to God's chosen nation, were taken with a pinch of salt by the drunkards. Even them with the most colourful imaginations thought these tales to be far-fetched and jeered instead of cheering.

After Juan had left the village in disarray, and the elderly villagers had each died with the passing of time, I had grown into anonymity and happily succumbed to a quiet life on the church grounds where I tended for a few chickens and two cows. Also, over the course of ten years or so, I had renewed the entire perimeter stone-wall, and even kept on top of the weeds every two or three months.

The place looked good and the village population had managed to recover well-enough in the almost-twenty years since I had been back. Changes in the monarchy did not much affect our isolated economy and from time to time, from the recluse of my church ground haunting, I would be volunteered by the locals to hunt the errant wolves that continued to snatch sheep and chickens from farmer Jack's paddocks.

I didn't mind the business of hunting, I had a proclivity for revenge and killing and exaction, and anyway the villagers kept my whiskey barrel topped up, and so we lived in a state of respect and tolerance. But for the rare quarrel down at the tavern, nothing dangerous or discerning had happened upon the village since the day Father Game was murdered and the abbey burnt down. And even that passing had been lost to memory. So, you can imagine the reaction of the villagers when six yeoman warders arrived with orders to bring the 'Eternal Lord Protectorate of the Church of England, Henry Game' to the summons of the *rightful* Queen of England.

The locals peered from behind curtained windows and between the gaps of doorframes – not a single soul out in the open as they marched on to the church grounds and knocked upon my door.

The sun shone high in the sky and the day was hot and dry. I heard the thunder of hooves long before they arrived, and through the absence of noise, the worry of folk and frightened children. I decided before they even asked me that I would leave, peacefully, so as not to inflict another disaster on the village. And as I left, I felt the eyes of the village watching in fear of losing my protection and their seclusion.

I was called to attend Her Highness Mary Tudor because she believed that she had the right to the throne of England. And after she had explained the line of succession to me, I couldn't help but also agree with her claim. Not that I actually gave a king's turd, but taking the job gave me the tingles for adventure and promise of riches.

I had been maintaining the lawns of monotony for too long. I craved direction, and direction led to purpose. The villagers would soon take my cows and chickens and then I would have nothing to return to anyway...

I spat my distaste upon the chequered tiled floor of the lobby as I passed the men and woman of aristocracy, all of them looking down their elongated noses at me as I arrived at Mary's temporary residence. They clearly thought of me as nothing but a trumped-up peasant. But, of course, Mary remembered me from her father's court. She knew the legends were more than myth.

I was summoned to her private residence in East Anglia, and we met alone. And when I say alone, I mean just me, her, and her small army of loyalists. But I really didn't care how many silver-spoon toffees she had with her: they could never get to me. Well they could, but they didn't know they could.

She told me how the Grey Lady now sat in her seat, "in my

fucking seat, the fucking protty-slut-bitch!" I think were her exact words, explaining that her half-brother had somehow skipped past her in the line of succession because he was a "protty-little bitch too", apparently.

I reckoned it was because of her religious denomination, but she spoke in angry bursts and half-sentences. I was quickly getting annoyed by her.

'Get to the point, I didn't travel all this way to listen to you moan.' I said my words loud and with as much disrespect as I could engineer into the sentence.

I smothered a smile as her towering first knight bristled and looked from me to his queen with short shakes of his head and reddening cheeks.

I returned my attention to the lady with all the money, but the knight's bruised pride must have kicked in and triggered a death-wish as before another word was spoken, he cursed and attempted to draw his sword on me but before the tip of his blade was pulled free of its scabbard, my bone-handled-dagger hissed through the ligaments and cartilage in his throat and gave him a liquid-red cravat over his shiny polished breast-plate.

He reached out to his queen-to-be with mournful eyes and stumbled, finally to his knees and then onto his back, choking and expiring louder than anyone should. I just wanted him to die already, but I was more interested in what Mary would make of the development, so I waited, my dagger still in hand and a big smile on my chin.

After a moment of disbelief, the remaining guards all reached for steel in a desperate panic. Mary clapped, slow but clear, her eyes alive and excited. The knights looked on at me, at her, at each other, everyone dumbstruck, swords half-drawn and fighting feet forward.

'Yes, Lord Game, yes!' Mary laughed. 'You will win back

my throne and help me cut off that bitch's head, just like Father would have wanted. Now tell me what your price is, and I promise that it will be yours. You can have it all, Lord Game, all of it. The world will be your oyster and you can have it all. Anything you want. *Anything.*'

I shivered a little at her use of my title, but more so by the way she pronounced the word *"anything"*.

Carefully I re-sheathed my knife, stepping over the still spluttering former first knight. The rest of the guards were still half-drawn and more confused than a snake at a shoe-shop; I allowed myself to dream and wonder – I was young and unencumbered, and feeling rather pregnant with a favour that would soon be owed to me by the most powerful person in the known world.

And I reckoned that if the world was in fact an oyster, then I was the biggest, angriest, crabbiest motherfucker on the seabed, pincers sharpened and ready to crack that bitch open and do with the slimy bastard whatever I will.

The Longest Day. Ever. (L. S.).

The deeper we went the colder I became, and Ian said not a word in our narrow glass cube as we descended into the mantle of the planet, and then some. Yet, despite given everything I knew about the arrogant prick, I couldn't help but respect his confidence and composure. And in the silent moments that passed, I wondered if he too had experienced an overcast day that sent him ricocheting down the path that led him to be with me, wounds itching like crazy but too proud to scratch at them, and going deeper and fucking deeper into the centre of the earth. As we continued to pass the dark shimmer of rock, I started to wonder at what point we would stop travelling down and start travelling up, or, as I thought about it more, perhaps sideways.

'A little elevator music wouldn't go amiss...' my words trailed off the end of my facetious comment as suddenly a bright light and whirling vibration opened up to show a huge chasm through the glass floor of the lift beneath our feet. From the bottom up, rock gave way to an entire metropolis contained within a cavern.

We must have been around two-hundred and fifty feet away from the white floor far below. We were descending fast, too fast for me to take it all in even, but at a brief assay, we were entering down into a high-tech underground city that seemed to have no end. Roads and buildings fading away to the curve of the inside of the world. No shit, it was like something out of a Ridley Scott movie, minus the flying cars.

I could see hundreds, possibly thousands, of people scurrying around on them electric two-wheeled things with the handles on, zipping down sterile alleyways and along pristine pavements, darting from building to building, all zippy like.

Shiny tarmac with white lines marked out the roads, and the pavements appeared to be cut from the same white stone as the cavernous layer of rock that formed the ceiling that was now over a hundred feet above me as we continued to plummet. And yet, the most eye-catching feature of all, dominating the subterranean skyline, if you could forgive such phrasing, was a glittering black pyramid, and a short distance to the side of that, an equally breath-taking bone-white obelisk with a golden tipped peak, like a strawberry dipped in chocolate fondue.

The twinkling black walls of the pyramid shivered in continuous waves, mechanical movements coordinated across each façade, in sequence, like a Mexican wave. I thought of a blackbird ruffling its feathers.

Hanging from the white-rock ceiling and soaring away from my vantage point in the lift were gigantic rectangular box-prisms that looked way too big to not be safely on the ground. The suspended units showering a sterile lighting over everything and everyone.

As the tops of the single storey buildings passed around our feet, I realised the vibrations in the air were almost untraceable and the humming noise from the ceiling lights, and I assumed filtration units, was faint and easy enough to ignore, especially with so many other distraction everywhere else.

The lift cushioned to the ground and the doors separated. I stepped out onto a landing pad that was made from a circle of slate-grey marble and inlaid with golden pattern that depicted a snake nailed to a cross.

Ian breathed deep and patted my shoulder. 'Welcome, brother dearest, to Atlantis.'

The people on the ground were dressed relatively normal, and not at all cultish or ardently zealous.

I saw regular looking folk in polo shirts, professional dresses, even yoga pants and boob-tubes; I saw Arabic robes, fully fledged three-piece suits, and military attire – both the decorative and the standard issues; I even thought I saw a guy in last season's Manchester United home shirt, but all of them were busy with purpose and completely comfortable with being wherever the fuck we were. It reminded me a little of London Waterloo if not for the repeated displays of deference in our general direction.

All around us the men and women, without invitation or permission, began touching two fingers to their foreheads and bowing a quarter or so, all of them still walking mind you, but only as they passed my brother and I.

This subservient display sure set my cultism alarm bells ringing and I looked back to the lift as a possible route of escape, but the door had already closed, and it was around thirty or so feet in the air on its way back up to a more reasonable negative altitudes.

A parking bay by the side of the road with a big brass plaque reading "Segway Bay" housed half a dozen of the two-wheel electric machines that looked rather appealing to me at that moment in time, but I just wanted what was mine and then to get as far away as possible. I wasn't down here for a site seeing expedition.

I had questions about this place, a fucking plethora of them, and I could practically feel Ian's giddiness wagging around like a pup about my shins. I reckoned he was desperate to impress me, and the truth is I was impressed; or rather I was surprised, which is tantamount to the same thing. But I wasn't going to tell him that, certainly not then.

'Atlantis…' I scratched the tip of my winklepicker against the smooth white stone on the pavement causing a rubbery black stain that looked perfect.

'Are you going to finish that sentence?' he said, shaking his head.

'Without sounding rude, brother,' I held a pre-emptive, apologetic hand up, 'well, I just expected more originality from you. Atlantis is done to death. Have you never seen a hollow earth action film?'

Ian chuckled a fake retort, opening his mouth to speak, except I beat him to it.

'Although, you could say one thing about it.' I threw out my line.

'Oh, you could, could you? What's that then?' His eyebrows raised at me a fraction higher than I thought possible, or even safe.

'You will never, ever, not ever, need a raincoat,' I nodded and rubbed my hands together, rather pleased with myself.

'I suppose the legends are true then,' he set off walking at an unforgivable pace.

'Which ones, I have many?' I followed, leisurely, painfully.

Ian stopped suddenly and I almost collided with him. 'Look, no offence,' he said. 'But for centuries I heard it that Henry Game was the most arrogant and self-righteous bastard alive.'

'You don't know the half of it, dickhead.'

I stepped up beside him, wrapping my arm around his shoulder, treating him to a quick and vicious squeeze. 'Now you look here, my fucking book better be down here, some-where, for everyone's sake, brother.'

Ian squirmed off, quick as a cricket. I smiled even wider at his weakly hidden discomfort.

He said, pointing over toward the black pyramid in the distance, 'I'll do you one better, Pope Slayer, I'll take you to the Cube myself.'

I looked over the tops of the buildings at the pyramid and was about to correct him that a cube has six facets with twenty-four right angles when he spoke again:

'And once you've seen the truth of all things, if you so

choose, you can have it. And this time we won't save you from your own ignorance. How's that, brother?'

Within his laugh I suspected an edge, and I honestly didn't know what the fuck he was jabbering on about, "saving me from my own ignorance". I paid no attention because a lot of what had happened over the last two days had confused the shit out of me anyway. I decided that one more vague reference wouldn't spoil the soup.

We continued on toward the pyramid that he called the Cube, passing long white domes at almost every other intersection.

'You have no idea what the manuscripts have shown us, do you?' Ian had stopped walking again, and I suddenly realised that we were at the base of the obelisk, Ian looking, his hand resting on the flawless cut of the stone. He looked like he had all the secrets to life in his breast pocket.

'What do you mean, *manuscripts?*'

'Well, brother, the "s" brings plural to the singular-'

'Plural? There are more books?'

Ian laughed and then continued on his way. 'You really are like an ignorant child. Sheltered from the truths of the world beneath your blankets. Oh yeah, and another thing, why are you always so angry? Always needing, wanting, like a child. All I hear from you is "Me, me, me, me, me".'

It was clear to me that he was enjoying this and had probably rehearsed the whole thing over and over in his head. I felt like the butt-end of the joke one too many times with this fucker and as we walked beyond the Obelisk, I promised myself that I would have the last laugh.

'There are thirteen in total,' he said, sparing a look around at me before continuing. 'We knew that each one held power, potential, but even the doctor had no idea of the connection between them.'

He continued to talk as we crossed a huge parade square that spanned from the obelisk to the black pyramid, and I continued to hobble after him, both physically and cognitively.

'We thought there were only twelve of them. We had no idea of the true connection before the so-called Voynich came to the fore. That was the catalyst. Then we knew it pertained to ancient geometry and the architect's cube.

'It was then that we knew that we needed to bring in all the books, including the one you held. All very interesting stuff Henry. The Codex. Vortex equations. The ruling: Three, Six, Nine; an infinite sequence of doubling patterns: one, two, four, eight, seven, five, one, two, four, yada, yada, yada…'

I kept my mouth shut, as for the first time in my long existence, I realised I didn't know as much as I thought I did. I believed I held the secrets and truths to most, if not all, modern histories. I even considered myself a mover of the power pieces, but it seemed I wasn't even aware of the real game being played.

I reckoned that owning up to my ignorance would not serve me best, so I carried on with my eyes open, through the subterranean of Atlantis, and on toward the great pyramid that was apparently a cube, even if it didn't look like one.

Summer. 1553. Decadence in Desperation.

'Ah, look at the wee darlins, will yee? Hic!' The oval shaped man was clearly talking to the snake-plant over in the far corner of the room.

Mary rolled her eyes and smiled, crossing her arms beneath her ample bosom. She introduced the egg-shaped man as Claruc when I entered the lounge. And from there it had taken me less than two sentences to work out that he was a bona fide lunatic. However, clearly the lady was fond of him, and the lady was fond of less people than I myself was, which left me wondering after the court jester big enough to strangle a polar bear, with curiosity.

'Humours are nything' an' brewin' an' nything' an' concoctin' an'-hic!'

'Is he always drunk?' I asked Mary, keeping my voice low so as not to draw his attention, again.

'And herein presents the paradox: for Claruc works tirelessly at his state of inebriation. 'Tis the curse, and the key that grants him the ability to access the window of infinite possibilities,' she said, and much louder than I wanted her to. 'But between you and me, I think he just talks utter bollocks and bullshit.'

At the mention of his name, the bumbling Irishman turned from the plant and made a beeline for us.

I sighed at both Mary's whimsical answer to a very simple question, and then, of course, because Claruc was shuffling his way over and his attention was solely on me.

'Is it the *Game* o' lords, or the *lord* o' games?' He tapped my shoulder, 'watch as the blue-blood washes into red an' makes purple,' he made fussing hands towards Mary as he spoke of red and purple.

'An' if yee not careful, queens will, will even, will-hic!' he glugged at his flask like a man most desperate, 'swell into mothers. Be warned, seduced into the madness o' destiny quicker than most. Both o' yee will! An' it will set the wheels in motion for-hic!'

'Claruc, leave us!' snapped Mary, suddenly not smiley and instantly bored in only the way true royalty can be.

He winked at me, and for a moment I saw something different from the drunken idiot, but then he hiccupped again and set about his drunken retreat like every drunken fool I ever saw.

I watched him leave with fresh eyes. The drunken act was played well, but the words he spoke riddled around my mind like a tick on a rat. I watched as he stumbled, unbalanced, into the guard at the door, causing a bit of a clatter and a lot more gibbering and creative cursing.

"Blue blood", this term triggered a memory of the nickname Father Game gave me on account of the seemingly red-blueish tinge to my blood. I wondered how this fool could possibly know about my curiousness.

We sat in silence for a few moments, listening to Claruc's long and drawn out retreat, a tuneless whistle echoing through the hallways beyond our decadent chambers, and when the noise finally faded, suddenly it was just the two of us. Mary and I, and no small amount of unfathomable tension.

The silence stretched on, and with it, so did the wordless intent of my royal employer. In fact, I was beginning to feel uncomfortable. I knew the measure of what caused such tension and with that truth came an unabashed shyness that I had not experienced before.

The emotions and sensations coursing through my body

were totally new to me. Although it is true that I was perhaps fifty summers to the good, even though I looked little older than twenty, in my haste for revenge and status, I had not yet found the time to entertain any sort of romantic feelings or desires or physical pleasures of any kind. Least not like the kind surging over me on that chair.

I stood up and helped myself to the goblet on the table besides the glowing fireplace, relieving the mounting pressure and momentarily turning my back on her. I tried my best to prepare myself for the intimacies of human flesh, succumbing to the situation, gulping down the wine like it was going out of fashion and I had just purchased the world's largest collection of it. If this was to be my first time, then wine would be my guide and blinding light. I stayed by the side table with the nearly empty goblet of wine until I felt her breath on the nape of my neck.

'Since the moment I saw you defy my father, I knew that you were not like any of the other men, and none of them like you. I knew, even as a young girl, that I must have you, Lord Game. If there would ever be a man to fulfil me, it would be you. And so it will be.'

I turned away from her to put some distance between us again, but it didn't work. She was the intellectual predator and I the predictable prey. Now, judge me not as a coward for I had slaughtered many a foe, scores of men, some women too I might add; I had free climbed tall towers into the darkest of skies with murder through my heart; nor had I blinked when faced against the odds of revenge over large distances – but, in all the devilish deeds and intention, through all the horrors I'd witnessed and orchestrated, I'd never been intimate with a woman, not ever, not once – not even in my dreams. To be clear, I was somewhere around fifty years old, and I was a virgin.

Again, she advanced, and I noticed a small yet crucial change in detail: she had loosened the front of her blouse and was now flashing her ample cleavage at me. I reassessed the situation: we were alone, the fire was glowing romantically, wine was in abundance and again, we were alone.

I squared my shoulders to hers and had a long look down her blouse and into her dilated pupils. A hunger was growing in me also, and it wasn't for food. I moved back half a step and put forward my terms:

'I will not be removing my weapons. If you want this, I come armed.'

And she clearly did because in just a few moments she had managed to slip her blouse down to the tiled floor and stepped out of it to be before me in all of her coppery glory. I nodded my head once in approval before she closed the distance between us, and my heart fluttered like a hummingbird in the rain.

I was no-more in control of the entanglement as any gentleman ever were, or would be, for that matter. She showed me things, feelings, I never knew I could feel – purely physical, but completely overpowering at the same time. I knew I was clumsy and sweaty and too impatient – and I suddenly realised that I needed to rethink my life priorities. Sex was almost as good as revenge, and still head and shoulders above all else. More sex would be good for me and I was absolutely certain from the moment I entered her.

* * *

'No, I have decided,' Mary stood up from her chair in a fury of fabric and frills, 'Lady Jane Grey is practically an innocent in all of this…' she washed her hands in the air, searching for the right word, 'debacle. No, it is clearly that inbred lot: the

Dudley's of Suffolk that sowed the seed of contempt. They are the real guilty party and wholly to blame. I see that quite clearly now.'

This was a side I had not seen, Mary being reasonable and logical. Maybe our shared experience had softened her up a touch, I worried for the consequence of my most recent and sweaty actions. I know it had sure opened my eyes. It had been almost ten days and although my cock didn't hurt anymore, it still burned when I needed to piss...

'But, my queen, your reign is in its infancy, just too fragile to risk publicly taking on the Dudley's right now...' Sir Ecgbriht began his counter from the seat directly opposite Mary at the table.

The mad queen's chief advisor in diplomacy was a resolute weasel of man, who had a wispy-point white beard below a little piggy nose and splash-bright green eyes. He was thinking, he always twiddled with chin-pubes when he was in thought, I noticed.

'Guildford! Yes, Guildford will serve, he is *technically* a Dudley, so-'

'And he is also the husband of Lady Jane Grey, you feckless moronic beardsplitter. No, the two of them will not be harmed! I forbid it. I will not condone such barbarity, such *punishment* upon the naivety of commoners...' her eyes wandered across the table to me, again. I was starting to think I was in trouble.

Sir Ecgbriht must have noticed Mary's love-struck glances at me also because he made a noise most unpleasant and of the disapproving tenor. It was a tut of impatience and disgust and sanctimony, but in short, it was precisely the wrong noise to make at that exact moment for the queen's chief advisor was advisor no more. Only he just didn't know it yet. It was made official when his head fell off two days later.

'Leave us, everyone. Sir Ecgbriht, you are to personally ensure that Jane and her spouse are kept comfortable at The Tower. You will treat them as an extension of my family, which they are. Now go!'

He was dismissed, and after a minute dip of his head, and a dirty look my way, he left, taking his holier than thou attitude with him. And again, it was just we two, Mary and I and the tingle of another kind of pungent bodily humour.

I had been under Mary's employment for two days when I set forth and spearheaded her loyal force upon the infamous glory of London Town. And to my most merry surprise, the crazy bitch had insisted that I take her drunken fool, Claruc, with me on our quest to bring back her crown.

I scoffed and told her it was folly, but of course, she wasn't asking me to take him, she was telling me. At first, his egg-like appearance, the annoying and persistent whistling combined with the drunken behaviour had me leaning towards total despair, and I promised her that I would not be responsible if he didn't survive. Yet, at the first sign of trouble my mind was settled as I saw him snap a soldier's head back, almost ripping it off even. Only thing, it was one of our soldiers… After that I did not ever again question Claruc's lethality, nor Mary's judgement in dangerous bastards.

Word of Mary's challenge to the throne spread throughout the land as surely as truth poisons a court of aristocracy. It was executed perfectly by our legion of bards, each of them armed with well-versed scripts, preaching from tavern to tavern throughout the length and breadth of the nation, and thus helping gather the required support needed to mount a successful coup – and it was no accident that our bards focused primarily on the waterholes known to be frequented by the serving Royal Guard.

The bards' songs had it that the 'rightful' queen placed a higher value on her standing army, every man one of them.

And, that every Royal Guard would have greater rations and higher pay and a half-sovereign paid on to them as a loyalty bonus. Also, they sang that Mary could not be stopped as she had the legendary Henry Game beside her – a man-demon raised from Hell for one purpose only: to put right the injustice and restore the rightful ruler to her correct place. Anyone foolish enough to stand in their way would be dragged down to Hell by Henry himself. Therefore, it was with very little further encouragement that the standing army decided to turn swords, so to speak, and join the righteous quest to the palace to dethrone the unfortunate Lady Jane Grey.

Within two days our advance had morphed into an ever-growing snowball of swords. We set forth with fifteen hundred, by the time we reached the outer limits of the capital, our numbers had grown ten-fold and there wasn't a force in all the land that would dare stand in our way.

It took nine days for the Lady Jane Grey to be removed from the seat of power. I keep this fact as the brevity of her reign is a personal source of pride for me. Did I win this war without having to slay a single foe, or stage a single battle on my way to victory? Maybe, but I'm not the boasting type. Triumph came peacefully and forcefully, if ever a statement could be said in earnest.

Back in the war-room it was just we two, and Mary was doing that thing again: that staring thing – deep black pupils and shallow breathing and glistening red lips. I felt no more confident than I had the last time this had happened. In fact, I felt more anxious and vulnerable.

I stayed exactly where I was, locked in the grip of weakness and humility. I looked little older than a boy after all. Her breasts were showing a little more, she knew I had a weakness for breasts. But I was determined that my job here was done, or so I tried to convince myself. All I now required was payment for services rendered. The whole endeavour had been a welcomed distraction from the monotony of farming and maintenance of church property, but it really was time I was going.

'Now you are queen, Your Majesty, I believe I am due the payment of one warship and crew.'

She stopped in her leering. A hesitation, perhaps doubt, flickering across her hard face. Perhaps all of her recent victories had managed to soften her up a little.

'Of course, my Lord Game. As agreed, you will have the pick of the fleet.' She put her long finger on my shoulder and slowly circled a line around to my face.

'However, you still have one more duty to fulfil.' The silk garment dropped to the stone floor around her ankles. I couldn't help but follow her curves down as my other member raised up.

'Me,' she clarified and clearly it was an order. Her hazelgreen eyes deadpan; not to be disobeyed.

And that, I'll have you know, was the very first time I shagged a reigning monarch. And let me tell you, she was certainly worth the work: my ship, of course.

The galleon I had selected from the offerings available was a majestic wonder of nautical prowess and unrivalled craftsmanship… It came with a crew of merchants and a balding cat. And apparently, the feline was absolutely non-negotiable in the deal.

The ship's cat was called Tricks, and it seemed she was the longest serving and most revered sailor of the entire Merchant Navy – and "should she not be permitted to stay aboard and join us on our quest, I would be hard-pressed to find a sailor in all the land of the world willing to crew my ship, gold coin or otherwise".

I figured that if the old and scabby sailor protesting before me was so adamant in his argument – the queen introduced him as Captain Skelton – enough to risk being thrown out of my employ for such a bloody trivial thing even, well, then I would be shrewd to let him have his way and so the cat stayed. It is wise to pick the battles you fight, or so my father would say to me…

The boat was perfection. Or, perhaps, I concede now that I was biased in my initial assessment. To a stranger she looked nothing more than an aging and neglected carrack that had not seen oil nor a paint brush in maybe a decade, but beneath the flaking scallops of withered daub lay a ship built to sail the seven seas and then some.

The queen smiled when I made my selection. I suspected she thought I may have chosen a newer ship or robbed her of her very own beloved *"Peter Pomegranate",* but instead what I had chosen seemed to please us both.

Shortly after, as the sails and masts were stripped of Tudor naval flag and colours, Captain Skelton introduced me to the rest of the crew: a middling lot that looked somewhat unstable on the still docks, and in desperate need of a leech or two hundred, and probably a witch doctor, and even a miracle.

I stepped out on to the snoring deck of my ship and turned to the men, and in a tone of grandiosity I asked the former captain and crew if they would sail with me to seek new worlds, and that a fair distribution of the profits and spoils of adventure would be bestowed upon each of them.

If anything the former captain looked rather unsure about my proposal, in fact, he looked unsure about everything in general, but one thing he was sure about was the malevolent stare-down from the new queen as she stood waiting to wave me off, and how the future of his head's attachment to his neck depended on his swift decision.

In my relatively short existence, I had known nothing but harsh times. Death had followed my trails like a shadow follows those who walk in the light. Hell, sometimes the darkness even got in front of me. But things being what they were, I ploughed on regardless and exacted my duty, took my lumps, bloodied my brow.

I had never spent any real time on the water of course. But the idea of the ship filled me with positive and clean energy. I once again had a spring in my step as my new venture offered the opportunity to start over. I had earned the possibility of true escape.

I looked still a boy, and I felt no older than I looked. I truly had no anger left within me and all I wanted was to see the wonders the world could show me. Seemed to me that only way to make a thing happen was to make a thing happen.

Legend of the boy abandoned within the well in the dead of winter, only for him to become the slayer of popes, the piper in the forest, the maker of kings and queens, were now in full circulation and whispered throughout the land via all of her frothing taverns. Of course, once the songs had reached the bards, the tales they spoke of were virtually set in stone and oral history.

The time had come for me to find myself again and I had no appetite to remain and be chased by those who sought to test the mettle of legend. Anger and revenge had taken enough of my time already. This was the occasion to make a new legend. I only hoped that this time it would be a legend of discovery and adventure and sea monsters and exotic treasures of the golden and jewelled and female variety alike.

There was a wide world out there, yet to be tainted by me.

The Wayside.

I was circling a dark and destructive drain at a time when blood polluted the oil of the Gulf and insatiable greed corrupted the west. And after four-hundred and fifty years, it was still yet a world of surprise to me.

My time in the Middle East had shown me fresh layers of reality. I had long since stopped believing in fairy tales, but, when you are in the heat of war and lives are being lost without pause, and it is all for the possession of a symbolic weapon, you too would question your own convictions when faced with elemental energies that do not conform to our primitive understandings of life – but this is for another time.

"The Spear of Destiny", to my surprise, was believed to be the blade that pierced the side of Jesus Christ as he drooled, limp and defeated upon his frame of self-fulfilled prophecy. The legends foretold it that the one to yield the spear-tip would be in possession of the most formidable weapon on Earth, imbued by the blood of the Almighty, with it they would be able to anoint themselves to ultimate power.

Up close and personal with the Spear of Destiny, I recognised it for what it was. The way that everything burned around the metallic tip of the dagger like it was magic. It was more familiar to me than anybody would know. I reckoned that Pope Clement VII would recognise it too if he was still with us... I said nothing to my employer and ploughed on regardless: hands out for coin and mowing down any motherfucker that was put in front of me on my quest.

With sand particles in my ears and nostrils and eyes and even up my arse once, I came to think of the region as a paradise of discovery, and annoyance, and heat, and authenticity. A place where the layers of the world we think we know peel away before our eyes to reveal that there is more to everything, and in that moment of actualisation, suddenly the cultures of the West seem abhorrently flamboyant and narcissistic.

My skin peeling from my arms, feet, face, shoulders, and back, desperately fleeing across the cooled sands of Nowhere, I came to learn that there were other beings that lived on Earth as different to me as I am to the rest of humanity. It was amidst my distractions that I took my finger off the pulse and was forced to choose between saving my best-friend and doing the right thing.

But of course, in the crunch of the moment I relented and handed the spear over to the Tyrant. I was done being a part of their game, but still, the plummeting tower of Grim Catspaw toppled and crumbled with what should've been a neck-breaking injury, as he hanged from the rope like a ragdoll was enough to call it a day on our adventures.

The world seemed darker than I had ever known it to be. And I was perhaps the darkest instrument of them all. I saw all this, and even more, and I saw the only way to stop the evil from ravaging my every experience was to not expose myself to it any longer. Pretend it doesn't exist, even. Then I saw myself as the common denominator and crumpled beneath the weight of guilt for my losses and cursed permanence.

Memories tainted my every waking moment. Each second derivative. It was as though my life was on repeat, and I was just running through the years. The circular nature of it all. The patterns; the connection of all things related plagued and festered; stuck in a rut, again. In the darkness that was my mind a voice stirred the shadows that suffocated my light, like sharks ringing around me.

From all of the time I have spent on this earth, my greatest shame is that you were deprived of the wonderful woman that was your mother. Her disappearance will haunt me through every gateway and beyond. The biggest mistake your mother ever made was loving and believing that a bastard like me could keep her safe. Keep us anonymous...

Her name was Helen. And she was quintessentially perfect. What she saw in a shadow-dweller like me I'll never know. I heard her voice in a period of darkness. Your mother was little older than twenty at the time, and she was perfectly, devastatingly, innocent; she was worlds away from the corruption, and guilt-ridden festering duplicities of my life. I should have left the tavern and ran as far away as I could, maybe your mother would still be here if I had not been so selfish and absorbed in my own shit.

She was a singer, your mother, believe it or not, or at least part-time she was. She bartended mainly, but for the bi-weekly occasion when the landlord would let her sing to the patrons.

Nestled in the clinches of late autumn, I'd traipsed back up to the far-removed reaches of northern England. I had just arrived in the quiet town via the new trainline I'd heard so much about on the news. The train carriage had that new vehicle smell, and I sat in first class, alone.

My head prickled from yet another skull crushing wound, and my skin was still burnt and peeling from the harsh Arabian sun. To say I was tired was an understatement, and not just physically. But I felt more at home in the northern reaches of England than anywhere else. I had to rethink my life, again. The clean air, the overcast skies, and the brisk winds were exactly what I needed.

The first guesthouse I happened across was a nice little whiskey tavern called The Wayside. The place had recently since been converted from an old barn and was surprisingly high-end quality, being idyllically sat amongst the roots of a long since dead volcano, or so the elderly landlord liked to tell me, more than a few dozen times. And although it was pretty remote, it regularly managed to draw a mixed crowd of locals and travelling mountaineers that created an atmosphere that brought me right back to my days spent on the road and my failed quest to kill a king. Times change, buildings change, even the beer changes, but people, for the most, stay the same.

I arrived at the reception and requested a guest suite for the foreseeable future. But the landlord bristled like I'd just shit in his cereal bowl, flicking the pages in his guest book back and forth, shaking his head, regrettable and not at all accommodating or sorry about it.

I often drew this kind of reaction, especially since shedding the iron mask. I slapped a bundle of crisp notes atop his turning pages and told him that I have my eggs runny, my coffee black and my toilet paper triple-ply, and that nobody was to enter my room without my permission; I was paying up-front, full-board, alcoholic drinks included, for the remaining three months of the year.

Registering the thick wad of sense, the landlord suddenly had no further qualms and he offered an available suite that was annexed from the main part of The Wayside. For me, that was perfect.

The first couple of weeks passed with little to remark upon. However, I do fondly remember the crowing of Eric the rooster just before first light. During the days I re-lived the events of what I had just been through; during the evenings I drank to forget and enough to make me smile as I slept, if ever I were lucky enough.

Not sleeping, however, has always been a frustrating trait of mine. I sleep maybe one or two nights a week. And even then, it is only ever for a couple of hours at a time. Yet, when I did manage sleep, presumably from the copious amounts of whiskey consumed back then, my dreams were dark and gritty, my skin feeling burned again from the scorching ball of fires in the skies of my nightmares – the Trojan horse dripping blood from its underbelly as the gates opened to Hell before me and I led the charge.

Down in the bar of an evening, I had barely shared anything other than a grunt or a nod with anybody else, including your mother, but for this one night, as the clouds blanketed our nights from the claw of ice, the landlord seconded Helen to sing for our evening's entertainment.

It was the first time to happen since I had been resident. I welcomed the change from the predictable route I was surely, and sourly, about to travel down, and was intrigued enough not to turn in early, as I often did on the busier nights such as this night was shaping up to be.

Helen inaudibly set up her chair and guitar over by the bay window, that in the daytime framed a picture of the steep rise and heather covered terrain – quintessential of the Lake District. At a signal to the landlord, the early 90s bubbly-pop music was turned down and the sudden quietness drew the attention of everyone in the throes of socialising, including and excluding myself, of course.

For another few moments she continued to tune her plain-pine guitar. Everyone watched on, silently sipping, until finally her tuning turned into a strum and she tapped her foot to a beat that complimented the chords.

The song was not anything familiar to me, not that I listened to much chart music, yet I found that her voice soothed like honey over the wounds that were my recent experiences. Her tones massaged the atmosphere and allowed my thoughts to ease. For the first time in forever I was able to clear my mind of the memories that bedevilled. I was listening and present in the moment, forgetting the anxieties that come from the past and the future, respectively.

I cannot tell you how long she sang, only that the spell was broken when a boisterous hiker uncouthly shouted his admiration for the singer over the top of the modest applause. I found his tone most disrespectful and I sank back the rest of my whiskey.

The punk in question was a young fellow, probably mid-twenties, clearly inebriated and from the clothes he wore, inexperienced in the mountainous terrain of the North; I figured he was most certainly a city dweller, and obviously a gigantic dickhead. And his two travelling companions looked to be cut from the same cloth as he, as all together they whooped and whistled their appreciation for the singer over the song, encouraging her to give them a private show back at their lodgings.

I recoiled back from the edge of my booth, deeper into shadow and signalled to the landlord for a refill, to which he acknowledged my request and poured another tumbler of single malt.

My thoughts were turning as dark as my corner when I spotted the landlord on his way towards me, and just as the next song was starting to the pacey strum and beating foot taps. He passed the table of the three amigos, collecting empty pint glasses on his way and placed my drink before me, removing my own empty tumbler in the process.

'So, if Freddy Kruger over here gets table service,' said the loudest of the noisy bunch, 'how about you fetch us another round too?' His tone drew a sudden stop to the new song, and also the attention of everyone in the bar, but this didn't seem to bother him or his table in the slightest.

The landlord stopped in his tracks and rounded on the

speaker. 'We don't offer table service, young man. If you want another drink, you can go to the bar, like everyone else, quietly.'

'No, you clearly do.' The little prick was growing in volume. 'Fucking Scarface over here just got his drink brought over to him, didn't he? Or is this freak your boyfriend?' The atmosphere was mutating into something like that of a cowboy movie.

The landlord looked over to your mother with apology in his eyes. 'Helen, please continue-'

'Not until you've fetched me and my boys a drink, old man.'

'I think maybe you three should leave,' suggested Helen, the fire in her eyes more interesting to me than anything else.

I noticed that the rest of the bar was still holding its breath over the confrontation. A few of the local guys were far more interested in their drinks than ever before. Cowards.

'Who the fuck asked your opinion, luv? You just play that guitar and keep out of it, alright? An' maybe I'll get a drink for you an' all, if you're lucky.'

The cocky prick winked at Helen and his friends laughed and started banging their nearly empty pint glasses on the table chanting "drink, drink, drink".

One or two people were getting their coats on, to which the landlord dashed away in an attempt to prevent them from leaving. In the commotion of growing hostilities, I quietly slid out of my corner and joined the table with my new friends, my back to Helen. As soon as they realised that I was actually joining them their chants stopped dead. Their limited attention spans now fully focused on my hideous scars, and the quick risk assessment of me severely underestimated.

'And what the fuck do you want, Elephant Man?'

Again, his friends laughed. One of them even reaching over to relieve me of my drink, his hand freezing in mid-air as I fixed him with a look that many a dead man would recognise as their very final moment. These guys were funny as fuck and the cold silence in the bar held testament to that.

'Boys,' I started, my tone soft and calm despite my rising adrenaline, 'I want to listen to the nice lady's song but you're causing a scene that is making her and the rest of the tavern uncomfortable.

'If you don't settle down, and I mean right now, you will all be leaving together and never coming back.' I tried to keep it respectful, though I couldn't quite mask the menace behind the pretence.

The threesome were suddenly all frowns and seriousness. The smug and mocking laughter evaporated. A tenseness in their movements and the delayed response told me that violence was not far away from his next words.

'An' are you going to fucking make us leave, Frankenstein?'

I shook my head at their ignorance, knocking back my whiskey before responding. 'It's Frankenstein's Monster, not Frankenstein. Frankenstein is the doctor, he creates the monster, idiot. And yes, if I have to.'

At once all three of them stood and towered over me, threatening but not at all intimidating. All I wanted was to hear the lady sing. I was tired of all the drama, but slapping a few cock-faces around might help me burn off some of that restlessness I'd been dealing with-

'Police have been called,' warned the landlord. 'You should get on your way, before they get here, don't you think?'

'I think this freak needs to step outside with us right now. See if he's as tough as he thinks he is. Won't be so confident out there, will you?'

'If he steps out, then I'll follow him.' The landlord stepped out from the side of the bar with an iron pole in his hands.

'And me!' piped up one of the regulars, who up until this point had been trying to climb inside his empty glass.

'I'll be coming out too,' another voice, not unfamiliar but I didn't see his face.

'And me!' Another four or five shouted out as the pledges of solidarity echoed around the tavern until finally your mother spoke up also, again the fire in her promise chilling.

With smiles wiped from their faces, the trio of shit-bags exited the premises and disappeared out into the night to the jeers of the brave remaining patrons.

'A round on the house!' declared the landlord to an even louder response and predictable surge to the bar.

I returned to my dark corner, meeting the eye of the landlord, even amongst the onset, signalling for another whiskey. Moments later the guitar strummed back into life, no song, just melody.

I looked over to your mother, who was now looking directly back at me and I felt the heat rush to my face. I was about to look away when she smiled and mouthed a "thank you".

* * *

Enamelled from the backing of the regulars, I had begun to feel more comfortable than I had felt in an age. The commonplace grunt and nod had been replaced with a traditional "good morning" and "good night", but only to those faces that I had come to remember, and only after they had acknowledged me first, of course. I felt welcome, and on the evening when Helen would delight the patrons with her music, I would leave the obscurity of my corner booth to adopt a more open and central position, but only for the duration of the set.

To avoid a repeat of recent hostilities, an accord was struck with the landlord that I should approach the bar from my four-fingers of pre-paid single malt. I agreed, although it did not serve me in the slightest, and I found to my surprise that giving for no gain released a feeling deep within that made me feel much better about, well, everything. It was wonderful, truly. A sensation I had not experienced since before my overcast day, since before that even. Not since Francis... Maybe never, actually.

The weather was turning and quickly, and as winter froze the grasslands and coating of heather outside my window, my guilt and sadness began to thaw and settle within, like a balancing of the good and bad humours. An internal neutralisation. Although I knew my regret could never leave me, living in symbiosis with all I had done would only ever be the best outcome for the bearer of a ledger such as mine. Acceptance, I suppose, is what I had found, and in such a relatively short time, I could only put it down to environmental factors: total severance from the forces of global manipulation; complete anonymity amongst my fellow whisky drinkers, and a faint sense of belonging, almost a familial energy that had embodied The Wayside since our shared experience had galvanised our comradery, collectively.

Christmas approached and for the first time since it had taken on its relatively modern paradigm, I was free to observe as one amongst the masses; free to be 'caught up' in the tides of Christmas Spirit and revel in the Christmas pop-song culture that dominated the radio waves. Hits from popular artists such as Shakin' Stevens, Slade, and Wham, but to name just a few, had somehow managed to worm into my subconscious, and on the odd occasion I would find myself whistling a tune only to clamp my mouth shut immediately and bite my tongue until it bled.

Snow was indeed falling, and all around me, and the boys of the NYPD choir were still singing Galway Bay, but Helen was committed to her own music, that I determined as Celtic in origin. And whilst she did enjoy the Christmas hat, and I think I saw her picking away at the complimentary mince pies and mulled wine quite regularly, she sang her own stories of a life without the sun or skies, and she mesmerised us all with her despondent imagery of a subservient life far removed from the sun-kissed ground and freedoms that we all took for granted. The tavern was quiet during the days, and even quieter in the evenings when Helen was allowed to sing.

I'd taken to spending less and less time in my room, once even climbing to the top of the late volcano, one cold and crispy morning. The grass and shrubbery crunched underfoot as I had stridden out even before the world turned toward the sun again. The seasonal changes had never really affected me, and I decided that a t-shirt and shorts was sufficient enough for me to make the hike. However, upon my return to the tavern, as I descended down the steep slopes, I stumbled across Helen, just as she was unloading trays of fresh vegetables from the boot of her car.

Eric heralded my return just as the skies washed a pale blue and I realised that such lack of winter clothing, especially when mountain hiking in December, may come across as a little strange, maybe even suicidal, to the regular warm-blooded human.

Helen had clearly seen me coming down the mountain, and I didn't know how long she had been unloading, but she knew I was out and amongst the altitudes in summer clothes. With no way to avoid her, especially not without looking even more bizarre, I decided to try a little more of that potent altruistic medicine and headed straight for her car.

'Please,' I said as I jogged the final few meters, making sure to blow into my hands for the effect of normality, 'let me help you with that.'

'Hey, you!' Just her smile warmed me more than a summer's day. 'Thanks, but I only have one more anyway-'

'I insist.' I lifted the crate from her boot and turned toward the kitchen entrance. I heard her close the boot and lock with a bleep and a flash. The early morning sun had yet to start thawing any of the grass, and I could hear the crunch of footsteps as she hurried to catch up.

'What a gentleman. I'll get the door for you; you must be freezing.' She hurried on and held open the door, closing it as soon as we had stepped through, removing her gloves at once and rubbing her hands. I put the crate down besides the others and lingered for a moment, suddenly not sure what to say next.

'Is that the first time you've been up the mountain then? You picked a cold morning for it, and in just a t-shirt and shorts, you bloody nutter!'

I rubbed at my exposed skin and nodded. 'Yeah, and I won't be making that mistake again. I'll see you later.' I turned to leave, and she reached out and brushed my arm leaving tingles where our skin made contact.

'You look frozen. I'll make us a cuppa. Go and sit down in your booth.' It wasn't a question.

'Have you eaten? I'll make some teacakes.'

'I've eaten already, thank you,' I lied.

'Well I'm making some anyway, and you need to eat them. Go and sit down, the lounge should already be warm. It's a new central heating system, one of them "combi-boilers", it has one of them automatic timers built into it.'

She seemed awfully interested in the heating system and I didn't know what to say to that, but I did as I was told and positioned myself in 'my booth' and waited, good humours continuing to neutralise the toxic ones.

I wondered how far, for how long even, I could exist in this space of happiness. I hate to admit it, but I was waiting for my past to catch up and destroy everything good about my new life. It left me teetering on the fence.

Several minutes later and she arrived with a teapot, two cups, sugar and milk, and a healthy pile of teacakes, completely drowning in salted butter. Suddenly I felt nervous again in her company.

'That should warm you nicely. Now, I'll never eat all these teacakes on my own, will I? Don't you bloody dare leave them all to me.'

I smiled and reached out to turn the cups over.

'No, sir, you've done enough. I'll take care of this business.' She put a teacake on a saucer and slid it over to me. 'Do you take milk and sugar?'

I realised that I was staring, perhaps a little too intently, and diverted my eyes to my food. 'No, no thank you. Black is fine.' I replayed the words over in my head, mentally kicking myself for being such a bumbling buffoon.

'Your name is Henry, right?'

I blushed. Good job my face is scarred up to shit, otherwise my embarrassment would have been hers.

'Yes, and you're Helen.' I sipped at my tea, steaming as the near boiling fluid went down. I again realised my mistake as Helen's eyes widened.

'Temperatures don't bother you at all now do they?' she laughed, and I joined her. She had no idea.

'I wanted to thank you, again, for standing up to those three pillocks a few weeks ago. You were very brave, and decent.'

'It was nothing. I just wanted to listen to...' I'd gone and put my foot in it. Fuck.

'To me?' she acted all shy. 'Aww, you're cute – and eat your bloody teacake before it goes cold.'

I looked down and obeyed. Looking anywhere but right at her was a relief from my extreme foolishness. How could a beautiful woman such as Helen ever be interested in a hideous creature like me. It wasn't possible, surely.

For the next ten minutes or so we enjoyed our breakfast in comfortable silence, the occasional smile and gesture for tea refills in between eating and sipping, when finally, as the last of the tea was poured, she adopted a slight frown.

'Tell me to mind my own business, but I cannot help but wonder…' she touched her cheeks. I felt my heart race a little and looked back down at my crumb covered saucer.

'Wars never end, instead they hide behind the eyes of men. Was it the Gulf?'

I was impressed with her astuteness. 'Yes, in a manner of speaking.'

She nodded and sipped at her tea. 'Your face then,' again that little frown that only made her more interesting to me. 'That was an injury from the battlefield?'

I thought about it for a moment, eventually meeting her eye. 'Yes, you could say that.' Lies were easier than the truth, far easier.

'May I?' She held her hand out now, halfway across the space between us.

I nodded and my heart raced into full gallop right until the moment when her fingers flitted across my jigsaw skin. And suddenly I was more interested in her reaction to it, far more than my own embarrassment.

She lowered her hand and returned to her tea, smiling furtively. 'I'm glad you came here, Henry,' She stood up and started gathering the plates and cups on the tray.

It seemed breakfast was finished, and I belatedly

helped, our hands brushing one another's causing us both to pause.

'This was nice,' she said, continuing the stack the tray. 'We should do it again, but next time you decide to go bloody hiking, wear something sensible, unless you want to freeze to death, of course.'

'Agreed,' I nodded, 'and thank you. I'll see you later?'

She smiled and walked back to the business end of the kitchen, humming a tune along the way. I knew I would see her later. Christmas was in two days' time and I'd overheard the landlord asking her to work both Christmas Eve and for a few hours in the afternoon of the twenty-fifth.

For the first time in my life the festive spirit was as intoxicating to me as any Disney movie, and it was in that moment, as Helen disappeared through the door with the bones of our breakfast that I decided that I would truly embrace the culture and buy her a present. Only I had no idea what she would like, or, what would be proper, if anything at all. We had barely just shared our first words. Was buying her a present an overstep into the realms of weird and creepy?

I pondered over my latest dilemma as I returned to my quarters with a new sense of adventure. I had a plan to borrow the landlord's bicycle and ride into the local town of Ravenglass, from where so many of The Wayside's regulars hailed from. My sole purpose was gift hunting. Honestly, I'd had less anxiety scaling crumbling towers into the black skies and fighting naked Frenchmen with tomahawks than I was experiencing at that moment. Going gift shopping was a terrifying concept for a man over four-hundred and fifty winters to the good.

* * *

Christmas day came and the tavern was decorated appropriately.

The landlord explained that every year they would open the doors from lunch to dinner, and the day was promised to be a merry occasion for regulars, staff, and family alike. I wondered where I fitted in exactly. I wondered if long-term patron counted as 'regular'.

Mistletoe hung from the ceiling lights and over the tops of booths. The usual table arrangement had made way for a long and ceremonial centre bench laid out with complimentary mince pies, ginger cake, a cauldron of mulled wine, pretzels and other nibbles, and of course, a heaping of Christmas crackers.

I was allowed to enter through the front entrance, whilst the patrons of the pub had to enter from the rear, and as the doors opened, in spilled many a face that I had grown familiar too, and in the rare instance: quite fond of.

I had the present in my hand, the shiny silver wrapping paper and crimson bow tightly atop. Of course, I had paid for the thing to be gift wrapped, dropping a crisp fifty-pound note into the charity box to the exclamations of the two nice ladies volunteering their time for no other reason than altruism was a feeling more potent than any drug I had sampled, and I'd sampled them all. Being good felt good because it was good, but, as I waited for Helen to appear, I had never felt so unsure, so anxious, such a fraud, and so full of self-doubt. Whilst I waited, I drank twice, maybe three times faster than usual, almost convincing myself that to give her a present was unequivocally disturbing and wrong-

'Merry Christmas, Henry.' She was standing behind me and I coughed as the whiskey went down the wrong hole.

'Merry Christmas,' I eventually managed, supressing the urge to cough and splutter, turning from the bar to face her.

The fire was well-bedded in and had warmed the place up nicely, but as soon as I laid eyes on her, and saw her eyes twinkling with that joy she always possessed, my skin goose-bumped and my veins contracted. I felt like I needed a seat for fear of falling.

She glowed with radiance, lighting of darkness. Her eyes a soft black; her skin apple pale; her lips and hair wet ruby and inviting my affection. Getting her the present was wrong. I could see that now and as I tried to hide it behind my back she looked down, that twinkle all too alive with curiosity and compassion.

'Ooo,' she teased. 'What did Father Christmas bring you? I was almost convinced that you were on the naughty list.'

I looked down, heartbeat in my throat, in my ears, my thumbs, my stomach.

'Actually,' I croaked, not meeting her eyes. I offered the small box forward. 'I got this for you.' I only dared to look up again as her pale hands accepted the gift, and she was beaming, all eyes and teeth.

'I, I don't know what to say.' She sat down beside me at the bar, her cheeks flushing a little. 'I mean thank you, Henry, this is so kind.'

'It's actually the first Christmas present I've ever given someone.' I don't know why I told her that. All I was doing was making her feel even more uncomfortable.

'Anyway, merry Christmas.' I turned away and retreated to my decorated, yet shady, booth in the corner, ignoring everything and everyone around me.

Although the distance from the bar to my booth was little more than twenty steps, I swear I've had years pass quicker as I walked over, her eyes no-doubt piercing my back. Should the floor have split open wide enough, I would have dived right in, no hesitation.

I sat in my booth and made sure my back was to the bar when Helen slipped in seconds later, opposite me. Just us, and the unopened present. She had that little frown on her face again.

'I'm embarrassed,' she finally confirmed.

It was my worst fear coming to life before my eyes. I knew it was a mistake. 'It's okay, you don't have to take it-'

'Oh no!' she interjected. 'Not embarrassed about receiving a gift, no, I'm embarrassed that I didn't get you one, in return.'

The twinkle in her eyes told me she was a pure being of truth and love and purity and as different from the rest of the human race as I am. I had let the silence stretch on a little too much.

'Don't be silly. I never expected- plus, it's nothing really. A token. I just wanted to give something to a person that I like, at Christmas. Please, open it. Or not, no pressure.'

She laughed and continued to carefully undo the bow then peel back the tape, careful not to tear the shiny plastic-coated paper. What she was left with was a plain white box, small enough to fit in one hand. She smiled at me as she opened the box and revealed the present that I had spent an entire day deliberating over, torturing myself even.

'A snow globe!' she sounded surprised. 'Muncaster Castle in a blizzard.' She gave it a shake and looked at me with deep appreciation.

'Oh look,' she pointed over our heads to the decorations hanging over our booth. 'Mistletoe…'

I looked up and without warning she kissed me. It took me a microsecond to realise what was going on and when I did, I reciprocated and felt the bounds of trepidation peeling away. I knew in that moment that this woman was the most precious thing I had ever encountered in my many years. I knew that I could love her. I think I already did.

'Where have you been all my life, Mister...' she trailed, that slight creasing on her forehead, again only adding to her beauty.

'Game, Henry Game,' I offered, my lips still tingling from where she had kissed me. 'And I was just thinking the exact same thing, Helen...?'

She laughed and placed the globe between us, the whirling snow settling around the castle and miniature castle-stocks.

'Oh no, it's just Helen. I don't carry a family name, not anymore. The Wayside family is all I need these days.'

She loved everything and had endless patience and compassion. I wondered at her often and for hours on end. She revealed to me that she had been drifting too. Been all over the country before coming across The Wayside, and it was very generous of the landlord to give her a job with boarding. She wanted for nothing other than simplicity and happiness. So naturally I vowed to give her everything and more. Eventually she told me that she had run away from her home but did not offer to tell me where that might have been, nor for what reason. I suppose fear stopped her from telling me more. The same fear kept me from insisting she told me.

Yet, and for all her qualities, I must say that your mother held no sense of danger. Absolutely none. She was like a child in that respect. Honestly, it was as equally infuriating as it was endearing. I think out of my own fears I tried to toughen her up, make her see the darkness around her, realise that evil nestled within everyone, especially me, but she refused to see the ugliness of my scars — mental and physical. She couldn't even if she wanted to. I regret that I tried to bring her down to my level now. As of course, angels do not need boots, not when they don't get their feet dirty.

* * *

It was perhaps just over a year later and our lives, our worlds, seemed complete and I believed that my past was forever behind me.

I had never been so happy. I didn't think it was even possible, if I'm honest. I thought of Francis and of Father Game and I wondered how my life might have been different if it wasn't for the events that had passed, but grateful for it all as I had met Helen.

In the first few weeks and months after we had left The Wayside, I remember thinking how everything was destined to come crashing down at any moment, forcing me to wake up from my dreaming like the desperate fool I would always be. But the persistent love and optimism of your mother had started to change me. Perhaps I was deserving of a happy life. Maybe this was my path now, and that having a child would see the next chapter of my life and close the book on the old ways once and for all.

We had squirrelled away into a beautiful little cottage, right on the shores of Coniston Water. I paid for the property through a private transaction, at almost twice the market value to ensure the deal was brokered anonymously and as discreetly as possible. We had four chickens, a rooster of our own, and some sheep. We even had a silly old goat that was completely insane. I named him Claruc, and often I would see him licking up the chicken poop. Dirty bugger.

One sunny morning, following an early cold spike in the weather, I left your mother in bed to go into Ravenglass and gather more supplies in preparation for your arrival. Shopping wasn't so scary once I had practised it a few times.

Helen was two weeks over term and not coping well. I tried everything I could to make her comfortable. My paranoia stopped her from going to a proper hospital. Instead she made arrangements to see an old family friend that she said she trusted. I still didn't feel easy about any of it.

When I arrived home, the front door was sitting ajar. The cold spread down my arms the moment I saw it. I burst in and immediately noticed her coat absent from the rack along with her new boots. In the kitchen her teacup was cleaned out and turned upside down on the draining board. The back stable-door locked, and everything looked like it had been professionally cleaned.

I shouted out to her but already knew the house was empty. My panic dashed into critical and I ran upstairs to check our bedroom, your mother's wardrobe. Mostly empty. All of the winter clothes missing and the snow globe from her bedside cabinet gone too.

She had left me, clearly. I was gone little more than two hours. I convinced myself that her disappearance was somehow connected to my past. Shock and fear metamorphized into rage as I relived all the times that I had warned her about trusting people. I had told her again and again and again and again and again until I was blue in the face.

But still she had trusted me. I should have protected her, always. That was my duty. I assumed she was abducted, but when I later turned the house upside down and discovered a note... it was undoubtedly Helen's handwriting. The heat of my fury extinguished like lava falling into the ocean. It read:

Henry,

They found me. All I can do now is run, I believe that if I lead them away, they won't come back for you, either of you, but regardless you must not ever return to this house, especially not with our child.

You will have no-doubt torn the house apart to find this note, but I couldn't risk leaving it where others may have found it.

By the time you read this I will have left our precious son, Francis Game, for you at Mary Hewetson Cottage Hospital, Keswick.

Ask for Dr Isaac Nane. He'll be expecting you.

I am scheduled for a caesarean procedure this morning. From there I will need to disappear. I wish I could explain.

I told the Dr that you would collect Francis this afternoon. I promised him a payment that I will need you to pay, give the good doctor whatever he needs, now and always he is a trusted friend to our family. Without him, both Francis and I would surely have not survived the uniqueness of our pregnancy — I think you know what I am talking about.

Tell our baby that I love him with all my heart. Tell him that I died shortly after childbirth. It will be easier that way.

Thank you for showing me how to love and be loved, how to be happy, how to fight, how to hope again. You are the only one for me in this life, it was always going to be you. I am so happy that I found you and have been able to give you a son. Take care of each other for as long as you can, I will be in your hearts.

Love you until the well runs dry.

Thank you for the memories.

Forever, your Helen.

Static. White noise within a soul consuming black hole birthed within my chest. I let the note fall to the floor amongst the wreck of my shattered heart. Something, someone, had taken her from me, and with it, the person I had become was gone too. The old me, the bastard, the monster, was clawing his way back and in total control.

This was the only thing I had ever known: vengeance, righting a wrong, violence and bloodshed. The person I had become around your mother was nothing more than a veneer, a memory, and also a failure. Trying to be happy and a 'good' person had done nothing but let us both down.

I allowed the anger to consume me in an attempt to flood the fires of anguish that were desolating my heart. Only fury and pure revenge could overpower the void that is left when love becomes lost.

I searched for hours in the surrounding areas, in the huddle of trees that flanked our cottage from our neighbours. I found multiple footprints, snagged branches and what looked like drag marks, scrapes through the mud that could've been anything. And in all my rage I had never felt so afraid. My fear was of claiming you and how my past would eventually take you too if I let it, and I had.

Having a family had made me vulnerable. Love leads to weakness. I couldn't see a way through the hurt. I had to give you the safest opportunity to grow, innocently, normally. You deserved better than me. That was when I knew the only way to ensure your safety was to send you as far away from my circle as possible, and I could never know where you would be sent to grow.

For years I tried to find her. For years I only prolonged the agony. I embraced the darkest parts of myself in order to fuel the inferno of injustice that propelled my search.

Acceptance finally came when it seemed I had come full

circle. But by this stage you were an adult. The good man that I had convinced myself I was capable of being was long and since consumed and forgotten about. Not even the shadow of memory in my recollection.

Yet despite my failings, I maintain that keeping you for myself would've been a sin even beyond my darkest capabilities. I am sorry for what you have had to go through alone. I am. I am also sorry for everything else, but sorry is only a word after all. I trust that you see the action of what I must do as the greatest sign of my love and quest for your forgiveness

Subtropolis Bonfires. (L. S.).

Ian marched a lengthy stride ahead. Arms swinging. Back straight. Head high.

I, on the other hand, hobbled and cursed through snot and healing wounds, physical and emotional, I hesitate to say, falling further and further behind him, deeper and deeper into the great shadow of the pyramid before us; its pinnacle blocking out the warm glow from the electric suns high above.

The temperature dropped dramatically in the shade. In shadow breath plumed; under the whitewash lights, skin twinkled with fresh sweat. The constant cooling and warming effect were a thing that nobody else seemed to be paying any attention to. I felt like I was in a microwave that had a freezing option, and some bastard was turning the dial one way then the other.

Ian arrived at our destination before I could catch up. I fantasised about poking out one of his eyeballs as I sucked it in and crossed the final distance, across yet another pristine courtyard of white pavers. The path I trailed after had skirted around the edges of an elaborate water fountain that was shining, bare golden tree. Water trickled out of the tips of the branches and into a clear pool covering a mosaic tile pattern beneath.

Meanwhile, Ian watched my efforts to catch up, smiling at me from upon his high horse, one hand flat against the black shiny stone base that projected the monstrous pyramid up and away into the sub-zone stratosphere, his other hanging limp by his side. I hoped that he was suffering.

'This is where the magic happens, *Lord Game.*'

He looked up toward the glimmering black peak. Dozens of the windows lining the walls were in the midst of rotation. It reminded me of a crow ruffling its feathers. And as far as architecture and construction engineering, it was impressive, I must admit. I fought down the urge to ask questions, even though I wondered if the panel rotation was for ventilation. A question that I was never going to give him the satisfaction of asking.

'Yep, this is where the real decisions are made. The world over I mean, of course. We're still excavating, but we are now proud to boast that there is at least one terminal in each and every one of the great continents – except Antarctica, but, of course…' he finished his sentence with a shrug and pushed open the etched golden door, square and compasses of freemasonry framed a gothic "G" in the centre of the panel.

'So, hang on a minute,' I had to ask, one foot over the threshold. 'This place-'

'Atlantis,' Ian corrected, being the sanctimonious cunt that he is.

'*Atlantis*,' I wanted to smash his smiling face with a shovel, 'it spans around the world, like, inside the earth, beneath the ground?' This I found hard to believe.

'Well of course not, silly! That would be physically improbable, not mention, counterproductive. Just think about it: excavating the entire mass area in relation to the surface above. We would end up filling it all back in with supportive frames, not to mention the sheer number of columns and braces – the additional excavation for the astronomical sum of piers and footings. There would be absolutely no benefit.' He switched arms on the door he still held open for me. 'No, I said we have terminals, or, in layman's terms: access points.'

I thought about stabbing him again, but this time in his throat, and I probably would have done if I still had my blade.

The wound area on my leg was beginning to tingle and itch. It was in the pleasure/pain phase of regeneration. Soon I would be back to full strength. I didn't find the idea of repeating the process of injury appealing. However, I did find great pleasure in fantasising ways of inflicting pain on the snake that is my brother.

'Listen, Henry, just relax. *We* are not your enemy—'

'Go and get my book, and also, I'll be needing my blade back too, dickhead.' I barged past him and into a well-lit corridor with tiled floors and dropped ceilings. It was all I could do not to head-but him on my way past.

Ian let the door swing shut, patting me on the shoulder as I passed him. 'All in good time. I have much to show you. You simply must see what we have built. It is a part of your heritage too, after all.'

I followed him to another elevator a couple of hundred yards in. We entered and he pressed the top floor: number 9. Again, no music. A couple of moments later and the door slid away to a wastefully furnished space that had clear glass walls on all four raking angled sides.

Through the glass walls I could see for miles in every direction. I noted back from where we had come: the lift mechanics and track frame stretching from the ground and up beyond the lights hanging from the rock ceiling. I wondered how deep we were and shivered, being so deep into the earth felt wrong. Like I was too close to Hell, if such a place once existed. The depths of the earth were sure to hold many wonders and secrets.

As we exited the lift, I immediately noticed the most peculiar placement of lecterns and chairs. The lecterns were set out in a complete circle and at equal distances, the woodwork carved out as double-headed eagle tabernacles, and each one standing around five-feet tall. Open books lay on the backs of spread wings. I counted thirteen of them in the circle and my zealot alarm was going ballistic in my head. The only thing this place was missing now was robes and sacrifices of the flesh.

The floor itself was a deep mahogany parquet. The area around the lecterns and positioned seats inlaid with fine golden patterns and bands, circles forming with lines that overlapped and crossed at every angle. The chairs were bolted down, each being centralised within its own circle. Every seat faced inward, toward the centre of the design. Lines connected everything.

I had seen this pattern before on the computer screen back at the heart attack café that was stuck in the 90s. I reckoned the whole set up was some sort of sadistic board game for sure. The chairs were clearly the positions of the would-be players. I saw no dice, but still it was some full-on freaky shit that I wanted no part of.

We passed the elephant in the room without comment and on toward the desk, deciding that what happens in underground secret cities is probably not worth pondering over.

Against the far end, and finally some semblance of normality, was an old-fashioned writing desk, behind which offered a great view of the obelisk and panoramic of the city at three-hundred and sixty degrees.

Ian pulled back the chair on the business end of the desk but did not sit.

'Top of the totem pole, Henry. I'd ask you to sit, but...' he looked over my shoulder at the centre piece, 'well, there are no spare chairs.'

Finally, he sat down and leaned back on his seat, that easy smile of his shining out. 'You made it. Tell me, how does it feel after all these centuries of struggle?'

I looked around, giving my very best appraisal face. I even ran a finger across the polished surface of the black writing desk. 'Not bad, if you like sadomasochism, or whatever the fuck that kinky shit is behind me.'

'My ignorant brother. You do not know what you look upon: this, in here, is the machine that runs it all. The device that turns the world to see the sun each morning; the place where prayers are received and answered and ignored.'

'All I see is a lonely desk, and maybe musical chairs or, well, you know, the type reserved for old and incestuous money, like you sick and bizarre cunts.'

Ian laughed and stood from his seat to perch on the edge of the writing desk. 'My point precisely. From here, the world's wars are declared, executed and ended. Cultures demonised and ascended. Governments instructed; and all of them, every last one of them, die, happily fulfilled in their ignorance to the real agenda. Life is a code of our creation.

'Tell me, how do you suppose that the god-forsaken Vatican could ever hope to assassinate me, when we created their regurgitated, recycled religion? And not just that one either, *we* created them all: Judaism, Islam, Hinduism, Taoism, Buddhism, Sikhism, Asatru, Wicca; the polytheistic worshipping of ancient Egypt, Greece, Mesopotamia… but of course, there were many more of *us* back then.'

We were back on to the subject of his wellbeing from a would-be assassination, it seemed. But truthfully, I was never really concerned for his safety. And especially not after I had realised that this wasn't the first time we had met.

Ian was a fucking snake – is a fucking snake – and he deserves everything that comes his way. And I mean that. But damn it if I didn't feel dwarfed by his achievements. In less than an hour he had made my five centuries of frolicking look like child's-play. I mean, I'd never built a city before…never created a secret underground organisation that apparently runs the whole world. I'd joined one once, but…

I shrugged. 'It's not my problem, Ian. I couldn't give a shit what you do. But you know as well as I do that you and I are not invincible.'

I strolled over to one of the tabernacles and glanced down the opened page, noting the symbols that seemed both familiar and alien at the same time. This seemed to be the way with powered inscriptions. Everything is information, and information is represented by symbols that we assign meaning to. We all have the understanding deep within us. A couple of the stands were vacant of reading material, I noticed.

'And that reminds me, where's my dagger?'

'Safe-enough. You'll get it when I decide you're not going to try to attack me again.'

Ian set himself down behind the desk again and opened a drawer. He was clearly enjoying himself.

'Do you think we will live forever?' I asked the question that I had always kept inside my heart and fears, all the while still fingering down the same page of a book that seemed to be more concerned with the eco-system than anything actually interesting.

'Are you afraid to die?' He laughed as he placed a package on the desk.

I knew what it was straightaway. I sensed it was mine. Made for me. I knew this as well as I know my own cock and balls. My book. It held the key to unlocking my power. I had learned of its potential many years earlier. I looked around and wondered if Ian had a book of his own.

Forgetting the manuscript on the wings of the mutant eagles, I approached the desk and reached out for it when I noticed a symbol beneath the gaze on the writing desk. I took a moment to study the image further: two horse riders, each one sporting shields painted with the blood-red cross of St George. They rode with swords drawn, facing in opposite directions. Fuck if I didn't recognise what I was looking at. It took me a moment or two – a lot had happened in the last four-hundred and eight years or so.

I moved on to my book and Ian watched as I gathered the package and peeled back the cloth. Meanwhile my mind was reaching through my earliest memories like a junkie through a friend's medicine cabinet.

The familiar bronze symbols that had been burnt across the leather jacket of my book spoke to me. I recognised it straight away as my long-lost companion. I wanted to smell it; to crack open the pages and skim through it again, but something big was bothering me about that symbol on his desk and I just couldn't let it go.

I looked back down, my fingers tracing across the lacquer for another moment or two until lightning struck and I finally remembered. But the question was whether or not Ian knew what it meant to me.

The grin on his face supported my road of thought as he stood and turned to look out over the vast dystopia of his sub-tropolis. I tucked the book into the inside of my soiled dinner jacket and breathed deep. The fire within growing.

'When word arrived that you were coming, I went to see the Ruling Council. I didn't know how they would react. You have created quite the blaze through history – sometimes even defying our intentions. But in your defence, you knew not whom you were opposed to, and that was your saving grace. It's ironic if you ask me. The doctor decided to take a chance on you-'

'Humour me...' I said, trying to hide my blistering rage, and clearly not listening to a word he was saying.

Ian turned toward me again, frowning.

'How long have you known about...me?' I asked as he hesitated, my eyes not leaving the insignia on his desk.

He snorted and cocked his head. 'That again? I thought we'd established that this evening isn't the first time we've-'

'Earlier, you called me by a name.' I looked him in the eye.

'Yes, and you have many names. Most amusing. Monster. Ripper-'

'No, one specific name.'

He hesitated. Eyes deadpan. He was thinking. It was an act, and I saw the veneer peeling. I know fear, know it better than I know my own teeth.

'Pope Slayer, you said.' I stepped forward and past the desk.

Ian took half a step back before seeming to remember himself. He watched me like a shark might watch a crocodile on the waves overhead.

'You are the legend, the living legend. The man maketh the myth, and so on.' He backed up a step and stood tall, defiant, an attempt to re-shift the sliding balance of power.

'Where are you going with this nonsense? Didn't you hear me? The doctor has given you permission to be inducted.' His words rushed out as I brought myself within arms' reach.

'Fucking inducted?' I poured as much venom into my words as possible.

He was cornered now, and he made a move, steadying his footing and within a blink of an eye he'd produced a dagger much like my own *Abatu,* but longer. Symbols down the glimmer of the sharpest, darkest, edge of metal you could never imagine.

He tossed the dagger; from one hand to the other, catching it by the modified handle with the ease of practice. His arm still hurt him; I took a miniscule of satisfaction in that apparent fact.

'Pope Slayer, though… I've not heard that one since before my running with them bastard Iroquois cunts. I figured, what with you being the Illuminati and all that, you knew things, but then I see this.' I tapped a finger against the varnished desktop. 'This helps make sense of a few things.'

Ian looked down, a heavy frown troubling his flawless face. I took another step forward. Close enough to see the calculation behind his eyes as he readied against what was coming, the business end of the dagger toward my general direction.

'Now listen Henry, I already told you, we are not your enemy. Mirabilis has given you the opportunity of a-'

The sole of my scuffed winklepicker cut him off mid-sentence, striking him square in the diaphragm whilst I hammered my fist down onto his good hand and relieved him of the weapon.

He looked up, his torso hurtling toward the glass panel behind him, microseconds snailing between us like sap happens upon the mosquito. But, bound to the physics of this universe, human or otherwise, my action had decided his immediate future and he was going through the fucking glass wall. And although the surprise on his face seemed quite genuine, for once, it brought me no satisfaction as my revelation had turned my convictions into contempt and anger.

The symbol was the very same one upon the ring of the guardsman who'd slain Father Game. It was the symbol of the Knights Templar. And that name: "Doctor Mirabilis", I'd definitely heard it before, but I didn't have time to trace old memories any longer.

Ian had taunted me, deceived me, manipulated, and I was certain I hated him, but even as I possessed the weapon to execute him, something other than a fury had stepped in to snuff my rage. Perhaps it was mercy that initiated the kick that sent him flailing backward, out of the wall he was so fond of looking from.

I watched his body streak through the air in a crescendo of broken glass until he impacted with the cut-stone ground, hundreds of feet below. From where I stood, he looked a little like a snow angel. His fancy fitted suit decorated with glitter; his halo a red-blue crimson in the hum of white light. He wasn't getting up, at least not anytime soon.

Dozens of nondescript faces looked up to the top of the pyramid where I stood, and after a few seconds, their shouts of panic reached me and brought a familiar smile to my lips. Grief and anger did not mix well together at all – but satisfaction and anger, well, that was a cocktail that I was most fond of.

I waved down at them and shouted that I'd be down there in a minute. It really was a great view. Seconds later and harsh smoke found my nostrils, breaking me out of my incessant grinning. I looked down and realised the dagger was blistering the lacquer from the flooring. I picked it up and lay the blade to the desk. The varnish bubbled and hissed and there was plenty of smoke, but it did not strike into flame.

An alarm like an air-raid siren set off, the echo bouncing from the buildings to return to me in a crackle. I strode to the devil-birds and lay waste to the open manuscripts, one-by-one, until each and every one of them shrieked in blue-fire, but not mine. No, I had my book with me and safe. It was most definitely a welcomed surprise to be back in possession of it. I thought it was lost forever.

Calm as you like I pressed the elevator button and hesitated a moment when the door opened, belatedly I remembered who Dr Mirabilis was – only I had presumed he had died almost five-hundred years since.

I recollected that when I last saw him he was over the shoulder of Henry VIII, guardian and pet magician. In fact, he was the one who identified the ring as belonging to the Knights Templar…

Hundreds of years had passed, and my journey had taken me, at times dismembered in several pieces, to be scattered amongst conspiracies and tall tales, amongst the four corners of the world and beyond. I had been the greatest evil, the hero of the tale, the ruthless and selfish mercenary, had been resurrected from a dormant state and sent to assassinate the opposition of the capitalist world, and then some. I had been raped by multiple extra-dimensional consciousness and held lengthy conversations with intelligent beings of no physical matter or tangible substance. To sum it all up though: half a millennium of shit had happened, and mostly to me. Safe to say that my memory was not quite the sharp tack it once was, until I stepped on it, and in the rush of pain I remembered it all.

I remembered something else about the one they called 'Doctor Marvellous', a thought that made my bones chill. Rumours of the time claimed he was the master of death. Not only was his unnaturally long-life evidence of this, but also, he had performed many a ritual for the wealthy and powerful families of old.

They used to whisper that he was, or is, a Necromancer. But more specifically that he could return anyone back to life and also trap and control the decaying corpses like a puppeteer. If ever there was a man not to be provoked, it was him. But I was never one for taking advice, especially when that advice was my own.

The lift doors closed again, and I pressed the button to open them. I needed another minute. I had just realised that it was totally plausible that the whole fucking 'Pope Debacle', the multi-national-corpse-strewn-episode, my overcast day, every-thing, had been a set-up.

I was so mad I had a little laugh and squeezed Ian's blade tighter than a duck's arsehole in white waters. Ian had men-tioned something about a council. I decided that this was the place to start. Allowing the doors to shut, I pressed "G". I needed to know how much they knew about my life and those for whom I cared about.

I stepped out of the pyramid and stood still for a moment whilst the bees busied in every direction. Alarms whirred and buzzed in distraction. Ian was gone too; all that remained of him was a couple of pints of oily-gloop and glass.

Smoke plumed from the top of the pyramid and was efficiently being extracted in a tornado of light. It really was a beautiful night and the fireworks were just getting started.

This Way, That Way, Forwards and Backwards. Autumn, 1553.

'Woooooo!' The air snatched from my lungs as the cold Irish Sea slapped me pink and washed away the old injustices that I carried with me.

My footing and positioning beneath the bowsprit was precarious at best, and my chances of slipping into the dark blue increased with each fresh wave that rose up valiantly to smash itself against the staunch hull of my beloved, beautiful ship – but my god, I was enjoying myself and relishing the experience of life without a score to settle or revenge to be had. That was until I heard Skelton's snivelling approach from up on the forecastle, for what seemed like the tenth time that morning already.

He'd been approaching, lingering, then turning away and leaving, only to return and linger again. It was a process on repeat for the best part of thirty minutes; I could smell his hesitation and it was distracting me from my enjoyment, but as another wave obliterated itself against the hardwood and gave my pink, raw chest another heavy coating, I tried my best to ignore the ignoramus.

'Cap'in,' he peered down at me from above the bow, 'crew's growin' a bit rowdy.'

Another wave doused me and stole my breath before I could congratulate him on finding his balls. I continued to peer forth from my perilous position beneath the beak of the ship and away toward new undertakings.

'They wanna know when all these adventures 'll be comin' nythi' that ye' promised?' He was growing in confidence, and so too was the volume of his open challenge. 'All th' gold, th' tropical pussy, th' *'adventures'*, and wha'ever else ye' swore t' deliver.'

I knew this moment was coming, but didn't expect it to be this soon, barely half-way through our first day. It was time to start taking the business of sailing seriously. And although I didn't need any more gold, my men clearly did. They also needed tropical pussy too, and not necessarily in that order.

The business of queen making had seen me obesely compensated. So much so in fact, that before I set forth on my great adventure upon the seven seas, I needed to stash my bounty, including my bone-bladed dagger, in the safest place I knew: the derelict crypts of St Oswald's.

I returned to the village of Horton in Ribblesdale aback the finest horse that money could buy, and also tethering at a short leash, the second finest horse that money could buy. My bounty was so great that I needed another mule to cart it away with me in the dead of night, and the royal stables housed only the best, of course.

The new Queen of England had been quick to offer me a "deposit-safe" in a new establishment that she said was touted as the "Royal Exchange". But whilst plans were finalised and premises secured, she would happily keep my gold safe in her personal vaults.

I declined, and then she offered her personal armed carriage, with escort, to "deposit my wealth" wherever I saw fit. But again, I declined with a shake of my head and made private arrangements to take care of my business in the dark hours.

Overcast skies welcomed me back and I noticed the tavern had closed its doors, but that was a sign of the times. I nudged open the main door of the abbey and was surprised to see a new monk lingering within the whale bone carcass that housed my childhood memories.

I could smell the mead before he spoke, he was obscenely drunk. For a moment I thought this was the new Juan and reached for my blade but when he saw me, he threw his arms in the air in celebration, his eyes bright within the soot and shadow of his face.

He shouted my name in a slur like we were old friends, but I couldn't say the same in return. He said that The Order had sent him, and he had waited almost six weeks for me, returning each day. Said the locals had told him that I'd been carted away by the Royal Guard, but he knew I would return, that he had something he needed to give me. Something precious. Something very important. He darted away to immediately go and fetch it. Said I shouldn't leave before he returned to give me what was rightfully mine.

I admit that I was intrigued by his suspenseful energy, but I had business to take care of and as soon as the drunken monk was out of the door, I set to work on prizing the nails loose from the base of the altar.

After a few minutes I had pried enough room to get my fingers underneath and I lifted the ornate box enough to slide it to one side. The crypts had always been the worst kept secret at the abbey, and as the stale air wafted from the open stone cut stairwell down into the bowels of the under-abbey, I was suddenly filled with a memory of when Francis came to get me from my rooms one stormy, hot, summer's night.

Little Franky held a finger to his lips as he entered my chambers and I had lain awake. Without a word I followed him, and we crept to the main hall and saw the altar had been moved, we saw a dark and intimidating hole in the stone floor that pulled us toward it and downwards and beneath the abbey.

After a few minutes we risked moving closer. Francis didn't want to go down the hole. He shook his head; his eyes were wide and glistening, but I was too curious not to see what was down there.

Francis held his breath as I stepped in and as my foot hit the first step, the outrage of Father Game echoed, almost scaring the skin off our bony frames, and we ran back to our chambers to hide beneath the safety of our blankets.

Of course, the next day Father explained to me that the basement area was a crypt and had long ago been used for the burial of ancient important people. He said that the skeletons down there were mostly Norman invaders and that the most famous Norman of all, Duke Rollo, was the first to be placed at rest down there.

As I reached the bottom step I peered through the dusty and stale air to the end of the narrow corridor. The crypts were much smaller than I had imagined, and I could touch both walls with my arms outstretched. Along the walls were dozens of narrow pigeonholes containing dust, skeletons and decomposing iron. At the end of the corridor, however, was a very fine burial chamber that had been cut from a bright white stone and held only one corpse. The Nordic markings around the surround told me that if Rollo was down here, then this was probably his.

I decided that Rollo had hogged the space for entirely too long and I pulled out as much of his dust and bones as I could hold and stuffed it all into one of the other generic holes along the wall. My treasure laden saddle packs quickly filled the space left by Rollo and the remainder of the gold, along with my dagger, I left piled neatly at the very end of the corridor, at the foot of Rollo's burial hole. I climbed out and re-fixed the altar into place.

There was still no sign of the inebriated monk and I had been there for perhaps an hour already, maybe less. I waited for another few minutes but could not shake off the growing feeling of foolishness. I figured that the new queen would be wondering where I had gotten to, and I didn't want my ship to leave without me, so I thrashed the queen's finest horse to within an inch of his life to make London in good time.

I gulped in a ragged breath as another ice-cold wave sprayed me. Balancing upon the cusp of oblivion is an addiction I have never been able to shake. Skelton hawked up above me and spat into the waves. I could hear his impatience and figured that it was time to get a hold of my men.

I swivelled about and shimmed back up the bowsprit to the dragon figurehead that spurred out from the outer most point of the forecastle. I balanced along the long beam and vaulted up and over the handrail to stand besides First Mate Skelton.

Tricks watched my balancing act from her usual position at the base of the foremast with very little interest. I still did not care for cats, no-matter how big their eyes may be. Cats had a way of seeing through people, and I didn't have the patience to be analysed by a fucking animal, not even if they did look adorable when they wash their own faces with the sides of their paws...

Skelton adopted a look of mock-outrage on his bearded, haggard face. 'Cap'in, do ye' wanna feckin' catch ye' death?'

He had a disgusting habit of biting his bottom lip. The wound was starting to ooze, but he bit it anyway, tongued the puss and looked on, demanding to know the truth of my intent.

He was making a power play, and with Tricks suddenly deciding to rub along his wooden shin, it looked like he had the support of the entire ship.

These men didn't know me. I'd requested it that way, which was why I chose a boat that had been out at sea the longest. My return to the fold had been swift and meteoric. I reckoned that any sailor who'd been at sea for the previous three months would not have heard anything of me. To these men, I'd still be assigned to stories and legends. I wanted a fresh start and to be treated like anyone else, under such circumstances.

'Maybe I do.' I responded, looking him deep in the eye and throwing the cat a dirty look.

Truth is, after asking for anonymity, I realised that I didn't like being treated like everyone else. Especially not when I was the subject of disrespect, and mutiny.

'And remind me again why I made a slug like you my first mate?' With wet feet I slapped past him as I approached the aft of the forecastle, resisting the urge to kick Tricks overboard on my way.

I leant over the handrail to address my men, two dozen of them squandering on the main deck, as expected, doing much of nothing and getting paid for the pleasure of it.

'Who's ready for adventure?' I exclaimed in my half-naked magnificence. It seemed none of them were in a participating mood, however, they looked up at me with contempt upon unkempt faces.

Their response was spitting on the deck. After a negative silence I heard a tuneless whistling somewhere down below. I peered over the rail even further and realised it was Claruc, sprawled and virtually catatonic between two empty barrels, his flask never far from his lips. The sun winked from his smooth scalp.

I cleared my throat and repeated the challenge, 'WHO'S FUCKING READY FOR ADVENTURE?'

'Feckin' heard yer first time, *Captain*. Now just fuck off will yer?' A brave sailor stepped forward, I couldn't remember his name, so I renamed him Fuckbag.

A sniffle from behind me, Skelton again. I turned on him. 'And what are you so pleased about?'

'Me? No-no, not me.' His words carried louder than normal.

He bit his lower lip again and pulled hairs from his chin in small clumps. He was thinking.

I folded my arms, turning my back on the men below and leant against the deck rail whilst Skelton continued to gather his balls.

'Well, seems to me, *Cap'in,*' Skelton began to a chorus of chuckling from the squibs.

He pulled another small clump from his beard, cleared his fingers then fished for another. 'P'raps ye'd be best served disembarkin' with ye' friend down there, drownin' in th' barrels.' He nudged his head toward the hiccupping egg-shaped pile beneath us. 'When we get t' Ireland, of course. I mean, no hard feelin's *Cap'in*, eh? Some o' us are just not meant fo' th' water.

'But look on th' bright side, I'm sure our new queen will soften your, ahhh, transitions back in t' court an' such.' He spat a wad of puss over the side of the ship, again.

I let him finish. I almost started laughing but managed to control myself and settled for a stretching smile. Normally he would have been picking up his teeth before his first dramatic pause. But I had to remember that these men didn't know anything about me. And neither did he have many teeth left.

The jeers had settled down on the main deck. I spared a long glance to each of the men, bathing them in the brilliance of my amusement. They looked happy enough. Confidence in numbers, I reckoned.

Claruc started snoring again. One of the men, it could have been the one who had the nerve to tell me to fuck off, turned and hoisted the mop bucket ready to throw at the sleeping Irishman, except he wasn't sleeping anymore, and as he turned around to launch, he stumbled backwards in shock and slipped on his arse, the bucket falling nicely over his head. And suddenly the crew weren't laughing at all, only I was.

Claruc had somehow closed the distance between them in no more than two seconds and nor did he act the drunken fool anymore. In fact, and I don't say this lightly, but the big bastard looked frightening.

The dozen or so crew members peered up at him with new-found fear, waiting for him to speak as he looked down at them from his full height, not quite so oval anymore: a mountain amongst anthills.

I clapped and casually leapt over the balcony, falling a good eighteen feet to land softly on my bare feet. This seemed to scare the men more than Claruc's murderous alter ego had.

Half-naked and soaked, I walked over to Claruc and slapped him on the shoulder before turning on the crew. 'Where is the brave cunt who told me to fuck off then?'

Fingers quickly pointed to the soapy fellow with an empty bucket on his lap.

I smiled. It wasn't a nice smile. 'You, get up.'

I looked around to address the whole crew as the soapy sailor slipped to his feet. 'From this moment on, sailor Fuck-bag is now in Claruc's service. And he will depart our company upon reaching Ireland, penniless. He will continue to serve upon Claruc, until Claruc decides to release him.'

The crew drew deathly silent and still. Sailor Fuckbag looked on with wide eyes, shaking his head in a wordless protest.

I closed the distance between us and spoke in a low voice. 'The alternative is to jump overboard, right now. Take your chance at a long cold swim.'

Fuckbag looked around and found no friends. Even Skelton avoided his desperate eyes. Meanwhile Claruc had wandered away, back to his barrels in the shadow of the forecastle, chugging deeply on his flask.

'Decide now.' I was still inches away from Fuckbag's sheet white face.

Without another word, he scurried off after Claruc and hovered besides him awkwardly.

I suppressed a smile as I turned on the remainder of the crew. 'The rest of you, well, after Ireland, should you wish to stay aboard, can remain so with me as your captain. I go west and in search of discovery.'

They didn't look convinced, but I was never one held back by fear. I stepped through the curve of men toward the quarterdeck, my back to them and pointed over to the starboard side, not sure that it was anywhere near the right direction, but still I continued with my speech: 'Now, who's ready to see the New World?'

'Yeargh!' Their response meagre at best, but it was a scurvy ridden group.

I took it as a victory. Considering the contempt harboured since our departure, a reasonable man might be very happy with the change in social climate.

'Well fucking ship-shape then you pod of wriggling crab-dicks!' I encouraged the bunch of useless cunts.

Claruc was bedded in his corner, flask upended in his bleary face. Meanwhile, Fuckbag slowly shook his head as he looked down at his wet shirt, still stationed besides the hiccupping Irishman. His wrung-out hands suggested maximum un-comfortableness with his new assignment and that made me happy.

Skelton sensibly performed an echo of a whispered bow as I reached the top of the steps and climbed back to the forecastle. It wasn't the boot licking act of contrition that I'd hoped for, but I appreciated it all the same. And besides, Skelton's joints had almost completely calcified.

'After Ireland we go west. I want to see what this New World is all about. What do you say?' I looked down and almost kicked out as I noticed Tricks rubbing herself up against my shin, her tail wrapping about my calf.

'Aye Cap'in, aye, lads 'll be glad o' it.'

'Aye they will.' I bent over to scratch behind her ear and she started purring. I found it calming. 'And you, do you want to see this new world too, as first mate?'

Skelton looked up at me and spread a cracked smile. His lip was positively infected. 'Aye, Cap'in. I'll be glad o' that an' all.'

* * *

'Hold up,' I pointed to the tray of food in the approaching sailor's hands, 'Taffy, if that is salted horsemeat and hardtack, with that god-awful cat piss cider-'

He stopped in his tracks, tray still in hand, waiting by the threshold of my quarters.

I continued, 'for our main evening meal, again...well, you'd be best throwing that, along with your sheep-shagging body, over the fucking rail and allowing the sheep of the west to sleep easily!'

Taffy looked down at the plate then back at me before hobbling into my room, adjusting his balance with the sway of the ocean. He slammed the tray of salted horsemeat and hardtack on the table before me like he was dropping a bucket of shit from the poop deck.

My empty stomach gnarled, and in spite of protests my hands wasted no time in breaking the biscuit and stuffing it into my mouth in pieces too big to chew decently. It doesn't matter what you eat when the hunger has you – it tastes fantastic.

'Aye Cap'in. How about I fetch ye' a menu fo' t'morra's scoff when I fetch yer fuckin' puddin', Cap'in.'

He was joking, of course he was joking. We ate the same shit every day, and the only pudding I had seen since we left the newly crowned mad bitch was Tricks' black pudding toward the aft of the lower deck.

I smiled, 'Why, that would be fucking marvellous, my extraordinarily Welsh friend.'

'I could season it with a good ol' oceanic turd, Cap'in?'

I considered it for a moment then sighed. 'No, thank you, you sheep shagging cunt, I couldn't possibly accept such favours. The men would grow jealous. It would be too much.'

Laughing, Taffy withdrew, but not before bowing so low that his pubic beard brushed the piss stained plank of my deck.

'Ye'll win the hearts o' men wi' steel on these tides,' riddled Claruc, who still hadn't left, nor had he accepted a plate since we'd set sail from the Thames.

Ireland was just over the horizon. Skelton had informed Claruc and I that we would be docking in Cork, to which Claruc started singing "with the dawning of the new day, Claruc would be on his way."

I offered him a repulsive piece of hardtack, which he declined and hiccupped loudly. In truth, I had never seen him eat a single thing, yet he was rather on the morbidly obese side of the scales.

'And what does this bloody puzzle mean to me now, as I settle to feast?'

He laughed a hearty laugh before answering me. 'Wi' the dawning o' the new day-'

'Yeah, Claruc, I know. And it's getting a little old, to be honest. Won't you let me dine in peace?'

'Soft men are won wi' warmth; hard men wi' steel. New tides bring the catalyst. An' wi' the dawning o' the new day, Cap'in Game will be betrayed. Blood will stain the waves.'

He was doing that thing again, the thing that was very confrontational and, to most people, scary. Not to me though, I just turned my back on him and shivered, ploughing another piece of cold horsemeat into my mouth.

Claruc predicted lots of things, true, but I realised that being relatable and striking up friendships was just not in my character. If anything, I judged it to be desperate and sad.

Claruc saw this, I think. Having friends and allies produced nothing but weakness. The man with no friend will never know betrayal. Unless of course he betrays himself…

Honeymoon period was over. It was time to get back to being me: a right old bastard. 'Fuck off, Claruc, I need to rest.'

The bumbling mountain got up and left, slamming my door and saying not another word, not even a whistle. His silence left concern in his wake as I thought about his latest prediction that someone was going to betray me.

* * *

Silence echoed amongst the fluid groans of the ship, her presence intruding upon the flaccid, still night. I dared not sleep. Not now, whilst things were too quiet, and my paranoia was spilling over like an over-filled teapot over the fire.

Claruc had successfully managed to destroy my bliss, my serenity. And in the recess of my own fears I wondered if I was turning soft or merely just losing my wits.

Rome was but a memory now. Maybe nothing more than a dream I once had. And the anger I had sagely cherished, deep within, was not even the ghost of a memory, not any longer. But still I could not rest whilst prophecies and nestled suspicions ran amok in my thoughts.

I remembered a time before all of the treachery and falsities, a time of hot meals, wracking laughter, a time of mucking out, herding sheep, and playing tag with little Franky, our bare feet fleeting across the haemorrhaged boulders that formed the roots of the mountains. Life was simple and pleasant. Hard work favoured the needy and the needy did not go without. Father Game taught me that much before his...

I blinked away that memory. I could feel it uncoiling within me like a filthy robe of rain-laden cloud. Except the heavy clouds wore ominous with threat, but not from the rain as you know it. I knew what hung heavy inside them dark, dark skies: blood looks black at night.

I strained my ears and held my breath as something approached my chambers. From the scuff of wood on wood, I recognised the approach of the one to betray me. I couldn't think of any other reason why one would come knocking me up before the sun was on the rise.

A rapid succession of raps on the door quickly followed by his voice. 'Cap'in, we have a problem. An' it's a bloody big 'un,' Skelton sounded nervous.

I pulled open my cabin door and he immediately lowered his gaze when he realised that I wasn't wearing any clothes, and instead he was focusing on the splintered deck beneath his feet, almost as if he had finally grown some semblance of respect for me. Unless, of course, he hadn't, and was only trying to lead me into a trap, as Claruc had predicted he would.

'Ye' need to come an' see fo' youself, out on th' fo'c'stle, Cap'in.'

This was it. I had made my mind up and Skelton was about to commit his last mistake. 'Lead on then,' I said, and as he turned about and headed toward the main deck, I retrieved my sword, the same one I had pried from the guardsman's dead grip on that consecrated hill, the day that the world became dangerous and real and awful; the day that all of this started for me – and as I followed with the sword gripped tight enough to swing, it seemed that my coming into possession of the weapon was also the same day that brought about the end for First Mate Skelton. I kept the tip sharp and free from divots as I knew what killing a man entailed. Blades needed to be sharp, and so it was.

The deck was deathly still. Something unpleasant hung in the air. I realised the moment I stepped out onto the main deck that it was not a ploy of mutiny. The looks on their faces were not of discontent but of fear.

I followed their muted stares into the dark waves of our starboard side and saw what was keeping the men out of their beds: a carrack, and a bigger one than my own. Distances in the dark can be deceiving, but luckily my eyesight is better than most and I judged that the ship was around four hundred yards off from our anchored position. The men knew as surely as I did that the only warships in the waters of the Irish Sea were that of the Tudor Navy. And without a single word we had all come to the same conclusion that the warship was sent after us for a reason.

I suppose I should have been relieved that the men had not betrayed me but I was somewhat rattled by my deductive theory, eventually coming to the conclusion that that if the Tudor Navy's carrack was in fact sent after us, then it was sent by the commander in chief, ergo the new Queen of England.

The betrayal made no sense and just as I had started formulating a plan to destroy the pursuant battleship, I saw another, fucking enormous, Spanish galleon flanking us from our port side.

I imagined the rolling lawns of Ireland reaching out to me from just beyond the limiting veil of darkness. We all held our breaths as the flanking warships slowly drew closer; we naively hoped the ships would pass us by until Claruc emerged from some dark corner, whistling, belching, and hiccupping with not a care in the world.

For once Claruc was correct in his prediction. I just didn't anticipate that the betrayal would come from Mary. I had served her well and fully, had given her everything she wanted and still the fucking mad bitch had sent her ships to sink me!

I felt more than betrayed: I felt insulted. Claruc continued to whistle as shouts of English and Spanish orders could be heard across the waters all around us.

Skelton leaned in close, whispering. 'Orders, Cap'in?'

I continued to look on across the waters, across the frightened men aboard my company.

'Ye' want me t' assume command?' Skelton whispered even lower, looking me straight in the eye. He still had no idea who I was.

I smiled and looked over to Claruc, who looked to be in a giddy mood. I knew he wasn't drunk, not at all, he was very much like me: he lived to kill. I was still naked, surrounded by frightened sailors, in the middle of autumn, somewhere in the Irish Sea and surrounded by enemies. The mask of sailor Henry fell away as I spoke loud enough for all to hear me.

'Hoist the white flag. Let them aboard. I do not want a single fucking plank of my ship to be damaged by cannon fire!'

Their silence was challenging. Again, it was Skelton who spoke to me but this time he did not make an attempt to lower his voice.

'An' have us surrender? They'll take th' ship an' make feckin' slaves o' us, all o' us. If we're lucky, tha' is. No, we run, surely, we're lighter an' rested?'

I rounded on him. 'Run, fucking run?' It was time they knew who I was. 'And what the fuck makes you think I want to run? And no, I will not let them, or any other cunt, take this ship away from me.'

I stared around the pale faces on the main deck and climbed the short steps up to the quarterdeck.

'And when they board, they will fall where they stand and be fed back to the sea. Tonight, their blood will settle on the seabed, nourish the sand.' My voice carried across the waters, stirring up courage. The men set their mouths tight, fists tight, brows locked.

I walked amongst them. 'Today you get to meet the real captain of this ship. All those who fight for this wood will have a place beside me when this is over. Today we will show them what it means to face death and tell that crazy bitch to fuck off!'

I never intended to make a dramatic speech, but I guess I did anyway, because they were loving it. All of them, even Skelton had brandished a weapon and cheered.

Claruc watched me with level eyes that knew the reality of what I spoke only too well.

I let the storm of my words quieten for a moment, bringing a hush to the men with a raised palm. I had them now. Fear tinged the excitement and brought it all to life as I relayed my simple plans for Skelton and the rest of the men to follow.

* * *

The wind dared not breathe. Not a sneeze, a blink, or a whistle. Even Tricks had disappeared to the lower decks.

The horizontal white and green stripes, topped in the upper left corner by the cross of St. George was significant, even to me. And the lads had served the realm long enough to know a naval battleship when they saw one. I couldn't help but wonder if Queen Mary was aboard the distant carrack, watching me. I more than wondered, in fact, I hoped for it. Give me the opportunity to show her what I do to those who try to double-cross me.

However, what really had the boys white-knuckled right now was the accompanying standards bearing the jagged red X topping the masts of the ridiculously large galleon flanking our port side, holding my ship at a disadvantage from the south.

Whispers of the Armada creaked through the knotted hardwood deck beneath my knees and into my bones. And as I waited, I wondered what business this was to the Spanish-

Skelton nudged me in the ribs to warn of the Spanish's imminent boarding. I was ready. My bonds were all for show, but the dripping red-blue blood from my crooked nose wasn't. I had to make it look convincing. And I had one last look around and realised that Claruc had vanished, again. I hoped he was ready too. I never knew if he was listening to me when I spoke. Only time would tell.

Spanish commands barked across the still water between us as our lads assisted in tying them aboard the port side. They lowered a plank and Skelton rested a long knife in my hand and backed away from me with a kick to my kidneys.

'He's th' one ye' after!' Skelton sounded so convincing that I almost believed that he wished me detained.

'Not yet,' I urged beneath my breath as the crew watched on, my shackles staged abound my legs and wrists, my bleeding head hanging.

A finely dressed Spanish officer stepped aboard with his polished, pointy boots, and his waxed moustache. His face the essence of contempt, like the deck was a pile of shit that he had the misfortune of stepping in.

Suddenly, and very much off script, Claruc reappeared, singing and laughing, belching and being the drunken buffoon that he is. Everyone stopped in their tracks, my crew and the Spanish alike, to assess the whistling and belching oaf as he stumbled back on the main deck like he didn't have a clue what was going on.

Claruc stopped a couple of feet away from the Spanish officer and started to re-cork his flask at a sway although the sea was calmer than a shooting star. The Spaniard dismissed the threat of Claruc with flick of his waxed moustache.

'Me cago en el decimocuarto kilómetro de los cuernos del cornudo de tu padre-Hic!'

I did not understand what Claruc said to the man, but the Spaniard's face began to darken, and he turned away from me, drawing his sword. Naturally Claruc wasted no time in reaching over and twisting his head all the way round, giving him the opportunity to clearly see his own back for the first and last time.

With things developing not quite as per my well-laid plan, I figured it was time to drop the charade and I roared for my men to take up arms as my bonds fell and I sprang forth and into the oncoming tide of angry Spanish, hopeful that my crew were behind me.

The Irish coast must have been close enough to swim, because when I turned around to see how my crew were faring, half of them had deserted us. But not Claruc or steadfast Skelton, nor Taffy, or the African, can't write his name down, it was a series of clicks …oh, and also the guy who once told me to fuck off, yeah, he was still there: his real name was Kevin, or Kelvin, or Calvin, or something like that; my name for him was easier to remember: Fuckbag.

Anyway, so there we stood, we six, and as the dance un-folded we rolled, and slipped, and slashed, and slid. We fought for each other. We had no idea why they were attacking us still, but the confusion only brought a sense of righteousness that spurred on the killing.

The decks of my ship were properly christened with the blood, piss, and shit from the tip of the Armada. Twenty-seven Spanish men watered the planks and washed away the memories of past endeavours, cleaned away the sin that my ship bore prior to my stewardship.

There was a whole domain out there that I had not yet explored. It was a kingdom upon which I could be ruler: The Oceanic Empire, and I would be a hard bastard of a leader, but a fair one, tolerant of differences and opinions, yet not quite so for the deliberately foolish, nor for the opinions and differences that were at odds with my own.

I was expecting the Queen's Observer to board at any moment throughout the slaughter, but it didn't. Mary kept her distance. She fucking knew better. The four remaining Spaniards surrendered as we closed in on them with bloodied glee.

For my first act of mercy, I declared that two of them would be allowed to join my crew, but only after they'd proved themselves worthy of our respect. The test was to pit them against one another to the death.

The whole world knew that the Spanish were good sailors, and I clearly needed more men, but the whole world also knew that the Spanish men were about as tough as wet bread. And not only had I been deserted by half of my crew, I now held two ships to command, and the galleon was a big bastard.

Claruc was whistling amongst the corpses of foreign enemies, looking for a live one. I saw him take a piss on the face of the stiffening Spanish captain before reaching down and lifting him by his shiny shoes and tossing him into the icy blue.

The green and white flag remained at a set distance from us. No canon fire, no signal of intent. After we had cleared all the decks of living enemies, except the Spanish ship cat, we decided to give the Royal Observer one last show, and on my command, we each bent over and presented Her Majesty with a rounded display of our bloodied arses. Moments later the Royal Observer pulled anchor and returned to Liverpool docks, tails tucked, and we cheered.

I needed more men and the greenery of Ireland was within reaching distance. Plus, I would be hard pressed to find a land of people who hated the English monarchy nearly as much as I did. Ask and ye shall receive, as they say.

'Cap'in, the Armada red cross, what'll we do wi' it?' It was Skelton. He had survived and I was surprisingly glad of it. Clearly there was more steel in his spine than I had initially thought.

Men were bleeding all around me, some silently dying, some howling: the choirs of war are always the same. Enemies and allies die identically, and it is in that moment that you realise that we are all just people, even me. But just as quickly it is forgotten and the lust for achievement takes over.

Sadly, Taffy had collapsed on top of the white flag we had used to feign surrender. I knelt beside him and gently freed the new standard of my company. The white square was dominated with dark red – profoundly signalling death like nothing I had ever seen. I liked Taffy... Now, with two formidable vessels, I had the beginning of something special. I had an idea but first I needed to unite the men, my men.

'Rip the standards down and replace them with this.' I handed over the blood-soaked sheet. 'Mop the decks if you have to.'

Skelton nodded once and began barking orders. Blood usually makes people think about things.

'Both ships, Cap'in?' he asked, eyes lowered and full of respect.

I turned and nodded back to him. I knew I had chosen well. The Queen's Observer had almost passed from view. I spat into the stirring waves. Now I was captain, and this was my company.

* * *

We travelled west of Ireland.

To the crew's merriment and my own regret, Claruc departed our voyage at the port of Cork, but not before blessing us with numerous drunken insults and one or two offensive hand gestures. Got to love Claruc and his foolery. However, once upon his homeland, and as per his promise to me personally, he managed to recruit a disreputable looking lot of nine, to help us continue our adventure westward.

How a gigantic drunken riddler of a man could convince a group of Irish sailors to board with a crew of English explorers will forever elude me. Claruc was definitely a puzzle to all aboard, and me chief amongst them.

The Irish recruits were all named some variation of Michael or Mark, but I couldn't really understand most of what they jabbered on about. I thought they were teasing me with the similarity of their names and as I started to get riled up, they swore that their names, respectively, were Mick, Mucka, Mitch, Mike, Mark, Micky, Michael, Marcus, and Mikey.

To make things easier for everyone, I instructed the crew to call them all Mick. And not trusting them as far as I could throw Claruc, I decided to spread them amongst the crew as evenly as possible, splitting them out over the two ships.

The rest of the lads didn't give a damn about any of it. They needed strong backs. The Micks certainly gave us that much. We needed to be leaving and quickly, and I was trying to put as much ocean between us and the English-Spanish vendetta as possible. Naturally, I assumed that the infamous Spanish Armada would be chasing us down. I wasn't confident that they would fall for a similar rouse, and therefore instructed the crews to make like shepherds and get the flock out of there, and hopefully long before our enemies caught up with us, again.

The word onshore was that Queen Mary was recently affianced to King Philip II of Spain. The recent engagement was sudden, and a diplomatic arrangement. The wedding was scheduled to happen within the next month or two, but it was rumoured that the mad queen had fallen in love with one of her knights...

They said that Philip had demanded this 'knight's' head on a platter before the marriage could be sanctioned. So that explained that, and I shivered at the thought of that mad bitch making my evening meals, scrubbing my back, breastfeeding our children...

Spanish Philip clearly had a case of the jealousy bug. And now I'd relieved him of one of his vessels. I imagined that such an act would only enrage him further. I figured he could cry into my sloppy-seconds and get fucked, literally. However, needless to say that my visit to Ireland was brief, remarkably brief.

The victory against a lonesome Armada galleon was brilliantly executed, but perhaps a touch fortunate. I had more to think about than just myself, for once. I had a company and just enough strong backs loyal to the promise of gold, warmer waters, and exotic pussy, to take me to new worlds and fresh discoveries.

We arrived in the port of Cork just after the break of dawn and before the sun came to set, we had departed once more. Our destination was the land of opportunity and for the first week or so the ocean slept as motionless as a corpse, allowing us to skate smoothly upon her shimmered flesh. However, our collective bad humours and mistrusts must've served as the necromantic catalyst to awaken the horrors of the deep, as by the break of day eight, she suddenly woke up to play.

That was when I learned the true meaning of seasickness. Fuck, we all did, well not all of us, probably just me. However, there was one who learned the final term 'sea-deathness'. We lost the African as wave after wave battered us senseless and snatched his soul.

I was the only one aboard who didn't know anything about sailing, or the sea, or the ship, or swimming long distances, and my curiosity to see if I could drown had been properly washed away with the ferocity of the Atlantic Ocean. I did know the business end of a dagger, however. Didn't help much as we toppled from the most rancorous of fluid cliff edges, rolling over waves that would dwarf even the Tower of London!

Somehow, quite miraculously actually, both ships made it through and on to the great beyond. The standards had been washed-out by the storm to leave a flag of pink-orange. In the sunlight I decided that they would not do, even Skelton commented on the femininity of our once fearsome company colours.

The nine Micks sure did like them though. One of them even suggested that we keep them and go by the name "Pink Pirates". He got to swab the decks for the rest of the voyage. The Irish were a bit weird if you ask me. Very weird, but they knew how to guide a ship through the mouth of hell. If it weren't for them, my company wouldn't have made it.

Skelton was determined to stay the course, sail through the storm, and if we had, it surely would have resulted in breaking us apart. The storm was too strong. The Micks convinced him to surrender to the winds. Eventually he agreed and I agreed with my first mate, and that was how we ended up in the fucking polar regions, in a hellhole called Newfoundland. And yes, it is a real place. Colder than an Eskimo's shit, but still, far away from anyone who wanted me dead. Or so I hoped.

* * *

There was ice. Mountainous and copious amounts of it with the odd sprinkle of fresh snow, just to break up the monotony.

For a moment I thought we had passed through a Bermuda-like portal and ended up in Niflheim. We had blown off course, way, way off course. I was most disturbed to find that the island already had a healthy population of Irishmen… So naturally, my Micks fucked off to mingle and frolic and get drunk amongst their fellow countrymen and women.

Newfoundland, as I learned in the first and only tavern I could find, was the very first British colony. England and Britain, as it was, had now become a global nation. I was horrified and plagued with the sudden thought that I may never be able to escape the feudalist societies: the tea, the fine china, the superficial culture of greed, and cowardice, and corruption; Queen Mary and her betrothed Spanish twat of a cunt that wanted to cure his jealousy by mounting my head upon a plaque.

Ice melting fizzes softly, and spits and cracks and hisses, gently. Ever so soft. From my teapot position on the docks, ice melting is what I heard. Huge pieces of ice buoyant atop the romping waves. I didn't know the sea could freeze.

The Micks, however, were definitely in their element. Three of them didn't even come back as I ordered the ships to be restocked and ready to sail again by the first glimpse of dawn. The miscalculation of destination had quickly developed from grumbling and sulking to almost mutinous levels.

The threat of losing my company was more than a foreboding shadow in the dying light, it was almost tangible, or at least it was to me. I knew the lads weren't happy. Neither was I, but no cunt ever asked how I felt about things. And despite my vulnerabilities, I responded to their complaints by telling them to eat lemon snow and get back to fucking work. We were leaving before the sun set and sea refroze again, or no-one would be getting paid and they could stay cold forever and live amongst the ice if they wanted.

The ships were re-provisioned with ice and fish and we were straight back on the water. I didn't have time to wait for our missing crew and left as the sun hailed from beneath the horizon. South, we travelled, as my promises must be kept. Promises with warmer climates and less ice, much less ice.

We travelled as a company with no nationality. And to any passing merchant ship, we promoted ourselves as chance traders. Sooner than expected, and with very little else to comment on other than sourly looks and sourly tides, we arrived at New City.

Upon the loose lips of great explorers, it was known as the mouth to the New World. Only drunken tales didn't warn that the mouth was filled with sharpened steel and evil tongues ready to trick you into your deathbeds.

It seemed the locals did not take too kindly to us English speaking folk, regardless of our emancipation from the country and her interests. We spoke the language of our ancestors and as such, we were as evil as they were...

What ensued was not for the faint hearted. I didn't know it, but I was walking into a place more sinister, more fucked up, than anywhere I had ever visited before.

This New City was the gateway to the New World; and this New World was a brand-new kind of fucked up.

Saxon.

My brother first entered my life in the guise of Father Saxon, and he spoke more splendidly than the queen herself. He came at a time when I had spiralled down to greater depths than ever before, and my painfully healing wounds still smarted as I withered away within the tatters of my moth-eaten robes. Moths had to eat. I couldn't begrudge them that.

As the country was busy re-building itself in the wake of World War Two, and with nowhere else for me to turn, I'd scurried back to the halls that raised me, or what had become of them. I was the haunting of Pen-y-ghent. My abbey was gone, all that remained was the main hall and chambers that had been de-escalated to become the Roman Catholic Parish Church of St Oswald's.

The local children must have heard my nocturnal moans as I re-lived the torments of my recent sins. I distinctly remember hearing light footfall and children's frightened laughter, pounding about the perimeter of the exterior. But none ever dared to enter, not ever. The haunting was too real.

In the wake of what I had done, and what I had discovered, I needed the time to reassess everything. Not only my perspective and allegiances, but my entire reason for existing. I had entered as The Bastard of Bolton, but The Bastard needed to die; the mask had to be broken and peeled off then buried.

Often, I would stare at the stained-glass window set up high within the gable-end wall and ponder the real meaning of its intended depiction. God being seated high and mighty on a throne above all others. Angels straddled beneath Him, and I, the scavenger, the pissant, the pawn, sat huddled and hurting beneath them in the cold and damp, surrounded by feathers and the inescapable stench of urine. For when the smell of human shit fades, the stench of piss lingers on.

Darkness followed light and my thoughts followed the same pattern. And for a time, that was all. Days morphed into weeks; weeks blended into months, but none of it held any meaning to me as I was forever young. I came to the conclusion one day that I had perhaps been squatting in that place for a year or more, but again, I had the good sense to also realise that it could have only been days, and I would never actually know and that it didn't matter in any event. Light followed dark and my thoughts followed suit. That was all, but my mask was peeling away, and as it did my truth bled out and formed into a scab that healed into new flesh, and that, the scar tissue, that was the real me. Ugly and raw and not a thing to look at and admire.

After the mask had been completely shed, I realised that my borrowed robes suddenly hung loose from my bones. I hadn't given myself a second thought for the longest of time. And although the wounds over my face were healed, the scars prickled and nipped at me in torment.

My memories could not be cut away however, and I accepted that they would have to become the part of me that went ignored, an unwanted reminder of something from before…something that did more than just exist like a curse, existed eternally and watched like a haunting as night followed day into night, again, and again.

After the pain had passed into a place more acceptable, I would look forward to the occasional optimistic and totally ignorant passing of mountain walkers. I quite enjoyed listening to their buoyancy. I followed them as they started by the east corner of my hall, eventually making their way around to the southwest.

They followed the public footpath; I hugged the cold walls, barely even daring to breathe. I wanted to hear every last word. But I feared that something terrible must have happened as suddenly the frequency of travellers grew less and less until finally, they stopped passing all together.

In the cold and damp, looking up at the fallacy of God, I feared that perhaps the children's ghost stories had stretched on to the elder generation of Horton in Ribblesdale…perhaps the children became the elder generation.

After a cruel period of silence, the day came when I heard the key turn in the big red door, and I had to cover my eyes from the blinding light of everyday. With a creak and a shove, white light spilled upon my filthy habitat and for the first time in a long time, I felt humility, embarrassment, and rejoiced for I knew that I had not become lost from all that it means to be alive. However, I had become so detached from civility, I worried as to what I must look like to any passing stranger, but regardless of my concerns, the door was opening, and I was doing nothing to stop it.

After a final shove, a young and very healthy-looking man walked in. He did not dress like a monk but instead wore a white collar on a pious black suit that matched his curly black hair covering his ears. He stopped in his tracks when he saw my tattered rags draped over my leather-bound bones from my huddled position opposite the stained-glass window.

'You must be Henry.' His accent was impeccable and his tone soft.

I hopped to my feet and grabbed a sharpened bone that I had made to kill my next meal. I didn't reply with words as I wasn't sure if I remembered how.

He left the door open as he navigated the garishly cleaned, long-since consumed pigeon carcasses, discarded about the place. After watching his shiny shoes for a few seconds, I realised he was coming straight for me. He didn't seem afraid, if anything he bore the look of pity.

Meanwhile my feet were rooted, and I held my breath as he reached me and held out a hand. I looked at it, thought about stabbing him. Waited.

'Henry, everything is going to be all right. The Order has returned. We have been looking all over Europe for you. Some believed you had escaped with Hitler, sided with him even.' He shook his head. 'I argued against them. Henry Game is a winner, I said. So, they sent me to find you and to assume this post as the new bishop.' He looked at his outstretched hand and smiled at me.

I let the bone drop to the stone floor and I placed my hand in his and let him shake it. 'What is your name?' The first words that the real Henry Game had said in almost fifty years.

'Saxon,' he smiled again, perfect teeth. 'Call me Father Saxon, and I'm here to help get you back on your feet. The world needs you, Henry. The Order knows how special you are and…' he trailed as he looked around the hall, 'merely existing in such squalor is not fitting for one of your infamy, is it?'

I ignored his question as I took a step past him to look upon the deep blue sky, beyond the arched doorway. I remember noting the position of the sun, the rusting leaves hanging heavy from the sycamore by the drystone walling I had once re-laid; and for the first time in forever, I knew it was midday, and autumn, and that gave me a tremendous feeling of peace.

Saxon explained that The Order had flourished Stateside,

and that following the forced disarmament of the Germans, it had taken him almost an entire year to find me. He had even had mass burial grounds exhumed in his efforts along the way.

I listened and kept my suspicions to myself as I wasn't sure that I was so important to The Order, or ever had been, but the way Saxon was speaking of his mission to learn my fate, he made me believed that The Order must've cared for me… in their own way, and that was enough to get my self-esteem engine turning over again.

Saxon was good for me and getting the church community up and running again was especially good for the village. I busied myself with rebuilding the section of drystone that had been decimated by a Luftwaffe bomber, and also re-landscaping a section of the graveyard that was more of a gigantic crater now than burial ground.

As I cut into the earth and barrowed into the hole, mound after mound of mud, stone, and, most probably, bones and shattered skulls, eventually bringing the level consistent and even again, I was surprised when a few of the locals turned up day after day to work alongside me in returning the grounds to as they once were.

We didn't speak much, but I couldn't help but be irritated by their incessant staring when they thought I couldn't see them. I heard them whispering about my facial scars, and how they invented stories that I had been captured by one of Hitler's generals and tortured for almost two years. I left them to their imaginations and continued to fill the wheelbarrows, shovel after shovel.

Before long it was all starting to look like the place I had once known, and after the service on a Sunday, Saxon would encourage me to share my stories of my childhood whilst we ate a hot meal at the local tavern. Usually I was not one for regaling the horrors of old, however, Saxon's bright eyes and easy smile had a way of making me open up. It was healing, to share my experiences and have another understand what I went through.

Winter came fast and before the first snowfall on the lower grounds, Saxon was gone, replaced by Bishop Ramsey, whom was decidedly the most miserable cunt I ever met.

With the colder months came longer nights, and Ramsey explained to me in monotone heavy laden with despondency, that Saxon had been mysteriously taken ill by a rogue strain of the Spanish influenza, and that he'd been transported by aeroplane to the United States of America. He said that Saxon would get the best medical treatment available, but that only God could save him now...

Weeks later and news arrived of Saxon's death. I prayed for him, I even mourned him, in my own fashion. I decided to turn over a new leaf and even helped out at the church for a while, as I knew that Saxon would've wanted me to. I stayed to preserve the memory of a man that I had grown to care for.

* * *

Years pass quickly in the servitude of others. Being submissive is submersible and creates space for ignorance and serenity, but it is not a full or woken life. Regardless, I was content in my small corner of the world and at ease with my designation in it.

Decades later, in the aftermath of "We landed on the Moon", when questions of deep space were being asked, even in service, I sensed that times were changing in a way that I never saw coming.

With the advancements of science, theology was losing

its potency for restricting the imaginations and curiosities of mankind. But in service I held my tongue and I tried to not point it out that God himself, should he exist, was quite clearly an alien.

I aimed to live simply and aspired to be much like the two great men in my life: Father Game and Bishop Saxon. I hate to admit now how foolish and sentimental I was. With the church back up and running, Ramsey was able to re-establish The Order of St. Oswald's on home turf once again and for the first time in almost a hundred and sixty years.

However, times had changed, and instead of regular Mass and seated evening meals, as I had ever known them, The Order would hold communitive meetings which openly took on a new medium, blurring the lines between religion, politics, and commerce. These meetings were held in the Town Hall where the mayor and local constabulary were usually present, along with other, more disreputable types even.

For the most I was a silent spectator at these business-driven meetings, and I felt like my legend had turned me into a mascot. I imagined that most of them regarded my fables as a fantasy or honorary, and me as a complete nut-job.

Saxon's altruistic nature had inspired me to try living a life of servitude; I preached that I treasured no possession other than my faculties and good humours, but that was a lie. Decades must have passed without me so much as even thinking about Abatu, my exo-blade, nor had I thought of my horde of golden sovereigns, or my book, all of which were safely stashed in the crypts beneath the altar.

Scripture attempted to replace my curiosity, but sharpened pigeon bones made more suitable substitutes. I always carried a couple with me to the meetings, and I smiled piously as I delivered piercing stares to the new capitalist kings and queens, fantasising how I could make them bleed and feel as vulnerable as I felt amongst them and their unquenchable greed.

A general feeling of stabbery and brutality was always present behind my mutilated face and broken smiles – and although it was there, it had been so long that even I started to doubt my own capacity for violence. I started to believe that perhaps I was a living mascot; a symbol of times gone by, and now all that remained was the soft version of everything I tried not to be.

I prayed often and mostly unobserved. But when I prayed alone, I always kept my eyes open. I woke up every day and watched the world turn toward the sun. I listened to the birdsong coming from the lone sycamore by the drystone walling beneath the looming shadow of Pen-y-ghent.

Sometimes I couldn't even chew my food properly for the taut scars on my cheeks and often it would re-open and bleed down my face. But within the next day or so the wound would form back into scab and then thick purple chunks, like elbow patches, but all over my face.

Ramsey merely dismissed my insistent wounds as a clear sign of God's mercy. I often fantasised about impacting one of my sharpened bones through his eye socket when he said shit like that. But regardless of his miserable energy and lethargic idiosyncrasies, I believed he was, although as blunt as a spoon, a decent person.

He genuinely believed that God was up there to protect him and all those who accepted the teaching of the Bible. And although I tried to believe, I knew better.

Intelligence almost always stands between people and faith in the divine, as I observe that only those willing to suspend logic and curiosity will find the faith they yearn for. Blind, *dumb, illogical and borderline delusional. But to each their own, as they say.*

I didn't witness the Ramsey's barbaric execution, but I did get to find him before the altar, reverse crucified, and skinned from the waist down to his head, with an ominous and thick black candle burning not four inches beneath his cooked and smoking skull.

I had seen this kind of thing before and it set my heart racing. It was called the ritual of enlightenment. And although I didn't have much in common with the guy, his death by the hands of my former comrades, the Iron Mask, was enough to resurface the old me in many ways that I had missed. Anger has something comforting about it and can shield you from the business of caring when not caring suits you better than the alternative.

I decided that the message was meant for me and was a big "fuck you" to The Order and everything it stood for. Never would Henry Game be allowed to fade into a normal existence. I knew that in order to protect the people closest to me, whether or not I liked them very much, I needed to keep them as far away as possible, lest they get to know me and ultimately pay the price for my discretions.

It was then that I peeled back the altar and retrieved my tools and resources, rolling my shoulders to the satisfying crack of understanding: the door stood wide open…it always had, and it always would, key or no key.

I reached toward the feeling of purpose and revenge once again. And although the purpose was red, and even for a guy I didn't think much of, I set out to exact justice for the miserable bastard and I latched on to the chord of retribution like a tick on a rat.

With the better fitting clothes on my back I took to the road with a new face, an old temper, and a familiar proclivity for violence. They knew me, or at least one version of me, but I had the advantage: I had various resources stashed away in small deposits. Alone I knew I could change and blend into whatever I wanted to be to get back to where I needed to be. My face was barely recognisable anymore anyway. My eyebrows and facial hair had persisted to grow in awkward clumps which could not decide which way was up.

The downside to looking like a patchwork quilt of flesh was the audacious attention it drew from the inexcusably rude. What was important was that I knew my enemy. I knew their safe houses, their lodges, their function rooms and palaces and therefore: I knew where they would be.

But the paradox in all of this was that, of course, they too knew that I knew where they would be.

* * *

It was mid-morning and I was a day into my travels, hitting the coastal routes toward London. I had traipsed into Lancaster, recently passing the newly formed university and into a sparsely populated forest when I heard the suspicion of company in tow.

Tensing, a coldness entered my step. Straining all of my senses whilst still trying to keep my cool, I no longer walked, but stalked through the woods as the industry of the town ahead plumed above the naked treetops like a merciless beast of gluttony.

A dead branch snapped behind me and without thinking I dropped to the ground and rolled to my left, feeling a tightness tear across my back and sharp whistle by my ear.

I knew from the burning across my right shoulder blade that I had taken a hit, and from the immediate hot trickling down my spine, bleeding, but not too heavy.

Another snap drew my attention to my left again but this time I didn't dodge in the correct direction as a jolt of red flashed across my eyes and my thoughts swam in treacle for a moment or two.

Opening old wounds on my face brought a stretched smile to my lips. Warmth oozed down onto my neck. I fell forwards and span around into a crouch to clearly see my attackers, or at least the ones who had stepped out from the trees.

My smile grew wilder and my skin tore on my face.

There were four metal-faced assassins before me, and one large fellow in the hat. I recognised the silhouette of the big one; I had not seen him for what seemed like a lifetime, mortally speaking of course, which it seemed he wasn't after all.

'Game, you've grown soft, weak. Where is The Bastard, or did he lose his balls the same time you did?' Grim stepped out of shadow, frowning as he posed the question. He was holding a thin branch, stripped of leaves, and was in the process of stripping what little bark the twig possessed.

I contained my surprise that he was as impervious to the aging process as I was and instead listened hard for any further movements from my flanks. Grim was a tactician and would undoubtedly have me surrounded and outnumbered.

'Grim.' I straightened up, touching a hand to the cut beneath my right eye. 'Back at the abbey, that was your doing, the sadist execution?'

Grim understood my meaning. I saw it in his remorseless expression. Meanwhile I continued to slowly back away in order to get all of my attackers into my field of vision.

Grim snorted an ugly sound and threw an object that landed in the dirt a few paces in front of me. It was a cross that bared Jesus on a heavy golden chain. I recognised it as the Ramsey's and that confirmed it.

'I see you finally shed the mask,' he said, the twig being nothing more than thin strings of green. He dropped it to the floor and pulled a pipe from out of his pocket and started to stuff the end with tobacco. 'Game, again we find that our nation is in crisis. I need you to accompany me back to the-'

'Stop!' I cut him off, flaring with a heat I'd not felt for an age. I kicked at the necklace, scattering it to the shrubbery that flanked our path. 'Ramsey was a miserable fucker, yes, but he didn't deserve that.'

'Did he not?' Grim bounded a couple of steps closer as he set a lit match to the end of his pipe and puffed.

'And Saxon? Please don't tell me that was you too.'

'Saxon?' He frowned at that one, and almost looked me in the eye as he puffed a thick cloud of smoke into the space between us.

The surprise on his face was genuine and I felt myself cooling a little. For Saxon I would've ripped the big cunt's head off and stuffed his stupid fucking hat down his stupid fucking wound of a neck. But it seemed he knew nothing of that particular tale.

Grim continued to chug on his pipe and gradually closed the space between us to a more murderous distance, as if tensions were not high and the threat of death and violence promising like thunder follows lightning.

I stood my ground, ready. I still counted four of the iron masks, five including Grim. The masks would die, of course. But Grim: I hadn't decided.

Something flickered across his face as I readied myself to attack, and in his moment of weakness I saw a plethora of vulnerability. My smile widened to its painful capacity and fresh fissures opened up my face, hot blood trickling down *toward my mouth as I allowed the thrill of the hunt to take over me. I unsheathed Abatu just as Grim retreated a step. The time for talking was over.*

My adrenaline picked up as half-time kicked in, and as I crossed the dusty space between us, the iron face painted a paradox on to my first victim as he had barely even begun to lift his arms in defence when I happened upon him like fulguration destroys the flesh.

I stabbed him once in the groin with a hiss and a smoulder of fabric, then stepped aside in an attempt to avoid the fountain of blood gushing from his severed femoral artery.

He dropped to his knees with an "oof" and proceeded to lose his lifeblood amongst the dried mud and loose stones of the dusty pathway, and all the while his mask looked ready and willing to fight.

Grim was the first of them to react. However, he had already lost one of his pawns, or was mere seconds away from doing so, and I couldn't help my smile from growing wider and wider as the blood on Abatu crackled and dried in a wisp of smoke.

The dying mask collapsed flat on to his back and into whimpers, and then nothing, but the crimson of his vitality leaked evermore and made the possibility of muddy boots increasingly likely.

'What was his iron mask designation then, Leaky?'

I sensed the fear of the remaining three and focused squarely on Grim, who no longer held a pipe but instead a shiny and hefty looking pistol. He held it levelled at the ground and half-time returned to normal.

'Game, I didn't track you down to go to sodding war with you.' Grim looked serious. 'The truth is that we need you.'

'And you're sure you didn't want to fight?' I retorted, gesturing to the dead assassin by my feet.

'I only brought them in case things got a bit tricky...you know, with the bishop. I knew you'd over-react and start trying to avenge before you would even listen to reason!'

'Reason? What fucking possible reason could you have to put a man through that Satanist bullshit?' My anger was getting the better of me and I set my feet at shoulder width apart and readied for another attack.

Grim stepped forward as an island and took off his hat. 'That bastard was abusing his position and power. He was selling children from the orphanage to the highest bidder and kept a couple for himself. But not only that, his allegiances had changed recently, and aligned with the new power that threatens these borders.

'Trust me when I tell you that the enemy has infiltrated almost every branch of government. They are already here, and this is a fight that I cannot hope to win without you!'

I blinked in surprise, deflating at his gesture of desperation. I had never seen Grim so open and vulnerable.

'Tell the masks to piss off and I'll hear you out, okay?'

Grim smiled, hat still in one hand, and the pistol in the other, but the threat had left his singular eye. I reckoned he knew me better than I knew myself. I re-sheathed Abatu. The time for talking had returned, briefly. Times change like the wind and always will do. That's how things are. No use being soft in a hard world or vice-versa.

The Collector (L. S.).

I awoke to a dark space of body and mind, and as I levered my arms against the hard surface beneath me to sit upright, I realised that this time I was properly shackled, as a prisoner should be.

I stayed lay down for a moment as my head was still woozy, but from a brief assay, I could see that my chains were anchored onto a dark and slick piece of sharp rock that formed the walls of my jail cell.

I recalled my last movements, coming out of the pyramid, alarms whirring, people running, smoke, shattered glass everywhere and oily blood. The rage had me and I was along for the ride. I get reckless when the red takes over and I obviously went and got myself recaptured and, well, chained up like a rabid dog.

I still had my clothes on, but my shoes had been removed, and as I patted my pockets and waistline I could've screamed in weariness as I had once again been relieved of both my book and Ian's exo-blade. For the pithiest of moments, I allowed myself to feel like the whole universe was against me. But, as you have probably deduced, I am not one to dwell in self-pity, nor self-adulation, nor self-abnegation, or any station between the extremes. I like to think of myself as well balanced with a proclivity for righteously driven homicide.

My ingrained GPS system had me feeling that wherever they had brought me was deeper still than Atlantis – not that determining my altitude in relation to sea level has ever done me any good, but there it is. Everyone is good at something and my thing was sensing my altitude positioning in relation to sea level. If not for my overcast day, I probably would've been a fantastic land surveyor or cartographer.

The rock walls around my cell were sweating for me, and I noticed a few dozen thin stalactites reaching down from the dark ceiling to grab me up. I doubted my chains would allow me to reach them, even if I tried. My hair pulled tight before peeling away from the slab as I sat up, and this was followed by another wave of dizzy rocking my eyes.

My scalp tingled and itched, cautiously feeling around the back of my head, my nerves caught fire as I traced across the patch of jellied glob that stretched from my crown to my neck. I reckoned the wound was almost four-fingers wide. I traced the hardened ridge on the wound that had split open the back of my skull like a jelly-zipper.

After my eyes had stopped swirling, I dropped down to the uneven rocky floor with a clatter. It was much further below than I had initially estimated, and as I fell, I cursed as loud as my head would let me as the hinge on the shackle dug into my ankle bone and set my foot slick and warm with blood. More pain. The rock floor was sharp, not something you could easily walk over in bare feet; not without slicing your soles off in the process.

The room held no windows, lights, or toileting facilities. The only form of light available spilled in from around the narrow doorframe opposite the high stone table I had just taken my nap on. Both of my ankles were bound tight, and the chain that attached was clearly well-maintained.

I tried yanking against the hook in the wall, but it was hopeless to break or pull loose. Whatever the metal, it was strong, and I quickly realised that I wouldn't be bending it with my bare hands to get out of this mess. I had to think, as I had a very unsettling feeling that this place was a purpose-fully built prison for those like me and my kin. With little other option, I returned to the table and vaulted back up, pulling as much of the chain slack as I could in order to allow my ankles some semblance of relief from the cutting weight of the cold metal.

I lay back down facing the glow from around the doorway until my eyes felt heavy again. It felt like I had been in the dark, far below the surface of the planet for the longest time. I wondered how long I had been unconscious and decided that finding my brother was a mistake. I needed to keep my focus on what was important, in protecting the secret. I allowed my eyes to close, gathering my thoughts by circumnavigating the various pains in my body until I eventually rediscovered my past.

Images flashed upon the backs of my eyelids of the recent rampage in the aftermath of my enlightenment. It seemed that I had been played since day one and as I dwelled, I felt the fire warming inside me again and I welcomed the memories, the flickers of a bygone fury returning to me in angry stings.

I remember stepping out of the doors of the great pyramid, touching the blade to the doors and watching it burn as outside destruction conducted the chorus of screams like an apocalyptic symphony.

Smoke was thick and low on the ground like a fog, and I bounded out amongst the hundreds of sheeple, scattering in an all-out panic, everybody fleeing in every direction.

I set off toward the closest of the acrylic domes, my blade hissing as I slashed into the side and created a new doorway for myself. Cool clean air washed over me like vapour as I stepped inside, the sounds of panic and alarm and destruction faded.

I remembered a lot of dwarfed trees, green shrubberies and colour from the blossomed flowers all around. I remember hearing the song of bird and buzz of insects, the lap of water even somewhere inside the bubble. I joined the gravelled path as it spiralled on a radius toward the centre.

The screaming from outside had completely fallen from the edge of my awareness, but despite the serenity of the underground botanical project, my thoughts were red, and my vision blinkered.

Mirabilis had played me like a fucking run of dominoes, and I had dashed off to Rome to kill the pope that he wanted dead. I wouldn't be totally surprised if he had also orchestrated the death of Father just to entice me and bring me down to the capital to kneel before the king.

I passed nurseries containing varied stages of vegetation and other exotic plant life before coming to the end of the path, at the centre of the dome. A small laboratory built from metal frame and draped in clear plastic stood before me. The sign on the door advised that all personnel must wear full hazmat suits and breathing equipment. I saw another sign that read "Danger: Biohazard", and I looked through the clear panel in the door and was surprised to see that there were still people inside, moving around in sky blue and pink hazmat suits, most probably oblivious to my recent rampage.

I cut through the plastic flap that was the main entry door and was met with another clear plastic door with the words "DECONTAMINATION UNIT" on a black and yellow background.

I looked up and realised that there were multiple rows of jets sprouting from a skinny metal frame, and a big green button that pulsed softly. Ignoring the invitation to get myself 'decontaminated', I started to cut into the last doorway when there came a heavy crunching on the gravel clearing behind me. I turned as suddenly the birds were screeching and crowing in wild scatter. I stepped back out of the lab and readied myself for whatever approached when all went black again.

Red and black. A sharp and long flash of red and the rever-berating sound of canon fire aboard my vessel.

My rampage of destruction was extinguished by curiosity, and then, judging by the wound on the back of my skull, being shot by a shotgun. But thankfully it wasn't the first time I'd had a part of my brains blown out; I'd heal in time.

I reckoned that I was more scar than flesh these days, so the latest dent in my skull would hardly look out of place, but my hair had just grown out to a good length and the big hole would mean that I have to shave the bloody lot off, again.

In another moment of spite, I hated how Ian had managed to keep his face free from the injury and hazards of centuries. Just thinking of my brother riled me up again. But as much as his angered me, he intrigued me too, and annoyance gave way to curiosity as I wondered after him some more, ponder-ing upon what trails the centuries had prepared for him. He was too fucking perfect in his perfect little underground city, safely away from the real dangers of the world. Of course, he had never had an overcast day. And my own was nothing more than the inciting incident in Mirabilis' morbid playbook.

Thinking of my brother and his last words had set my thoughts and my mind racing again with calculation and the search for answers. I wondered how he was connected to Mira-bilis, and what did he mean by "join them" when suddenly the sound of bolts screeched against iron, and my cell door swung inward.

A silhouette dominated the open door against a backdrop of warm light.

'Mister Game, you are summoned by Ruling Council.' I recognised the speaker as Mr Serious.

'I take you now. You come, calmly. Release his shackles…' he entered the room followed by three fully suited guards, all armed with shotguns. Every caution pointed at me.

'And what if I don't want to go see this fucking council, eh?' I did, I really did, but this guy's mannerisms and arrogance just pissed me off. I found him intolerable.

Mr Serious flashed his sharky grin and shrugged. 'Not problem: I tell them and they shoot, break, cut into small pieces, then drag. When Council summons, I bring.'

I looked around and nodded as he explained. 'Well, I do like to know my options,' I slid to the edge of the table.

The four of them stopped for a moment, all shotguns raised my way.

'Fucking chop, chop! As Mister Serious over here says: "when council summons, we go". So, let's go, vàmanos! And someone please tell me that one of you had the good sense to bring a ladder…'

Late Autumn, 1553.

My company arrived at the New City, a place very much in transition in the year of our Lord, 1553. Even looking at it from the waves, it was quite clearly a wretched festering wound of a place, choking between the clutches of the old world and the ruthlessness of neocolonialism. It was a desperate paradise for chancers and the likes that found themselves without a country to call their own. In summary, it was a place of foes, a place welcoming to the right kind of horrible bastard.

I was disappointed to see that the French already had their dirty digits firmly embedded in the so-called New World and were in the process of negotiating an establishment of power, a kind of treaty with the native tribes collectively known as 'The League'.

The French called them the Iroquois, which sounded remarkably French to my ears, but the native bastards had a leader of their own and if the power was shared, it was he who had the lion's portion. I can tell you now that this bastard was the most horrible cunt I ever met. And he was ironically named Peacemaker.

A spokesman, of sorts, that represented the indigenous people introduced himself to me in broken English, a kind of performance of animated body gestures, bouncing squats and hopping, clapping and voodoo dancing, all combined with no small amount of spitting.

I was truly mesmerised by the oddness of it all. Meanwhile my beloved fleet of two remained anchored at a safe distance, several hundred feet from the bay, waiting to see what kind of reception awaited us before truly abandoning the decks.

I judged the situation to be relatively welcoming, and so called in the rest of the men. They arrived ashore upon two rowboats, mooring against the rotten piers. Our cannons and warships still out in the deep of the bay. A troupe of French soldiers supervised their landing, making sure to excessively expectorate all the while.

A skeleton crew had been volunteered to remain with the ships, someone had made the call and I couldn't argue with the logic or caution of it. Meanwhile, I was joined by my finest and bravest in Skelton, another large African fellow we picked up on Newfoundland who could name every star in the sky; the remaining two Micks that I still didn't trust, and the spooky Spanish fellow with yellow sclera, who made far too much eye-contact with me for it not to be weird.

Disembarking on to the piers, we allowed ourselves to be marched off into the tangle of naked forest. The French commander did not lower his weak cannons from my company still out in the bay, but my ships were safe enough, and at the first sound of cannon fire, I would be coming to wreak revenge and I would love it.

However, the crew were clearly in no condition to fight. Provisions were low, too low to chance being turned away without re-stocking. But most important of all: the morale needed lifting.

The truth is I had no choice but to parley with Peacemaker, regardless of his French connection, distasteful as it may be. It was either that or risk losing the men to abandonment, or perhaps both the men and ships to another round of mutiny.

Since the moment we departed the journey had been harsh. And I had been about as useful as a teaspoon in a knife fight. Truth is, and I'm not ashamed to say it, I'd spent most of the way in my chambers, trying to keep dry. And as I kept reminding the men: I was the captain, the owner of the boat, and would therefore remain in my captaincy chambers for as long as I should see fit. But of course, subsequently, the mood amongst the men was dour and most certainly drenched. Yet they hung in there and worked to the relentless barking of my brilliant first-mate, Skelton.

We were escorted down a heavily trodden path into a forest guarded by spearmen with painted faces and feathers in their hair and hanging from their elbows. Fucking birdmen. I reckoned they judged our shit-rag band of nationless sea-bandits with an equally prejudice name too.

I noticed several others climbing through the bone-bare branches above us and all along our trail, following our path, ready to drop down on us, I suspected. I watched them with wary eyes, but just by the sheer numbers, I figured peace was the way to go. After all the rollicking I yearned for a soft bed and, perhaps, a softer woman. Queen Mary had opened the door to the world of sexual delight and encounter, and, try as I may, as the ship rocked and rolled throughout the storms, I could not shut the door on my desire and imagination... it was a damned good job my chambers had a lock on the door. Like the rest of the crew, I had calluses on my hands, but mine weren't from tying or pulling on any ropes.

The trees opened out on to a clearing of dozens of tall tepees and smoking cook fires. Heaps of children milled across the flat encampment, with small clusters of them chasing each other down in mock-butchery of war. I wondered at the savagery of kids and how they would only grow crueller. In the centre of the camp, beside the only standing tree, was the highest and most colourfully decorated tepee of them all, and it was to this centrepiece that our Indo-French guard stomped to a halt and a syllabic bellow.

As we waited, I noticed that the children had cleared out back amongst the fringes of the tree line. I wondered why they would behave in such a way when suddenly Peacemaker stepped forth from his canvas establishment with an almighty fucking flair.

'Welcoming of you, to this New World.' He sang the phrase, almost. 'Where do your hearts of love belong, where are your dreams?' Shaking his bony arms in the air, feathers and beaks clacking on his multitude of necklaces about his leathery, wrinkled neck. He locked onto me with black eyes and crouched, apparently quite comfortable, but making me feel all manner of emotions to the contrary.

After a moment I crouched too, not sure of the etiquette. 'Well met Peacemaker, I am Henry Game, friend to no king, and captain of the…' I let my opening address trail away as our chaperone French commander stooped down to whisper poor manners into the ear of the colourfully decorated Peacemaker.

Peacemaker laughed, harshly, and suddenly the tension in the clearing was thick with uncertainty. In particular the native warriors around our gathering seemed to stiffen the most. I wondered if laughing was a bad sign.

The French commander stepped aside, red faced and eyes wide, his jaw locked tight. Clearly not as anonymous as I had previously hoped. I was hoping for a fresh start in the New World.

Peacemaker stood, extravagant – all beak, bone and paint – then spat into his palm and offered it toward me, palm out, fingers spread like a challenge of mercy. 'Be welcoming, Henry Game, slayer of the demon pontiff!'

The tepee erupted with celebrations, all except the Frenchman of course, but I once heard a rumour that French men didn't know how to clap.

I stepped forward, looking him in the eye and spat into my own palm, my spit against his, fingers locked. Spit brothers.

Peacemaker grinned, leered even, and thrust our hands up high to show the whole clearing. Bleeding gums and what looked like bits of eggshell jutted at angles in his teeth. That kind of shit would just drive me crazy. I almost started picking my own gums before he released me and threw his arms in the air, uttering high-spirited gobbledygook.

Children came running toward us in numbers. Scavenging fingers grabbing for any loose items. And just like that we were welcomed to the New City and at ease with the established order.

I suggested that the French cannons should be lowered, and the commander stomped away, but not before spitting on my boot. Within the hour the remainder of my crew had disembarked and were all filling their bellies with hot meat.

I overheard Skelton suggesting that some men return to the ships, to keep the company active, just eight men, just in case, he said, and I said nothing to the contrary, but neither did anyone offer to return to the decks. He had earned my respect, and after all, he did have good sense did that old and diseased bastard.

Clearly the French weren't happy by our acceptance. But a sour Frenchman is not uncommon in my experience, so I let it go and took my party into the encampment under the promise of friendship and a calm and dry night.

* * *

We slept beneath the glazed black and twinkled sky. Well, everyone around me did. I lay awake, listening as the universe flirted with me over a hundred and twenty degrees of motion, releasing a cooling breeze from the heat of the late afternoon and a foreboding chill.

Peacemaker and company had wailed and danced all evening for us, apparently guaranteeing that it wouldn't rain – I wasn't holding my breath – I could taste the promise of moisture coming. And meanwhile, the distant lapping of the river did little to quell my paranoia regarding the angry Frenchmen. They knew that I was the assassin that killed the pope, so I figured that they would surely be seeking revenge as they were as pious as any European outside of Britain.

I concentrated on my breathing, consciously drawing each breath, the lull, then exhaling again. My guarded mind almost had me convinced that I could smell the dirty Frenchmen in their plots; and my equally suspicious imagination even had them picking their way through the network of tepees to get themselves into position around our camp. But in the dead of night I believed my paranoia to be getting the better of me. So, I did nothing and continued to harbour my fears as distant stars blinked and fell away into the black that was infinite and pure and unattached.

When my men were too tired to hold their pelts of fermented fruits, and the craze of novelty gave way to lust and slumber, we were ushered to another camp of tepees, over in the next clearing along, with only a small flurry of trees dividing our camps. Long after we called it a night however, our hosts partied on, in their continuing praising to the gods.

I traced the constellations that the African had shown me, deep in thoughts and memories. And if I looked at any particular stars for a certain length of time without blinking, I noticed how other stars would disappear and morph around the main feature of my vision when all of a sudden everything went dark, and I could see no stars at all.

At first, I thought that a colony of bats were passing overhead until I recognised the slowing momentum of the arc. At once my limbs jolted through with the shock of realisation and I sat up, blinking away my doubts. I looked upon the dark flock swarming before the stars and moon like a murder of crows, blotting the cosmic clouds in waves and yet could find no breath within me to raise alarm.

The promise of death held suspended, gracefully, before hailing down toward our camp without remorse, and the moment passed within a single breath. Inside a second, several swishes and thuds landed in the dirt around me, and the nightmarish cries and screams of my men followed thereafter. The choirs of terror being further harmonised by the unfortunate natives that had chosen to bunk down with my men, mostly in exchange for items of little to no value other than mild fascination.

My suspicions were coming alive, and it was raining after all, just not in the way you might expect, and I belatedly gave the call to battle – but the screams were already thundering in the storm.

An arrow sunk through my calf just as I rolled and attempted to spring to my feet. I snapped the tip off and dragged the shaft out clean, and that was when I knew just how fucked we all were: the arrow was Iroquois and not French, as I had suspected.

I climbed to my feet and set forth toward the dark tree line from where the arrows had been sent when the first tomahawk lodged deep into my left shoulder, just beneath the collarbone and to the side of my armpit. Pain was slow to arrive to the party, so I continued running, or rather hobbling, my way across the killing field. There were dozens of armed Frenchmen scattered amongst the tepees, swords swinging, men screaming. My men dying...

Feeling betrayed and desperately afraid, my first thoughts of retribution were reserved for Peacemaker, and he wasn't hard to miss under any circumstances. I zeroed in on him as he spread his winged arms and howled at the moonless night in a war-cry, the rest of his warriors bounding from the tree line with weapons glinting back the deception they had hatched. There must have been hundreds of them, but I only wanted one to pay for this dishonourable betrayal.

Seconds later and more French war cries rang out from the tree line to our eastern flank, and another score of the frog fuckers split through the line of crouched Iroquois archers, swords aloft, charging on us as we continued to writhe from our waking nightmares.

I stopped a moment and spared a look around me, some of my men had reached their feet and screamed defiance with notched swords and haunted faces; but most, gurgled in the mud, squirming like overturned woodlice-

Another tomahawk whistled past me and I pulled my focus back together. I turned, heading straight for the treacherous bird-cunt-fucker, who was flanked by two Frenchmen and currently facing off against one of the Micks.

The confrontation was well underway, and I shouted to him, scrambling as fast as my leg would allow me, taking the opportunity to open a Frenchman's spine from the base of his skull to his pelvis in one vicious slash, just before he did much of the same to one of my men.

Mick held his weapon at the ready, making himself as small a target as possible by turning his striking arm forward, braced against a possible three-way attack, and as the first filthy French twat stabbed bold, Mick parried the clumsy swing and hacked out the hamstring of his enemy before turning to meet the blade of the other Frenchman, high above his head.

Each second slowed to a trickle as I sent my sword up through the gaping underjaw of one of the painted Iroquois, and punched a deep crater into the side-neck of a French-man, and all the while, I couldn't take my eye from Mick in his struggle but as he began to overpower the his French adversary, a tomahawk struck him just above the knee, passing straight through fabric flesh and bone in the process, and his leg was halved and now he stood on one foot.

I stopped my advance as the wind blew from my sails and another arrow sank into my gut, but still I was looking on at Mick as he let his sword drop to the blood-churned earth and he fell after it. His severed leg somewhere beneath him.

Observing his demise was all the help I could spare, and his resigned gaze found mine in that moment, through all the carnage and screams and laughter around us both, he shook his head as if to say he didn't expect that or something. I shouted to him to pick up his weapon, but the fight was lost, and he spat at the Frenchman who'd recovered and was poised to stick him through.

I continued my advance, cutting away at anyone or anything that stood in my way as I closed the distance. I saw Peace-maker instructing his French companion, and the Frenchman walked away, leaving Mick to water the field with his blood. That was when Peacemaker stepped up like the vulture of evil and set to work on the prostrated Mick, forcing an eruption of shrieks from him in the process.

The feathered bastard had turned him over and pinned down in the blood-soaked dirt with one of his bony knees, hunched over, working at something. The silver gleam of steel caught in the glint of starlight.

I was still several tepees, and several lethal obstacles away from the scene, and I certainly wasn't quick enough to stop it. But as Peacemaker continued his work and Mick screamed in a way that I have never heard before, I felt tears falling down my cheeks and everything became red and distant, but for the Iroquois fuck's scrawny arms thrashing in short controlled stabs.

I sent up a silent prayer to end Mick's suffering and meanwhile he gurgled his hell out for the whole world to witness. I had halved the distance again when I finally saw Peacemaker's work and he wailed as he held up the Irishman's scalp into the darkest of nights and the white of skull shone and prominent to my eye, dull and forefront amongst the misery of deceit.

I was almost there, a few feet more and I would have the horrible cunt bleeding beneath my blade. I would make the cruelty shown to my man look like a kindness in comparison. I was going to turn the Peacemaker inside out, and as slowly as I could.

Something heavy and final sunk into the side of my head, sapping my strength. Killing my fire and sending me blind into the mud to be swallowed up with the rest of the slaughter that was once my company.

* * *

There is a peacefulness about being settled and buried in soft, warm mud.

Limbs spangled, members and hair beautifully interwoven; my company decimated and forgotten in a mass grave beneath the feet of the dancing French and Iroquois party, slaughtered and scattered like the seeds of the decimated. But still, it was peaceful, and I had crawled back into consciousness just before decomposition set in.

They thought they had won. Our enemy thought they were the last ones laughing as they wailed and fraternised upon our mass grave and I came to with a bitter taste of boldness deep in my intent.

The wounds to my neck had closed up enough to allow me to suck in and cough, suck in and cough – and if one of them had put their ear close to the freshly dug earth, they may have heard me as I plotted my retribution.

Oxygen was in scarce supply, thankfully I don't need much to keep going, and the lazy fuckers had dug shallow graves. I reckoned that I was one of the last bodies to be tossed into the ditch, so I wasn't too far from the surface.

My head throbbed; my neck burned; my gut ached and itched; my shoulder tingled; and my calf stung like a bitch. Truth is, I was in a bit of a state. However, ever the optimist I am, I took comfort in knowing I was at least a couple of shades pinker than the guys around me, and a good couple of degrees warmer.

Vibrations and cold fluids oozed through the clumps and clots of clay, releasing pockets of death-drenched air for me to feast upon as I clambered, slowly. The disturbances serendipitously lubricated the branches of cold stiff flesh that penned me in like I was the marble caught in a sadistic version of KerPlunk, but I kept myself moving and my eyes at a squint. I did however pause as I put a handout and felt Skelton's putrefied mouth and beard beneath my fingers, and instead chose another way up – I didn't have it in me to climb over the face of my late, brave first mate.

Thankfully, but also regrettably, they had reclaimed the tomahawk from my shoulder before throwing me in, as they tend not to bury their weapons, but in doing so they had unwittingly given my flesh the opportunity to begin knitting back together again. My tendons were still intact, and I knew this because I could still make a fist, and so, setting my fingers into scoop position, manipulating rigor mortised limbs this way and that to get myself closer to the surface. I made it a point not to look upon their dead faces, and instead focused on the sections of light between inter-crossed arms of my former crew. Each limb of a comrade's corpse acting as a rung on the ladder of vengeance. Each arm and torso reinvigorated my determination to get out of that pit of defeat and take my revenge on the swine responsible.

The ground grew colder and wetter as I neared the surface. The cackle and insidious celebrations blurred on as I scraped my way nearer still until I managed to get as close to the surface as possible.

I froze as a hand-span sized pocket of earth collapsed in besides my face, and to my surprise the sun was high in the blue, but the sickly slap of sex could not be mistaken, even from my lowly position.

I waited a few more moments before reaching forwards but then froze again as another person's hot flesh brushed against the top of my knuckles. I heard a high-pitched scream like that of a little girl and I remained inanimate in my position amongst the dead.

Words were said that I couldn't clearly make out, then quickly cut across by a deep voice, booming, nonchalantly. After another moment or two, accompanied by the clear shrill song of a blackbird in the distance. Laughing erupted and the sticky slap of sex resumed.

I coughed, my whole-body racking with the movement and more of the earth fell in around me. Again, the deeper voice spoke, but suddenly sounding a little less nonchalant. I picked up one or two of the words: the deeper voice was a Frenchman.

Scuffs in the ground above and immediately around my crouched position revealed more of the sky; revealed more of the Frenchman and his male, yet feminine, Iroquois partner. The homosexuality didn't surprise me as after all, he was a Frenchman, and those Europeans were up for anything.

I closed my eyes and continued to wait, but my cough irritated tremendously, and I couldn't help but wheeze and croak as I breathed. There was an overpowering smell of arse and sweat and death above ground. My feet were in position to spring. It was going to be glorious and I would rise, leaping free like the fucking Dolphin of Doom. I waited, a mere six inch from the surface.

'Ce qui la baise?' Nerves trembled through each syllable of the question, like the plucking of a harp string, as grubby fingers testily began uncovering my head and neck, one small hand at a time.

The rumble of a withheld cough nestled deep within my solar plexus, reverberating in my throat, leaking through my nose. I had waited long enough. And, I decided, either I had grown accustomed to the smell of arse sex, or the epic-ness of the moment was transcending my disgust. Either way I was ready to go again.

'Merde, je pense qu'il respire!' Suddenly snatching his hand away from my now fully exposed head and shoulders.

I kept my eyes closed, meaning I had to listen to the moment unfolding around me. They knew I was breathing. They could probably hear the wheezing buried in my throat. Yet, I don't think that they could actually believe I was alive.

'Voyez si vous pouvez le sentir. Vérifiez son nez,' suggested the softer one, the more feminine of the two, from a little further back, I estimated.

I was ready to pounce, my footing was solid – probably on the backs and necks of my fallen comrades, but it was for them that I needed to do this. The smell of arse intensified as another hand came to rest under my nose, and I couldn't help myself from crinkling up my nostrils then coughed, deep and chesty.

They both screamed in tandem, harmoniously, even. I opened my eyes, half-croaking, half-growling in a state of hysterical fury. Still shrieking, they shrivelled away from me, falling over one another's naked, soiled bodies as I took them into my sights.

With feet set I pushed up with all of my strength, the mud falling from me as I leapt free at an angle and collided with the smaller of the two, and he crumbled like a thin biscuit dipped into a hot cup of tea.

Using my thumb, I pushed down into his eye socket, hissing, spittle and clay clumping around the corners of my mouth as his eyeballs burst apart and my thumbs sunk in, clear fluid oozing from beneath his pulped lid. I realised that I must have knocked him unconscious because he didn't even moan, no struggle, nothing.

In a heartbeat the dirty Frenchman was on me. Kicking at me, slashing at me with his muddy blade while his soiled chopper sloshed around, and all up in my face. It was all I could do to keep myself from getting clubbed by the damned thing as I slipped and rolled, but not quick enough as he struck me with something pointy and stabby.

I stumbled back. He'd got me right in the soft spot, in the crook of my neck. Where the clavicle embeds itself into your throat region, but this time on my right side. More fucking agony, and suddenly I couldn't breathe again.

Pain lanced throughout my entire body. My vision blurred. Each breath was getting harder and harder to suck up now and I felt like liquid fire was filling my lungs and I dropped to my knees, at the mercy of my naked enemy.

I looked down to the unfamiliar dagger lodged into my throat and I could only guess at how big the blade was. Time was running out fast for me. The sky was darkening. Whipping out the dagger in a frenzied cry I stuck the flailing Frenchmen right in the gooch: the area delicately poised between a gentleman's balls and his arse hole.

His reaction was a simple gasp.

I didn't hesitate with my intention as I knew I had already dragged in my last breath, so cleaving the dagger handle upward and toward his pubic region, I jaggedly hacked through his balls and cock to leave them separated and flapping loosely. I reckon I must've caught an artery and his bladder because I haven't ever seen that much fluid drain out of a single person.

A blackbird with red tipped wings passed overhead just as the Frenchman stopped living and I was washed by a wave of dizziness. My revenge was done. But I had only managed to get two of them, and Peacemaker was still out there and free to live and sing and dance and betray good, honest, adventurous people.

My eyes swam into my skull and I dropped back into the very same grave I had literally just climbed out of.

The world switched to black and the fire left me again and I was falling down into my very own version of death.

On the Dock (L. S.).

After giving me a final shove on to a small platform, Mr Serious fastened my shackles to a considerably chunky hoop of metal that was anchored into the ground and dressed around with carpet. Then, assuming he was satisfied that I was secure, he bowed to the vacant space, holding two fingers to his forehead then backed out through the leather studded door that we had entered through and into the so-called "Council Chambers". The door was belted with iron bands, criss-crossing every eight to ten inches, and I reckoned that it was a door not to be broken down without tremendous effort.

I had been fastened to a dock that seemed dead centre of the chamber's total floor area, elevated from the pool of benches that lined up, in ranks, perpendicular to my position. Opposite my platform, on the other side of the benches, was another station that housed a long desk with three empty chairs. This point was highest of all in the court, and took power position, each chair ornately ringing of absolute authority. The benches looked like church pews and my platform didn't have a seat at all, whereas the thrones behind the long desk were cushioned and maybe even carved from gold. Fabric adorned the walls and a thick, stiff carpet bristled my grazed soles.

I didn't have to wait long before a shadow-figure detached itself from the curtains draped behind the high, long desk. It pulled back the left-most of the three thrones and sat in a swoop of black robes and mystique.

Now I was cold, and I clamped my jaw tight to stop my teeth from chattering as the robed figure lifted his hood back to reveal himself. His skin wrinkled around his eyes and mouth like raisin flesh, and his fingers curved into leather claws, topped with pointy yellow scabs, resting upon the desk. His frame looked brittle, but his eyes sharp and strong, eating into me from his position thirty yards away. It was a stare that brought memories from a very distant past to the fore.

I didn't even want to guess how old this ancient bastard was.

'And so, we meet again, Lord Game.' His voice resonated with a strength that his appearance keenly betrayed.

'I'm sorry, you are?' I played it casual, keeping it cruisy, as they say. The truth is that I just like winding people up. I knew exactly who he was, and the role he'd played in the pantomime that had been my life.

He shook his head and took a long blink, and I thought I saw a smile through his ridiculously long and white beard. I wondered if he had ever cut that horrible thing in his entire life. Then I wondered if scissors were even a thing when he was a young man, maybe a thousand years ago.

'True to design, you play the part intended for you: the loose cannon; the ace up the sleeve; the anarchist.' He adjusted his robes a little and pulled his seat up. 'But from the moment we brought you in, you have been tested. A test you failed when you tried to destroy the scriptures and put your brother in the medical-.'

'Listen, old man-'

'No, you listen, *boy*!' His hands had curled into fists and his eyes widened. 'What you know about the world, about life, about anything, I could write down upon the head of a sewing needle. If those books were the originals The Cube would've been redundant and impossible to replicate. Technological stalemate would be the future. Zero progression.'

He sighed. 'But even now, at the end of the show, you cling to the role as was cast for you. Afraid to accept that you do not know yourself, and in hindsight, you never did, only the version we created.'

His words irritated me, but I held my tongue. Not knowing as much as I should has always been a pet-peeve of mine. Being in disadvantaged situations and not knowing as much as I should is my fucking worst nightmare.

'You were probably too young to remember when your function was decided in the strategies of empires. But even then, as an infant, you were always too concerned with the small things.' He steepled his fingers and blew out, hard. 'But still, you have had your moments. And alas, here we are, and finally you discover the truth of-'

'Hang on, go back a second,' I waved my shackled hands counter clockwise, trying to rewind the moment back, forgiving the chink and pinch of iron. 'Let me get this right. Are you saying that *you*,' I gestured, animating, clinking in his direction, 'left *me,*' this time toward myself, 'back with the brothers at the abbey, and took my sanctimonious fucking brother away with you,' I did my best to finger play a bird in flight, 'to live here?'

The old man had a hard look about him that only matured as my words echoed out.

'Your foremost problem is your arrogance, which is swiftly followed by your remarkable aptitude for stupidity and ignorance. Even when the truth shackles you to a dock and tries to ram it down your unenlightened throat, you still can only see small frames, tiny sections of the bigger picture and idea.

'But hear my words now when I say that you are a pawn, and you always have been. Your brother however, he is a player. He always did show remarkable propensity for-'

'Deception? Deceitfulness?'

'Yes, amongst other things. But not everything is black and white. I trust you at least know that by now. But enough of all that, the past is gone; you served your purpose, did what was needed. But now,' he raised his arms wide. 'Henry Game, you reached the end of the board, and thus: the pawn evolves.'

That confirmed it. These bastards had played me like a jack in the box. Wind me up to watch me pop. Well no more... Blood pounded behind my ears; wrists biting into the oiled shackles as I tested its metal.

'One of you cunts took my book. Was it under your order?'

He said nothing. I knew that getting angry would only play into his hands again, of course.

'Knights Templar, that definitely was you.' It wasn't a question and the old man's smile was all the answer I required.

'You do have it in you,' he said, 'the ability. You are blue blood, Henry.'

Given the poor lighting my eyes had adjusted and I could see that we were not alone, not by a long shot. Several shadows still hung back by the curtains around the peripherals of the chambers, and I realised that the room resembled the House of Lords at Westminster. I tried again but the metal at my wrists would not give way.

'So, I have been a tool for your games? All this time, a weapon wielded...'

'There were times when you carried out the wishes of this council, yes. Other times when you strayed. But such is the way with unruly things. Yet all things, even you, are a part of the masterplan.'

More shadows separated from the peripherals and took their places amongst the benches. I counted seven in total.

'Not submitting to a master makes me unruly, then? I'm not one of your puppets, Doctor Mirabilis! You may have my brother under control, but I promise you this: I'll never join your incestuous boyband. No matter how catchy your choruses might be!'

'But, Henry, you are already one of us.' A new voice, and that of a much younger man with an eastern European accent.

The newcomer had taken the far right-hand position, opposite the central vacant throne. He kept his hood drawn. His hands were pale like snow, and tiny sparkles glowed out at me from beneath his robe.

'Count Saint Germain is correct,' said Mirabilis, 'all of us are blue blood, and of the First,' and then he raised two fingers to his brow and muttered something unintelligible.

St. Germain was the next to follow suit, and the fetish repeated around the room and amongst the benches which I realised were now almost filled with robe wearing zealots.

When the freaky ritual finished, St. Germain spoke again. 'Have you not ever wondered why you age so slowly? Or why time and decay doesn't affect you consistently with the rest of the world?'

This was a question I had toyed with for almost as long as I could remember.

'Well, I make sure I drink plenty of water; take multi-vitamins as often as I remember, which isn't…that…often.' When I started my response, I thought I was being a smartarse, but even as I heard myself, my words sounded childish and I regretted them.

'It is the same reason your blood runs so dark, you imbecile!' He faced Mirabilis, clearly annoyed. 'Why do we waste time with this one? There are others, and much more suitable.'

The doctor frowned at the count. 'Tell a hammer that it was only made to smash things, and it will only ever be a tool for destruction. But show that hammer that it can do more, that it can build too, that it can create new things,' he said, now turning toward me, 'and it will show you what it is truly capable of accomplishing.'

St. Germain lowered his hood. His features sharp and rather

sinister. He was much younger than I expected. He returned his unpleasant attention back to me, his eyes twinkling with a light unnatural.

I kept my silence. St. Germain and Mirabilis made a formidable team but there was still the empty seat between them, and I could only wonder as to whom that may belong.

The (Living) Dead of Night.

I was in the black. In a state between sleep and death, and neither at the same time.

An undefinable period had passed. Somehow, I knew this. It was more than sleep. I call it suspended. I don't suppose I could ever really understand, and I gave up trying centuries ago.

To put simply: I was gone. Not dead and not living, but still a part of the great consciousness that flows through every living thing. I was still in existence, still me, yet not as I am now or ever was before.

I orbited the vacuum of now, neither aware of reality nor ignorant to it. There was no I. My possessions, including my mind and body were confiscated. Bereft of the tools of expression I became the current, the wind, the blazing glory of sunlight, and nothing, all at once, and never at all.

There was no time, only happenings and events unfolding then refolding, and all to a perpetual rhythm of design. It was a state of comfortable torque, a momentum that slowly began to unwind until I was finally falling against something real, something tangible, again. I didn't know I was reaching for it until I touched it and the *I* came back.

I opened my eyes to the flicker of candlelight, snotty sniffling, and the sound of leather tensioning to a rhythm. It was a kind of pulling sound that comes only from human flesh being sewn together.

Pain brought my estranged mind back to the present. My limbs weighed down like mountains, each one frozen and bound to a table or slab. There was also a good deal of excruciating agony around my neck. It felt like a collar of molten iron choking my skin, pulling me, head down into damnation. I tried to make sounds but could only muster a ragged gurgle.

Suddenly the sniffling stopped, and the blur of a body swept the air around me and hovered over my head. My vision focused and I realised that it was an old man with a patchy, flaking beard. His weathered face hording patches of pink, peeling skin. He looked malnourished, like most of my crew had, like Skelton in particular...

A single glistening gem of mucus hung from the tip of his nose. I clamped my mouth closed and tried to suck in air through my itchy nose, but it was no use – my nose didn't work. The mucus hung heavy, and if I wasn't careful, it would be landing in my mouth. I tried sniffing again, but I couldn't even crinkle my nostrils to get at the itch, never mind breathe.

The old man wore a crystal-clear glass screen that was currently lowered across his eyes. The look of it disturbed me. But whatever the apparatus was, it looked to be attached to his head by an impossibly thin and cylindrical metal frame, fastened around the circumference of his cranium upon a neat leather crown.

The levers and springs on display made me feel uneasy, but what the glass did to his eyes and forehead, left an altogether different impression. Although it spooked me a little, the effect that the glass had on the old fellow's appearance was comical and his watery eyes bulged back at me as one blue, one brown.

Making an indistinguishable grunt, he disappeared from view and continued stitching, sniffing. I lay awake and paralysed as my body was tugged at and manipulated, tightened, but I think I had it figured out, and as my leg was jerked and clamped and tensioned, I figured that I was dismembered and my thoughts trailed back to Peacemaker and his first scalp. I wondered with a sick feeling as to how many chunks I had been separated in to.

Contemplating my bodily division, as one does in situations such as these, my attentions were drawn to the lustrous globes that hung up high, suspended from the ceiling. The light was encased within a metal lamp and glass walls, and it showered the entire area in a bright and unnatural yellow ambiance. I knew it was no candle-flame. I presumed a magic of some description, and I noticed it made a sinister hissing noise that set my heart at a quickening pace.

My eyes pressed heavy against my concentration and I welcomed slumber and hoped to wake from my nightmare in a new place.

* * *

'Damn it, Doc, even though I think you're super creepy, I thank you from the bottom of my toes – literally.' I rolled my right wrist and flexed my fingers with fluid motion, then scratched my nose again, but gained no relief as the itch was deeper than the surface.

The old man looked at me, his eyes still magnified through the glass device craning from his forehead. From the crinkle around his eyes, I assumed he was pleased.

I reckoned I had been conscious for about a week, and over that time it had taken a good four days, and a gallon or two of a sweet and gloopy concoction, for me to find my voice. But still, it was little more than a croak at that. And in all that time alone, the goggle-eyed doctor had said not a single word, and not a single legible syllable.

I noticed, that as each fleshy section of my person was repositioned to be sewn up tight, the doctor would first attach the most curious of contraptions both to the wrinkled, pale and detached part of myself, and also the part of me that was a lot healthier in colour and revived.

The device was a wooden cylindrical instrument, about twelve inches high, and it housed a large pile of silver disks in its open middle section. It had a polished wooden circular lid and bottom plate, and was fixed apart by thin copper tubes, that appeared to also stop the silver disks from falling out. Although it was peculiar in itself, the most interesting part was the two thin copper plates that were attached by a wire directly to the top and bottom of the silver disks. These plates were the only part of the contraption to touch my skin, and where it did, my flesh would blacken and smoke a little, but regardless, the doctor methodically set up each part of my estranged body, and connecting the device to my flesh appeared to be a critical step in putting me back together again.

I said nothing as he continued stitching my left foot to the bottom of my leg. The doctor had been occasionally pausing in his work to drip feed me the potion of sweet slurry that made my limbs tingle with pleasure. The feeds were intermittent and without warning. Sometimes it was the good stuff, other times it was dirty warm water.

On several occasions I attempted to converse with the surgeon but the most I had achieved was a prolonged grunt and a hard frown. That grunt told me he was displeased, I'm sure of it.

It seemed that the stronger I became the faster I healed, and now I could move myself enough to get almost into a full sitting position, almost, but not quite as still the pain across my waistline was tremendously prohibiting. But from my elevated position, I was able to see a lot more of my surroundings.

The first and most obvious items were the eight rusted iron boxes of different sizes and shapes. Some rectangular, arm length, some small and box-like, one head size. I deduced that these were the boxes that once contained my severed and estranged body parts. I at least took comfort in the knowledge they were lined with fur, and that they didn't just burn me to ashes and scatter me to the wind. But it seemed that cutting me into several pieces and separating them is a good way to keep me down, if not permanently then certainly indefinitely, unless someone pieces humpty back together again, of course.

I was clearly in a very old building and I suspected it to be a tower because the walls formed around us in a circular movement. Also, the walls random stone and the eaves of the pitched roof bared its rafters in a shameless fashion, flirting with pigeons, even. And other than the doctor's cot bed, the room was pretty bare and derelict.

I reckoned that I was in a castle tower, and by the sound of wind and rain howling beyond the stone and slate shelter, back in the motherland. There were no windows I could see anything useful from, and only one door.

Looking down at the doctor I "ahemed" as loudly as I could manage. I was dangerously close to being bored, and with only pain for distraction, I was losing my patience for the silent act that we had been playing for the past week.

The old man stopped his stitching and looked at me, all of me. Then, giving a peculiar grunt he stood from the end of my stretcher and finally wiped the jewel of snot from the tip of his nose that just kept recurring. Then, gripping my foot between a long and bony forefinger and thumb, he gave it a turn then let loose a satisfied grunt and a nod.

'Seriously Doc, I need you to talk to me.' My words were once again met with a groan. This groan reeked of frustration.

Somehow, I was beginning to interpret his guttural dialect. I tried to watch his path as he stalked away behind me, groaning myself as I accepted that my head could not fully turn yet.

After a moment of scratching and equipment crashing, he reappeared with a very short piece of chalk, and a slate that had fallen in from the roof, in hand.

'You can't talk,' I realised.

His eyes crinkled around the edges again. Lifting the glass away from his face he wrote on the slate: Dr Kratzenstein.

'Henry Game,' I offered, stupidly.

He frowned again. I asked the next most important question I could think of.

'How long have I been…' I trailed then almost choked as I saw the chalk scratch a number into the slate.

259 years, they estimate, he wrote.

I did the math. If Kratzenstein was telling the truth, then the year was 1812. Fuck. No wonder I was so thirsty.

The sounds of a key scraping in a lock drew my attention to the other side of the room. Kratzenstein dropped the slate to the stone floor and hurried away from me as the door opened. A large and round looking fellow wearing a long and dripping wet coat entered at a bit of a stagger.

My arm, neck, stomach, leg, chest and back were all screaming at me to lie down, so I obliged. The tension was positively wound as this new person entered, still unannounced and eventually the sound of the door swinging shut then the bolt sliding to lock, reverberated around the circular purgatory of silent men.

Kratzenstein shuffled even further away from me as the stranger approached and sat down in the doctors sewing chair, now by my head. Luckily that was my good side and I could turn my head just enough to look into his face. He smiled. I recognised him: Claruc.

He produced a stoppered wine flask from inside of his coat and offered it, however briefly, in my direction. Before I had the chance to refuse, he'd withdrawn it, removing the bung with his teeth before giving it a long and satisfying chug.

'There ye are me darlin', it's bin too long.' A hiccup.

I realised he was addressing his wine skin. I laughed, or I tried to, but my stomach hurt too much.

'Powerful enemies, Henry Game, power-full names-' another hiccup, his jewel eyes seeing past his vice and resting upon me.

'Claruc, it's been a while old friend…' I propped myself up once again despite the agony. 'The chances of running into you up in this lonely tower of mine – it boggles the mind. Tell me, must be going on a couple of centuries since I last saw you? To what do I owe the pleasure?'

Now it was Claruc's turn to laugh, blue liquid spraying from his nose and mouth.

'T'what indeed?' He stoppered his flask and leaned in close. 'Nothin' makes more o' an enemy than ye greatest ally. Henry Game: king o' pawns!' he lifted his stoppered flask and made a toast to his own proclamation then realised the bung was still in.

I lay back down. For a guy that had just slept the last twenty-six decades I sure was tired of the same old half-truths and riddles.

'Kratzenstein, is Humpty-Dumpty back together again?' Another hiccup.

Scratching on a board. A shadow passed over me and away.

'Well, ye' best get on wi' it then. All the king's horses an' all the king's men won't wait much longer! Doctor, finish your creation, an' bring him back t' life!'

I opened my eyes just a crack and saw Claruc unstopping his flask once more then upending his never-ending supply of, whatever the hell it is he consumes.

Kratzenstein had picked up thread and needle and was

lowering his enhanced spectacled screen before leaning back in to continue working on my foot. The sickly rip and pull of dried flesh were a timely reminder of why I was lay there.

Claruc was making for the door and I closed my eyes for just a minute.

1888.

Through the act of writing these accounts, I must confess to gleaning some semblance of clarity, and therein a modicum of peace, as I have committed to laying out my misdeeds and histories for you. A most serendipitous consequence for sure, but admittedly one that I am finding a guilty comfort in. And whilst this may sound odd, planning my own death has finally given me something to live for again.

My plan is to burn, along with the rest of my kind. This is the only way to ensure that you do not become a pawn in their games as I have been. I have so much to tell you but so little time to do it. One can only write so fast. I must be selective with the words, selective with the stories. My accounts are meant to show you the darkest parts of who I am in order to help you avoid the same mistakes. Forewarned is forearmed, and so on.

You have it all before you. See these accounts as the catalyst to set you upon your own path through the ages, although most likely you will not live as long as I have, due to your mother's DNA, I expect you will live at least as long as I have by the time I do what must be done.

However, I do not see your shortened life as weakness anymore. In fact, I have never felt stronger than I do when I write these words and plan my final moments. I am literally living to die, but I suppose we all are.

I was never fit or good enough to raise you. If I could go back and change anything, it would be to have hidden you and never trusted your whereabouts to anyone still breathing. Being who I am and also your father was never an option, especially not when I am so receptive to the darkest aspects of our existence.

You may notice that many of my confessions have since been used as the origin of myth and legend, or that my history has been used as the horror stories told at night to scare children to sleep. I have many more in the closet, many more that I hope will burn to ashes with me, but some, I dare say, are too notorious to let die:

I was back in England and the year was 1888. I had travelled far and wide but always I returned home. This time I settled into a sparsely furnished and dubious flat above the finest Gentlemen's club in all of east London. It was a grubby little spot where I attempted to keep myself hidden from the powers that be and their games. The district was Whitechapel, and it was a place of lust and filth in a pit of sin. And I figured it was the perfect place to find oneself the right kind of lost.

I was the new kid about town and trying to find the niche between the whoremasters and the opium dens. I had enough money to be viewed as aristocracy, whilst baring enough scars and dents to be seen as a self-made man.

I was often approached by the puppeteers behind both major games: drugs and sex. I even considered combining the two, but trust me, when the opium has you, sex is not easily achieved. I kept my options open, as it was still early days and I was already knee deep in filth and overflowing street gutters.

I'd spent plenty of silver crowns upon my fair share of street girls, my unfair share of alcohol and poppies, and I was just finally starting to lose myself. It seemed that I was everyone's novelty. I was even starting to feel at home when the nightmarish cold sensation nipped at the nape of my neck and trickled over me, again. Centuries had passed since I last felt this sensation, but when I felt it, I knew what it was, and I was raped.

An absence and darkness ensued for the most. I recall snippets of imagery; surgeon's tools and sharp instruments; moonlight spilling across a lady's throat. Syringes and grapes dressed in blood and the pleasurable moan of asphyxiation...

The first time my faculties returned to me I realised I was in the back of a moving carriage. With operating devices in hand, and my shirt sleeves rolled tight about my elbows and blood up my forearms I panicked.

Before me, and completely spilled open, was a whore that I didn't recognise. Her stomach and chest spread neatly on the floor of the carriage. A surgeon's tool bag open beside me and I dropped the sharp blade I was holding into the bag and closed the silver clasp. The leather had three initials stamped in gold leaf "".

With a shock I abandoned the carriage and sought the shelter of my recently purchased flat, scattering through the dank alleyways like a red-handed ghoul across a graveyard.

News of the gruesome murder rumoured around town. I, of course, being a newcomer, always smartly dressed and with enough coin to make an impression on all classes and walks of life, was a current source of public opinion anyway. If the gossipers weren't talking about the recent murder, they were almost certainly speculating about the newcomer. I just happened to be both in this scenario, so naturally others made the same link.

Like Hamelin, the spectres of Whitechapel must have been served a great injustice as they raped my consciousness again and again upon the ladies of the alleys. I tried to resist them but could form no semblance of defence as I didn't yet know how. The murders were committed by my hand, but I felt no sense of responsibility for them, only a great shame.

Over the next few months the days grew shorter and colder and I was carried through, little more than a passenger. My clothes hung loose around my waist and my beard had grown out to an unruly length. The suspicions of the locals had all but isolated me, and the fortune in my safe had all but kept the law enforcement satiated and distant too.

In what time I did have to consider my situation, I feared that they would never let me go until one quiet evening I returned to consciousness, again sticky with dark blood. I was in my flat, thankfully, but coagulated clots of death draped down the front of my apron. It was spattered all about me and mostly upon the defiled bed sheets which I had returned to once more.

My face felt tight, but my limbs buzzed and tingled in ecstasy, like I could run around the city, twice. New energy vibrated through every fibre and bone. Whatever substance I had taken, whatever narcotic, the feeling was vaguely familiar, and somewhat similar to the sweet potion given to me by Kratzenstein, some several decades earlier.

My stomach was heavy, which was unusual as the spectres care not for my well-being nor need for sustenance. The nape of my neck tingled, and I shivered. They weren't finished with me yet. I could feel their influence all over. My skin prickled and rose like goose flesh. Whilst I felt physically stronger than I ever had, my emotional and mental states were disturbed and fragile, inflamed.

I walked over to the mirror to see what made my face feel so peculiar when I observed that upon my writing desk was a dinner plate with an uncooked liver, and two large bites out of it. Blood was smeared over every inch of the desktop and chair. I noticed that the inkwell was full to the point of overflow, and a saturated quill lay scattered amongst the bundle of tarnished parchments, bloodied fingerprints over white sheets.

I peered into the mirror, angling the frame so as to illuminate my face by the white of the moon and my stomach turned and threatened to rebel. My face was tight because of the dried-up blood on my chin, my cheeks, around my lips. My stomach felt heavier than ever before and a sour saliva flooded into my mouth, sending the room into a spin. Dropping to my knees I noticed a crumpled piece of parchment beneath the desk. I reached out and opened it whilst trying to keep the contents of my stomach from deserting me. Whatever it may be, I thought it was best staying in there.

Dear Boss,

the letter began. I started to read the opening line but the ink, or blood, had smeared when it was crumpled. I could only make out the opening and ending. My hands were shaking. I vomited in my mouth and swallowed again when I recognised the salty, metallic tang of blood.

The signature was a name as chilling as the night is black. A name that lives in infamy even to this day. A name that stalks the streets of Hell:

Ripper.

With the borrowed strength I felt in my veins I abandoned my flat along with my money and possessions and ran into the night, fleeing the city in a desperate attempt to rescue both my sanity and to preserve what remained of the whoredom of Whitechapel.

1814. Why I Was Returned.

It branded itself upon the moonless night, eclipsing each star in its wake. A sight to behold and one that hinted of the big things happening beyond our skies and domed prison.

I closed my eyes and breathed in the humidity, turning my back on the soft lapping of the shores of Lake Windermere. The meeting was set by the old waystone on the eastern shore, and as instructed, I had waited, patiently.

My left ankle clicked like knitting needles when I rolled my foot in a circular motion. It had since become quite the habit. But, click or no, my functionality was a damn sight better than it had been for the last couple a hundred years or so, give or take a decade or three. I was whole again and Claruc warned that I had to be grateful, had to be compliant. I was back amongst the living again and lucky to be breathing in the freshwater air.

I couldn't stop thinking about the Humpty Dumpty rhyme. I propose that whatever it may be about, it certainly isn't an egg and never was. The rhyme doesn't ever mention an egg, nor any animal that lays eggs! And if it was possible to put a shattered egg back together, the contents would surely be ruined and lost. A hollowed and fractured shell would be the absolute best you could hope for. An egg-man. It's ludicrous and just downright irritating, even if only for a children's skipping rhyme.

Whatever Humpty was, this supposed "king" was mightily concerned when it fell from the wall. And thinking along more practical avenues, perhaps the infamous Humpty Dumpty was actually a cannon, or a very large piece of artillery… far more likely than an egg man, but likely still not accurate. And in a book of truths, one well-placed lie can corrupt them all.

As my mind mulled over the fallibility of nursery rhymes, my eyes lingered upon the burning inferno trailing across the cosmos beyond our world, hurtling through the distorted reflections of the lake in a trail of illumination. It sure was spectacular.

Doomsayer's were rife with prophecy and how we all should abandon our sinful possessions and money and beg for mercy. I knew where my money was, amongst other treasures, and given the first opportunity, I would be collecting it all.

The comet heralded a change in times. In hindsight it may be looked upon as the usher to the dawn of the industrial revolution. It was stark to my perceptions of how the world had blissfully moved on in my absence. Miraculous inventions of technology and leaps in science had begun to make up a part of everyday life. It was almost like the idea was to make living as easy and effortless as possible. The way I saw it, we had already fallen into the vice, and every man was now just another shiny cog in the age of the machine.

If the idea was for the world to continue to invent devices that made every day living easier and easier, then the counterpart to that argume would be that easy living brought easier ways to die. Or, if you are as sinister as I am: kill others.

Easier to live; much easier to die.

Perhaps the novelty of smart living will never be outshone by the comet of quick-death, or de-evolution, or a growing of mass ignorance, least not by those who continue to grow rich from it. They are the new kings and queens, self-made royals.

It seemed that the great comet heralded a change in me too, or at least in my perspective of self. The French had taught me the most valuable of lessons, for which I could never thank them enough, as they taught me that I was stoppable. Perhaps even killable, but that there are things worse than death, and a fire that can destroy everything.

Pebbles crunching drew my attention from the astronomic brilliance in the sky. Two shadows approached, one of them egg-like. The other being a somewhat narrower shadow beside him, I did not. I rolled my foot in anticipation, bones clicking.

Claruc and the stranger stopped short, lingering around ten feet away, speaking to one another in hushed tones. After several minutes I grew impatient.

'Ahem!' I declared, tactfully. 'Would either of you know what the difference is between a French man and a sack full of shit?'

The two men stopped their whispering and drew silent.

'The sack.' I said.

Claruc laughed and playfully slapped the back of the other man, whom did not laugh, I observed. Together they approached. I could see Claruc's face, yet his companion remained darkened beneath his drawn hood. I continued to wait. My instructions were to wait and behave myself: a note passed to me by the dumb doctor, several days ago and signed by Claruc.

I had traipsed the breadth of the country, mostly on foot, to get to this specifically desired spot for the required time. If the idea was to make sure all my limbs and joints were in working order, a sort of test run, then they could tick the box, I reckoned. I felt good and ready to go. The world was the same place, no doubt about it, but it had changed beyond my wildest dreams.

'Take it in, Ross,' Claruc spoke first. 'It's ne' often ye' catch the Game wrong footed.' His words were more slurred than usual.

I rolled my foot around again, testily; it clicked and clicked and clicked. 'What am I doing here, Claruc?'

Finally, the small man spoke. 'He's a bit cock sure o'

himself. Ey, Claruchaun?' Another Irishman, I noticed. Now I was outnumbered and too many Irishmen made me uncomfortable, especially when in England.

'Claruc, who the fuck is this little fopdoodle?' Heat was rising in my face. I didn't care for a man who wore a hood, especially when it wasn't raining, but I was on my best behaviour.

The "fopdoodle" stepped forward. His face about as serious as any I had seen before. 'I am General Robert Ross, Mister Game, and as o' tree days ago, the Empire is declared at war on both side o' the Atlantic. You, Mister Game, will fight under my command and squash the threat quickly.'

'General?' I frowned, directing my question at Claruc who was quietly sipping at a hip flask. If he heard me, he chose to ignore it.

General Ross advanced another step. 'Listen t' me closely, as I'm only gunna say it one more time, you've been brought back t' help us win these wars.'

I took note of the plural. However, I was still totally at a loss, almost two hundred and sixty years had passed since I was last knocking around. Back then Britain had virtually ruled supreme. I wondered whom these multiple enemies might be. Maybe the Spanish, more likely the French, but I couldn't think who else. "Both sides o' the Atlantic," he had said. Maybe my face gave me away as he pulled his hood back and smiled.

'Ah, but you know nothing do you?'

I didn't appreciate his tone, if I'm honest, but he was correct, so I kept my mouth shut. You won't ever catch me owning up to not knowing everything I need to, and then some. Nor would you catch me beating the living shit out of those who helped bring me back to life, least not on the first date.

'It hasn't been 'officially' announced,' the general air-quoted the officiality for clarity, I presumed.

'But, the United States o' America have attacked two o' our

major trading vessels, an' have made plans t' occupy Canada. They've officially declared war on us. On fecking us!' He laughed and looked up to the trailing comet. 'They passed it through Congress, earlier in the week, or so they tell me, feckin' cock-sucking yank-twats!'

'United States of America?' I let slip, accidentally.

'Two-hundred an' sixty years is a time fo' countries t' be birthed, yet still the game can't die-Hic!' charmed Claruc, between sips.

'Two hundred and fifty-nine,' I corrected him. 'So, who's the other enemy then?' I asked the general. He looked back at me like he had just seen me eating shit.

'Napoleon, of course!'

'Two-hundred and...' I trailed, giving up to frustration. I turned to Claruc instead. 'What the fuck is Napoleon?'

Claruc's face lit up as he gazed at the comet, not looking at me as he spoke. 'Fatefully French. Ye' have a perfect game fo' the imperfect Game-hic!'

'So, let me get this right, my enemies are the French and the Americans, really?'

'A re-birthday gift,' slurred Claruc, still observing the skies.

I smiled, breathing in the warm and humid night. The comet really was a beautiful sight. Almost like a cosmic birthday candle perhaps, trying to make all my wishes come true at once.

I vowed I would play nice and earn my life back. And if I got to exact my revenge at the same time, well, that was just bloody marvellous.

*   *   *

'Is this really necessary?' I pleaded. 'The cat didn't drown. I saw her and she's absolutely fine. Just a bit wet is all-' I tried but the hatch dropped down with a crack, leaving us in the dark amongst the rickety bowels of the naval frigate as we set sail for Canada. They stowed us so deep that not even the rats would hide there.

'Don't take it t' heart, Ga-' Claruc hiccupped.

'Take it to heart?' I said, pinning Claruc across the space with a point of my finger. 'What is it with you and fucking cats, eh?' He was over there somewhere; I just couldn't see him was all.

'Horrible creatures-'

'The crew almost abandoned the ship. You're lucky we hadn't left the docks and that the bloody cat could swim.' I was still incensed by the injustice of my poor treatment.

'The fucking riddling and belching alone is enough to curse any damned voyage. Especially with a bunch of superstitious fucking sailors! But to stow me away with you... I didn't do anything wrong!'

He laughed and burped at the same time then went on chugging on something wet.

'Ye', well, sometimes, us mythics are nought but the whispered tales told from books an' from the dregs o' empty barrels, an' mainly t' frighten' wee darlings. Only few know what we are. Sea-folk wouldn't sail with monsters like we... 'specially not the ones shitting an' fightin' beside 'em...hic!'

As far as Claruc went, that might have been the clearest, most coherent bit of conversation I had ever had with him. I was stunned by his lack of riddle, so I didn't speak for several minutes, thinking while the vessel lurched to one side.

Something heavy bounced across the planks, sliding hard against my arse cheek. I picked it up. It was unusually heavy, and I could feel a stopper bung in the neck. Claruc's hip flask.

Suddenly a great thirst seized me, and all I desired was to taste the contents that never ran dry... Claruc's fumbling in the dark stopped. Silence pressed against me. I located the stopper and eased it free. The smell that hit me took my mind reeling back to my days at the abbey: sweet beor. Raising the flask to my mouth, I hesitated as I detected Claruc's nectar breath hissing hot against my cheek.

'I wouldn', Game, unless ye' wanna be a Claruchaun. An it's a thirsty honour for sure. A life suspended between truths t' come, and the ones that don't.'

I lowered the flask, my arm feeling almost weightless as Claruc took it at a snatch and noisily glugged at it like a man lost in the desert.

I realised that I had been holding my breath as I heard Claruc's scuffed retreat back across the cargo deck.

For a time, we sat in dark silence. The ship steadied as the sails were lowered and the wind took a hold of her and guided us out amongst the deep ocean.

* * *

Through the distant walkways above, I could make out the orders given to man the oars. We had been at sea for the best part of a month, and for the most, Claruc and I had remained down below. The marines aboard did not trust us one bit.

I watched Claruc, staring into the depth of his flask like a dying man searches for the meaning of life in everything, and suddenly felt an excessive sense of pity for the great egg. Contradictory to my emotions, I wondered if we were all slaves to our past. Claruc stuck in the bottle, me stuck in a vengeful existence.

The hatch lifted, showering us in a salty vapour. If Claruc felt the stark cold, he showed no sign of it. I, on the other hand, cursed and threatened vehemently.

A smooth faced marine looked down at us for a long moment, spat to his side, then slammed the hatch shut again.

The chill on the wind was familiar, I recognised the distinct lack of pollution to it, we had indeed arrived, and the soft hissing of Claruc's intermittent whistle haunted us into the land of Canada.

Soon enough my feet would be back on frozen ground and ready to march south to fuck the Americans in the arse hole with my sharp steel. And if I had to straighten my own men out along the way, well, then so be it.

'Everythin' changes when the blood starts flowing. The Game knows the players, the pieces-hic!'

It was the first thing he had said in weeks, and again I understood him completely. I wondered if maybe I had spent so much time around the old fool. It seemed his riddles were becoming clearer and clearer by the sentence – but damn if he wasn't right. Everything does change, and never quicker than when the first head topples.

For now they shunned us because they feared us. But when the bodies begin to drop, it will be us that they hide behind. Years pass, technology advances, ideologies change, but never men. Not in my experience.

* * *

It was a clear dark night, not a cloud in sight. The boarder traipsed miles behind us, along with a steady trail of dead American scouts. Breadcrumbs.

We crept through the outer reaches of the nominated capital, Washington DC, with the dark on our side, and a darker intent about our objective. A moonless night, and all that shone through the tarred pin-pricked canvas were the stars of those who had died before us. Overlords would not bless our actions or make things easy for the men with poor lighting. But I needed less light than most.

The remainder of General Ross's men approached from the east. We took the northern and most direct route whilst the rest of the navy oozed slowly from the west. Resistance was pathetically futile and thin.

The fat Americans thought themselves too far away to be touched by the evils we harboured, but they knew not that I was there when the Iroquois settled with the French and the purest form of evil was born here.

Fuck, it had practically mass reproduced and infected the whole sodding country. And now it had come full circle; now the return of which had evolved and flourished into something spectacular, astonishing even. It was quite beautiful in a sadistic light that I should be the one to return to punish them.

My ankle still plagued me, and it was cold. Bad combination.

The regimental navy men of the Royal Marines were a tough bunch for sure. Not a peep from even the weakest of them as we blistered through the ice and into the obscurity of a densely packed woods. Every one of them would have had a place amongst my company, if I still had it. Bad memories of my previous visit here only proved to fuel the fire that burned eternally in my heart for revenge.

Truth, or Lip Service (L. S.).

And whilst the benches were overflowing with black robes, the seat between St. Germain and Mirabilis remained empty. It was almost as if the two of them leaned away from one another to emphasise the vacancy that made the vacuum between.

Whether my still returning grey matter was showing me more of my own frailties, or they actually were leaning apart, I'll never know, but it was felt keenly on my end, and for reasons I could not fathom. I could only imagine that one of great influence claimed the seat between them. But in any event, such a person was clearly too busy to attend my hearing, or intervention, or whatever the fuck the charade was supposed to be.

Often enough, I'd found myself a passenger on the train of life. I hate being in the dark. Ignorance is for the dead; enlightenment is lifeblood, oxygen, sustenance.

'The great secret of it all is actually explainable. It is basic science, Henry,' explained Mirabilis. 'The red-blue pigment of your blood is the most obvious and compelling indicator, and while you were young, your uniqueness was a closely guarded secret. It is the case for all of us, as while we have the biological advantage, they have the numbers.

'We have several subtle and varied differences to the *Homo sapiens*. And the long and short of it is we do not need as much oxygen as they to function at our optimum levels. And I suppose, in such light, you could simply deduce that humans were designed to expire much more quickly than we. Think of humans as having a shelf life, so to speak, because the truth of it is, they do.

'The main difference between us is their dependence on oxygen, and restricted capacity for intellectual advancements and self-actualisation. But of course, it is the oxygen rich atmosphere that eventually kills them. A calculated design that served a purpose for the mining of precious elements and other such things that are long since ancient history to us.

'Age is what kills them, and the passing of time. And it is true that time kills us all eventually, even we, but for humans specifically, with a ninety-nine percent oxygen saturation level, they bleed bright red; they burn out much quicker than we, like a struck match, but we, the *Homo primoris,* descendants of the *Anunnaki*, we burn like stars among the fireflies.'

Mirabilis' eyes shone like it was story time around a cosy camp-fire. Meanwhile, I couldn't pull myself away from the fact that I knew that what he said was probably the closest thing to the truth that I had ever heard, and, that perhaps I really did belong alongside them, as one of them. But of course, too much water had passed beneath the bridge for me to forgive and forget.

'The *Homo primoris* oxidise at a significantly reduced rate, and therefore age at a lesser velocity. It really is just basic science, and it is from the uncommon pigment of our lifeblood that the term "*Blue Blood*" derives, and of course, its associated connotations to royalty and old power and influence. Compared to the rapid processes of humans, we seem immortal. To them we are gods. Which is not too far a stretch from the truth of it all.'

Mirabilis ran his pointy fingers through his beard, lost in thought, for a moment, before continuing. 'I sit here before you all, a little over eight hundred years old. Count Saint Germain,' he gestured to his seated companion, 'approaches three hundred and fifty, even. He is young; I am old. He looks young, and I look old, and that is down to the variance in purity of our respective bloodlines.

'The rate of one's molecular degeneration is dependent upon this factor, and quite significantly. Wherein the purer the bloodline, the slower the rate of oxidisation occurs, which ultimately translates to the slow corruption of our flesh.

'The Anunnaki hailed from a world of harsher realities to Earth, making their dominance in strength, agility, intellect, seem all the more supernatural to the indigenous genus. As an advanced species, they have been around for almost a billion of Earth's years. The stories tell it that through exploration and science, they came into possession of the *Greater Truth*, and have been able to expand their lives almost indefinitely thereafter.

'Hundreds of thousands of years ago they colonised this planet by creating a subservient species in their own image. The scientists that arrived here were surprised to discover that even though Earth was so young, a primitive form of intelligent life had evolved naturally.

The *Homo erectus* was dominant and fierce and capable of empathy and socialism. They had already discovered how to use controlled fire, and they made weapons and tools and formed communities of hunter gatherers.

'This was huge news to the Anunnaki, as in all of their years of space exploration, they had never come across an intelligent form of *Homo*. And using splicing technology, the Anunnaki rulers approved the creation of a new labour force, the *Homo sapiens*, to replace the troublesome and rebellious Igigu. After decades they eventually achieved the "Human Being". It was accomplished by combining the DNA of both the primitive, and the ultimate evolution of the genus, the *Homo primoris* with the indigenous *Homo erectus*.

'Following the successful creation of the new slave race, great ethical and political debates ensued within the upper echelons of the Anunnaki society. Some factions believed that in creating such an intelligent form of life, they were also creating a threat to their own species and as such, in the end, further precautions were taken to ensure the new sapiens were restricted and expendable, and easier to thwart should they eventually try to follow the footsteps of their predecessors: the recently decimated Igigu race in attempting to raise rebellion against their creators and masters.

'The primoris required something specific from this planet, and once their mission was complete, further debates raged on over the future of Humanity. Due to mankind's genetic makeup, some saw the human race as being too similar to the primoris to terminate, and it wasn't long before lethal conflicts arose amongst them.

'A great deluge was created by the militant faction of our people lead by El, forcing an equally desperate rescue attempt by the scientific faction lead by Ea. The result was almost total extinction of the human race.

'And just as Ea prepared to retaliate against El, the ruling council of the Anunnaki intervened and decreed that Earth and its humans would be left to develop naturally, and without hinderance. Free to choose its own path.

'Subsequently the ruler of the Anunnaki announced the great exodus from Earth. They had achieved their target and it was time to replenish their home planet. However, there were some, mainly from the scientific faction of Ea, that volunteered to remain on Earth. And so, as our histories show, those that remained became the rulers of mankind as the gods of myth and legend.

'Yet staying on Earth was not as luxurious as it seems, as those that remained did so knowing full well that the oxygen rich atmosphere would drastically shorten their life expectancy, and that the *Greater Truth* would forever be beyond their reach.

'Yet still they remained, some even professing their love for mankind, even seeing them as a second chance to start over. Others stayed for the lust of power and dominion; the chance to play god amongst the less enhanced.

'Shortly after the great departure, a new and all conquering civilisation of humanity was born. The remaining Anunnaki assumed their place as ruling kings and divided the land up equally. But of course, even in time gods die. And so the depths of deceit among the Anunnaki eventually set brother against brother, and father against son, until fewer and fewer lived long enough to produce pure-blooded successors. We in this room are the descendants of that most ancient order of rulers-'

'We are the masters of this planet, and all who dwell upon her,' St. Germain interjected, locking stares with me, daring me to challenge his conviction.

'Surely it serves as no surprise to you when I tell you that you are not like the rest of them?' The body language of the good doctor juxtaposed the bad count. A trick not lost on me.

'I've not been hiding beneath a fucking rock; I know what I know. What I don't know is why I am here, shackled before... well, you zealot cunts: a bunch of robe wearing swingers.' Something about St. Germain unsettled me so I directed my insults at Mirabilis, while continuing to push against the manacles abound my wrists, with zero success.

'Truth is we thought it was time to bring you in to the fold. The world is not what it was and the need for brute force,' he shrugged, 'well, is just about redundant. The time approaches when in order to maintain the Ruling Council, we must replenish the fountain, for posterity-'

'Time to bring me in?' I cut across him as my bare feet discovered a hard lump of something covered by a cloth. It was stashed away into the corner of my dock. Whatever it was, it was tucked in tightly.

I flipped it over with my toes and almost jumped for joy as I recognised *Abatu*. Seemed somebody down here was on my team after all. I just needed to pick the damned thing up without making it obvious or burning my toes off or burning anything else that might give me away.

'You are filled with anger, Henry. If you cannot learn to transform that energy, I promise you now that we will destroy it for you...' St. Germain sounded like he had his own anger issues if you ask me.

'Please, let us make peace, the fighting is over. Do not let anger consume you any longer. Join us and your enemies will become nothing more than avatars on the board game of reality. But be under no illusion when I tell you that right here, right now is the time to decide your future.' Mirabilis played the hard sell as well as any I had seen.

Using the gap between my big toe I managed to secured the handle and was slowly lifting it, all the while trying to keep my torso from bending forward to grab it. I admit that it would have been much easier if I'd bothered to learn yoga in all my years. I promised myself in that moment that should I find peace once more, yoga was top of the list.

'If I agree to join you, what then?' I struggled to keep the strain from my voice as I lifted the blade slowly.

'You will learn of the greater truth and we will show you the path to true enlightenment, but most importantly, together, along with your twin brother, you will take your rightful place beside us.'

'And what will become of my book?' I had my blade in my hand now and pressed the cut of it against the hinge of my shackles to the immediate hiss of smoulder.

'The manuscripts do not belong to one person!' St. Germain shouted and caused an echo in the chamber. 'Why are we wasting time with such foolery?'

Murmurs around the court seemed to be agreeing with St. Germain's frustration and I wondered what that might mean for me.

St. Germain controlled himself with a deep breath before settling his gaze back on to me, teeth clenched. 'The manuscripts are relics left by those who came before us. And when collected, and recited under the correct circumstance they complete the-'

'Now, now, all in good time!' said Mirabilis, holding his hand up at his companion to stop him from finishing his rant.

The cloth was still about my toes and baptismal smoke wafted about my head, lucky for the poor lighting, none seem to notice my prison escape. A moment later the smouldering metal gave way and the hinge latched open to hang loose upon my wrists.

'The manuscripts only form part of the key, Henry. It is a-

'You mentioned something about my enemies?' I tactfully returned the subject. 'I have many. Obviously, first thing I want is to see them dead and preferably burning.'

Mirabilis laughed. 'As I said, you needn't worry about them anymore. You are better than them. Superior. They don't deserve the time spent thinking about them.'

'But what if the enemies I speak of are not the pieces on the game, but the actual players. Well, you know, like you bunch of cunts?'

I dropped the chains to the floor and raised my arms, enamelled by *Abatu*. Finally, I was free and of a mind to cut these motherfuckers to pieces.

'Henry, No!' Mirabilis threw out his hands and suddenly I felt a weight press down on me from above, like magnetism or gravity, or something else hard to fight against.

It was as if my limbs were suddenly three-times as heavy as they were and my movements slow and clumsy. From my peripherals I noticed St. Germain bounding from his seat, straight over the parapet of his own platform and quickly closing in.

My heart set to pounding, whether with fear or excitement, I cannot say. Meanwhile, I thrashed against the pressure clamping down on me whilst more and more cloaks converged upon my dock when suddenly the pressure vanished from my right-hand side. I reckoned that it must have been as the blade swished, unintelligibly, more so just thrashing around, in that general area. Must have cut through whatever energy Mirabilis was enforcing, somehow.

With only half as much weight on me I was able to stumble backward through the dock cubicle and toward the iron-banded door when I noticed that it stood ajar. And now armed with half an idea of how to defend against Mirabilis' Jedi-Force attack, I resumed thrashing the blade dangerously around my left side, and all the way down to my ankles until eventually rolling to my feet as the weight disappeared entirely.

During my wild bouts of fits, St. Germain had leapt up to the front of my dock and poised at a crouch, barely ten feet away, poised but not attacking. Even this close his eyes held a glimmer, even in the obscurity and haze after the smoke.

Cloaks down each aisle to both flanks held back. I noticed over the shoulder of St. Germain, Mirabilis stood and was rolling up his sleeves. Seemed they were waiting for something.

Taking on St. Germain was a fight I wanted, but given the numbers against me, even armed with my blade, I reckoned my chances were slim at best and I didn't like the idea of being locked up again in the unbreakable chains, on a cold piece of stone, and shoeless over a sharp rock floor. With my mind made up, I backed up and then ducked out of the iron banded door, slamming it shut, then twisting the handle off for good measure.

The hallway was abandoned, which felt odd, as on the way in there were several people milling one-way or the other, most with heads glued to bright tablet screens. The sounds of furious scrabbling and thuds from the other side of the door was the next thing, followed by muffle pounding steady against the door slab, stronger and stronger. I reckoned it would give sooner rather than later.

I had absolutely no idea where I was, so going in either direction seemed both pointless and reckless at the same time, but of course, my only option and therefore inevitable. After a moment's hesitation I headed the same way I had been escorted down.

In one hand I still held the broken doorknob, one edge sharp and jagged, and my other hand, my knife, but as for the protective cloth, I had left that behind. The corridor floor was tiled in black and white, and the walls held wooden panels and scrollwork picture frames formed from plaster and painted in gold leaf.

I took no notice of the people or landscapes held within them as I continued, as calmly as I could with sliced soles and a tattered dinner suit, taking the route of little-known hazards.

After a dozen or so yards I heard a soft step behind me. My stalker was light footed indeed and I deduced that should it have been St. Germain or another member of the Ruling Council, they would not be creeping so lightly; therefore, I reasoned it was the one who perhaps planted my blade in the first instance, and probably left the door ajar for me too.

Regardless of my assumptions, taking absolutely no chances, I held my weapons fast as the corridor veered around to the right and given the momentary break in visual, I sprinted noisily on the spot and then tucked myself into a recess in the wall panelling, waiting for my mystery-aid to follow after the sounds of my fleeted dash.

I pressed tight and held my breath when seconds later a shadow slipped around the corner, whisking straight past me. My stalker was also wearing a robe, this one a dark gold and green colour and it stopped still as I stepped out behind.

In a flurry of fabric and pleasant perfume, my pursuer turned to face me, and my heart stopped beating in my chest. My secret Santa was a woman; a most beautiful woman; a woman that I had not seen for going on thirty years. The broken doorknob rattled off the tiles beneath my bare feet.

'Helen?' I couldn't believe my eyes but there she stood, more serious than I have ever seen her. More tragically perfect. She frowned at me. Lifted a hand toward my face before dropping it.

'No, err, not quite.' She looked down at my blade. 'Good, you got it with you.'

Not Helen, her accent was American. Whomever she was she looked identical to my memory of her. The sound of a door breaking some way down the hallway turned both of our heads and upped the ante once again.

'Quickly now, follow me,' said the woman that wasn't Helen, and with a swish of robes, she vanished down the hallway, and meanwhile many a heavy footfall stomped in our direction.

Given my options I followed her, blade still drawn, suspicion still heavy, heart still pounding with ache and hope.

August. 1814.

White wood, when it burns, is a story all to itself: flaccid flames tongue across the stubborn glaze, licking, dressing it, teasing a blister at a stroke lighter than a shadow's fall.

I watched the capital wood bubble and spit, burning in orgasmic reaction to such violation. Fighting against the fire. Fighting, yet burning all the same. The heat of battle still within me as I looked upon this new world of mine with clean eyes, again.

We had the surviving American resistance, the fighters, all rounded up and stripped to their briefs, and largely just for the amusement of their humility. The spoils of war. Yet, it was the prisoners of war's most principal duty to keep the bonfire that was their great White House stoked and raring. The clean and soft military clothing on their backs made for the kindling, but the rest of the fuel came from the White House itself.

I'll admit that I laughed along with the others, watching, glugging the whiskey by the barrel as the defeated men scramble to-and-fro. Slipping between the sections of the capital building not yet afire; wildly gathering chairs, curtains and, well, whatever they could handle, or risk being branded "a porky yank" and subsequently subjected to other forms of entertainment for the troops, entertainment of a more sinister calibre. I hadn't the pallet for such proclivities. But on the whole, it was refreshing to see that mankind hadn't yet lost its sense of humour and winning was still the most important thing in war.

General Ross arrived as the flames licked the lawns and we were forced to pull back the howitzers and 6 pounders. I immediately recognised the egg-shape man jittering beside the general on a horse that looked like a pony beneath his great shape. I actually felt sorry for the poor beast. I noticed an arm slip beneath his rain cloak and produce a hip flask. I noticed that he noticed me noticing him. He tipped his flask; I tipped my head.

The men let out a great cheer as one of the prisoners slipped in the mud-pit that had become the lawns of the White House, and was subsequently covered by a heaping of fabric, or an ejaculation of curtain.

The American scurried and scrabbled beneath the draping like a rat in a sock up the arse of a bull. The men only seemed to find this funnier, but only up until the moment General Ross stuck his sword clean through the struggling mass of draped fabric, through the prisoner's skull, by the looks of it. The laughter immediately evaporated. The only person still laughing was Claruc, although I guessed he was laughing at us, not the unfortunate prisoner.

Ross withdrew his blade, inspecting it in the firelight. 'Did I give ye' instruction t' capture a few yanks an' have a feckin' celebration, eh? A feckin' giggle or somet!' He wiped his blade on the curtains still covering the dead man. None spoke up.

'Not feckin' laughing now, eh, marines? Ye' were feckin' brought here to finish the feckin' job, an' finish it feckin' quickly. An' ye've done well lads, but remember, every one of ye': the fightin's not over, not while tha' pig-fecker-Napoleon is out there!' He re-sheathed he sword and jumped aback his horse beside Claruc, who was still churning away in his giggling and hipflask.

'Boots on ground at the port, ready t' depart no later than sundown, t'morra. There's a fair few miles between here an' there. Ye' be best buggin' out before ye' miss ye' ride home boys!' Putting spurs to his mount, he started away at a trot, calling over his shoulder. 'An' put that feckin' fire out, ye' bunch of feckin' pillocks!'

One or two "Sirs!" echoed across the killing field as I scratched my head, baffled by the sudden despondency. This isn't how I remembered a victory celebration. Where was the wine? The whores, even? Moreover, where was the squabbling and drunken homicide between fellow countrymen following the euphoria of winning something as bloody as a battle?

The remaining prisoners were quickly taken care of, with one or two left alive to dig graves for the others, and then themselves, of course. Doing my duty, as instructed, I approached the fire and reached deep, letting myself hang freely.

The most efficient way of killing a fire is at the base. I crinkled my nose as I whiffed my own odour before my piss hit home, hissing as it splashed against the burning white wood.

A marine stepped up beside me, following my lead, except, I noticed, his piss scattered wildly and across the fringes. Never going to put a fire out. I kept my thoughts to myself, however.

'They don't say much about you,' said the marine who would never make a fireman.

I'd finished pissing a while back but stayed where I was. Truth is I quite enjoy the feel of raw heat on my cock. Several seconds passed. He was still in full flow. I think I saw him look down toward me.

'They say that you were deep undercover, and that they had to dig you out to help the war effort.'

I laughed. I had to. Funny how close to the truth that statement was. 'You could say that.'

'I don't lend rumour much credit mind you, but the way you dealt with those yank twats up at the gate... Shit, you're not like the rest of us.' He finished his piss and tucked up immediately, no hanging around, I noticed.

I stayed where I was. 'Again, one way of saying it.'

The marine turned to walk away, and I stopped him with a non-specific grunt. He turned back eyebrows high.

'That fellow, the one Ross just mentioned…that Napoleon chap.'

The marine looked like he'd missed a trick or something. 'Yes, Napoleon, what about him?'

'Well,' I lowered my voice a little, 'who the fuck is he, and why do we not like him?'

The marine cracked up laughing. I frowned, which only made him laugh even more. I turned back toward the flame just about to tuck myself back in and teach the lad some manners when another marine pulled up on my other side, eyes darting low toward me and my decidedly dry and hot member.

I left it where it was and looked him in the eye. He startled and looked down quickly, piss spurting in short, nervous bursts. He was as ineffective as the last man, probably worse.

'Napoleon,' I hissed. The marine looked up at me. 'What do you know about him?'

The marine stopped pissing all together. I looked down. He looked down. We both looked up, eyes meeting.

'Tell me everything, and for crying out loud, aim your piss at the base of the fire.'

* * *

So, there we were, wounded, tails tucked, but safely back aboard the HMS Endymion, and racing across the Atlantic Ocean to regroup in London before dealing with the menacing resurgence of Napoleon head on, or so I was informed.

I figured that there must be others involved in my resurrection or I was as likely to go on a treasure hunt as I was to face off against this Bonaparte chap, I'd heard so much about. Even if he was a French.

The Americans rallied at Baltimore and chased us through to North Point. A little late as the damage was done, but clearly, they weren't happy about the little incident with the White House. Truth is, as we moseyed back to port, we all believed the fighting was over, right up until General Ross had his balls blasted off and the commanding officer was no more...

That had left the troops rather dismayed. And with lack of active reconnaissance in our ignorant victory march, we were suddenly a little flat-footed and ridiculously deep in hostile territory, outgunned, outmanned, outwitted, out angered, and a thousand times over, fucked up the arse by an angry rhino with an itchy cock. The Canadians were safe in their chalets with their moose and maple syrup. Meanwhile, we were being bum-rushed the fuck out of there, tout-suite.

The lads had straight up started saluting Claruc, before General Ross's balls had even stopped bouncing, and just like that, they deferred to his riddled and slurred commands and jibes.

It seemed in my absence he had been promoted from the humble rank of court jester of general foolery, to the general of lost fools in a land of evil. In fact, I heard one of the other officers call him "Admiral" at one point, right before ordering us to bug-out, straight through the night and on toward the aptly named Fort McHenry: the last bastion between us and safety.

The war was won of course, and the necessary documents had been signed, but damn it if the rest of the god-damned country didn't know that, or care to the contrary. Yes, the Americans were defeated. No, they didn't gain a single inch of Canadian territory, and instead only acquired losses and humiliation, but my god they were not of the mind to let us leave unscathed, or alive at all, if they could help it any.

We were barely more than a battalion strong; alone and

fucked if captured for sure. I reckon that the Americans rallied to boost their egos. We all needed some of that every now and then, and meanwhile a moderate portion of the British Navy were anchored just out of the bay. The British and the Americans knew we were fucked before we even got there, but of course the Americans were counting on our arrival to draw our ships closer to land, closer to their guns and death.

To Claruc's order we marched on Fort McHenry. The sounds of thunderous and prolific bombardment from our frigates strengthened each step we took. Shit, even a patriotic roar escaped my throat in the madness of it all. I marvelled as my own men screamed with tears in their eyes, full sprinting at the last of the American defences, convinced that the empire had really turned up for them, to bring us home, despite other engagements.

As Claruc lead the final charge, winking at me before knocking back a long chug of his flask, I started to believe that the world really had changed for the better in my long absence. The sense of brotherhood amongst the men was touching and I started to feel accepted by them. But alas the Americans claimed the final battle, sending the empire scurrying east to fight a more ambitiously tyrannical foe, and most of the men with whom I had started to feel comradery fell at the last.

But most devastating was when Claruc fell. I refused to believe it for a long time. And I often remembered in my waking nightmares as Claruc single-handedly entered the outer buildings of the fort, opened one of the port gates with the strength of ten men and took his lumps as we passed through.

In all the commotion I looked around for him, and the pang hit true as I realised that he would never emerge again. Even after the gates were reclosed and the breaches refortified, Claruc didn't re-appear. And as the artillery from the Endymion continued to reign down upon the ports fortifications and the great tower crumbled to the ground and was lost beneath the frolicking waters, I waited for him to re-emerge. But all that came to the surface of the deep blue was the mutilated corpses of British, American, and Canadian soldiers, dying for a war they had no say in.

The topic of immortality never actually came up between us, Claruc and I, believe it or not, but I knew that he was at least three-hundred years to the good. And I suspected he was older even than myself.

I never would have said we were traditional friends but losing him sure did leave a pang in my heart. And in the quiet moments that were to follow, I would wonder about where his hip flask lay. Wondering if it too had fallen to the icy depths of the harbour. I pictured his bloated corpse being pecked at by fish and crabs and the such. His flask being caught in a swirl of current and carried up-stream to rest in a shallow embankment. Perhaps some poor soul would find it one day and drink the sweet, cursed, beor.

* * *

The HMS Endymion quickly mutinied into a festering barge of egos and bullies, and straight up cunts. On the blue return to dutiful country, we had seamlessly de-evolved into brutish animals without honour or code or morals. The comradery was destroyed along with our leaders and fallen brothers. None of us actually knew why we were fighting the Americans, and the dissent for king and country only grew by the nautical mile we sailed.

If I were ever to make it back home to recover my property, I recognised that the crew needed a leader, otherwise we might never make it out of the Atlantic Ocean ever again. My fight has always been perpetual. Sometimes my foe is clear, obvious;

sometimes it is obscure; sometimes it is myself; but in this instance, my enemy was the potential for evil to rise aimless in the absence of strong leadership.

I emerged from the thin shadow of my cabin, the wet cutting across the steel of my purpose. The chief bully was a marine called Sergeant Sam Spike. He had taken the captain's quarters for his own 'war-room'. He had guards by his door. Smart man. They eyed me as I wandered close.

I nodded to them as I paused to peer out across the waters, not another vessel in sight. Our original orders, as given by Rear Admiral Claruc, or whatever they called him, were to return to London, gather fresh supplies and then topple the nuisance of Napoleon. The crew had voiced other ideas the moment Claruc didn't arrive on-board to assume command.

In the first day or two I was happy to hold my tongue, keep to the shadows, see how things unfolded without me, but nothing quite stirs the stomach like the harsh Atlantic, and the potential for losing our ways on the great ocean was deterrent enough for me to do something about my situation and intervene. Yet, and regardless of my belongings and treasures that I was still desperate to reclaim, I was owed a debt, and that was a promise of payment in French blood. The 'Americans' were not my enemy. I realised this as soon as I set eyes on one. The men we encountered were not the Iroquois. They were basically us; colonised English, Irish and Europeans.

Took me a little while to realise that 1812 was the first war of Capitalism. Capitalism sure seemed a force to be reckoned with. Turn brothers against one another in the name of financial prosperity, and just like feudalism: some were born with all the money, ergo all the freedom. Capitalism was no different to the earliest democracies of ancient Greece. Money and the inflation of ego corrupts all.

Meanwhile, I sought revenge against those that had stolen the centuries from me. Gold was a soft and relatively useless artefact when weighed against the ledger of vengeance.

The only way I could see my slate being wiped clean was to run through this Bonaparte fellow, an apparently little nerdy fucker who'd run amok throughout France. Seems a strange thing to me now, believing any justice could be achieved by making another bleed. Still, this was the old way, and God only knows how I enjoyed seeing a man's light snuffed with my own eyes. Bullets are too efficient, too detached. Bullets are for cowards. Give me a stiletto dagger any day over a long-range rifle. Give my hands a throat to squeeze, a rigid corpse to dance upon.

I straightened up from the rail, hawked up phlegm and grebbed deep over the side. Cracking my neck both ways then turning to the marines, all smiles, and none of them pleasant.

Their unsteady fingers twitched toward holstered weapons. A moment was all the chance they would ever get against me and they should not have wasted it.

The More You Know… (L. S.).

We hid away through a seemingly random non-descript door, amongst a plethora of entrances, somewhere amid the labyrinth of identical corridors that seemed endless and without distinction, leaving me as confused as a duck in a bubble bath.

Upon our swift entry, however, I found myself standing upon the welcome mat of a very tech-smart, luxury apartment, and totally not what I was expecting in a place like this.

Beneath my weeping feet a *Star Wars* doormat read "Welcome, you are", as spoken by the picture of Yoda in a stiff and bristled, brooding pose. From the corridor outside, the doors all looked so close together that once we had entered, the effect was literally like a TARDIS. We were standing in an open-plan kitchen, living, and dining area that completed the lower level, but for a walled-off area by the staircase in the furthest corner.

My heart was still thundering behind my throat, and I'm not sure if I was excited, afraid, aroused, disgusted, or all of the above, but from where we stood, our breaths held, I could see through the open door of the walled off area, what looked like a library, with tall shelves and the ladder rail and everything. It was classy, and brilliant, and the rail and ladder made from buffed brass.

Toward the back-left corner of the lower floor plan, nestled between the dining and library room was an iron black spiral staircase which accessed the mezzanine area that created a ceiling over almost half of the lower floor. The absence of windows felt a little strange, but we were deep underground…

The lights came on automatically and I noticed that the fridge-freezer was one of them smart fridges, and I have to admit to being just a little jealous of the gadgetry of it all.

The stampede of pursuers came bounding down our corridor and we both stiffened like the dead and breathed even less. My hostess and saviour still had her hood drawn but I could see a tinge of scarlet in her hair, just like Helen. The sounds of the riot passed beyond our passageway, and even then, we waited. A couple of minutes later and finally she stepped away from the door and she lowered her hood.

I followed her in a little, not once taking my eyes off her face, eyes, hair, her mouth. Then she looked at me with that sad smile, and her eyes averted from my own to elsewhere.

Whomever this woman was she was definitely not Helen. Helen had compassion and empathy; she had the kindest heart I had ever known, but I had never seen pity in her eye.

"Sympathy is reserved for the sanctimonious and arrogant", she used to say to me when I would drivel on about the appalling living conditions of people I encountered during my time in the Middle East.

I looked down, my heart dropped into my toes, along with any hope I still held on to. Still no shoes on and the cuts on my soles were smearing the polished wooden floors from the doorway in, even bloodying the welcome mat to a darker and more corrupted version of Yoda's inverted syntax. Although I found it odd that the welcome mat would be inside, not outside, I kept my opinions about I to myself.

'I'm making a mess.' It was supposed to be an apology, but it came out like an obvious statement, and one abundantly laden with stupidity.

'It took you long enough.' She was angry. 'For a minute there, I thought you were actually waiting for me to come in and get you out myself.'

I took a step back. I had no idea why she had any right to be annoyed with me and figured that if anyone should be miffed, it was definitely not her.

'Well I…' my words failed as my hostess planted hands on hips and finally looked at me, properly, full faced and filled with conviction.

'I had to be sneaky about it.' It was the only thing I could think of. 'It wasn't easy picking the blade up with my feet. I needed to free my hands before I-'

'Sneaky?' she laughed, but I knew she found nothing funny about the situation. 'I almost came in after you. That would have ruined the whole plan!'

She stomped past me and away into the kitchen area, and as she approached the fridge the digital display lit up: a message on a bright sticky note *"All or nothing. Xxx"*

I felt like a naughty boy again, back at the abbey, hiding in the stables with a quarter skin of beor, trying to get drunk before we turned in for the monotony of evening prayer-

'Here.' She threw a towel at me. 'How about you clean up your own mess for once.'

I dropped the towel and stood on it, wiping the floor whilst soaking up the leakage from my still bleeding feet. Meanwhile, 'not Helen' headed up the spiral staircase and out of sight.

'Who are you and why are you helping me?' I shouted.

'Clean that up, then we talk.' She had changed into a jumper and jeans and looked just as normal as Helen ever did, just as beautiful, but not. Her thick socks muffled her tread down the staircase and back to the kitchen where she started to gather a tea-set onto a tray.

'Just keep your voice down. I figure that they will come in here looking for you, eventually.' She turned to walk toward the far end of the living room. 'You can call me Selene.'

I was confused and hopeful, angry and heartbroken, I felt just about ready to kiss her, or slit her throat. She was definitely not my Helen, but she looked just like I remembered her.

I decided that the floor was clean, so I kicked the bloodied towel over toward the bare corner of the kitchen/dining room and joined my heroine over by the three-piece sofa set before the snuffed and remarkably clean cast iron fireplace.

She gestured to the empty chair and offered me a cup of fine china, its contents a cold brew of cloudy pink. I accepted and drank thirstily. It tasted salty and sweet – reminded me of the potion fed to me by Kratzenstein and immediately I felt the tingle of energy wriggling into my limbs. Naturally, I skulled the rest, sploshing it down the front of my ragged dinner shirt in the process.

'You shouldn't drink it so fast,' she said, frowning at me like she'd just seen me eating my own ear wax from a bulbous cotton swab.

There was only one cup, I noticed, but as my limbs buzzed and energy flowed through my veins, I resisted the urge to start doing star-jumps and instead let the deep and expensive chair fold up around me as I sank into it like a fly ready to sleep in a Venus plant.

'Ian wasn't with the Council, then?' She was frowning unreasonably hard, and still not meeting my eye, instead her gaze held on my shoulders, swapping intermittently.

At the very mention of his name I had the chill back into my spine.

'Probably having his bones manipulated into position again.' The buzz was growing, and I held out my empty cup for a refill.

'Sip it, slowly. And what do you mean, having his bones manipulated?' her eyebrows high, only half-filling my cup this time.

'Well, I sent the smarmy twat tumbling down the side of a fucking enormous pyramid he took me to. Somewhere down there, or there about.' I pointed through the floor somewhere over by her front door.

The look on Selene's face flipped from distasteful to outright panic.

'Oh please, don't fucking tell me he's a friend of yours.' I sipped up the last dregs of my sweet elixir and closed my eyes for just a moment, the pain in my leg and feet completely forgotten. My blade was still gripped tightly in my free hand, however, and resting upon the high arm of the chair that swallowed me.

'Why would you do such a thing?' she demanded, her eyes flaring,

I sat up again as wave upon wave battered my concentration. 'Come again?'

'He is the one person on the Ruling Council that doesn't want you chained up and harvested.' She looked at me as she said that last word then away again.

I didn't know what I had done wrong, but obviously on the defensive, again, I countered.

'Okay, well if whatever your saying is supposed to make sense to me, it doesn't. But let me tell you this piece of information, and I'll give you this for free: Ian Mulliti is a deceitful cunting twat of a bastard dickhead, and that is unfair to bastards, cunts, and dickheads. So, whatever you think my brother is, he is not, trust me on that, Selene.'

She looked at me hard, finally holding my gaze. 'He's my husband. And I think I know him quite well by now, you ass.'

I was lost for words, literally. I don't know what surprised me more: the fact that this woman looked so much like Helen, or that somebody would actually marry a shit like my brother, or that Helen's fucking doppelganger had married my own… I tried to say something, but nothing came out.

'Trust me, Henry, Ian is not your enemy and never was. He has goodness in him. But the Council, well, it has designs on you, on me, on all of us-'

'And Helen?' I held her eye.

She looked grey as she nodded. 'On all of us. Everyone. We all have a part to play.'

She wrapped her arms across her belly and stood up, facing the fireplace. 'Alone, you literally have no chance. But together, you and Ian, you can be stronger than the Ruling Three. They know that, that is why they have kept you apart for so long…'

Suddenly the fire erupted within me and I was on my feet as it dawned on me who exactly Helen had been running from.

'She was running from *them*, the fucking Council of Zealots?' I remembered her reluctance to talk about her past, but that only she had said that she lived without sunlight and I had thought she was being metaphorical, even melodramatic.

'Who was she?' I managed, a few moments after the fire had left me and I had sunk back into my chair.

'Helen was just Helen, it was you that was always the danger, but…'

She looked up and met my eye. There was an edge to Selene, a hardness that Helen never possessed. I found myself wishing that Helen had been stronger, fiercer. But then, she wouldn't have been the woman I fell in love with.

It was in this fracture that I realised that all this time it had been my own damned ignorance that had placed those around me in danger, including myself. I had loved Helen for her vulnerabilities and thought not to strengthen them for fear of corrupting her purity.

'There is so much you do not know, Henry. They kept you in the dark about what you are. They used you and your ignorance, your naiveties, in ways that you probably wouldn't even be able to accept as truth.' She turned back to the fireplace, her arms back across her stomach.

'But Helen and I, there are more of us,' she stretched her jumper longer, 'and we were selected to be the surrogates for the next generation of the Ruling Council. The Madonna Program is the official name. And the women selected, we are called the Posterities. *"For the future"*. An honour, truly.' She looked down to her hands and let them fall.

'What are you saying?' I fought to deny the sick thoughts riffling through my mind, gritting against my teeth. 'That you and Helen, what, that you're some sort of fucking sex slaves? Forced to mother the children of monsters like me?'

Selene smiled and shook her head gently. 'There really is so much you do not know and cannot understand right now. Your reaction is of disgust, but you clearly do not know our culture. It really is an honour amongst our people. The Ruling Council provide for our entire family tree, for the next millennia, my family will never want for anything, ever again.'

'The fucking Madonna Project. Are we expecting the next Jesus Christ or something? You're all brain washed, and totally messed up. This is wrong!' I had gone way past the point of trying to keep my voice lowered. The longer I stayed with these people in their underground circus, the more my skin crawled.

Selene pleaded with her eyes. 'Don't judge us until you know the whole story. Helen was my sister, but she sealed her own fate the moment she chose not to deliver on her purpose.'

My face must have asked the question my mouth wouldn't.

'You were her assignment,' she confirmed. 'And your brother, mine. Delivering your offspring for the longevity of the Council, is, and always, has been our primary objective.'

'Liar!' Blood washed cold through my arms and into my clenched fists. 'No way that my Helen was involved in this bullshit because she didn't take him to them. She left him at the...' I let the words trail before I said too much. But I clearly already had.

I was burning from the cold in my bones. I knew my fears to be true as I looked upon Selene. If ever I needed proof, it was right in front of me.

'She loved you. I know that much. And she never gave up her secrets.'

I noticed a tear in her eye as she offered a sympathetic hand on my shoulder. I shrugged her off.

'I am not your enemy either,' her eyes softened to a twinkle. 'And, as I said, Ian is not. But we cannot hope to overthrow them by ourselves. And while there are those who are tired of the Ruling Council's games, we remain too few in numbers, but with you on our side, Ian would easily convince the others to join the new order. Believe it or not, but you do have friends, Henry, even down here.'

Now I was surprised. 'I have friends?' I almost laughed; I had never had friends. 'Who?'

'Your experimental exclusion from our society turned you into a bit of a celebrity among us. The Ruling Council decided that your part in the game would serve little more than sport, but the rest of us watched on with interest. Listening out for information on your circumstances. Rooting for you as you followed the path they wrought.

'And although I suppose that doesn't make us friends, there is one being that they captured and kept locked-up in the higher-level cells, that you would perhaps class as a real friend.

'He's not a blue-blood, but something else altogether. And he has been a prisoner here for centuries. Ian once told me that he thinks that he is older than Doctor Mirabilis. He doesn't speak much anymore though, they say, except only to whistle, and occasionally whisper his curse and his name: Claruc.'

I had to take a second. I had not seen him in over two hundred years. 'Where is he?'

'Topside.'

'Topside? Does he know I am here?'

She nodded. 'Yes. But even if you had him on your side, it would not be enough to defeat them. A devil is much closer to your heart than anyone else,' she pressed on. 'And he will stop at nothing to see his plans through. Afterall, you are the game.'

'A devil?' I had to think but my thoughts and memories were still swarming back around to Claruc, and the tower of Fort McHenry as it came toppling down.

'No, now you're starting to sound like The Order. Fucking robes, dungeons.' I was losing patience.

She lowered her voice and knelt before me, a hand on my knee. 'You've been hoodwinked too, Henry. Your closest ally is not who you think he is-'

My closest ally would also be my only ally, and that was easy. 'Grim?'

Selene's mouth pressed tight and she gave a sharp nod. She looked afraid. 'Yes, and he has made a game out of you and your brother since-'

'Grim-fucking-Catspaw? Are you trying to wind me up?'

I couldn't believe that apparently this 'devil', my eternal enemy, was also my proven advocate and a person whose life I had saved more times than I care to remember. Selene tried to wave my noise down, but I was too enraged to see her warnings.

'If he was my great arch-fucking-enemy, and that is a big fucking "IF", I would annihilate him, without even breaking a sweat…'

Memories leaped between various times when Grim had stepped in to save me. The evening with the Black Hand, for instance.

'You don't understand, do you?' Her tone lessened from aggressive to impatient. Clearly, I didn't.

'He has played you since the beginning, Henry, both of you, all of us, everything. Ian was taken in as an infant and taught the doctrine from the Council directly. But even the Ruling Council are a part of his "Game". You, however, you he kept as a side order, entertainment value, an opponent to The Council's strategies as often as you were assisting them. He would often say that "there is no sport in progress without risk of regression".'

I had to admit that the Grim Catspaw that I knew was probably just about up his own arse enough to actually say such a thing. But still, it was Grim, my friend.

'Listen, Selene, I know you believe this shit, but I didn't meet Grim until just before the Great War. So, given the magnitude of shit that had happened to me prior to the early twentieth century how could Grim have been behind everything. Doctor Mirabilis, however, I met long, long before that. Have you considered that maybe Mirabilis is the one behind-'

'No.' She stood up now, arms still across her belly. 'He is older than Mirabilis, much older. He *is* the master manipulator, the devil in the detail. Nobody knows how long he has been here, but it seems that he has always been present. His blood is the absolute purest among us. It is probably true that the Council are all his offspring, or sometimes the offspring of his offspring. You call him Grim, but we call him Woden.'

A return of the search party approaching from the hallway beyond the door turned both of our heads. And they had started banging on doors, and by the sounds of it, we had mere minutes left.

'Quick, you have to leave. They can't know I'm involved, not yet. I need to find Ian first before we can...' She looked afraid, deeply afraid. 'In the meantime, you must go and find him and make him disappear, or all this: Helen, Ian, Claruc, the sacrifices you made, all of it would have been for nothing!'

The cold had me in a grip made of everything I ever feared. I already knew the answer before I asked. 'Make who disappear?'

There was a knock at the door. The handle rattled and protested against the lock.

Selene looked at me, eyes rimmed with pity. It disgusted me and scared me shitless, simultaneously. 'Your son, my nephew, Francis.'

She pushed a button within the fire surround and her black-iron fireplace released from the wall and swung toward us like a door. I saw the tail ends of a ladder shooting up and stalled, eyes searching desperately; stuck with a plethora of questions I needed the answers to, but absolutely no time to ask them.

For the first time in my long life I chose flight instead of fight. Selene's desperation and vulnerability made the decision for me. And by the way she protected her belly, I wondered if she worried for two.

* * *

I climbed into the hidden chimney flue, still buzzing with the tingle in my bones and purpose in my muscle fibres. Whatever that elixir was, it was good, and already I craved more.

'Take Claruc with you, if you can. He needs to be free,' she whispered and then the fireplace latch clicked shut followed by a quick dash across the room to open the door.

I had no fucking idea where Claruc was, and I scrambled up the ladder as fast as my sooty hands and feet would allow, but I was kicking myself for not asking Selene for some socks or slippers or something to cover my ruined soles.

I climbed the ladder for what felt like hours when finally,

my fingers scratched against a dark metal grate and peeled back three of my fucking fingernails in the process. I tested the manhole and it easily gave way to reveal a corridor that I had certainly been in before, and there was no-one in sight. The light at the end of the walkway was where I needed to get to and I slipped out of my escape chute and crouched in the plush, thick carpet, and gently placed the grate back into place, taking great care to make sure the carpet didn't look disturbed.

I recognised the passage as being the first dungeon I'd been held captive in since my meal with Ian. I also remembered that there was an unreasonably long and winding staircases that lead upward to the lifts. One went up, the other down. I had already been on the downward journey, so I figured that the only way was up.

Still carrying *Abatu* tightly, I carefully made my way down toward the lights when I noticed the emergence of desperate hands through the bars atop the cells that lined the hallway of dungeon doors.

Obviously, I had not been as silent as I would have wished; yet one cell had no reaching fingers, and I knew that this was the cell I had been in and suddenly I remembered the dark and bulky presence in the corner when a whistling started low, almost inaudible, yet, unmistakable for sure.

It was a tuneless whistle that I would recognise anywhere. I could only describe it as jazz for the soul, and I hadn't heard anything like it for a good long while.

I passed at least half a dozen wanting hands before I reached the cell that I had been in. No hands reached out from this one, but somebody was definitely in there, on the other side of the door, I could feel it. I tried the handle, but it wouldn't move or bend. Whatever it was made of was the very same stuff my bonds had been cast from. It was too strong for me but my knife however, had no earthly equal.

I pushed the tip of the blade into the keyhole as slowly as I could; twisting it round as it went deeper until eventually I had formed a hole straight through, the sounds of a spring bursting, followed by the drop of a pin, allowing the door to creep inwards. The fine carpet stopped on the threshold of the cell, and the hard, damp stone floor ramped up toward the shackled shadow of Claruc, still crouched, still smiling, still whistling even, in the highest corner of the jail.

Claruc's eyes were wide and not focused on me, and as I drew nearer to him, I realised that he wore the crispy remnants of a trench-coat, a pair of seriously threaded officer's trousers, and an almost completely moth-eaten officer's shirt. It was the same uniform worn by the British in the Napoleonic Wars.

I stood a few feet before him, absolutely stunned. Claruc had not had a change of clothes for over two-hundred years… But for all that, he at least kept his fucking shoes. The leather was barely clinging to his feet still, and he had no actual laces left, but still, shoes all the same.

Without a word I freed him from his bonds, pulled him to his feet and led him to the bastard staircase, and up until eventually we stood before two lift doors, panting. Or at least I was.

'Please, do the honours,' I gestured for Claruc to press the arrow up button in the silver panel on the wall, which he did, gingerly, and we waited for a few moments before a "boop" preceded the lift doors hissing open to admit us.

The interior was remarkably different from the glass one that Ian and I had gone down in. This one was lined with metallic panels around the lower half and littered with advertisement stickers: taxi companies, pizza takeaways, and night-clubs plastered on each wall except the doors. I stepped in, hoping that Claruc had the same sense of hurry.

'An' this is?' Claruc asked in a croak, clearly spooked, hanging back on the landing.

I realised that Claruc had no idea what a lift was. I'd also once been in the dark, only for a couple of hundred years. Funny how things go around.

'It's a mechanical carriage.' I explained, my arm across the threshold to stop the doors from closing. 'A lifting device that is operated by steel-wire ropes, but look, just fucking get in, and I promise it will carry us to freedom… I think.'

Claruc patted a foot out to test the stability of the lift floor before stepping in entirely and causing the carriage to creak beneath the stress, the whole unit dropping an inch or two.

'Everybody just calls them lifts though. On account that they lift people and…'

There were a lot of buttons and a big red keyhole underscoring everything. I pressed the "G" button and leaned back against the handrail, relieved as the doors closed and we slowly ascended to the soft sounds of piano music. The lift's hidden mechanisms were clearly unhappy with Claruc's bone density, and I was a little concerned that we might not make it for a moment or two but kept my fears to myself.

I looked at Claruc and marvelled how in the two hundred plus years, he still looked like an egg, except for now he had very long, white and shabby hair, and a ginger beard so long it made Gandalf's look like pre-pubescent growth in comparison.

'Don't folk wear shoes 'ne-more?' He was looking at my bloodied and bare feet.

'No. Times change. You can take your shoes off if you want.' I lied.

'So, what've you been up to then?' I was keeping it casual. Small talk.

Claruc coughed. 'Am thirsty…'

The lift slowed to a stop and I felt Claruc tense. Hell, I did too. I didn't know what to expect but as the doors opened my mouth dropped wide. What I saw…well, nobody could've expected that. Unexpectedly, I started laughing.

Hundreds, maybe even thousands of people rushed in every direction, most lugging a trailing suitcase, and some kids were even riding on them like wacky races, their parents pulling them along and looking up at information screens dotted everywhere.

After a few seconds, Claruc and I stepped out on to the tiled floor and looked up at the huge welcome sign suspended from the ceiling: Denver International Airport centralised over a vertically draped flag of America.

'An' what's an International Airport then?'

I noticed the growing level of attention we were receiving from the ready travellers milling by. I was used to drawing stares on account of my resemblance to Freddy Kruger, but it seemed Claruc was equally as popular today, and I presumed for his remarkable egg-like shape, but mostly due to his ancient and disreputable war attire. Then there was the fact that I was still not wearing shoes which probably didn't help the situation. But still, I needed a moment to digest that we were in an actual fucking airport and back in the real world, above ground, and it was daytime.

I gestured to Claruc that we should start walking. 'The airport is where these mechanical birds sleep. Big fucking birds, Claruc. Then, when these machine birds are ready and fuelled, and people have enough money to pay them, they fly all around the world, carrying passengers in their belly. A bit like a pelican, but without the water, if you can imagine it.'

'Aye? An' what do ye' feed the mechanical pelican then?'

'Oil.'

Claruc coughed again, rubbing at his throat. 'Really need a wee sip.'

We attempted to blend with the crowd. And when I say blend, we stood out like an iceberg dumped into the Red Sea. Yet, Claruc was thirsty, and getting a drink seemed like an excellent place to start for the both of us. Despite all I'd been through this very long day, including losing my dinner shoes and my bastard socks, I was mightily relieved to discover that my money clip, complete with the tight wad of dollars, was still secure in my trouser pocket.

We approached the first drinking establishment with its doors open and entered as a ragged and disgracefully shoe-less man and an undeniably egg-shaped fellow in re-en-actment war attire. The well-dressed barkeeper looked less than impressed and saw no funny side to our walking punchline.

'N, n, no guys, not, not, not in here…' he pointed a finger in lieu of the stuttering absence of words, 'd, dress, dressed like that!' he concluded, finally.

Claruc and I looked at each other for the briefest of moments before continuing onto the counter.

'Ye' strongest proof, landlord!' Claruc held on to the pol-ished brass that acted as a bull-bar against the swathing tides of patrons upon more lively occasions, or perhaps upon a more reasonable hour of the day.

I produced the money clip and met the incredulous look of the man serving us. 'We'll take it by the bottle. Along with two glasses and a bit of privacy, if you can accommodate?' I slid over a couple hundred-dollar bills.

'Privacy co-co-costs extra,' said the bartender, counting the money.

I liked him, his confidence anyway, so I held out another hundred-dollar note and grabbed his hand as he collected.

'Nobody disrupts us.' I smiled as cartilage and bones clicked painfully in his hand.

His cool quickly melted away and agony stepped in. 'No, no, no problem! This, this way.'

'Throw in a couple of packs of nuts and some salt and vinegar crisps too.' I pointed to the savoury snack section as he closed the main doors and showed us through to his office at the back. A few moments later and he served us nuts and crisp with a tall bottle of green absinth and two clean tumblers.

Claruc wasted no time in tearing the wrapping from the lid, chugging a good four fingers before I'd even taken my seat.

'There she is.' He was talking to the bottle and he smacked me on the shoulder as he swigged another four fingers.

'I need your help.' I sat down, suddenly exhausted. I had no appetite for the nuts but opened them anyway.

Claruc's head snapped to me and he lowered the bottle but kept a tight grip on it. 'More than ye' my eyes can see. An' clearly time has warmed ye' heart, hic!' Claruc knew I'd grown soft. No point asking him how he knew.

'I need to find my son and get him to safety, then I have to kill Grim Catspaw, Doctor Mirabilis, Count Saint Germain and the rest of that fucking Council. Along with my cunt of a brother, if it comes to it.'

Selene's warning came back to me and I wondered if any of it could be true: could Grim really be that old… thousands and thousands of years…

'No.' He burped and wrapped both of his meaty hands around the circumference of the bottle. 'Ye' don't win anything' alone. Perchance the wolf can fight wi' a knife o' persuasion instead. Fight wi' the knives of El.'

Claruc upended the bottle. Probably a third gone already. I think he was referring to my shit of a brother, maybe even forging an alliance or something along those lines. But "fighting with the knives of El", I was almost positive that he was talking about the same thing that Mirabilis was talking about, the Anunnaki.

'You think my twat of a brother would ever do something that didn't feed his own ego or serve his own ambition?'

'Henry.' He leaned in close to me and pulled the bottle into his bosom as if he feared I would try to take it from him. 'Ye' prob'ly know by now tha' I'm a Claruchaun.' He stared at me and I back at him.

After a moment he continued. 'An' to be honest, we're jus' not meant fo' ye' tunnel vision lives; ye' blinkered, mono-dimension existence. But fo' too long they kep' me parched down there. Fo' years all I saw was the same as ye' do, now.

'In the beginning they used me sight, kep' me simmerin', so t' speak. After a wee while, the flow o' juice stopped an' I was forgotten about by most o' them, except ye brother, Ian.

'Often, we had wee talks. He asked about ye', mainly: The legend-come-myth o' Henry Game. His eyes comin' t' life fo' a moment 'fore doctrine returned an' he closed me out again.'

I tried to imagine Ian asking after me and decided to shelve that line of thought for a more private, or confrontational, moment.

'What's a Claruchaun then?' I had to ask. I didn't fancy any other topic.

'Ha!' He chugged down another four-fingers and slammed the bottle safely within his reach and out of mine, but didn't say anything else.

'Are you a blue-blood?'

'Feck ye' and ye' blue-blood privileged swine!' Claruc's eyes grew dark.

I took his answer as a resounding no and decided to concentrate more on my own situation again. 'I need to find somebody…important to me before they-'

'Ye' already in the mousetrap. Forget the feckin' cheese, Game, an' jus' kill the feckin' cat first. Secrets don't exist fo' the likes o' ye'. Never did'. He was talking in riddles again.

'Do you know about Grim?'

Claruc took the contents of the bottle to halfway, smacked his lips and burped, loudly. 'Aye. Every single one o' us knows Him, one-way o' another.'

'Is he really thousands of years old? Selene said he is known by different names.'

'An' they all have jus' one eye.' Claruc looked grey of a sudden.

I nodded and felt a cold wash over me. Fuck, I needed a stiff one. Claruc tore a strip off his shirt and reached for my blade, that was when I realised that I still held it tightly in my grip… no wonder people were staring at us and the bartender wanted us to leave.

'What are you doing?' I pulled my hand away from him as he reached.

'Pure cotton does'ne' react wi' the exo-steel alloy.' He wrapped the cut of *Abatu* with the strip from his officer uniform and I couldn't believe that the shirt sleeve didn't immediately set on fire. Relaxing a little, I put the blade on the table between us.

I was dumbfounded but managed to find the words. 'So, you know what *Abatu* is?'

Claruc nodded and knocked back another chug of the green liquid. 'Reactive alloy from another solar system-hic!'

'Cotton, really? Of all things?' I had seen the blade cut through almost everything and react to most things with the same effect.

Claruc shrugged and cradled his absinth closely. His beard touched the table and his hair reached down his back and shoulders. I still couldn't believe that he had worn the same clothes for the last two-centuries-

We both heard a commotion from the bar area. It was the type of sound that rhymed with trouble. I looked over at Claruc and noticed he was carefully screwing the lid back on to the bottle. I stood, pushing my chair back in the process. Claruc rolled his head to one side then the other, traces of a smile hidden behind the grubbiness of his outgrown hair.

A series of crashes and smashed glass preceded the door of our little confinement being blasted open and off its hinges. A moment of stillness as splinters of wood and shards of metal pinged and drifted to the floor, I looked to Claruc and noticed he was baring his teeth. I think he was smiling. Actually, I think he was laughing.

A robed fellow appeared in the doorway, eyes glinting unnaturally: it was Count Saint Germain, and he looked just about ready to tear our throats out when the stuttering bartender barrelled straight into the side of his head with a dented, metal baseball bat, sending him for a homerun.

'Who the fu-fu-fu-fu' he was pointing his finger again, clearly annoyed by himself, 'fuck do you think, you, you, you are, mister?'

St. Germain dropped to the floor quite enthusiastically and was still for a few seconds. But now he was grumbling and quickly coming to his senses again.

'Stay down, cu-cu-cunt!' The bartender warned, his bat pointing at St. Germain's head.

'Is it fu, fu, fu, fucking fancy dress today or wha, wha, wha, wha-'

Before he could finish the question, he was slashed across his gut with a speed that made my blood cool even further, and now St. Germain was holding a remarkable looking blade. The sharp of it red with murder and runes carved along the flat of metal. The handle had been modified like the one Ian had, again with an ivory coloured graphite grip over the bone handle – but this was way longer than my own or Ian's, or both of ours combined. It was at least two feet in length, and I have to admit, I was both intimidated and in love with it in equal proportions.

After a sickly wet gasp, the bat, along with the bartender's innards, dropped to the linoleum floor in a splodge of finality. It seemed the three of us just watched him for a moment as he tried to process what was hanging out the front of him.

Claruc was next to speak. 'Ye' futures all lead into darkness. An' ye're outnumbered, Count.'

The bartender flopped into the soft pool of his own intestines and gurgled blood, but it seemed neither Claruc nor St. Germain noticed his wheezing collapse; maybe it wasn't significant enough to pay attention to.

'Fu-fu-fuck do you think you, you, you are?' The bartender looked more affronted than murdered as he persisted to protest against the indignity of the intruder in robes that had just shattered his office door off its hinges.

I recognised the lull that followed as the *possibility-space* between active realities, or, as the point where alter-dimensions of decision splice apart and run parallel. The moment is always piloted by choice and clearly, we had all made the same bloody one. Furthermore, it had always been my favourite part, for naturally I have a proclivity for killing motherfuckers that I do not like the look of, and also motherfuckers that creep me out, and St. Germain, well, he ticked both boxes.

Francis,

After all this time, I finally found out who and what Grim was. Yet even despite what Selene had told me, and even though Claruc confirmed in his own riddled way, I still held a place in my heart remained for the giant I had known only as Grim Catspaw.

The amount of times, the amount of opportunities even, that Grim had over the years to destroy me, but instead had taken action to the contrary. Also, and no small matter, he was the only living being I had ever entrusted your whereabouts to, and from as far as I could figure things out, the Ruling Council did not know about you, nor Ian, nor Selene, and if they did, it was one hell of a well-kept secret.

I personally handed you over to him. Big mistake that one. And I imagine he was rubbing his hands together at my unexpected request for him to make disappear the very thing that the Council desired.

In spite of all accounts to the contrary, I could not bring myself to see my closest friend in the world as the evil cunt he had been painted out to be. When you have bled with another, fought with them and against them, laughed with them and at them, held each other's eye when all is lost, you form a bond that is stronger than mere words or accusation. But still, the bell of truth rings in a way that cannot be unheard.

It had to be genuine, the coldness within had never steered me wrong. Even Claruc appeared afraid of him. I suppose it is comical that I had always seen Grim as the sidekick to my heroics. It sounds ridiculous now, but, well, I had always thought of our relationship as being a one-way affair: him needing me.

Of course, years would pass between our encounters. And it would always be the same story in which he needed me to help fight his wars. Feeding my ego for me to join the struggle and turn the tide, to play his games.

What did I get in return? Money. Scars. Pain. Sure, but not just that. No, I got the fraternity – the fellowship and comradery – to associate with a network of bastards just like me. Well, not exactly like me, but of the same proclivities for sure.

The picture had finally become clear and it was always Grim, one-step, or two, removed from the seat of power, like Mirabilis behind Henry VIII. It was always the Dr's hand that steered the ship of action, sending me on my way, to Rome, the Vatican.

But Grim was the puppeteer of them all, even Mirabilis. Pulling the strings from the shadows. They say that in chess the queen cannot be the most powerful or dangerous piece in the game for it is surely the hand that moves them. The player, but not the hand. The mind. Or, not the mind but the intellect. Not intellect but intelligence, and determination, and dastardly willingness to do whatever it takes to win.

That is who Grim has been all these years. To beat him I must become the same, or just kill the cunt in a blaze of glory and end it for good.

I realise that I was no more than a pawn now, and never was. I was the wild card, the loose cannon. But at least I was a puppet that finally became a real boy. A determined real boy with revenge in his heart and a desire to find the kitchen knife and cut the puppeteer's fucking throat as he slept. Or the puppet who garrottes his master with his own strings. Or both.

I wondered if my great enlightenment was a part of his game too and cut that string of paranoia before it dragged me down. The only way to save you, my son, would be to sever the head off the dragon and be done with it... The only thing was the dragon was a multiple headed cunt, and at least one of those heads was my own.

My sources informed me that Grim, contrary to my wishes, had decided to play an active role in your life. They reported to me about your relationship. Your uncle Oddy. Naturally, in light of this I couldn't trust anyone he had placed around you, and not even those he hadn't.

Should I be unsuccessful in my attempts to kill them all, I implore you to never again let Grim, or Oddy, anywhere near you or anyone you may care about. He will undoubtedly manipulate you into situations that force you enact his will, and all the while you will almost certainly be unaware of his hand controlling you, but control you it will, and always to the tune of his fancy.

In the clear light of hindsight, Grim Catspaw is a calculating bastard of epic proportions. And I will kill him or die trying. This is my promise to you. Perhaps you may find it in your heart to accept that what I have done – what I have put you through – it has only ever been done so from a place of good intention. But of course, the hammer of good intention forged many a sword that killed many a good man and I am long enough in the tooth now to hide behind such feeble defences and excuses.

I believe that love is the strongest weapon against the armies of evil. Let not your hatred rule your actions, as it did for me, for so many years lost to it.

November 1814.

Docked in at the Thames, and with feet back on home soil for the first time in almost two full years, I was immediately approached by two stalwart fellows with peculiar badges emblazoned upon the left breast pocket of their navy-blue jackets. They were definitely a constabulary of some sort. It was clear from the cut of their jib.

'Lord Game, ah…' said the taller of the two as they both bowed their heads fractionally.

I was both taken back by their use of politeness and affronted in equal measures by the incessant use of my unwanted title. It wasn't until several moments of silence had passed between our threesome that they realised that I was still waiting for the other shoe to drop.

The taller of the two hastened to fill the silence. 'Please accept our deepest apologies, ah, for ambushing you like this, but, your, ah, your presence is required by The Crown.

'I am Sergeant Slater, and this is Constable Wilson, and our carriage is, is this way, ah… If you would like to please accompany us to the, ah, the City of London-'

'Hang on a minute, stretch,' I showed him the flat of my palm, barely an inch from his nose. 'Maybe you two plum-sucking-cross-dressers don't know that I've been away for almost two years straight now. Been fighting and shitting in holes for this sodding country, so I'll give you the benefit of that doubt. But let me be clear: I'm not going anywhere 'till I'm good and ready, and especially not for the fucking King of England. That sheep shagging motherfucker should be coming to me, if anyone is going anywhere.'

The pair frowned and shared a look.

'Did you just say…' I just caught on, 'are we not already in London?' I looked around, suddenly unsure of where I was, despite being able to see St. Paul's Cathedral.

Again, the two officers looked at each other before frowning even harder than before. It seemed that I misunderstood something.

'Yes, ah, but we mean to escort you to the *City of London*. And, Lord Game, it is not King George who, ah, who summons you today…'

All around us disembarking marines milled passed our little event. One fellow whooped as he gathered his two young girls into his arms. His wife hanging back meanwhile, looking uncomfortable.

She met my eye for a small moment then quickly away again, pulling at the cuffs of her dark blouse sleeves. Her marine husband followed her gaze to me and my associates, and the relief and happiness on his face was washed off and replaced with dread. Without a word he picked one of his girls up and pulled the other as he ushered his wife from the dock until they became indistinguishable from the crowd.

In fact, most of the marines avoided looking in our direction. I avoided giving a fuck. Sure, we had fought alongside one another, even squatted over the same holes, but the essence of comradeship had abandoned us a long way back. If it had ever existed.

A month aboard the ship of despondency is longer than it has any right to be. I remembered only the prison like social complexity that accompanied us back across the choppy Atlantic Ocean.

The remainder of our sea journey back to the motherland had been a gloomy affair. The best thing for everyone aboard was to leave me well alone. I was in mourning for Claruc. I even tried to leave me alone. Not sure that worked out quite so well.

The peculiarly dressed policemen stood expecting, twitchy glances snapping back and forth. I wouldn't say they were nervous, but I don't know, something wasn't right about the oddness of these two.

I zeroed in on the one who hadn't said a word yet, Constable Wilson.

'Constable,' I had his full attention. 'Who has the audacity to summon me at the precise moment I step foot back on home s-'

'The Crown!' Wilson's cheeks flushing of colour and his posture stiffening like water in the artic.

Perhaps we were creating quite the scene as some of the marines began ushering their families away from our little gathering as quickly as they could, and I didn't blame them. I'd be legging it too, if I could.

'Begging your most humble of pardons, ah, Lord Game,' interjected Sergeant Slater, stumbling across his flustered partner. 'The ah, the note, ah, Wilson, give it to him, ah, to Lord...'

Wilson's cheeks suddenly started to refill with an anxious pink as he patted his breast pockets. After a moment or two he stepped forth, a fancy piece of paper in his outstretched white gloved hand.

I noticed the coat of arms on the letter head, and the words **The City of London** across the top, centralised. However, the page was blank but for one word scribbled in red ink across the middle: Kratzenstein.

Maybe I would finally find out who plucked me from the abyss of eternal unrest. I felt hopeful. But I also, belatedly, felt ashamed that I hadn't even spared a single thought for the tongue-less surgeon who stitched me back together. The click still persisted in my left ankle but the habit formed and had become quite comforting.

I wondered what the old doctor was doing now. Then I thought of Claruc again and forced myself to turn away from memories. Unease lives in the past, lives in the recollected, and also lives in the forecasted and fantasised futures of our best laid plans. I needed to stay in the present, worry cannot find me here, it doesn't have the time and never will.

I finally conceded my compliance to join them with a nod, and the officers deflated in unison. I mused that now they looked even shorter. I gave the letter back to the gloved hand of Sergeant Slater. Didn't much care for the little one, Wilson. And I say little one, but he was probably a shade shorter than myself.

'The carriage awaits us, ah, Lord-

'Look, it's just Henry, or Game, if you must address my name in every fucking sentence,' I interrupted him. 'No more of that Lord or Sir shit, okay?'

They smiled as I barged past them and into the waiting carriage, also festooned with the coat of arms of the City of London.

The Count Down (L. S.).

Two things happened in the void between decision: first, two more random bad guys barrelled through what remained of the shattered door to face off against Claruc and I – only the new bad guys were dressed in the more acceptable attire of shorts and t-shirt, and jogging suit, respectively – and second, the bartender belted out his final gurgle of outrage before succumbing to his death upon his bedding of guts. Outrage over guts for his final act.

'You will not be going back into the cage this time, Leprechaun.' St. Germain looked down the length of his bone-sword at Claruc, creating what could only be described as an insane amount of emphasis, before murderously switching to me.

'But you will be, Game.' Now the sword levelled on me. 'And in as many fucking pieces as I choose to cut you-'

'Hang on, Count-fucking-Dracula, for just a second, please.' I turned to Claruc, the penny finally dropping.

'Tell me the truth now, and no more riddles. Are there really such things as leprechauns, or is this jumped-up-twat being facetious?'

I couldn't believe that I had never made the link, and in doing so I naturally dwelled upon the whole liturgy of mythical beings. It was a moment of great awakening and wonder. It was a bright glimmer of possibility that gave me a renewed passion for adventure. A new world to explore and discover and-

'Aye,' Claruc was frowning about something. 'Them feckin' leppy shits are out there, alrigh'. Meddlin' wi' timelines. Undoin' truths, makin' new pasts. Feckin' pain in the arse is what they are!'

I was stunned into silence, and for a moment forgot the pregnant situation at present, still on pause by virtue of my raised palm. The room was about to give birth to a great and unholy evil that manifested itself as an undeniably egg-shaped guy by the name of Claruc and the bright-eyed cunt called Count Saint Germain. And Claruc liked a drink. Clearly, St. Germain was getting in the way of this thirsty truth.

'Instructions are not to kill Game. They didn't say anything about-'

I interrupted St. Germain again, this time with just my finger: the pointy one. I had too many questions for my long-time associate of unknown mythical ethnicity.

'So, what, you're a…' I struggled for the word, and all the while Claruc kept his darkening eyes on St. Germain. 'A fucking fairy or something?'

Claruc looked at me. Meanwhile the other three seemed to have just stalled or something. It was actually quite funny, if you were a fly-on-the-wall.

'We are faerie. Jus' not like ye' are thinkin' is all. We're in'er-dimensionals. An' I have told ye'. Lots o' feckin' times, if you'd jus' stop an' listen for once.'

Presumably St. Germain had finally lost his patience as his two associates dived towards us with mal intent. One-on-one, and each clearing the pretzel corpse of our late bartender with quick leaps, sinister looking weapons in hand.

I suspected the knives to be of the burning metal and bone handle variety. I figured it was just my luck that Mr Shorts & T-shirt chose me to fight, what with him being the more murderous looking of St. Germain's backup dancers.

I saw Claruc place the absinth beneath the table before somehow avoiding a slash of a blade that would've likely unzipped him from collar bone to pelvis. It was so close that for a second I thought Claruc had been hit, but he was nimble on his feet, and the sheer weight of the assault had set Claruc's attacker off balance and giving the beloved killer-egg the upper hand in the duel.

Simultaneously, across the breadth of our table, less than two meters away in the confined staff-come-storage room, my own assailant was locked in on me. Presently it wasn't possible to worry about my faerie friend any longer.

I lifted the table up to act as a shield whilst the nuts and crisp, my cotton wrapped blade, and both empty tumblers scattered to floor, just as the point of the hook-like-scythe embedded into the table.

Using the momentum of my upward thrust, I rammed the table top back down on top of him, but not before he dislodged his weapon as the table began to smoke and burn, and he rolled backwards, quick as I ever saw a fucker move, smoothly returning to his feet, fighting-position, as menacingly-impassive as the moment he'd entered the fray. The table was still between us except now the four legs reached for the ceiling.

The gutted bartender was in a slushy pile, only a meter or so behind Mr Shorts & T-shirt, and St. Germain inaudibly sneering less than two-foot from him.

The sounds of Claruc's fight was a touch distracting, but I had no time to engage before my guy was back on me, swinging his weapon, thrashing and stabbing. I worried that he was somehow getting faster and faster in the fight, and did my best to squirm backward, twitching away from an arcing slice but not quick enough to avoid a stiff and unpleasant boot to the chest.

The force of it sent me rolling into the modular shelving that held dusty file boxes. The shelves smashed and fell apart around me as I clattered amongst the debris. I caught a moment of similar despondency from Claruc when he too collided back against an old fridge-freezer, his hand barely holding back the hatchet pressing down toward his face, and his skin burning at the grip.

This was the moment when I remembered who the fuck I was. And, that I would not be defeated by any kind of underling, especially not by one dressed so casual and ordinary.

Brushing the splinters of wood and cobwebs from my shredded dinner shirt and trousers I climbed back to my feet. It seemed Mr Shorts & T-shirt had decided that I was not threatening enough as he was now closing in on Claruc.

'Hey!' I shouted. I didn't have a degrading nickname, so I just straight up resorted to one syllable.

I was really starting to feel underrated and underappreciated as a direct enemy, but Mr Shorts & T-shirt turned around, his pale face as readable as the wind.

'Fucking chicken legs!' It was the best I had, and as I insulted him, I pounced, dodging his one-trick slice, then the follow-through elbow as he scrambled to meet my attack with one of his own.

I knew he was fast, and clearly aggressive, but fast only gets you so far when up close and murderable, and I figured that if his defence was to attack, then he had no defence at all, or so I hoped. And although he could move his arms and legs very quickly, moving the abdomen is much trickier.

A fact proven as I tackled straight through his midsection, slamming him to the floor and pinning his weapon beside his face with my left arm, my right anchoring his other hand by the other side of his head. It was perfect tea-bagging position and if I had the time, I definitely would've taken the opportunity to demonstrate the aforementioned.

St. Germain snarled as he saw me abreast his casual assassin and rallied toward us, his smart-as-fuck sword in hand. I had very little time to react and not enough free hands to crush the assassin's skull with – the only available weapon remaining, not including my blade, somewhere amongst the wreckage behind me, were my teeth.

The fury had me and this cunt had to die by my hands, not by any weapon, but my own hands, just like my first time… I sunk my teeth into the soft flesh of his neck, clamping around the mass of his throat before ripping my head away, simultaneously snatching the scythe from his hand and rolling backward as the spray of red-blue blood collided with the swipe of blade from St. Germain, precisely where my neck had just been.

Spitting the casual cunt's throat amongst the guts of the bartender seemed the tidiest, and most decent thing to do. Blood was dripping from my face and chin, and more was gushing from the prostrated, throat-less motherfucker I had just dined on. The place was quickly becoming a bit of a mess, truth-be-told. Good job the bartender was already dead, or he'd be surely having a heart attack by now.

Claruc had managed to create a bit of space between himself and Mr Jogging Suit, blood dripping from both of them, but one of Claruc's hands looking like it had been flash-fried on a barbeque and then dropped into a blender. But other than that, he looked alive.

We faced off as two against two, and I figured that there was at least three gallons of blood on the linoleum floor, just to add to the drama. I spared a look and it seemed that none of us had escaped the taint of gore as even St. Germain had a fancy stripe across his torso and face. His sword dripped, and the blood bubbled and hissed on the cut with a poetry that can only be translated through image.

Nuts, crisps. And my blade were lost amongst the carnage and destruction. However, thankfully, the bottle of absinth remained untouched by the chaos. In the momentary respite, Claruc moved it to the highest shelf he could reach without having to avert his gaze from the two that stalked.

'What about elves then?' I hissed through the side of my mouth in the brief interval that felt like the eye of the storm as oppose to any kind of cease-fire.

'Elves?'

'Don't tell me Father Christmas is real too!' I could hardly contain my excitement.

'Elves are fo' wee children's stories, ye' pillock!'

'Ah.'

'There's no way you two leave this room of your own accord.' St. Germain gestured for Mr Jogging Suit to go at Claruc as it seemed that he and I had some unspoken score to settle.

I span the hooked blade in my hand like a cowboy from a John Wayne movie. It was made of the same element as *Abatu*, and the blood that had sprayed onto it had bubbled and sizzled into a crusted coating where it met with the metal. The handle however was still sticky with congealed blood and every time I tried to spin it to get the blade facing up, it didn't quite work out. Safest bet was to keep it firm in my grip and pointy end facing toward the enemy.

Mr Jogging Suit snapped one of the legs from the upturned table and launched at Claruc before immediately following up with a jumping knee, intended for the head if not for Claruc's mobility, prowess, and foresight.

Claruc caught his attacker mid-air with just his neck and shook him like a ragdoll until his head went all floppy and his arms and legs limp. Then he reached for the absinth and downed another few fingers, still holding his assailant in the throes of a neck-break grip. When he had supped his fill and removed the bottleneck from his mouth, he let go of the decidedly sporty assassin and burped loudly.

Mr Jogging Suit knocked hard against the floor like a regular old sack of potatoes, leaving we two against St. Germain. And if he felt concerned any, he sure didn't show it. But if he had looked contemptuous before, back when the numbers were in his favour, he now looked purely malignant and his eyes burned brighter than reasonably explainable.

'Your fool of a brother made his case for you, back before you tried to burn everything down!' St. Germain spat on the floor between us, perhaps not a fan of Ian either. That made two of us. Seemed I was in good company after all.

'He didn't have me fooled though, and after this debacle, Mulliti and Mirabilis will be finished. When I bring you in, *He* will elevate me.'

The time for words was gone. And during St. Germain's latest declaration of promise, Claruc had finished the last of the absinth and the bottle dropped to the floor with a clatter, then hiccupped and before I could even register an action, he made a move toward St. Germain.

For a giant egg, Claruc moved with frightening speed and agility. I had often thought of him as shark-like the way he moved to kill. It was almost as if he were made entirely of cartilage and could fold himself sideways, doubled over on himself if needs must.

St. Germain met Claruc's advance with his weapon thrust out to cut a hole straight through Claruc's chest with a speed akin to a lightning strike.

However, Claruc had other intentions and somehow managed to roll to his extreme left to be directly by my side and in a fine position to take advantage of St. Germain's wide-open right flank.

But as Claruc shifted his great mass to strike his enemy down, something else entirely happened that left me paralysed in disbelief.

It seemed that in sensing his vulnerability, St. Germain forgo his chances of defence and instead concentrated a new strike toward me with a further step and forward thrust of his magnificent sword.

In the blink of an eye Claruc had stepped across and into the path of danger. As a pain erupted inside my heart, I recoiled back a step, realising what had almost happened, and also what did happen.

The blooded end of St. Germain's sword had torn straight through Claruc, and bedded into the muscle of my left breast, if not just a shallow and superficial wound, but a wound that burned like molten iron against my skin and I fell back another half a step, in shock, almost losing my balance amongst the rubble of broken shelving and cardboard boxes.

The tip of the sword slowly withdrew and Claruc coughed, a plume of dark blood hanging in the air, and I caught him as he slumped and became as still and heavy as a rock.

At the time I didn't quite realise that he had given his life for mine, and in the micro moments between lowering him to the ground and St. Germain withdrawing his scorching weapon from Claruc's chest cavity, I hadn't the time to blink, never mind appreciate the sacrifice he made for me.

St. Germain grinned like a bully on a day trip to a special school as he stepped forward and straight onto the offensive. Numbers had finally evened out in a room stacked high with death.

Time slowed down to a gloop, the way it does when killing is at hand and I anticipated his charge, sword swinging down from over my high right, the attack closing the space between us to less than a foot.

I tried to parry but was dumb-founded and wrong footed with the pointy end of the scythe blade rounded toward myself instead of... Truth is I had moved beyond panic, acting by shear instinct instead of using the weapons at my disposal and, well, the stupid hook knife was never any match for that sword of his. And, if I figured correctly, I couldn't dive toward him, Claruc's rock of a corpse eliminated that option for me; nor could I move backwards, the broken shelves presented danger in the form of painfully sharp stakes.

As St. Germain closed in to strike me down, in a flash of bygone times I remembered being out on the open fields by the abbey. I remembered young Franky stepping into another of my blows, against his more innocent nature. I remembered the lesson I was trying to teach him. Sometimes you need to take a hit to be able to hit back.

The fields were gone, and my mind was presently back in the storeroom of corpses. Knowing what needed to be done, I brought my empty left hand across to block the slash of the sword, whilst spinning my entire body around and lashing out with my right, the hook blade, furiously weighted, arced at a neck-high-slice that would have cut down General Sherman in a single blow.

The result was a flash of agony and several wet thuds to the swamped linoleum, immediately followed by an intense burning sensation from my left hand. I span again to my left to clear the space between us when I realised that my enemy was down and currently missing the top half of his head.

The scythe had taken him at a diagonal slice from the bottom of his right ear, straight through his left eye, and scalloping over his opposite ear.

St. Germain's severed skull, matted with blood and wispy thin golden hair, including the fabric from his severed hood and purple-goo brain matter, was spinning on its circumference and coming to a gentle stop.

The rest of his body had dropped and lay as motionless as frozen fish, toppled to one side with the bulk of his torso over the bottoms of Claruc's legs and feet.

Lay besides what remained of St. Germain's head were four

scattered stumps that I painfully recognised as my own fingers. I looked at my hand aghast: a hand with only a thumb and a long, thick red smile.

More unfortunate was the sword lay wedged beneath his torso and Claruc's shins. There was a severe hissing and popping sound that spelled the beginning of a fire, which was already causing quite the choke of corpse smoke.

I had to take a moment but with nowhere to sit I leant against the remains of the shelving, and within less than two minutes the fire was beginning to rage betwixt St. Germain and Claruc, quickly spreading toward the other three corpses splayed colourfully around the store-room-come-battlefield.

Claruc and St. Germain were already cooking, but regretfully I didn't have time to snatch the sword to safety, and in the process of retrieving my cotton covered *Abatu*, I dropped two fingers and before I knew it, the whole room was lost to flame and smoke.

Sparing a glance to the depleted bottle of absinth by the fridge freezer, I knew that Claruc would've been happy that not a drop was wasted, but by this point his body was shrouded in thick smoke and bright orange flames deep within.

I wondered if the strike through the heart would've killed him permanently if not for the fire. I still couldn't believe that he was an actual faerie, after all the time I'd spent with him too! Regardless, there was nothing I could do for him now. The fire would take him as it does for us all, mythical or not, whatever you may be. Fire is the great leveller.

The inferno was devouring the room quicker than any blaze I had ever seen and I spared one last thought for my old comrade, taking my severed fingers, *Abatu*, and still shoeless, I fled into the busy airport terminal, smoke chortling out of the doors as I escaped, panic and alarm rising in my wake.

Cities Within Cities, 1815.

We were stopped at least twice before being allowed to continue on through, passing beneath an ancient archway at a snail's pace, and I was desperate for something rotten.

It was an oddly busy little spot this place they called "The Bar". Officers tall and timid had announced our arrival as a matter of pride. Meanwhile I looked on from the carriage hatch completely ignorant to the significance of it all. But, metaphorically perhaps, I supposed it made sense that a deeper meaning resonated behind the loosely draped chain, spanning, between two opposing sentry towers that framed the archway and gatehouse. Clearly the chain couldn't hold against the feeblest of aggressors. So, therefore, it merely functioned little more than pomp or decorum. Even the thought of having to endure yet more entitled silver-spoons got my ring flaring even further. I wasn't sure if I should be impressed or disappointed or indifferent, so I kept my thoughts to myself and my legs crossed tightly.

The guard on my side of the chain eyeballed me as we passed. I noticed the futuristic looking bilateral sidearms he used as hip-handles. A lot like one of them cowboy outlaws from the Wild West.

As far as I was concerned, we were still in the London Town I had spent many a night in, but apparently, this was not true, or not quite. We had entered the sovereign territory of The City of London, one square mile of independent state. It made me think of the Vatican. So, naturally, I didn't trust the place or any person in it, or anywhere near it for that matter.

'Right you are, Lord, ah, Henry. If you would just hand over your weapons and we can be-'

I rounded my bemusement on Sergeant Slater, snatching the remainder of the sentence away from his expectant hand, and to my surprise, the officer's other hand decidedly moved to hold the carriage door closed at my refusal. He saw me look at his hand and swallowed his trepidation.

Military boots approached the carriage door but stopped short of opening it. More and more tough boots scraped against cobbles, taking up positions all around the carriage, waiting. That was when I figured that the carriage was entirely surrounded. The sounds of bated breath and steel sole plates resonated through my caution, continuing to delay in conflict against my baser requirements.

'Not a fucking chance that you are getting any of my weapons,' I informed both of the officers, Wilson once again in the process of flushing a royal burgundy. I don't think he had the balls for dealing with the likes of me.

I looked back at Slater's gloved hand. 'If you're not going to open that door, Sergeant, I suggest you get the fuck out of my way before I end up shitting down your-'

'Don't you know where you are?' blurted Wilson, the purple one.

I sighed and decided to give them one more chance. 'Look, dick jockeys, you jumped me before I'd even had the chance to take a dump. And I really needed a dump way back then. Now, I am positively desperate. I didn't ask to come here, and I have so far caused you no physical harm. So, if you don't kindly get out of my way, I'll shit down your throat,' I pointed at Slater, 'and use your colourful tongue to wipe my arse,' I switched to Wilson, 'right here, in this carriage.'

Sergeant Slater, despite the contrary looks on his face didn't move his hand; the purple one stiffened in his seat, making himself larger, it seemed.

After a moment of staring and breath holding, I produced my blunted fruit knife from my pocket and immediately Sergeant slater reached for it. I stabbed it through his soft hand, sending both blade and extremity, firmly lodged into the roof of the carriage. To give him his due he didn't scream, well, not immediately.

Wilson's mouth smacked open and his hands flustered inside his jacket to produce a dull-black, next generation looking pistol, and he drew back the top of the chamber in one fluid motion like he knew exactly how to handle it.

Usually I have no taste for firearms but this one looked interesting enough to make me curious. Sadly, it was at this point when officer with hand impaled to ceiling began to wail and I guesstimated that I had mere seconds before the carriage would be overrun.

Without further hesitation I acted. The pistol just about fitted in Wilson's gob. Truth is, I had to smash a few teeth out to get it in there properly, and I smiled as his eyes flickered upward into his soft-shell brain.

Just then the door to the carriage was torn open and light beamed in. Suddenly I was met with a larger and heavier version of the futuristic-firearm Wilson was sucking, and the one holding it was wearing an all-black, slick-fashioned military uniform.

I considered surrendering as the weapon levelled to my head. My boots however, clearly had other ideas and before you could smell a fart, the young soldier had an eleven-inch depression in his chest, roughly the same shape as my boot. Bones and organs reconfiguring violently as the man went flying backwards from the door of the carriage and sprawled onto the cobbled courtyard amongst the dozens of other black-clad soldiers.

A barked order was given from somewhere outside. Solid steps advancing. Perhaps fighting wasn't the way out of this situation, I reckoned. An odd notion for sure, but I did have an extremely urgent matter that was distracting me and corrupting my every thought. When you got to go, you got to go.

Constable Wilson sounded like he could have possibly swallowed his tongue. I considered helping him. But instead shut him up with a perfectly weighted headbutt.

'Look, I'll come out…peacefully, on one condition,' I bellowed through the open wound that was formerly a carriage door.

The advancement halted. Another moment passed before a deep voice responded. 'And what is this condition, Lord Game?'

I cringed. 'You take me straight to a fucking toilet, before anything else happens – oh, and my weapons stay with me. Nobody dies as long as nobody does anything stupid.'

A deep laugh rumbled in the echo. I relaxed, a little pip of wind escaping me, threatening to follow through and turtle head right there and then.

'Nobody's fucked either way then?' asked the deep voice, now followed by a small chorus of laughter.

I laughed too as I thought about it, and as I did, a soft mass hatched beneath me and I realised right then and there that I definitely shouldn't have laughed.

* * *

No sooner had I freshened up, did they have me before The Crown.

And there I was, in a city within a city, I had passed The Bar, literally, not legally or metaphorically, I had even changed and removed my underwear entirely, and now stood, flanked by two super policemen with big guns, standing at a large table, before a conglomerate of unhealthy middle-aged businessmen.

The youngest of them sat at the head of the table was the first to speak. 'Welcome, Lord Game. It is your correct title, I believe?'

'Do you?' I eyed them all, individually. Thirteen of them in total, excluding the chaperones that continued to watch me at a close distance.

The speaker looked just a smidgen uncomfortable. 'I am Nathan Rothschild, and we are The Crown. First of all, we wanted to congratulate you on a job well done in the United States of America.' A smattering of affirmations croaked around the table.

Nathan continued. 'However, we now face an unprecedented threat from this side of the Atlantic, and…well, your country needs you. Will you save us, Lord Game?'

I smiled, wider than usual, which is why I think there was such a long pause. It was all I could do not to laugh at them and their professional seriousness, but I held my tongue and waited for the beans to spill.

After several seconds of silence, an uneasy murmuring started to grow around the table. I watched as whiskey noses and overgrown eyebrows curated a growth of brooding dissent. All I had to do was wait, I could sense it as soon as I entered the fray.

'The war with America had to stop!' Nathan stressed to his peers, clearly exasperated.

I cleared my throat. I think they were expecting me to say something so I took my time as I looked at each face and made up a nickname for them all; the process must have taken me at least fifteen seconds and yet they waited, baited.

'Don't let me stop you,' I said, holding my smile, wide.

All eyes redirected back to the head of the table, who began to colour a little in his pasty cheeks.

'The embargo on our Atlantic trade was just too great.' He searched his acquaintances like a man soaked in gasoline might look at an arsonist holding a battery and a strip of paper foil.

'Napoleon is the *real* enemy; we all know that. He cannot be reasoned with. He doesn't have the capacity for trade, nor does he know when he is defeated. He is coming back, and stronger than ever. If we do not act now, we will all soon be answering to him!'

His words dropped flat against my heavy sighs as I grabbed the back of an empty chair and stretched my back at a right angle to my legs.

Rising from his hard chair, all formal like, Nathan turned his attentions back to me. 'Did you really need to hurt our officers? Especially given all that we have done for you, I would expect a little gratitude-'

'There you go. Finally!' I cut across him. 'Doctor Kratzenstein. The ace up your sleeve.'

Their collective silence and intense frowning were confirmation. Sometimes the body speaks a language that words cannot translate. It was subtle but noticeable; the gentlemen at the table all seemed to grow an inch or so at my mention of the tongue-less surgeon.

'So, where was I?' Despite the loathing I felt for the men in the room I was grateful for the small favour of stitching me back together.

'Half of you was in the Polar North, deep in the ice. The other half, down in the Antarctic. It took a long time, Lord-'

'Don't call me Lord.' I was just about sick and tired of this charade now. 'Henry, or Game will do. Please, just tell me why.'

'Why we exhumed you?' chortled Nathan, clearly a thousand times more comfortable with the current topic and conversational dynamic.

My body language must've taken a step towards the aggressive as the clacking of raised machine guns behind me resonated around our small chamber. My back ached already, it had since these cunts put me back together again, I didn't fancy getting shot in it too.

I needed to sit down. 'Yeah, that. Also, what took you so long?' I pulled out the chair and plonked my arse. 'And please, everyone, stop sweating, you're making me nervous.'

'Well, Mister, Mister, Game,' Nathan sat down smartly, 'the truth is we purchased your locations from the French. It's ironic that you will be their downfall. I mean, of course, we all knew of the legends. But...'

'None ov us believed zem!' announced another fellow, a real stick of a man, seated three up from my right. His accent decidedly Germanic. His breath odour strong with sausage.

'It was Claruc who initiated proceedings with the French for us,' clarified Nathan. 'Though he spoke in riddles for the most.'

I brought my fist down on the table and gripped my fruit knife beneath. 'Claruc died fighting your war, you trumped-up twats!'

Nathan's eyes widened, his brow furrowed, he was shaking his head as discreetly as possible, beads of sweat flicking this way and that as a boot struck the polished stone floor behind me. Then another step. I stood, sending my chair skating back and into the one advancing on me.

I decided that the room needed an example and I turned just in time to see the approaching officer fold over the heavy block of chair backing, his firearm dropping to the floor with a clunk and I lashed out. Blunt fruit knife sticking him just beneath his right ear. Cartilage and bone clicked apart as I dragged the knife sideways, unlocking his jaw, permanently, and unzipping the flesh of his cheek down one side.

Chaos erupted around me as I withdrew my weapon, doors bursting open and two-dozen other black-clad soldiers storming in to take aim on me. Without a second thought I crouched to leap forward-

'Stop!' Nathan Rothschild slapped at the table-top like a ball sack slapping against a fat arse. 'For Christ's sake, Henry we need you. We're allies, our interests are aligned!'

I straightened up, fruit knife dripping bright red. The officer with half his jaw hanging off choked and twitched, then dramatically toppled back from the chair and all over the expensive floor with a squelch and a pitiful moan.

'Edvards, gets Pinberry out ov here!' ordered the bearded stick, addressing the guard closest to me.

The officer eyeballed me and hesitated for just a moment before hurrying over to his fallen comrade. I turned my attention back to the table.

'The French, you say.' I had a score to settle with them cunts. 'You want to pay me to stop this Napoleon?'

'Help us do zis and ve are square.' The stick man sure did have a deep voice for such a wisp.

'Square?' I laughed. 'We're already square for what I did in America; for what Claruc gave you. No, I do this, and then you will owe me as much gold as I can fit into my vaults. Agreed?' I didn't have vaults, but I did have a hidey hole beneath the altar at the abbey, I just hoped it was still there.

I wiped the blade clean on the tablecloth as they conferred, re-sheathing my fruit knife as it seemed civility had returned. My seat was soiled with the officer's blood, so I decided to stay standing.

The speaker also stood up, nodding before leaving his

position at the head of the table and starting toward me, his pasty hand offered before him.

'As the current chairman, I hereby welcome you officially to The Crown. Your previous debt to us is settled. The new agreement is for you to destroy Napoleon, from which point we will owe you our favour.'

'And lots of gold.'

'And gold. As much as you can fit into a vault.'

Thing is, I'd happily kill this French cunt, payment or not. But money is money, and it makes the world go around. The French owed me a debt of blood. I was cashing it in one-way or another, and I figured the debt they owed me had accrued a good couple of hundred years' worth of interest.

'Count me in then, Mister Rothschild.'

I looked down to his hand but did not take it, and my counterpart hovered for a moment before dropping his smile and his girly hand.

Returning to the head of the table, he resumed his place. 'Excellent. Next order of business, gentlemen.' The room had crept back onto the chilly side.

'Claruc,' All eyes turned toward me. Nathan continued, 'You said he perished.'

He was safely back at his seat and I locked him with my death stare.

'Our sources say differently-'

'Well your sources are wrong!' my fruit knife wobbled as the blunt metal sunk into the expensive looking mahogany top.

The room drew quite again, nervous eyes and overgrown ear hair not daring to disagree. After another minute or two, it was Nathan who spoke again:

'Right you are. Next order of business, gentlemen.'

New York City, Present Day.

Rapping on the hotel room door brought Frank out of his reading with a start. The light was low, sun almost set. He'd been reading for going on eight hours, he realised with disbelief.

More overt knocking on the door brought his senses fully back to the present and he stretched his arms and back in the process. All day he'd been absorbed, horrified and infatuated in the accounts Henry Game had prepared for him, and he was probably only about halfway through.

Distraction wasn't the word. His thoughts were alive and swimming with everything from hatred to wonder and relief, at finally being given a logical explanation for what he is.

Not quite human after all. Maybe now he could find the space necessary to be at peace, and not be torn by conflict and confusion in a society not meant to contain him.

From what he could hear there were two people at his door, whispering and hissing at one another in hushed but argumentative tones.

He approached the door and set his hand on the handle. Maybe the book was already teaching him caution.

'Who is it?'

'Francis, it's me, Dad. Your mom's here too. Open up, we've all been worried sick about you.'

Frank hesitated. 'How did you find me?'

This time it was his adopted mother to speak. 'Your uncle called us. Please, we've been so worried. Don't leave us standing out here, it's embarrassing, open up!'

Putting his foot several inches back from the door he opened it. His adopted parents gawped back up at him, both looking very worried indeed – too worried, Frank suspected.

He let them in and checked nobody else was out there before closing the door and double locking it this time. His parents noticed the books on the table and looked at each other.

Frank suspected their interest with caution.

'Why are you here?' He wanted to keep them as far away from the books as possible.

'Woden said that you were in danger,' exclaimed his mother, suddenly turning on the waterworks and reaching out to hold Frank's limp hand.

Something wasn't right. She had never shown even an ounce of emotion towards him, especially not in such a dramatic and superficial sense.

'The fire!' interjected his dad, a little too loudly.

'What of it?' Frank folded his arms to stop his mother's pathetic attempts to show compassion. It was embarrassing for the both of them.

'Woden has contacts in the police – you know that – anyway, he called this morning and said that the causation report determined that the fire was a deliberate act. They think that it was meant for you instead of your girlfriend-'

'She wasn't my girlfriend. And anyway, what's it to you two? I haven't seen either of you since…well, it must be going on three years now. Why show up today, right now? I clearly don't need you, and you obviously don't care about me so…'

His parents looked at each other again. They didn't look upset by Frank's words, more worried if anything. Frank felt a pit open up in his stomach as he remembered the telephone conversation that morning to his uncle. Maybe whatever Henry had planned had not worked…he looked back at the stack of journals.

'I tried calling but your cell phone wouldn't connect. We

have been trying to find you ever since the fire happened. We thought the worst.' She wrung her hands and tried her best to be the distraught mother, the haunted father standing beside her, a consoling arm about her shoulders.

'I have a new phone, it's really old. Switches off all the time.'

'Let me make you a cup of tea, hey?' Frank's dad had always been kind to him, if not distant and completely uninterested, but he had always been kind.

Frank nodded. 'Yeah, okay. I don't have any milk though, just black, and the hotel's tea bags are terrible.' Frank's head was starting to hurt, and an intense anxiety was building.

'How about I make it, dear, and you two go and sit down. We're just both so happy to see you.' Frank's mum fussed and dashed to the kitchen, smiling but not completely at ease.

Frank sat opposite his adopted father, who was suddenly very interested in his life. With his suspicions still high, Frank collected the pages and the ancient leather grimoire, and started returning them into the cardboard packaging it had arrived in.

'What's that you're reading, son?'

Frank looked up. This must have been the first time he had ever called him son. Now his suspicions were rising through" his throat. 'Son? Am I your son all of a sudden?'

The look on his father's face looked genuine and Frank felt a pang of regret.

'We know we're not your biological parents,' said Frank's mum, two cups of tea in her hands before passing one to Frank and his father, adopted father. 'But we have always loved you as if you were.'

Frank's head was splitting. He just wanted things to go back to some semblance of normality; he wanted the ticker; he wanted them to leave and he really wanted to find out what happened to Henry... His real dad. He needed to know.

Was Grim coming for him now? Maybe even the Ruling Council? Selene…he remembered the name. Maybe his 'Claim handler' was the Selene: Ian's wife – his real aunty, he supposed.

'You've a funny way of showing it.'

'Raising you wasn't easy, you know.' Frank's father leaned forward, sipping at his drink.

Frank leaned back and looked out of the window. He'd heard this one before, and just wasn't in the mood to be made to feel guilty for being born and becoming a burden for them.

His tea tasted just as bad as it always did, but he drank it all anyway, and quickly. Reading for eight hours straight was likely to drive up a thirst in you.

'You're not exactly 'normal' Francis. You know what you put us through with the behaviour at schools and-'

'Look Dad,' Frank had heard enough already, 'Just, just… just…' a dizziness washed over him and swept his pounding headache away, but also his ability to speak, see clearly, and move properly.

He could hear his mum and dad mumbling to each other by the kitchen, followed by the sounds of furniture moving, but his vision was like he was under murky waters. Sleep was calling to him but at the same time his anxiety levels were rising fast. He felt like he wasn't getting enough oxygen suddenly as shapes moved in front of him, laying him down to look at the ceiling. Frank's legs were pulled tight together and then his hands.

The world was bleeding away from him, blinking, slower and slower. The last thing he remembered was the sound of heavy footsteps and a low tuneless whistle before a dark rest claimed him and dragged him away to slumber.

* * *

Sounds returned, and also whistling.

Frank opened his eyes and saw the smoke-stained ceiling of his hotel room. He was lay down beside his bed, but his arms and legs were not bound as he remembered.

He sat up, and as he did the headache returned, but this time ten-fold and like he'd done something personally to upset it.

Perched on the edge of the kitchen counter was a very large man holding his *Lord of the Rings* ticker box, minus the ticker. The tin was completely empty, cleaned out in fact.

That was when Frank noticed the torn sealer bag besides the kitchen sink, the tap still running. Naturally he thought the worse.

'What did you do?'

'Ye' gonna need all o' ye' time, boy.' The man had a strong Irish accent.

For a moment Frank wondered if he was still dreaming until he felt the strong pull of a substance that bereft him of all dream and time in which to suffer.

'I need...' Frank's words trailed off, suddenly realising that it was just the two of them. 'Where are my parents?'

The man produced an antique looking hipflask and unclamped the top.

'Not a thing ye' 'ave t' worry abou' 'ne-more.' He drank deeply.

Frank got up and sat on the edge of his bed, still a little groggy. 'Are you Claruc?'

The egg man frowned at that, taking another sip before answering. 'Depends on who ye' ask, boy.'

'But you died, burned...'

'Sometimes, aye. Also drowned before-hic! But tha' also depends who ye' ask.' Claruc walked over to the cardboard box and peered inside.

'Many miles t' go fo' the pair o' us on this path. Take ye'

words, an' hold ye' comfort in 'em. Heed the advice as if ye' own mistakes were teachin' 'em to ye'. 'Cause He's comin' for ye'. An' right now, we have t' leave.'

'Who's coming for me?' Frank knew the answer already, of course.

'He's many o' names. Yet always one eye.'

'Woden.' Frank stood up and tried to massage the cold creeping into his veins. 'Is he really as bad as-'

'Worse.' Claruc sprang to his feet again and the bed frame stayed in a half-crushed state.

'We best be off then, boy. Ye need t' gather ye stuff, an' quick. He's almost here.'

TO BE CONTINUED.

ACKNOWLEDGEMENTS

First of all, I have to thank my wife for being my proof-reader, my co-editor, my muse, and my biggest fan. I must thank you for allowing me to commit to my writings, for giving me the time I need, and for being an awesome mother to our two boys. You are the best and I love you.

I want to thank the friends that have helped me in my writing over the years – not just on this book. I appreciate your efforts, guiding words, and patience: Jason, your encouraging words and detailed notes spurred me on; Garry, your feedback is always most brutal and honest and exactly what I need to hear. I am lucky to have you both.

I have to thank Graham for handing me Terry Pratchett's *The Colour of Magic* on that cold morning when I was boarding the train to join the army. And of course, all the subsequent recommendations for my reading list over the years.

And finally, I want to thank Henry Game for making this journey so fun and interesting and educational and shocking and enlightening.

I can't wait for the next instalment.

ABOUT THE AUTHOR

Anthony hails from Bolton, England.

He has a passion for research and history, picking at the seams of documented events to unravel fresh perspective.

He now lives in Australia with his wife, two boys, dog, cat, & three chickens.

Printed in Great Britain
by Amazon

45531344R00253